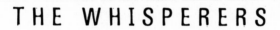

THE WHISPERERS

THE
WHISPERERS

A CHARLIE PARKER THRILLER

JOHN CONNOLLY

ATRIA BOOKS

NEW YORK   LONDON   TORONTO   SYDNEY

ATRIA BOOKS

A Division of Simon & Schuster, Inc.
1230 Avenue of the Americas
New York, NY 10020

First Atria Books hardcover edition July 2010

ATRIA BOOKS and colophon are trademarks of Simon & Schuster, Inc.

For information about special discounts for bulk purchases,
please contact Simon & Schuster Special Sales at 1-866-506-1949
or business@simonandschuster.com.

The Simon & Schuster Speakers Bureau can bring authors to your live event.
For more information or to book an event contact the Simon & Schuster Speakers
Bureau at 1-866-248-3049 or visit our website at www.simonspeakers.com.

Extract from *A Terrible Love of War* by James Hillman © 2004 Penguin Books.

Designed by Level C

Manufactured in the United States of America

10   9   8   7   6   5   4   3   2   1

Library of Congress Cataloging-in-Publication Data is available.

ISBN 978-1-4391-6519-5
ISBN 978-1-4391-6529-4 (ebook)

To Mark Dunne, Paul O'Reilly, Noel Maher,
and Emmet Hegarty: princes all

PROLOGUE

War is a mythical happening . . .
Where else in human experience, except in the throes
of ardor . . . do we find ourselves transported to a
mythical condition and the gods most real?

James Hillman, *A Terrible Love of War*

It was Dr. Al-Daini who found the girl, abandoned in the long central corridor. She was buried beneath broken glass and shards of pottery, under discarded clothing, pieces of furniture, and old newspapers used as packing materials. She should have been rendered almost invisible amid the dust and the darkness, but Dr. Al-Daini had spent decades searching for girls such as she, and he picked her out where others might simply have passed over her.

Only her head was exposed, her blue eyes open, her lips stained a faded red. He knelt beside her, and brushed some of the detritus from her. Outside, he could hear yelling, and the rumble of tanks changing position. Suddenly, bright light illuminated the hallway, and there were armed men shouting and giving orders, but they had come too late. Others like them had stood by while this had happened, their priorities lying elsewhere. They did not care about the girl, but Dr. Al-Daini cared. He had recognized her immediately, because she had always been one of his favorites. Her beauty had captivated him from the first moment he set eyes on her, and in the years that followed he had never failed to make time to spend a quiet moment or two with her during the day, to exchange a greeting or merely to stand with her and mirror her smile with one of his own.

Perhaps she might still be saved, he thought, but as he carefully shifted wood and stone he recognized that there was little he could do for her now. Her body was shattered, broken into pieces in an act of desecration that made no sense to him. This was not accidental, but deliberate: he could see marks on the floor where booted feet had pounded upon her legs and arms, reducing them to fragments. Yet, somehow, her head had escaped the worst of the violence, and Dr. Al-Daini could not decide if this rendered what had been visited upon her less awful, or more terrible.

"Oh, little one," he whispered as he gently stroked her cheek, the first time that he had touched her in fifteen years. "What have they done to you? What have they done to us all?"

He should have stayed. He should not have left her, should not have left any of them, but the Fedayeen had been battling the Americans near the Ministry of Information, the sounds of gunfire and explosions reaching them even as they sandbagged friezes and wrapped foam rubber around the statues, grateful that they had at least managed to transport some of the treasures to safety before the invasion commenced. The fighting had then spread to the television station, less than a kilometer away, and to the central bus station at the other side of the complex, drawing closer and closer to them. He had argued in favor of staying, for they had stockpiled food and water in the basement, but many of the others felt that the risks were too great. All but one of the guards had fled, abandoning their weapons and their uniforms, and there were already black-garbed gunmen in the museum garden. So they had locked the front doors and left through the back entrance before fleeing across the river to the eastern side, where they waited in the house of a colleague for the fighting to cease.

But it did not stop. When they attempted to return over the Bridge of the Medical City they were turned back, and so they stayed with their colleague once again, and drank coffee, and waited some more. Perhaps they had remained there for too long, debating back and forth the wisdom of abandoning what was, for now, a place of safety, but what else could they have done? Yet he could not forgive himself, or assuage his guilt. He had abandoned her, and they had had their way with her.

And now he was crying, not from the dirt and filth but from rage and hurt and loss. He did not stop, not even as booted feet approached him and a soldier shone a flashlight in his face. There were others behind him, their weapons raised.

"Sir, who are you?" asked the soldier.

Dr. Al-Daini did not reply. He could not. All his attention was fixed on the eyes of the broken girl.

"Sir, do you speak English? I'll ask you one more time: who are you?"

Dr. Al-Daini picked up on the nervousness in the soldier's voice, but also the hint of arrogance, the natural superiority of the conqueror over the conquered. He sighed, and raised his eyes.

"My name is Dr. Mufid Al-Daini," he said, "and I am the deputy curator of Roman Antiquities at this museum." Then he reconsidered. "No, I *was* the Deputy Curator of Roman Antiquities, but now there is no museum left. Now there are only fragments. You let this happen. You stood by and let this happen. . . ."

But he was speaking as much to himself as he was to them, and the words turned to ash in his mouth. The staff had left the museum on Tuesday. On Saturday, they learned that the museum had been looted, and then began to return in an effort to assess the damage and prevent any further theft. Someone said that the looting had commenced as early as Thursday, when hundreds of people had gathered at the fence surrounding the museum. For two days, they were free to ransack. Already, there were rumors that insiders had been involved, some of the museum's own guardians targeting the most valuable artifacts. The thieves took everything that could be moved, and much of what they could not take they attempted to destroy.

Dr. Al-Daini and some others had gone to the headquarters of the marines and pleaded for help in securing the building, for the staff was fearful that the looters would return, and the U.S. Army tanks at the intersection only fifty meters from the museum had refused to come to their aid, citing orders. They were eventually promised guards by the Americans, but only now, on Wednesday, had they come. Dr. Al-Daini had arrived just shortly before them, for he had been one of those assigned the role of liaison with the soldiers and the media, and he had spent the previous days being passed up and down the military ranks and providing contacts for journalists.

Carefully, he raised the head of the broken girl, youthful yet ancient, the paint still visible on her hair and mouth and eyes after almost four thousand years.

"Look," he said, still weeping. "Look at what they did to her."

And the soldiers stared for a moment at this old man covered in white dust, a hollow head in his hands, before moving on to secure the looted halls of the Iraq Museum. They were young men, and this operation was about the future, not the past. No lives had been lost, not here. These things happened.

After all, there was a war on.

DR. AL-DAINI WATCHED THE soldiers go. He looked around and saw a swatch of paint-spattered cloth lying by a fallen display case. He checked it and found it to be relatively clean, so he placed the head of the girl upon it, then wrapped the cloth carefully around her, tying a knot with the four corners so that he might more easily carry her. He stood wearily, the head now hanging from his left hand, like an executioner bearing to his potentate the evidence of the ax's work. So lifelike was the girl's expression, and so troubled and shocked was Dr. Al-Daini, that he would not have been surprised had the severed neck begun to bleed through the material, casting red drops like petals upon the dusty floor. All around him were reminders of what had once been, absences like open wounds. Jewelry had been taken from skeletons, their bones scattered. Statues had been decapitated, so that the most striking aspect of them might more easily be carried away. Curious, he thought, that the girl's head, exquisite as it was, should have been overlooked, or perhaps it was enough for whomever had broken her that her body was ruined, enough to have removed a little beauty from the world.

The scale of the destruction was overwhelming. The Warka vase, a masterpiece of Sumerian art from about 3500 B.C., and the world's oldest carved stone ritual vessel, was gone, hacked away from its base. A beautiful bull-headed lyre had been reduced to kindling as the gold was stripped from it. The Bassetki statue base: gone. The statue of Entema: gone. The Warka mask, the first naturalistic sculpture of a human face: gone. He passed through room after room, replacing all that was lost with phantasms, ghosts of themselves—here, an ivory seal, there a bejeweled crown—so that what had once been was superimposed over the wreckage of the present. Even now, still nearly numb at the extent of the damage that had been done, Dr. Al-Daini was already cataloging the collection in his mind, trying to recall the age and provenance of each precious relic in case the museum's own records might no longer be available to them when they began the seemingly impossible task of recovering what had been taken.

Relics.

Dr. Al-Daini stopped walking. He swayed slightly, and his eyes closed. A soldier passing by asked him if he was okay and offered him water, a small gesture of kindness that Dr. Al-Daini was unable to acknowledge, so grave was his disquiet. Instead, he turned to the soldier and gripped his arms, a movement that might well have ended his troubles on the spot had the soldier in question had his finger on the trigger of his gun.

"I am Dr. Mufid Al-Daini," he told the soldier. "I am a deputy curator here at the museum. Please, I need you to help me. I have to get to the basement. I must check something. It is very, very important. You must help me to get through."

He gestured at the shapes of the armed men ahead of them, beige figures in the darkened hallways. The young man before him looked doubtful, then shrugged.

"You'll have to let go of my shoulders first, sir," he said. He couldn't have been more than twenty or twenty-one, but there was an assurance to him, an ease more appropriate to an older man.

Dr. Al-Daini stepped back, apologizing for his presumption. The name on the soldier's uniform read "Patchett."

"Do you have some identification?" asked Patchett.

Dr. Al-Daini found a museum badge, but the lettering was in Arabic. He searched in his wallet and found a business card, Arabic on one side, English on the other, and handed it across. Squinting slightly in the poor light, Patchett examined it, then returned it.

"Okay, let's see what we can do," he said.

DR. AL-DAINI HAD TWO titles in the museum. As well as being deputy curator of Roman Antiquities, a job description that did insufficient justice to the depth and breadth of his knowledge or, indeed, the additional responsibilities that he had shouldered unofficially and without remuneration, he was also the curator of Uncataloged Items, another name that barely hinted at the extent of the Herculean labors involved. The museum's inventory system was both ancient and complicated, and there were tens of thousands of items that had yet to be included. One part of the museum's basement was a labyrinth of shelves piled high with artifacts, boxed and unboxed, most of them, or most of the tiny fraction that had been cataloged by Dr. Al-Daini and his predecessors, of little monetary value, yet each one a marker, a remnant of a civilization now changed beyond recognition, or departed utterly from this world. In many ways, this basement was Dr. Al-Daini's favorite part of the museum, for who knew what might be discovered here, what unsuspected treasures might be revealed? So far, in truth, he had found few indeed, and the trove of uncataloged items remained as great as it ever had, for with every shard of pottery, every fragment of a statue that was formally added to the museum's records, ten more seemed to arrive, and so, as the body of what was known became greater, so too did the mass of the unknown. A lesser man might have regarded it as a fruitless task, but Dr. Al-Daini was a romantic when it came to knowledge, and the thought that the store of what remained to be discovered was forever increasing filled him with joy.

Now, flashlight in hand, the soldier Patchett behind him with another light, Dr. Al-Daini passed through the canyons of the archives, his key redundant, for the door had been smashed open. The basement was stiflingly hot, and there was a sharp smell in the air left by the burning foam that the looters had used as torches, since the electricity had stopped working before the invasion, but Dr. Al-Daini barely noticed. His attention was fixed on one spot, and one spot only. The looters had made their mark here too, overturning shelves, scattering the contents of boxes and crates, even setting fire to records, but they must have realized quickly that there was little worthy of their attentions, and so the damage was less. Yet some items were clearly missing, and as Dr. Al-Daini moved deeper into the basement, his anxiety increased, until at last he came to the place that he had sought, and stared at the empty space on the shelf before him. He almost gave up then, but there was still some hope.

"Something is missing," he told Patchett. "I beg of you, help me to find it."

"What are we looking for?"

"A lead box. Not very big." Dr. Al-Daini held his hands about two feet apart. "Plain, with a simple clasp and a small lock."

And so together they searched the unlocked areas of the basement as best they could, and when Patchett was recalled by his squad leader

Dr. Al-Daini continued to look, all that day and into the night, but there was no sign of the lead box.

If one wants to hide an item of great value, surrounding it with the worthless is a good way to do so. Better yet if one can swathe it in the poorest of garbs, disguising it so well that it can remain in plain sight and yet not attract even the slightest of glances. One might even catalog it as that which it is not: in this case, a lead casket, Persian, sixteenth century, containing a smaller, unremarkable sealed box, apparently made of iron painted red. History: unknown. Provenance: unknown. Value: minimal.

Contents: none.

All lies, especially the last, for if one got close enough to that box within a box, one might almost have thought that something inside it was speaking.

No, not speaking.

Whispering.

CAPE ELIZABETH, MAINE
MAY 2009

THE DOG HEARD THE call, and came warily to the top of the stairs. She had been sleeping on one of the beds, which she knew that she was not supposed to do. She listened, but picked up on nothing in the voice to suggest that she might be in trouble. When the call came again, and she heard the sound of her leash jangling, she took the stairs two at a time, almost falling over her own legs with excitement when she reached the bottom.

Damien Patchett quieted the dog by raising his finger, and attached the leash to her collar. Although it was warm outside, he wore a green combat jacket. The dog sniffed at one of the pockets, recognizing a familiar scent, but Damien shooed her away. His father was over at the diner, and the house was quiet. The sun was about to set, and as Damien walked the dog through the woods toward the sea, the light began to change, the sky bleeding red and gold behind him.

The dog bit at the leash, unused to being restricted in this way. Usually, she was given free roam on her walks, and she indicated her displeasure by tugging hard. She was not even allowed to stop and sniff scents, and when she tried to urinate she was dragged along, causing her to yelp unhappily. There was a nest of bald-faced hornets in a birch tree nearby, a gray construct now quiet, but in the daytime a buzzing mass of aggression. The dog had been stung earlier in the week when she went to investigate the tree's sap lick, where a yellow-bellied sapsucker had cleared the bark to feed, leaving a useful source of sweetness for assorted insects, birds, and squirrels. She began to whine as they drew close to the birch, recalling her pain and desirous of giving its source a wide berth, but he calmed her by patting her and changing direction, easing her away from the site of her mishap.

As a boy, Damien had been fascinated by bees, and wasps, and hornets. This colony had formed in the spring when the queen, roused from months of sleep after mating the previous fall, began to mix wood fiber with saliva, creating a pole of paper pulp to which she gradually added the hexagonal cells for her young: first the females from the fertilized eggs, then the males from her virgin eggs. He had kept track of each stage of its development, just as he used to do when he was a boy. It was the aspect of female rule that he had always found most interesting, for he came from an old-fashioned family where the men made the decisions, or so he had always believed until, as he grew older, he began to recognize the infinite subtle ways in which his mother, and his grandmothers, and various aunts and cousins, had manipulated the males to their satisfaction. Here, in this gray nest, the queen could be more open in her government, giving birth, creating defenders of the hive, feeding and being fed, even keeping her young warm by her own shivers, the warm air created by the actions of her body becoming trapped in a bell-shaped chamber of her own creation.

He stared back at the shape of the nest, almost invisible now among the leaves, as though reluctant to leave it. His sharp eyes picked out spider webs, and ants' nests, and a green caterpillar scaling a bloodroot, and each creature gave him pause, and each sight he seemed to store away.

They could smell the sea when Damien stopped. Had anyone been there to see him, it would have been clear that he was weeping. His face was contorted, and his shoulders convulsed with the force of his sobs. He looked round, right and left, as if expecting to glimpse presences moving between the trees, but there was only birdsong and the sound of waves breaking.

The dog's name was Sandy. She was a mutt, but more retriever than anything else. She was now ten years old, and she was as much Damien's dog as his father's, despite the son's long absences, loving both equally just as they loved her. She could not understand her younger master's behavior, for he was usually tolerant of her in ways that even his father was not. She wagged her tail uncertainly as he squatted beside her and tied her leash to the trunk of a sapling. Then he stood and removed the revolver from his pocket. It was a .38 Special, a Smith & Wesson Model 10. He had bought it from a dealer who claimed that it had come from a Vietnam vet who was down on his luck, but who Damien subsequently discovered had sold it to feed the cocaine habit that had eventually claimed his life.

Damien put his hands to his ears, the gun in his right hand now pointing to the sky. He shook his head and squeezed his eyes shut. "Please, please stop," he said. "I'm begging you. Please."

His mouth curled down, snot running from his nose, as he removed his hands from his head and, trembling, pointed the gun at the dog. It was inches from her muzzle. She leaned forward and sniffed it. She was used to the smell of oil and powder, for Damien and his father had often taken her to hunt birds with them, and she would bring back the bodies in her jaws. She wagged her tail expectantly, anticipating the game.

"No," said Damien. "No, don't make me do it. Please don't."

His finger tightened on the trigger. His whole arm was shaking. With a great effort of will, he turned the gun away from the dog, and screamed at the sea, and the air, and the setting sun. He gritted his teeth and freed the dog from her leash.

"Go!" he shouted at her. "Go home! Sandy, go home!"

The dog's tail went between her legs, but it was still wagging slightly. She didn't want to leave. She sensed that something was very wrong. Then Damien ran at her, aiming a kick at her behind but pulling it at the last moment so that it made no contact. Now the dog fled, retreating toward the house. She paused while Damien was still in sight of her, but he came at her again, and this time she kept going, stopping only when she heard the gunshot.

She cocked her head, then slowly began to retrace her steps, anxious to see what her master had brought down.

I

I fought single-handed, yet against such men no one
Could do battle.

Homer, *Odyssey*, Book 1

CHAPTER

I

Summer had come, the season of awakenings.

This state, this northern place, was not like its southern kin. Here, spring was an illusion, a promise made yet always unkept, a pretence of new life bound by blackened snow and slow-melting ice. Nature had learned to bide its time by the beaches and the bogs, in the Great North Woods of the county and the salt marshes of Scarborough. Let winter hold sway in February and March, beating its slow retreat to the 49th Parallel, refusing to concede even an inch of ground without a fight. As April approached, the willows and poplars, the hazel and the elms had budded amid birdsong. They had been waiting since the fall, their flowers shrouded yet ready, and soon the bogs were carpeted in the purple-brown of alders, and chipmunks and beavers were on the move. The skies bloomed with woodcock, and geese, and grackle, scattering themselves like seeds upon fields of blue.

Now May had brought summer at last, and all things were awake. All things.

SUNLIGHT SPLASHED ITSELF UPON the window, warming my back with its heat, and fresh coffee was poured into my cup.

"A bad business," said Kyle Quinn. Kyle, a neat, compact man in pristine whites, was the owner of the Palace Diner in Biddeford. He was also the chef, and he happened to be the cleanest diner chef I'd ever seen in my life. I'd eaten in diners where the eventual sight of the chef had made me consider undertaking a course of antibiotics, but Kyle was so nicely turned out, and his kitchen so spotless, that there were ICUs with poorer hygiene than the Palace, and surgeons with dirtier hands than Kyle's.

The Palace was the oldest diner car in Maine, custom-built by the Pollard Company of Lowell, Massachusetts, its red and white paint-work still fresh and spruce, and the gold lettering on the window that confirmed ladies were, indeed, invited glowed brightly as though written in fire. The diner had opened for business in 1927, and since then five people had owned it, of whom Kyle was the latest. It served only breakfast, and closed before midday, and was one of those small treasures that made daily life a little more bearable.

"Yeah," I said. "Bad in the worst way."

The *Portland Press-Herald* was spread before me over the counter of the diner. At the bottom of the front page, beneath the fold, the headline read:

NO LEADS IN SLAYING OF STATE TROOPER

The trooper in question, Foster Jandreau, had been found shot to death in his truck behind the former Blue Moon bar just inside the Saco town line. He hadn't been on duty at the time, and was dressed in civilian clothes when his body was discovered. What he was doing at the Blue Moon, nobody knew, especially since the autopsy revealed that he'd been killed sometime after midnight but before 2 A.M., when nobody had any business hanging around the burnt-out shell of an unloved bar. Jandreau's remains were found by a road crew that had pulled into the Moon's parking lot for some coffee and an early morning smoke before commencing the day's work. He had been shot twice at close range with a .22, once in the heart and once in the head. It bore all the hallmarks of an execution.

"That place was always a magnet for trouble," said Kyle. "They should have just razed what was left of it after it burned."

"Yeah, but what would they have put there instead?"

"A tombstone," said Kyle. "A tombstone with Sally Cleaver's name on it."

He walked away to pour coffee for the rest of the stragglers, most of whom were reading or talking quietly among themselves, seated in a line like characters in a Norman Rockwell painting. There were no booths at the Palace, and no tables, just fifteen stools. I occupied the last stool, the one farthest from the door. It was after 11:30 A.M., and technically the diner was now closed, but Kyle wouldn't be moving folks along anytime soon. It was that kind of place.

Sally Cleaver: her name had been mentioned in the reporting of Jandreau's murder, a little piece of local history that most people might have preferred to forget, and the final nail in the Blue Moon's coffin, as it were. After her death, the bar was boarded up, and a couple of months later it was torched. The owner was questioned about possible arson and insurance fraud, but it was just a matter of routine. The birds in the trees knew that the Cleaver family had put the match to the Blue Moon bar, and nobody uttered a word of blame for it.

The bar had now been closed for nearly a decade, a cause of grief for precisely no one, not even the rummies who used to frequent it. Locals always referred to it as the Blue Mood, as nobody ever came out of it feeling better than they had when they went in, even if they hadn't eaten the food or drunk anything that they hadn't seen un-sealed in front of them. It was a grim place, a brick fortress topped with a painted sign illuminated by four bulbs, no more than three of which were ever working at any one time. Inside, the lights were kept dim to hide the filth, and all the stools at the bar were screwed to the floor to provide some stability for the drunks. It had a menu right out of the chronic obesity school of cooking, but most of its clientele preferred to fill themselves up on the free beer nuts, salted to within an inch of a stroke in order to encourage the consumption of alcohol. At the end of the evening, the uneaten but heavily pawed nuts that remained were poured back into the big sack that Earle Hanley, the bartender, kept beside the sink. Earle was the only bartender. If he was sick, or had something else more important to do than pickle drunks, the Blue Moon didn't open. Sometimes, if you watched the clientele arriving for their daily fill, it was hard to tell if they were re-lieved or unhappy to find the door occasionally bolted.

And then Sally Cleaver died, and the Moon died with her.

There was no mystery about her death. She was twenty-three, and living with a deadbeat named Clifton Andreas, "Cliffie" to his bud-dies. It seemed that Sally had been putting a little money aside each week from her job as a waitress, perhaps in the hope of saving enough to have Cliffie Andreas killed, or to convince Earle Hanley to spike his beer nuts with rat poison. I was familiar with Cliffie Andreas as a face around town, one that it was sensible to avoid. Cliffie never met a puppy that he didn't want to drown, or a bug that he didn't want to crush. Any work that he picked up was seasonal, but Cliffie was never likely to qualify for Employee of the Month. Work was something that he did when there was no money left, and he viewed it entirely as a last resort if borrowing, theft, or simply leeching off someone weaker and needier than himself weren't available options. He had a superficial bad boy charm for the kind of woman who assumed a public pose of regarding good men as weak, even as she secretly dreamed of a regular Joe who wasn't mired in the mud at the bottom of the pond and determined to drag someone else down there with him.

I didn't know Sally Cleaver. Apparently she had low self-esteem, and lower expectations, but somehow Cliffie Andreas succeeded in reducing the former still further, and failed to live up even to the latter. Anyway, one evening Cliffie found Sally's small, hard-earned stash, and decided to treat himself and his buddies to a free night at the Moon. Sally came home from work, found her money gone, and went looking for Cliffie at his favorite haunt. She found him holding court at the bar, drinking on her dime the Moon's only bottle of cognac, and she decided to stand up for herself for the first, and last, time in her life. She screamed at him, scratched him, tore at his hair, until at last Earle Hanley told Cliffie to take his woman, and his domestic problems, outside, and not to come back until he had both under control.

So Cliffie Andreas had grabbed Sally Cleaver by the collar and pulled her through the back door, and the men at the bar had listened while he pounded her into the ground. When he came back inside, his knuckles were raw, his hands were stained red, and his face was flecked with freckles of blood. Earle Hanley poured him another drink and slipped outside to check on Sally Cleaver. By then, she was already choking on her own blood, and she died on the back lot before the ambulance could get to her.

And that was it for the Blue Moon, and for Cliffie Andreas. He pulled ten to fifteen in Thomaston, served eight, then was killed less than two months after his release by an "unknown assailant" who stole Cliffie's watch, left his wallet untouched, and then discarded the watch in a nearby ditch. It was whispered that the Cleavers had long memories.

Now Foster Jandreau had died barely yards from the spot on which Sally Cleaver had choked to death, and the ashes of the Moon's history were being raked through once again. Meanwhile, the state police didn't like losing troopers, hadn't liked it since right back in 1924 when Emery Gooch was killed in a motorcycle accident in Mattawamkeag; nor since 1964, when Charlie Black became the first trooper killed by gunfire while responding to a bank raid in South

Berwick. But there were shadows around Jandreau's killing. The paper might have claimed that there were no leads, but the rumors said otherwise. Crack vials had been found on the ground by Jandreau's car, and fragments of the same glass were discovered on the floor by his feet. He had no drugs in his system, but there were now concerns on the force that Foster Jandreau might have been dealing on the side, and that would be bad for everyone.

Slowly, the diner began to empty, but I stayed where I was until I was the only one remaining at the counter. Kyle left me to myself, making sure that my cup was full before he started cleaning up. The last of the regulars, mostly older men for whom the week wasn't the same without a couple of visits to the Palace, paid their checks and left.

I've never had an office. I never had any use for one, and if I had, I probably couldn't have justified the expense of it to myself, even given a favorable rent in Portland or Scarborough. Only a handful of clients had ever commented upon it, and on those occasions when a particular need for privacy and discretion had arisen, I'd been in a position to call in favors, and a suitable room had been provided. Occasionally, I used the offices of my attorney up in Freeport, but there were people who disliked the idea of going into a lawyer's office almost as much as they disliked the idea of lawyers in general, and I'd found that most of those who came to me for help preferred a more informal approach. Usually, I went to them, and spoke with them in their own homes, but sometimes a diner like the Palace, empty and discreet, was as good as anywhere. In this case, the venue for the meeting had been decided by the prospective client, not by me, and I was fine with it.

Shortly after midday, the Palace's door opened, and a man in his mid-sixties entered. He looked like a model for the stereotypical old Yankee: feed cap on his head, an L.L. Bean jacket over a plaid shirt, neat blue denims, and work boots on his feet. He was wiry as a tension cable, his face weathered and lined, light brown eyes glittering behind surprisingly fashionable steel-framed spectacles. He greeted Kyle by name, then removed his hat and gave a courtly little bow to Tara, Kyle's daughter, who was cleaning up behind the counter and who smiled and greeted him in turn.

"Good to see you, Mr. Patchett," she said. "It's been a while." There was a tenderness to her voice, and a brightness to her eyes, that said all that needed to be said about the new arrival's recent suffering.

Kyle leaned through the serving hatch between the kitchen and the counter area. "Come to check out a real diner, Bennett?" he said. "You look like you could do with some feeding up."

Bennett Patchett chuckled and swatted at the air with his right hand, as though Kyle's words were insects buzzing at his head, then took a seat beside me. Patchett had owned the Downs Diner, close by the Scarborough Downs racetrack on Route 1, for more than forty years. His father had run it before him, opening it shortly after he returned from service in Europe. There were still pictures of Patchett Senior on the walls of the diner, some of them from his military days, surrounded by younger men who looked up to him as their sergeant. He'd died when he was still in his forties, and his son had eventually taken over running the business. Bennett had now lived longer than his own father, just as it seemed that I was destined to live longer than mine.

He accepted the offer of a cup of coffee from Tara as he shrugged off his coat and hung it close to the old gas fire. Tara discreetly went to help her father in the kitchen, so that Bennett and I were left alone.

"Charlie," he said, shaking my hand.

"How you doing, Mr. Patchett?" I asked. It felt odd to be calling him by his last name. It made me feel about ten years old, but when it came to such men, you waited until they gave you permission to be a little more familiar in your mode of address. I knew that all his staff called him "Mr Patchett." He might have been like a father figure to some of them, but he was their boss, and they treated him with the respect that he deserved.

"You can call me Bennett, son. The less formal this is, the better. I don't think I've ever spoken with a private detective before, except you, and that was only when you were eating in my place. Only ever saw them on TV, and in the movies. And, truth to tell, your reputation makes me a little nervous."

He peered at me, and I saw his eye linger briefly on the scar on my neck. A bullet had grazed me there the previous year, deep enough to leave a permanent mark. In recent times, I seemed to have accumulated a lot of similar nicks and scratches. When I died, they could put me in a display case as an example to others who might be tempted to follow a similar path of beatings, gunshot wounds, and electrocution. Then again, I might just have been unlucky. Or lucky. It depended upon how you looked at the glass.

"Don't believe everything you hear," I said.

"I don't, and you still concern me."

I shrugged. He had a sly smile on his face.

"But no point in hemmin' and hawin'," he continued. "I want to thank you for taking the time to meet with me. I know that you're probably a busy man."

I wasn't, but it was nice of him to suggest that I might be. Since my license had been restored to me earlier in the year, following some misunderstandings with the Maine State Police, things had been kind of quiet. I'd done a little insurance work, all of it dull and most of it involving nothing more strenuous than sitting in a car and turning the pages of a book while I waited for some doofus with alleged workplace injuries to start lifting heavy stones in his yard. But insurance work was thin on the ground, what with the economy being the way it was. Most private detectives in the state were struggling, and I had been forced to accept any work that came along, including the kind that made me want to bathe in bleach when I was done. I'd followed a man named Harry Milner while he serviced three separate women in the course of one week in various motels and apartments, as well as holding down a regular job and taking his kids to baseball practice. His wife had suspected that he was having an affair but, unsurprisingly, she was shocked to hear that her husband was engaged in the type of extensive sexual entanglements usually associated with French farces. His time-management skills were almost admirable, though, as were his energy levels. Milner was only a couple of years older than I was, and if I'd been trying to keep four women satisfied every week I'd have incurred a coronary, probably while I was soaking myself in a bath of ice to keep the swelling down. Nevertheless, that was still the best-paying job I'd had in a while, and I was back doing a couple of days a month tending bar at the Great Lost Bear on Forest Avenue, as much to pass the time as anything else.

"I'm not as busy as you might think," I replied.

"Then you'll have time to hear me out, I guess."

I nodded, then said: "Before we go any further, I'd just like to say that I was sorry to hear about Damien."

I hadn't known Damien Patchett any better than I knew his father, and I hadn't made any effort to attend the funeral. The newspapers had been discreet about it, but everybody knew how Damien Patchett had died. It was the war, some whispered. He had taken his own life in name only. Iraq had killed him.

Bennett's face creased with pain. "Thank you. In a way, as you might have figured, it's why we're here. I feel kind of funny approaching you about this. You know, you doing things that you do. Compared to them fellas who killed and got hunted down by you, what I've got to offer might seem pretty dull."

I was tempted to tell him about waiting outside motel rooms while people inside engaged in illicit sexual congress, or sitting for hours in a car with a camera on the dashboard in the hope that someone might bend down suddenly.

"Sometimes, the dull stuff makes a pleasant change."

"Ayuh," said Patchett. "I can believe that."

His eyes shifted to the newspaper before me, and he winced again. Sally Cleaver, I thought. Damn, I should have put the newspaper away before Bennett arrived.

Sally Cleaver had been working at the Downs Diner when she died.

He sipped his coffee, and didn't speak again for at least three minutes. People like Bennett Patchett didn't reach their senior years in pretty much perfect health by rushing things. They worked on Maine time, and the sooner that everyone who had to deal with them learned to adjust their clocks accordingly, the better.

"I got a girl waitressing for me," he said at last. "She's a good kid. I think you might remember her mother, woman name of Katie Emory?"

Katie Emory had been at Scarborough High School with me, although we'd moved in different circles. She was the kind of girl who liked jocks, and I wasn't much for jocks, or the girls who hung with them. When I returned to Scarborough as a teenage boy after my father's death, I wasn't much in the mood for hanging with anyone, and I kept to myself. The local kids had all formed long-established cliques, and it was hard to break into them, even if you wanted to. I made some friends eventually, and for the most part I didn't cross too many people. I remembered Katie, but I doubt if she would have remembered me, not in the normal course of events. But my name had made the papers over the years, and maybe she, and others like her, read it and remembered the boy who had arrived in Scarborough for the last two years of his schooling, trailing stories about a father who was a cop, a cop who had killed two kids before taking his own life.

"How's she doing?"

"She lives up along the Airline somewhere." The Airline was the local name for Route 9, which ran between Brewer and Calais. "Third marriage. Shacked up with a musician."

"Really? I didn't know her that well."

"Good for you. Could have been you shacked up with her."

"There's a thought. She was a good-looking girl."

"Still not such a bad-looking woman now, I suppose," said Bennett. "A little thicker around the trunk than you might recall, but you can see what she was. Can see it in the daughter too."

"What's the daughter's name?"

"Karen. Karen Emory. Only child of her mother's first marriage, and born after the father took to his heels, so she has her mother's name. Only child of any of her marriages, come to think on it. She's been working for me for over a year now. Like I said, a good kid. She's got her troubles, but I think she'll come through them all right, long as she's given the help that she needs, and she's got the sense to ask for it."

Bennett Patchett was an unusual man. He and his wife, Hazel, who had died a couple of years ago, had always viewed those who worked for them not simply as staff, but as part of a kind of extended family. They had a particular fondness for the women who passed through the Downs, some of whom stayed for many years, others for only a matter of months. Bennett and Hazel had a special sense for girls who were in trouble, or who needed a little stability in their lives. They didn't pry, and they didn't preach, but they listened when they were approached, and they helped when they could. The Patchetts owned a couple of buildings around Saco and Scarborough, and these they had converted into cheap lodgings for their own staff and for the staff of a select number of other, established businesses run by people of a similar outlook to themselves. The apartments weren't mixed, so that women and men were required to stay with their own sex. Some occasional meetings of the twain did inevitably occur, but less often than one might have thought. For the most part, those who took up the Patchetts' offer of a place to stay were happy with the space—not just physical, but psychological and emotional—that it offered them.

The majority moved on eventually, some getting their lives back together and some not, but while they worked for the Patchetts they were looked out for, both by the couple themselves and by the older members of staff. Sally Cleaver's death had been a grave blow, but, if anything, it had made them more solicitous toward their charges. While Bennett had taken his wife's death hard, the loss of her had not changed his attitude toward his staff one iota. Anyway, they were now all that he had left, and he saw Sally Cleaver in the face of every one of those women, and perhaps he had already begun to see Damien in the young men.

"Karen's fallen in with a man, one I don't much care for," said Bennett. "She was living in one of the staff houses, just up on Gorham Road. She and Damien, they got on well together. I thought he might have had a crush on her, but she only had eyes for this friend of his, a buddy from Iraq by the name of Joel Tobias. Used to be Damien's squad leader. After Damien died, or it could have happened even before he died, Karen and Tobias hooked up. I hear that Tobias is troubled by some of what he saw over in Iraq. He had friends die on him, and I mean literally. They bled to death in his arms. He wakes up in the night, screaming and sweating. She thinks that she can help him."

"She told you this?"

"No. I heard it from one of the other waitresses. Karen wouldn't tell me that kind of thing. I suppose she prefers to talk to other women about these matters, that's all, and she knows that I didn't approve of her moving in with Tobias so soon after they'd met. Maybe I'm old-fashioned that way, but I felt that she should wait. Told her so too. They hadn't been together more than a couple of weeks at that point and, well, I asked her if she didn't feel that she was rushing things a bit, but she's a young girl, and she thinks she knows her own mind, and I wasn't about to interfere. She wanted to keep working for me, and that was just fine. We've been hurting a bit lately, same as everywhere, but I don't need to make more from the place than lets me pay my bills, and I can still do that, with money to spare. I don't need more staff and, I guess, it might be said that I don't need all the ones I've got, but they need the work, and it does an old man good to have young people around him."

He finished his coffee and looked longingly at the pot on the other side of the counter. As if by telepathy, Kyle looked up from where he was cleaning the prep station and said: "Go get that pot, if you want some. It'll go to waste otherwise."

Bennett walked around to the other side of the counter and poured us both a little more coffee. When he had done so, he remained standing, staring out the window at the old courthouse, thinking on what he would say next.

"Tobias is older than her: mid-thirties. Too old and too screwed up for a girl like her. Got himself wounded over in Iraq, lost some fingers and damaged his left leg. He drives a truck now. He's an independent contractor, or that's what he calls himself, but he seems to work pretty casually. He always had time to hang out with Damien, and he's always around Karen, more than someone who's supposed to be on the road earning a living should be, like money isn't a worry for him."

Bennett opened some creamer and added it to his coffee. There was another pause. I didn't doubt that he'd spent a lot of time considering what he was going to say, but I could tell that he was still cautious about speaking all of it aloud.

"You know, I got nothing but respect for the military. Couldn't help but have, man my father was. My eyesight hadn't been so bad, I'd probably have gone to Vietnam, and it might be that we wouldn't be having this conversation now. Maybe I wouldn't be here, but buried under a white stone somewhere. Whatever, I'd be a different man, or even a better one.

"I don't know the rights and wrongs of that war in Iraq. Seems to me to be a long way to go for no good cause that I can see, with a lot of lives lost, but it could be that wiser minds than mine know something that I don't. Worse than that, though, they didn't look after those men and women who came back, not the way they should have. My father, he returned from World War Two wounded, but he just didn't know it. He was damaged inside by some of the things that he'd seen and done, but the damage didn't have the same medical name then, or people just didn't understand how bad it could be. When Joel Tobias came into the Downs, I could tell that he was damaged too, and not just in his hand and his leg. He was hurting inside as well, all torn up with anger. I could smell it on him, could see it in his eyes. Didn't need anyone to tell me about it.

"Don't misunderstand me: he has as much of a right to be happy as anyone, maybe even more so because of the sacrifices that he's made. The hurt he's going through, mental or physical, doesn't deny him that right, and it could be that, in the normal run of events, someone like Karen might be good for him. She's been hurt too. I don't know how, but it's there, and it makes her sensitive to others like herself. A good man could be healed by that, once he doesn't exploit it. But I don't think Joel Tobias is a good man. That's what it comes down to. He's wrong for her, and he's just plain wrong with it."

"How can you tell?" I asked.

"I can't," he said, and I could hear the frustration in his voice. "Not for sure. It's a gut feeling, though, and something more than that. He drives his own rig, and it looks as new as a baby in the nurse's arms. He's got a big Silverado, and that's new too. He lives in a pretty nice house in Portland, and he's got money. He throws it around some, more than he should. I don't like it."

I waited. I had to be careful with what I said next. I didn't want to sound like I was doubting Bennett, but at the same time I knew that he could be overprotective of the young people in his charge. He was still trying to make up for failing to protect Sally Cleaver, even though he could not have prevented what befell her, and it was not his fault.

"You know, all of that could be on credit," I said. "Until recently, they'd let you pay a nickel down to see you drive a new truck off the lot. He may have received compensation for his injuries. You just—"

"She's changed," said Bennett. He said it so softly that I might almost have missed it, yet the intensity with which he spoke meant that it couldn't be ignored. "He's changed too. I can see it when he comes for her. He looks sick, like he's not sleeping right, even worse than he was before. Lately, I've started to see it in her too. She burned herself a couple of days back: tried to catch a coffeepot that was falling and ended up getting hot coffee on her hand. It was carelessness on her part, but the carelessness that comes from being tired. She's lost some weight, and she was never carrying much to start off with. And I think he's raised a hand to her. I saw bruising on her face. She told me that she'd walked into a door, like anyone believes that old story anymore."

"You try speaking to her about it?"

"Tried, but she got real defensive. Like I said before, I don't think she likes talking to men about personal matters. I didn't want to pursue it further, not then, for fear that I'd drive her away entirely. But I'm worried for her."

"What do you want me to do?"

"You still know them Fulci fellas? Maybe you could get them to beat on Tobias some, tell him to find someone else to share his bed."

He said it with a sad smile, but I could tell that there was a part of him that would really have liked to see the Fulcis, who were essentially weapons of war with appetites, unleashed on a man who could hit a woman.

"Doesn't work," I said. "Either the woman starts to feel sorry for the guy, or the guy figures the woman has been talking to someone, and it gets worse."

"Well, it was a nice thought while it lasted," he said. "If that's not an option, I'd like you to look into Tobias, see what you can find out about him. I just need something that might convince Karen to put some distance between her and him."

"I can do it, but there's a chance that she won't thank you for it."

"I'll take that chance."

"Do you want to know my rates?"

"Are you going to screw me over?"

"No."

"Then I figure you're worth what you ask for." He put an envelope on the counter. "There's two thousand dollars down. How much is that good for?"

"Long enough. If I need more, I'll get back to you. If I spend less, I'll refund you."

"You'll tell me what you find out?"

"I will. But what if I discover that he's clean?"

"He's not," said Bennett firmly. "No man who hits a woman can call himself clean."

I touched the envelope with my fingertips. I felt the urge to hand it back to him. Instead, I pointed at the Jandreau story.

"Old ghosts," I said.

"Old ghosts," he agreed. "I go out there sometimes, you know? Couldn't tell you why, unless it's that I hope I'll be pulled back in time so I can save her. Mostly, I just say a prayer for her as I pass by. They ought to scour that place from the earth."

"Did you know Foster Jandreau?"

"He came in sometimes. They all do: state troopers, local cops. We look after them. Oh, they pay their check like anyone else, but we make sure that they don't leave hungry. I knew Foster some, though. His cousin, Bobby Jandreau, served with Damien in Iraq. Bobby lost his legs. Hell of a thing."

I waited before speaking again. There was something missing here. "You said that this meeting was about Damien's death, in a way. The only connection is Karen Emory?"

Bennett looked troubled. Any mention of his son must have been painful for him, but there was more to it than that.

"Tobias came back troubled from that war, but my son didn't. I mean, he'd seen bad things, and there were days when I could tell he was remembering some of them, but he was still the son I knew. He told me over and over that he'd had a good war, if such a thing is possible. He didn't kill anyone who wasn't trying to kill him, and he had no hatred for the Iraqi people. He just felt sorry for what they were going through, and he tried to do his best by them. He lost some buddies over there, but he wasn't haunted by what he'd been through, not at first. That all came later."

"I don't know much about post-traumatic stress," I said, "but from what I've read, it can take some time to kick in."

"There is that," said Bennett. "I've read about it too. I was reading about it before Damien died, thinking that I might be able to help him if I understood better what he was going through. But, you see, Damien liked the army. I don't think he wanted to leave. He served multiple tours, and would have gone back again. As it was, all he talked about when he got back was reenlisting."

"Why didn't he?"

"Because Joel Tobias wanted him here."

"How do you know that?"

"From what Damien said. He took a couple of trips up to Canada with Tobias, and I got the sense that they had something going on, some deal that promised good money at the end of it. Damien began to talk about setting up his own business, maybe moving into security if he didn't return to the army. That was when the trouble started. That was when Damien began to change."

"Change how?"

"He stopped eating. Couldn't sleep, and when he did manage to fall asleep I'd hear him crying out, and shouting."

"Could you hear what he was saying?"

"Sometimes. He'd be asking someone to leave him alone, to stop talking. No, to stop *whispering*. He became anxious, and aggressive. He'd snap at me for nothing. When he wasn't doing stuff for Tobias, he was somewhere by himself, smoking, staring into space. I suggested that he ought to talk to someone about it, but I don't know if he did. He was back for three months when this all started, and he was dead by his own hand two weeks later." He patted my shoulder. "Look into that Tobias fella, and we'll talk again."

With that, he said his good-byes to Kyle and Tara, and left the diner. I watched him walk slowly to his car, a beat-up Subaru with a Sea Dogs sticker along the rear fender. As he opened the car door, he caught me watching him. He nodded and raised a hand in farewell, and I did likewise.

Kyle came out from the kitchen.

"I'm going to lock up now," he said. "You all done?"

"Thank you," I said. I paid the check, and left a good tip, both for the food and for Kyle's discretion. There weren't many diners in which two men could meet and discuss what Bennett and I had discussed without fear of eavesdropping.

"He's a good man," said Kyle as Bennett's car turned out of the lot.

"Yes, he is."

ON THE WAY BACK to Scarborough, I took a detour to drive by the Blue Moon. Yellow police tape flapped in the breeze from a downpipe, bright against the blackened shell of the bar. The windows remained boarded up, the steel door secured with a heavy bolt, but there was a hole in the roof where the flames had burst through all those years ago, and if you got close enough it smelled of damp and, even now, charred wood. Kyle and Bennett were right: it should have been demolished, but still it remained, a dark cancer cell against the red clover of the field that stretched behind it.

I pulled away, the ruin of the Blue Moon receding in my rearview mirror until at last I left it behind. Yet it seemed something of it remained on the mirror, like a smudge left by a blackened finger, a reminder from the dead of what the living still owe to them.

II

I thought about what Bennett Patchett had said when I returned to my house in Scarborough and sat down at my desk to make notes on our conversation. If Joel Tobias was beating his girlfriend, then he deserved to experience some grief of his own, but I wondered if Bennett knew what he was getting himself into. Even if I found something that he could use against Tobias, I didn't believe it would have much impact on the relationship, not unless what I found was so terrible that any woman who wasn't clinically insane would instantly pack her bags and head for the hills. I had also tried to warn him that Karen Emory might not thank him for getting involved in her personal affairs, even if Tobias was being violent toward her. Still, if that had been Bennett's sole reason for becoming involved in his employee's business, his motives would have been sound, and I could have afforded to give him a little of my time. After all, he was paying for it.

The problem was that Karen Emory's well-being was not the sole reason for his approach to me. In fact, it was a dupe, a means of opening a separate but linked investigation into the death of his son, Damien. It was clear that Bennett believed Joel Tobias bore some responsibility for the change in Damien Patchett's behavior, a change that had led, finally, to his self-destruction. Ultimately, all investiga-

tions instigated by individuals and conducted outside the corporate
or law enforcement spheres are personal, but some are more personal
than others. Bennett wanted someone to answer for his son's death
in the absence of his son being able to answer for it himself. Some
fathers, in a similar situation, might have directed their anger at the
military for failing to recognize the torments of a returning soldier,
or at the failings of psychiatrists, but, according to Bennett, his son
had returned from the war relatively unscathed. That claim, in itself,
warranted further investigation, but for now Joel Tobias was, in Bennett's eyes, as much a suspect in Damien Patchett's death as if he had
steadied Damien's hand as the trigger was pulled.

Bennett was a curious man. While he might have had a soft center,
the exterior was like a crocodile's plated carapace: Bennett was solid
now, but he had served time. As a young man, he had fallen in with
a group of guys out of Auburn who had taken down gas stations and
grocery stores before progressing to the big time, and a raid on the
Farmers First Bank in Augusta during which a weapon was waved
and shots were fired, albeit blanks. It hadn't netted them a whole
lot, about $2,000 plus change, and soon the cops had informally
identified at least one of the members of the gang. He was hauled
in, sweated for a while, and finally rolled over on the rest of his ac-
complices in return for a reduced sentence. Bennett, who had been
the wheelman, was facing up to ten years, but served five. He was no
career criminal. Five years in Thomaston, a fortress prison from the
nineteenth century, still bearing the mark of its old gallows as assuredly as if it had been burned into the earth, had convinced him of the
error of his ways. He had returned to his father's business with his tail
between his legs, and he'd kept out of trouble ever since. That didn't
mean that he had any great fondness for the law, and being ratted out
by someone in the past meant that Bennett wasn't about to rat out
anyone else in turn. He may not have cared much for Joel Tobias, but
hiring me instead of going to the cops was a very Bennettian compro-

mise, I thought, as was asking me to investigate one man in the hope that it might reveal the truth behind the death of another.

NOTHING IS SECRET ANYMORE. With a little ingenuity, and a little cash, you can find out a great deal about people that they might have believed, or have preferred to remain, confidential and protected. It's even easier when you're a licensed private investigator. Within an hour, I had Joel Tobias's credit history laid out on my desk. There were no outstanding warrants against him and, from what I could see, he had never been in trouble with the police. Since he had been invalided out of the military just over a year earlier, he seemed to have worked hard, paid his bills, and led what, to all appearances, was a regular, blue-collar existence.

One of my grandfather's favorite words was "hinky." Milk that was just about to go off might taste a little hinky. A tiny, almost inaudible noise in his car engine might lead to suspicions of undiagnosed hinkiness in the carburetor. For him, something that was hinky was more troubling than something that was outright wrong, simply because the nature of the flaw was undefined. He would know that it was there, but he would not be able to tackle it because its true face had not yet revealed itself. What was wrong could either be dealt with or lived with, but what was hinky would come between him and his sleep.

Joel Tobias's affairs were hinky. His rig, with a sleeper, had cost him $85,000 when he'd bought it. Despite what Bennett had said, it wasn't quite new when he purchased it from the dealer, but it was as good as. At the same time, he'd also picked up a "dry van," or box trailer, for another $10,000. He'd put 5 percent down, and was paying off the rest monthly, at a rate of interest that wasn't excessive and might even have been considered pretty favorable, but he was still eating about $2,500 a month in repayments. In addition, that same month he'd bought himself a new Chevy Silverado. He'd negotiated himself a pretty good deal on it: $18,000, which was $6,000 off the regular dealer price, and he was paying that loan off at $280 a month. Finally, the payments on the mortgage on his house in Portland, just off Forest and not far from the Great Lost Bear, as it happened, came to another $1,000 a month. The house had been his uncle's, and had already fallen into arrears when it was left to Joel in his uncle's will. Taken together, it all meant that Tobias needed to be taking in almost $5,000 each month just to keep his head above water, and that was before he paid for insurance, medical coverage, gas for his Chevy, food, heating, beer, and whatever else he needed to make his life comfortable. Add in, conservatively, another $1,000 per month for all that, and Tobias's annual earnings would have to be in the region of $70,000 after taxes. It wasn't completely unattainable, given that, as an owner-operator, Tobias could expect to earn about 90 cents per mile, plus fuel, but he'd be working long hours to do it, and would need to put in the miles. In addition, he was probably receiving compensation for his injured hand, and maybe for his leg as well. At a guess, he was pulling down somewhere between $500 and $1,200 tax free each month for his injuries, which would help some with his bills but would still leave him with a lot of cash to earn on the road. His credit rating remained steady, he hadn't defaulted on any of his loans, and he was paying contributions into his IRA.

But according to Bennett, or the impression he had gained, Tobias wasn't working all the hours God had given him. In fact, Tobias didn't seem to have many financial worries at all, which suggested that there was money coming in from somewhere other than what he earned by driving, or received in comp; that, or he had money stored away, and was subsidizing his business from his savings, which meant that he wouldn't be in business for very long.

So there it was. Joel Tobias was hinky. There was cash coming from elsewhere. It was just a matter of establishing the source of that additional income, and something that Bennett had told me meant that I could hazard an educated guess at the source. Bennett had said that Tobias traveled back and forth between Maine and Canada. Canada meant a border crossing, and a border meant smuggling.

And when it came to the border between Canada and Maine, that meant drugs.

ACCORDING TO AN ARTICLE in *The New York Times*, "To check smuggling along the Maine and Canada line would require a small army, so wild is the greater part of the territory and so great and varied the opportunities." The article in question was written in 1892, and it was as true now as it was then. In the late nineteenth century, what worried the authorities most was the loss of customs revenue from liquor, fish, cattle, and produce being smuggled over the border, but drugs were also becoming an issue, with opium being brought into New Brunswick in bond, and from there transported into the United States via Maine. The state had 400 miles of land border with Canada, most of it wilderness, as well as 3,000 miles of seacoast, and about 1,400 small islands. It was then, and still is, a smuggler's paradise.

In the 1970s, as the DEA began focusing increasingly on the southern borders with Mexico, New England became an attractive option for pot smugglers, especially as there was a ready market for it among the students in its 250 colleges. It was simply a matter of buying a boat, hitting Jamaica or Colombia, and then running an established route that allowed a ton each to be dropped off in Florida, the Carolinas, Rhode Island, and, finally, Maine. Since then, the Mexicans had established a presence here, along with assorted South Americans, bikers, and anyone else who figured he was hard enough to capture a share of the narcotics market and hold on to it.

I sat back in my chair and stared out of my window at the salt marshes and the seabirds scudding across their waters. To the south, a thin column of dark smoke raised itself to the sky before slowly dissipating in the still air, leaving a faint trace of pollution to mar the otherwise faultless blue of the gently closing day. I called Bennett Patchett, and he confirmed that Karen Emory was working. Her shift was due to finish at 7 P.M. and, as far as Bennett knew, Joel Tobias would be coming by to pick her up. He often did when he wasn't out on the road. Karen had told Bennett, after he had asked if she could work a little late that evening, that she couldn't because she and Joel were going out for dinner. She said that Joel had a bunch of Canadian runs lined up over the coming weeks, and they were unlikely to have much time together as a result. So, with nothing better to do, I decided to take a look at Joel Tobias and his girlfriend.

THE DOWNS WAS A pretty big place, capable of taking a hundred covers or more, assuming the kitchen was fully staffed and the waitresses were prepared to sweat hard for their tips. Large glass windows looked down on Route 1 and the parking lot of the Big 20 bowling alley on the other side of the road. A single counter ran almost the entire length of the room, taking a dogleg to the north and south to form a kind of elongated U. The walls were lined with four-seater booths, with another bank of four-seaters creating an island of vinyl and Formica in the center of the restaurant. The waitresses wore blue T-shirts with the name of the restaurant on the back, beneath which was an illustration of three horses straining for a finishing post. Each waitress had her name stitched into the fabric above her left breast.

I didn't go inside, but waited in the parking lot. I could see Karen Emory depositing checks on her tables in preparation for the end of her shift. Bennett had described her to me, and she was the only blonde working that evening. She was pretty and tiny, perhaps only five feet tall, and slimly built for the most part, given that, even from a distance, her T-shirt looked like it was at least a size too small for her around the bust. Guys probably came to the Downs just to dribble egg on their chins as they gazed upon the stretched material.

At 6:55 P.M., a black Silverado with smoked-glass windows pulled into the lot. Twenty minutes later, Karen Emory emerged wearing a short black dress and heels, her hair loose on her shoulders and freshly applied makeup on her face. She climbed into the Silverado, and it turned left on to Route 1, heading north. I stayed behind it all the way to South Portland, where it pulled into the Beale Street Barbecue on Broadway. Karen got out first, followed by Joel Tobias. He was at least a foot taller than his girlfriend, his dark hair, a little long and already streaked with gray, brushed back over his ears and away from his forehead. He wore jeans and a blue denim shirt. If there was any fat on him, it was well hidden. He walked with a slight limp, favoring his right foot, and kept his left hand tucked into a front pocket of his jeans.

I gave them a couple of minutes, then followed them inside. They were sitting at one of the tables near the door, so I took a seat at the bar and ordered a bottle of alcohol-free beer and some fries, positioning myself so I could watch the TV and the table occupied by Tobias and Karen. They seemed to be having a good time. They got a couple of margaritas with beer on the side, and shared a sampler plate. There was a lot of smiling and laughing, mostly on Karen Emory's part, but it seemed kind of strained, or that might have been Bennett Patchett's opinion coloring my own. I tried to blot out all that he had said, and just regard them as a couple of interesting strangers in a restaurant. Nope, Karen was still trying too hard, an impression confirmed when Tobias went to the men's room and Karen's smile gradually faded as she watched him walk away, to be replaced by a look that was equal parts thoughtful and troubled.

I had just ordered another beer, which I didn't plan to drink, when Joel Tobias appeared at my elbow. I didn't react when he squeezed in at the bar and asked the bartender for the check, pointing out that the waitress appeared to be busy elsewhere. He turned to me, smiled, said "Beg your pardon, sir," and returned to his girlfriend. I caught a glimpse of his left hand as he walked away: there were two fingers missing, and the skin was scarred. A minute or two later, the waitress arrived, picked up the check at the bar on the instructions of the bartender, and brought it to their table. A couple of minutes more, and they had paid up and left.

I didn't follow them. It had been enough to watch them together, and Tobias's appearance at my side had made me uneasy. I hadn't seen him return from the men's room, which meant that he must have gone outside through the side door and come back in by the main door. Maybe he'd smoked a cigarette while he was out there but, if so, he was strictly a two-drag guy. It was probably just a co-incidence, but I wasn't about to confirm any suspicions he might have had about my presence there by running out to the parking lot and taking after them with squealing tires. I finished most of the beer that I hadn't wanted, and watched some more of the game on the TV before settling up and leaving the bar. The parking lot was almost empty, the black Silverado long gone. It was not yet 10 P.M., and there was still light in the sky. I drove into Portland to take a ride by Joel Tobias's place. It was a small, well-maintained two story. The Silverado was parked in the drive, but there was no sign of Tobias's big rig. A light burned in an upstairs room, visible through the partly closed drapes, but as I watched, it was extinguished, and the house became entirely dark.

I waited for a moment or two longer, regarding the house, and thinking about the look on Karen Emory's face, and the way that Tobias had appeared at my elbow, before I drove back to Scarborough and my own quiet home. There had been a woman and a child with me once, and a dog, but they were in Vermont now. I visited my daughter, Sam, once or twice a month, and sometimes she came to stay with me for a night if her mother, Rachel, had business in Boston. Rachel was seeing someone else, and I felt awkward intruding upon her for that reason and, sometimes, resentful of her for doing so. But I also kept my distance because I wanted no harm to come to them, and harm followed me.

Their places had been taken by the shadows of another woman and child—no longer glimpsed, but felt nonetheless, like the lingering scent of flowers that have been discarded after the petals began to fall. They had ceased to be a source of unease, this departed wife and daughter. They had been taken from me by a killer, a man whose life I had taken in turn, and in my guilt and rage I had allowed them to become transformed for a time into hostile, vengeful presences. But that was before: now, the sense of them consoled me, for I knew that they had a part to play in whatever was to come.

When I opened the door, the house was warm and filled with the smell of salt from the marshes. I felt the emptiness of the shadows, the disinterest of the silence, and I slept softly, and alone.

CHAPTER

III

Jeremiah Webber had just poured a glass of wine to ease himself into the act of cooking his evening meal when the doorbell rang. Webber did not like his routines being interrupted, and Thursday evenings at his relatively modest home—modest, at least, by the wealthy standards of New Canaan, Connecticut—were sacrosanct. On Thursday evenings he switched off his cell phone, did not answer the land line (and, in truth, his few friends, aware of his quirks, knew better than to disturb him, mortality, impending or actual, being the only permissible excuse), and most certainly did not respond to the ringing of the doorbell. His kitchen was at the back of the house, and he kept the door closed while he cooked, so that only a thin horizontal shaft of light might possibly be visible through the glass of the front door. A lamp burned in the living room, and another in his bedroom upstairs, but that was the sum total of the illumination in the house. Bill Evans was playing at low volume on the kitchen's sound system. Webber would sometimes spend the preceding days of the week planning precisely what music he would play while cooking and eating, what wine would accompany his meal, what dishes he would prepare. These small indulgences helped to keep him sane.

On Thursday evenings, therefore, those who knew that he was at home were unlikely to interrupt him, and those who did not know for certain if he was there or not would be unable to confirm his presence or absence merely on the basis of the lights in the house. Even his most valued clients, some of whom were wealthy men and women used to having their needs met at any hour of the day or night, had come to accept that, on Thursday nights, Jeremiah Webber would be unavailable. His routine had already been thrown slightly on this particular Thursday by a series of extended telephone conversations, so that it had been after eight by the time he returned home, and now it was nearly nine and he had still not eaten. More so than usual, he was in no mood for interruptions.

Webber was an urbane, dark-haired man in his early fifties, good looking in what might have been considered a slightly effeminate way, an impression enhanced by his fondness for spotted bow ties, bright vests, and a range of cultural interests including, but not limited to, ballet, opera, and modern interpretive dance. It led casual acquaintances to assume that he might be homosexual, but Webber was not gay; far from it, in fact. His hair had not yet begun to turn even slightly gray, a genetic quirk that took ten years off his age, and had enabled him to date women who were, by any standards, too young for him without attracting the form of disapproving, if envious, attention that such May-December assignations frequently aroused. His relative attractiveness to the opposite sex, combined with a degree of personal generosity to those who found his favor, had proved to be a mixed blessing. It had brought two marriages to fraught ends, only the first of which he actually regretted, for he had loved his first wife, if not quite enough. The child of that marriage, his daughter and only offspring, had ensured that the lines of communication remained open between the estranged partners, with the result that he believed his first wife now viewed him, for the most part, with a certain bemused affection. The second marriage, meanwhile, was a mistake, and one that he did not intend to make again, now preferring casual to committed when it came to sex. So he rarely wanted for female company, even if he had paid a price for his appetites in broken marriages, and the financial penalties that come hand in hand with such matters. As a consequence, Webber had recently found himself with serious cash-flow problems, and had been forced to take steps to rectify the situation.

He was about to commence deboning the trout that lay upon a small granite slab when he heard the bell. He wiped his fingers on his apron, picked up the remote-control unit, and turned the volume down still further, listening carefully. He walked to the kitchen door and stared at the small video screen by the intercom.

There was a man standing on his doorstep. He was wearing a dark fedora, and his face was turned away from the camera lens. But, as Webber watched, the man's head moved, as though he were somehow aware that he was under examination. He kept his head lowered, so that his eyes were hidden in shadow, but from the brief glimpse of his face that he caught, Webber could tell that the man on the doorstep was a stranger to him. There appeared to be a mark on the man's upper lip, but perhaps that was simply a trick of the light.

The doorbell rang a second time, and the man kept his finger on the button, so that the two-note sequence repeated itself over and over.

"What the hell?" said Webber aloud. His finger hit the intercom button. "Yes? Who are you? What do you want?"

"I want to talk," said the man. "Who I am doesn't matter, but for whom I work should concern you." His speech was slightly unclear, as though he were holding something in his mouth.

"And who is that?"

"I represent the Gutelieb Foundation."

Webber released the intercom button. His right index finger went to his mouth. He chewed at the nail, a habit of his since childhood, an indication of distress. The Gutelieb Foundation: he had only engaged in a handful of transactions with it. Everything had been conducted through a third party, a firm of lawyers in Boston. Attempts to discover precisely what the Gutelieb Foundation might be, and who might be responsible for deciding on its acquisitions, had proved fruitless, and he had begun to suspect that it did not exist as anything more than a piece of convenient nomenclature. When he had persisted in his efforts, he had received a letter from the lawyers advising him that the organization in question was very particular about its privacy, and any further inquiries on Webber's behalf would result in an immediate cessation of all business from the Foundation, as well as some appropriately placed whispers indicating that perhaps Mr. Webber was not as discreet as some of his customers might wish him to be. After that, Webber had backed off. The Gutelieb Foundation, real or a front, had sourced some unusual, and expensive, items from him. The tastes of those behind it appeared to be very particular, and when Webber had been able to satisfy those tastes he had been paid promptly, and without question or negotiation.

But that last item . . . He should have been more careful in his dealings, more attentive about its provenance, he told himself, even as he understood that he was simply preparing the lies he might offer in exculpation to the man on his doorstep if it became necessary to do so.

He reached for his wine with his left hand, but misjudged the movement. The glass shattered on the floor, splashing his slippers and the bottoms of his trousers. Swearing, Webber returned to the intercom. The man was still there.

"I'm rather busy at the moment," he said. "Surely this is something that can be discussed during normal hours."

"One would have thought so," came the reply, "but we seem to be having trouble getting your attention. A number of messages have been left with your service, and at your place of business. If we did not know better, we might have begun to believe that you are deliberately avoiding us."

"But what is this about?"

"Mr. Webber, you're trying my patience, just as you have tried the patience of the Foundation."

Webber gave in. "All right, I'm coming."

He looked at the wine pooling on the black-and-white tiled floor, carefully avoiding the broken glass. Such a shame, he thought, as he discarded his apron. He made his way to the front door, pausing only to remove the gun from the hall stand and slip it into the back of his trousers beneath his cardigan. The weapon was small, and easily concealed. He checked his reflection in the mirror, just to be sure, and opened the door.

The man on the doorstep was smaller than he expected, and dressed in a dark blue suit that might, at one point, have been an expensive purchase, but now looked dated, although it had survived the intervening years with a degree of grace. There was a blue-and-white-spotted handkerchief in the breast pocket that matched the man's tie. His head was still lowered, but now it was part of the gesture of removing his hat. For a moment, Webber had a strange vision of the hat coming off and taking the top of the visitor's head with it, like an egg that has been neatly broken, permitting him to peer into the cavity of the skull. Instead, there were only loose strands of white hair like tendrils of cotton candy, and a domed head that came to a discernible point. Then the man looked up at him, and, instinctively, Webber took a small step back.

The face was quite pale, the nostrils slim dark holes cut into the base of the narrow, perfectly straight nose. The skin around the eyes was wrinkled and bruised. It spoke of illness, and decay. The eyes themselves were barely visible, obscured as they were by folds of skin that had descended on them from the forehead like wax melting from an impure candle. Below the eyeballs, red flesh was visible, and Webber thought that the man must have been constantly irritated by grit and dust.

But then, this individual clearly had other distractions when it came to pain. His upper lip was distorted, reminding Webber of those photographs in Sunday newspapers of children with cleft palates that were used to elicit charitable donations, except this was no cleft palate: it was a wound, an arrowhead incision into the skin, exposing white teeth and discolored gums. It was also grossly infected, red raw and speckled in places with purple dots darkening to black. Webber thought that he could almost see the bacteria eating away at the flesh, and wondered how this man could bear the torment, and what kind of drugs he would have to take just to allow him to sleep. In fact, how could he even bear to look at himself in a mirror and be reminded of his body's betrayal and his own, clearly imminent mortality? His age was impossible to surmise because of his illness, but Webber put him between fifty and sixty, even allowing for the depredations he was suffering.

"Mr. Webber," he said, and despite his wound, his voice was soft and pleasant. "Let me introduce myself. My name is Herod." He smiled, and Webber had to force his face to remain still and not register his disgust, for he feared that the movement of the visitor's facial muscles would tear the wound on his lip still further, opening it to the septum. "I am often asked if I am fond of children. I take the question in good spirit."

Webber wasn't sure how to respond, so he simply opened the door a little wider to admit the stranger, his right hand moving almost casually to his waist and resting there within easy reach of his gun. As Herod stepped into the house he nodded politely and glanced at Webber's waist, and Webber felt sure that he knew of the gun, and that it didn't bother him in the slightest. Herod looked toward the open kitchen, and Webber indicated that he should enter. He saw that Herod walked slowly, but it was not a function of his illness. Herod was just a man who moved with deliberation. Once in the kitchen, he laid his hat on the table and looked around, smiling in benign approval of all that he saw. Only the music seemed to disturb him, his forehead creasing slightly as he stared at the music system.

"It sounds like . . . no, it is: it's Fauré's 'Pavane,'" he said. "I can't say that I approve of what is being done to it, though."

Webber gave an almost imperceptible shrug. "It's Bill Evans," he said. Who didn't like Bill Evans?

Herod contrived a little moue of disgust. "I've never cared for such experimentation," he said. "I'm afraid that I am a purist in most matters."

"To each his own, I guess," said Webber.

"Indeed, indeed. It would be a dull world if we all shared the same tastes. Still, it is hard not to feel that some are better resisted than indulged. Do you mind if I sit down?"

"Be my guest," said Webber, with only a hint of unhappiness.

Herod sat, noting the wine and broken glass on the floor as he did so. "I hope I wasn't the cause of that," he remarked.

"My own carelessness. I'll clean it up later." Webber didn't want his hands full with a brush and pan while this man was in his kitchen.

"I appear to have disturbed you in the act of preparing your meal. Please, by all means continue. I have no desire to keep you from it."

"It's okay." Equally, Webber decided that he would rather not turn his back on Herod. "I'll continue after you've gone."

Herod considered this for a moment, as though resisting an impulse to comment upon it, then let it pass, like a cat that decides not to chase down and crush a butterfly. Instead, he examined the bottle of white Burgundy on the table, turning it gently with one finger so that he could read the label.

"Oh, very good," he said. He turned to Webber. "Would you mind pouring a glass for me, please?"

He waited patiently as Webber, unused to guests making such demands of him, retrieved two glasses from the kitchen cabinet and poured a measure for Herod that, under the circumstances, was more than generous, then one for himself. Herod raised the glass and sniffed it. He removed a handkerchief from his trouser pocket, folded it neatly, then placed it against his chin as he took a sip from the glass with the corner of his mouth, avoiding the wound on his lip. A little of the wine trickled down and soaked into the handkerchief.

"Wonderful, thank you," he said. He waved the handkerchief apologetically. "One gets used to the necessity of sacrificing a little of one's dignity in order to continue living as one might wish." He smiled again. "As you may have surmised, I am not a well man."

"I'm sorry to hear that," said Webber. He struggled to put any emotion into the words.

"I appreciate the sentiment," said Herod dryly. He raised a finger and pointed at his upper lip. "My body is riddled with cancers, but this is recent: a necrotizing illness that failed to respond to penicillin and vancomycin. The subsequent debridement did not remove all the necrotic tissue, and now it seems that further explorations may be required. Curiously, it is said that my namesake, the slayer of infants, suffered from necrotizing fasciitis of the groin and genitalia. A punishment from God, one might say."

Are you referring to the king, or yourself, Webber wondered, and it was as if the thought were somehow audible to Herod, for his expression changed, and what little benignity he had about him seemed to vanish.

"Please, Mr. Webber, sit down. Also, you may want to remove your weapon from your belt. It can hardly be comfortable where it is, and I'm not armed. I came here to talk."

Slightly embarrassed, Webber retrieved the weapon and placed it on the table as he took a seat across from Herod. The gun was still close if he needed it. He held his wineglass in his left hand, just to be safe.

"To business, then," said Herod. "As I told you, I represent the interests of the Gutelieb Foundation. Until recently, it was felt that we had a mutually beneficial relationship with you: you sourced material for us, and we paid without complaint or delay. Occasionally, we required you to act on our behalf, purchasing at auction when we preferred to keep our interests hidden. Again, I believe that you were more than adequately compensated for your time in these cases. In effect, you were permitted to buy such items with our money, and sell them back to us at a markup that was considerably more than an agent's commission. Am I correct? I am not overstating the nature of our understanding?"

Webber shook his head, but didn't speak.

"Then, some months ago, we asked you to acquire a grimoire for us: seventeenth century, French. Described as being bound in calfskin, but we know that was merely a ruse to avoid unwanted attention. Human skin and calfskin have, as we are both aware, very different textures. A unique item, then, to put it mildly. We gave you all the information required for a successful, preemptive sale. We did not want the book to go to auction, even one as discreet and specialized as this one promised to be. But, for the first time, you failed to produce the goods. Instead, it appeared that another buyer got there before you. You handed back our money, and informed us that you would do better on the next occasion. Unfortunately, it is in the nature of the unique that 'next time' never applies."

Herod smiled again, this time regretfully: a disappointed teacher faced with a pupil who has failed to grasp a simple concept. The atmosphere in the kitchen had changed since Herod entered, palpably so. It was not merely the creeping unease that Webber felt at the direction that the conversation was taking. No, it felt to him that the force of gravity was slowly becoming greater, the air heavier. When he tried to raise his glass to his lips, the weight of it surprised him. Webber felt that, if he were to stand and try to walk, it would be like wading through mud or silt. It was Herod who was altering the very essence of the room, releasing elements from within himself that were changing the composition of every atom. There was a feeling of density about the dying man, for dying he most assuredly was, as though he were not flesh and blood but some unknown material, a thing of polluted compounds, an alien mass.

Webber managed to get the glass to his lips. Wine dribbled down his chin in an unpleasant imitation of Herod's own previous indignity. He wiped it away with the palm of his hand.

"There was nothing that I could do," said Webber. "There will always be competition for esoteric and rare finds. It's hard to keep their existence a secret."

"Yet, in the case of the La Rochelle Grimoire, its existence *was* a secret," said Herod. "The Foundation spends a great deal of time and effort tracking down items of interest that may have been forgotten, or lost, and it is very careful in its inquiries. The grimoire was traced after years of investigation. It had been incorrectly listed in the eighteenth century, and by an arduous process of cross-checking on our part, that error was confirmed. Only the Foundation was aware of the grimoire's significance. Even its owner regarded it merely as a curiosity; a valuable one, possibly, but with no awareness of how important it might be to the right collector. The Foundation, in turn, nominated you to act on its behalf. You were required only to ensure that payment was made, and then arrange for safe transportation of the item. All the hard work had been done for you."

"I'm not sure what you're implying," said Webber.

"I'm not implying anything. I'm *telling* you what occurred. You became greedy. You had dealt in the past with the collector Graydon Thule, and you knew that Thule had a particular passion for grimoires. You made him aware of the existence of the La Rochelle Grimoire. In return, he agreed to pay you a finder's fee and offered one hundred thousand dollars more for the grimoire than the Foundation had earmarked in order to ensure that it would go to him. You did not pass on that full amount to the seller, but kept half of it for yourself, in addition to the finder's fee. You then paid a subagent in Brussels to act on your behalf, and the grimoire went to Thule. I don't think I've missed out on any details, have I?"

Webber was tempted to argue, to deny the truth of what Herod had said, but he could not. He had been foolish to think that he might be able to get away with the deception, but only in retrospect. At the time, it had seemed perfectly possible, even reasonable. He needed the money: his cash flow had slowed in recent months, for his business was not immune to the economic downturn. In addition, his daughter was a second year med student, and her fees were crucifying him. While the Gutelieb Foundation, like most of his clients, paid well, it did not pay well often enough, and Webber had been struggling for some time. He had made $120,000 dollars in total from acquiring the grimoire for Thule, once he had paid off the subagent in Brussels. That was a lot of money for him: enough to ease his debts, cover his share of Suzanne's fees for the next year, and leave himself with a little in the bank. He began to feel a sense of indignation at Herod and his manner. Webber did not work for the Gutelieb Foundation. His obligations to it were minimal. True, his actions in the sale of the grimoire were not strictly honorable, but such deals happened all the time. Screw Herod. Webber had enough money to get by on for now, and he was in Thule's good books. If the Gutelieb Foundation cut him off, then so be it. Herod couldn't prove any of what he had just said. If inquiries were made about the money, Webber had enough false bills of sale to explain away a small fortune.

"I think you should go now," said Webber. "I'd like to get back to preparing my meal."

"I'm sure that you would. Unfortunately, I am afraid that I can't let the matter rest there. Some form of recompense must be made."

"I don't think so. I don't know what you're talking about. Yes, I've done some work for Graydon Thule in the past, but he has his sources too. I can't be held responsible for every failed sale."

"You're not being held responsible for every failed sale, just this one. The Gutelieb Foundation is very concerned with issues of responsibility. Nobody forced you to act as you did. That is the joy of free will, but also its curse. You must accept the blame for your actions. Amends must be made."

Webber began to speak, but Herod silenced him with a raised hand.

"Don't lie to me, Mr. Webber. It insults me, and makes a fool out of you. Be a man. Acknowledge what you did, and we can set about arranging restitution. Confession is good for the soul." He reached out and laid his right hand upon Webber's. Herod's skin felt damp and cold, painfully so, but Webber was unable to move his hand. Herod's grip seemed to weigh him down.

"Come," said Herod. "All that I ask from you is honesty. We know the truth, and now it is simply a matter of finding a way that we can both put this behind us."

Those dark eyes glinted, like black spinels in snow. Webber was transfixed. He nodded once, and Herod responded with a similar gesture.

"Things have been very difficult lately," said Webber. His eyes grew hot, and the words caught in his throat, as though he were about to cry.

"I know that. These are hard times for many."

"I've never acted in this way before. Thule contacted me about another matter, and I just let it slip. I was desperate. It was wrong of me. I apologize: to you, and to the Foundation."

"Your apology is accepted. Unfortunately, we now have to discuss the matter of restitution."

"Half of the money is already gone. I don't know what sum you were considering but—"

Herod appeared surprised. "Oh, it's not a matter of money," he said. "We don't require money."

Webber sighed with relief. "Then what?" he said. "If you need information on items of interest, I may be able to provide it at a reduced rate. I can ask some questions, check my contacts. I'm sure that I can find something that will make up for the loss of the grimoire and—"

He stopped talking. There was now a manila envelope on the table, the kind with a cardboard back used to protect photographs.

"What is that?" asked Webber.

"Open it and see."

Webber picked up the envelope. There was no name or address on it, and it was unsealed. He reached inside and withdrew a single color photograph. He recognized the woman in the picture, captured when she was clearly unaware of the camera, her head turned slightly to the right as she gazed over her shoulder, smiling at someone or something out of the shot.

It was his daughter, Suzanne.

"What does this mean?" he asked. "Are you threatening my daughter?"

"Not as such," said Herod. "As I told you before, the Foundation is very interested in concepts of free will. You had a choice in the matter of the grimoire, and you made it. Now, I have been instructed to give you another choice."

Webber swallowed. "Go on."

"The Foundation has authorized the rape and murder of your daughter. It may be some consolation to you to hear that the acts do not have to be committed in that order." Instinctively, Webber looked to his gun, then began to reach for it.

"I should warn you," continued Herod, "that if anything happens to me, then your daughter will not see out this night, and her sufferings will be greatly increased. You may yet have use for that gun, Mr. Webber, but not now. Let me finish, then consider."

Uncertain of what to do, Webber did nothing, and his fate was sealed.

"As I said," Herod continued, "an action has been authorized, but it does not have to be carried out. There is another option."

"Which is?"

"You take your own life. That is your choice: your life, ended quickly, or the life of your daughter, taken slowly and with much pain."

Webber stared at Herod, dumbfounded.

"You're insane." But even as he said it, he knew that it wasn't true. He had looked into Herod's eyes, and he had seen nothing there but absolute sanity. It was possible that, with enough pain, a person might be driven to madness, but this was not the case with the man who sat opposite him. Instead, his sufferings had given him perfect clarity: he had no illusions about the ways of the world, only an insight into its capacity for inflicting agony.

"No, I am not. You have five minutes to choose. After that, it will be too late to stop what is about to occur."

Herod sat back. Webber picked up the gun and pointed it at him, but Herod did not even blink.

"Call. Tell them to leave her alone."

"So you've made your choice?"

"No. There is no choice. I'm warning you that if you don't make the call, I'll kill you."

"And then your daughter will die."

"I could torture you. I can shoot you in the knee, the groin. I can keep hurting you until you accede to my demand."

"Your daughter will still die. You know that. At the most basic level, you acknowledge the truth of what you have been told. You must accept it, and choose. Four minutes, thirty seconds."

Webber thumbed back the hammer on the revolver.

"I'm telling you for the last time—"

"Do you think that you're the first man to have been presented with this choice, Mr. Webber? Do you honestly believe that I haven't done this before? Ultimately, you must choose: your life, or the life of your daughter. Which do you value more?"

Herod waited. He glanced at his watch, counting the seconds.

"I wanted to see her grow up. I wanted to see her marry, and become a mother. I wanted to be a grandfather. Do you understand?"

"I understand. Her life will still be hers to live, and her children will lay flowers for you on your grave. Four minutes."

"Don't you have anyone whom you love?"

"No, I do not."

The gun wavered in Webber's hand as he realized the futility of his arguments.

"How do I know that you're not lying?"

"About what? About raping and killing your daughter? Oh, I think you know that I mean what I say."

"No. About—about letting her go."

"Because I don't lie. I don't have to. Others lie. It is for me to present them with the consequences of those lies. For every fault, there must be a reckoning. For every action, there is a reaction. The question is: who do you love more, your daughter, or yourself?"

Herod stood. He had a cell phone in one hand, his wineglass in the other. "I'll give you a private moment," he said. "Please don't attempt to use a phone. If you do so, our deal will be off, and I'll make sure that your daughter is raped to death. Oh, and my associates will also ensure that you don't live to see the dawn."

Webber did not try to stop Herod as he stepped slowly from the room. He seemed stunned into immobility.

In the hallway, Herod examined his reflection in a mirror. He straightened his tie, and brushed some lint from his jacket. He loved this old suit. He had worn it on many occasions like this one. He checked his watch a final time. From the kitchen, he discerned words. He wondered if Webber had been foolish enough to try to make a call, but the tone of voice was wrong. Then he thought that it might be Webber making an Act of Contrition, or saying some unheard good-bye to his daughter, but as he moved closer he heard Webber's words.

"Who are you?" Webber was asking. "Are you the one, the one who's going to hurt my Suzie? Are you? *Are* you?"

Herod glanced into the kitchen. Webber was staring at one of the kitchen windows. Herod saw Webber and himself reflected in the glass and, for just a moment, he thought that there might be a third figure visible, too insubstantial, Herod believed, to be someone in the garden looking in, and yet there was nobody else in the kitchen apart from the living, or the soon-to-be dead.

Webber turned to look at Herod. He was weeping.

"Damn you," he said. "Damn you to hell."

He put the gun to his temple and pulled the trigger. The sound of the shot made Herod's ears ring as it echoed off the tiled walls and floor of the kitchen. Webber fell, and lay bucking by his overturned chair. It was an amateurish way to turn a gun on oneself, Herod mused, but then Webber could hardly have been expected to be a professional in the art of suicide; after all, the nature of the act precluded it. The barrel of the gun had pulled upward with the shot, blowing a chunk out of the top of Webber's skull, but he had not managed to kill himself. Instead, his eyes were wide and his mouth was opening and closing spasmodically, rather like the final moments of the fish he had left on the slab. In a gesture of mercy, Herod took the gun from Webber's hand and finished the job for him, then drank the last of the wine in his glass and prepared to leave. He paused at the door, and peered back at the kitchen window. Something was wrong. Quickly, he moved to the counter and looked out upon Webber's neatly tended, and gently illuminated, garden. It was surrounded by high walls, and blocked off by gates at either side of the house. Herod could see no sign of another person, yet he remained troubled.

He checked his watch. He had already stayed too long, especially if the shots had attracted attention. He found the main switchbox for the house in a closet beneath the stairs, and killed all the lights before taking a blue surgical mask from his inside pocket and placing it over the lower part of his face. In a way, the H1N1 virus had been a blessing to him. Oh, people still sometimes stared at him in passing, but for one who exhibited such signs of illness as he did, they were looks of understanding as much as of curiosity. Then, concealed by shadows, Herod became part of the night, and he put Jeremiah Webber and his daughter from his mind forever. Webber had made a choice, the correct choice in Herod's view, and his daughter would be allowed to live. Herod, who worked alone, despite his threats to Webber, would not harm her.

For he was an honorable man, in his way.

IV

Far to the north, as the blood from Webber's body mixed with spilled wine and congealed upon his kitchen floor, and Herod returned to the shadows from which he had emerged, the sound of a telephone ringing echoed around a forest glade.

The man curled on the filthy sheets was dragged back to consciousness by the noise, and he knew immediately that it was them. He knew because he had unplugged the phone before he went to sleep.

Lying on the bed, he moved only his eyes, glancing slowly in the direction of the handset, as though they were already there with him and any significant shift in position would alert them to the fact that he was awake.

Go away. Leave me alone.

The television boomed into life, and for an instant he caught a snatch of some old comedy from the sixties, one at which he could remember laughing with his mother and father as he sat between them on the sofa. He felt tears spring from his eyes at the memory of his parents. He was frightened, and he wanted them to protect him, but they were long gone from this earth and he was all alone. Then the picture faded, leaving only static, and the voices came through the screen, just as they had the night before, and the night before that, and every night since he had taken delivery of the latest consignment. He began to shiver, although the air was warm.

Stop. Go away.

In the kitchen at the far end of the cabin, the radio began to play. It was his favorite show, *A Little Night Music,* or it used to be. He liked to listen to it just before he tried to sleep, but not anymore. Now, when he turned on the radio, he could hear them behind the music, and in the spaces between symphonic movements, and talking over the announcer's voice: not quite blocking him out, but loud enough that he could not concentrate on what was being said, the names of composers and conductors lost to him as he tried to ignore the foreign tongue that spoke so mellifluously. And even though he did not understand the words, the sense of them was clear to him.

But what they wanted, he could not give them.

At last, he could take it no longer. He jumped from his bed and grasped the baseball bat that he kept by his bedside, swinging it with a power and purpose that his younger self would have admired. The television screen imploded with a dull *whomp* and a cascade of sparks. Moments later, the radio was in pieces on the floor, and then only the phone remained to be dealt with. He stood above it, the bat poised, staring at the power cord that was not even close to the outlet, and the plastic connector cable that lay tantalizingly close to the box: not connected, yet still the phone was ringing. He should have been surprised, but he was not. In recent days, he had entirely lost the capacity for surprise.

Instead of reducing the phone to shards of plastic and circuitry, he put down the bat, and restored the power and the connection. He placed the receiver close to his ear, careful not to let it touch him for fear that the voices might somehow leap from the handset into his head and take up residence there, driving him to madness, or closer to it than he already was. He listened for a time, his mouth trembling, his tears still falling, before he dialed a number. The phone at the other end rang four times, and then a machine clicked on. It was always a machine. He tried to calm himself as best he could, then began to speak.

"There's something wrong," he said. "You need to get up here and take it all away. You tell everyone that I'm out. Just pay me what I'm owed. You can keep the rest."

He hung up the phone, put on an overcoat and a pair of sneakers, and grabbed a flashlight. After a moment's hesitation, he reached beneath his bed and found the green M12 universal military holster. He removed the Browning, slipped it into his overcoat pocket, picked up the baseball bat for added peace of mind, and left the trailer.

It was a moonless night, heavy with cloud, so that the sky was black and the world seemed very dark to him. The flashlight beam scythed through the darkness as he made his way down to the row of boarded-up rooms, coming at last to number 14. His father returned to mind, and he saw himself as a boy, standing with the old man outside this very same room, asking him why there was no number 13, why the rooms went straight from 12 to 14. His father had explained to him that people were superstitious. They didn't want to stay in room 13, or on the thirteenth floor of one of those big city hotels, and changes had to be made to set their minds at rest. So it was that 13 became 14, and everybody slept a little better as a result, even if, in truth, 14 was still 13, didn't matter what way you chose to hide it. Big city hotels still had a thirteenth floor, and small motels like theirs still had a room 13. In fact, there were folks who wouldn't stay in room 14 for precisely that reason but, generally, most guests didn't notice.

Now he was alone outside 14. There was no sound from inside, but he could sense them. They were waiting for him to act, waiting for him to do what they wanted him to do, what they had been demanding over the radio, and the television, and in late-night phone calls from a phone that shouldn't have worked but did. They wanted to be set free.

The bolts on the door were still in place, the locks undamaged, but when he checked the screws that he had drilled into the frame through the wood, he found that three of them were loose, and one had fallen out entirely.

"No," he said. "That's not possible." He picked up the screw from the ground, and examined the head. It was intact, and unmarked. He supposed that it was possible someone had come along while he was away from his trailer and used a drill to unscrew it, but why stop at one, and why leave some of the others only partially removed? It made no sense.

Unless . . .

Unless they had done it from inside. But how?

I should open it, he thought. I should open it and make sure. But he didn't want to open it. He was afraid of what he might see, and of what he might be forced to do, for he knew that if he only ever performed one more good act in his life, it would be to ignore those voices. He could almost hear them in there, calling him, taunting him. . . .

He returned to his trailer, found his big tool kit, and returned to 14. As he began to fit the bit into the drill, his attention was distracted by the sound of metal on wood. He put the drill down, and directed the flashlight beam at the door.

One of the remaining screws was turning gently, removing itself from the wood. While he watched, its length was at last fully exposed, and the screw fell to the ground.

Screws weren't going to do it, not anymore. He put the drill aside, and took out the nail gun. Breathing heavily, he approached the door, set the muzzle of the gun against the wood, and pulled the trigger. The force of the recoil jarred him slightly, but when he stepped back he saw that the nail, all six inches of it, was buried up to the head in the wood. He moved on, until there were twenty nails in the door. Removing them all would be a pain in the ass, but the fact that they were there for now made him feel a little more comfortable.

He sat on the damp ground. The screws were no longer moving, and there were no more voices.

"Yeah," he whispered. "You didn't like that, did you? Soon, you'll be somebody else's problem, and then I'll be done. I'm gonna take my money and leave this place. I been here too long as it is. Gonna find me somewhere warm, hole up there for a time, uh-huh."

He looked at the tool box. It was too damn heavy to haul all the way up to the trailer and, Lord knows, he might have need of it again before too long. Number 15 was secured only by a piece of plywood. Using his screwdriver, he prized out the two nails that held it in place, and placed his kit in the dark room beyond. He could make out the shape of the old cabinet on the left, and the bare frame of the bed, all rusted springs and broken posts, like the skeleton of some long-dead creature.

He turned and stared at the wall separating this room from 14. The paint was peeling, and it had bubbled in places. He placed his hand against one of the bubbles of paint, feeling it give way against his skin. He expected it to be moist to the touch, but it was not. Instead, it was warm, warmer than it should have been, not unless there was a fire blazing in the room on the other side. He moved his hand sideways, letting it trail along the wall until he came to a cooler patch, one on which the paint remained undamaged.

"What the—?" He spoke the words aloud, and the sound of his own voice in the gloom startled him, as though it were not he who had spoken but a version of himself that stood somehow apart, watching him with curiosity, a man aged beyond his years, damaged by war and loss, haunted by phones that rang in the dead of night and voices that spoke in unfamiliar tongues.

For as his palm rested against the paintwork, he felt the cool spot on the wall begin to grow warm. No, not just warm: hot. He closed his eyes briefly, and an image flashed in his mind: a presence in the next room, a figure that was crooked and distorted, burning from within as it placed a hand against the paintwork on its own side and followed the progress of the man on the other, like a piece of metal drawn by a magnet.

He pulled his hand away and rubbed it against the leg of his sweatpants. His mouth and throat were dry. He felt the urge to cough, but he suppressed it. It was absurd, he knew: after all, he'd just hammered twenty nails into a door, so it wasn't as if he'd been quiet so far, but there was a difference between those mechanical noises and the simple human intimacy—and, say it, frailty—of a cough. So he covered his mouth with his hand and backed out of the room, leaving his tool box behind. He replaced the plywood, but didn't bother trying to find a way of securing it again. The night was still, so there was no wind that might cause it to fall. He didn't turn his back on the motel until he was at his cabin. Once inside, he locked the door, then drank some water, followed by a glass of vodka and some Nyquil to help him sleep. He called again the number he had dialed earlier, and left a second message.

"One more night," he reiterated. "I want my money, and I want this stuff gone. I can't do it no more. I'm sorry."

Then he stamped the telephone to pieces before removing his shoes and overcoat and curling up in bed. He listened to the silence, and the silence listened back.

They were nickel and dimed, that was what he thought: right from the start, they were nickel and dimed. They'd even managed to spell his name wrong on his new identification tags: Bobby Jandrau instead of "Jandreau." Damned if he was going to war with his name messed up: that was bad karma right there. Way they'd kicked up when he pointed it out, you'd have thought he wanted to be carried to Iraq in a sedan chair.

But then the rich always screw the poor, and this was a rich man's war being fought by poor people. There was nobody wealthy waiting to fight alongside him, and had there been he would have asked them why, because there was no sense in being here if you had a better option. No, there were just men like himself, and some who were poorer yet, although he knew what it was to live short; still, by the standards of some of the guys he knew, who were on first-name terms with poverty before they joined up, he was comfortable.

The brass told them that they were ready to deploy, ready to fight, but they didn't even have body armor.

"That's 'cause the Iraqis ain't going to fire at you," said Lattner. "They'll just use sarcasm, and say mean things about your moms."

Lattner, who was a long drink, maybe the tallest man he'd ever met, always called them his "moms" and his "pops." When he was dying, *he asked for his moms, but she was thousands of miles away, probably praying for him, which might have helped. He was doped up to take away some of the pain, and he didn't know where he was. He thought that he was back in Laredo. They told him that his moms was on her way, and he died believing it.*

They scavenged scraps of metal and flattened cans to make their own sappy plates. Later, they took body armor from dead Iraqis. The men and women who followed would be better equipped: pads, eye pro, Wiley-X sunglasses, even pieces of green cards with answers to possible media questions, because by then it was all going to hell, jizzicked to fuck and back, as his old man used to say, and they didn't want anybody speaking out of school.

There were no showers at the start: they bathed out of hard hats. They lived in ruined buildings and, later, five to a room without A/C in 130-degree heat. No sleep, no showers, weeks in the same clothes. In time there would be air-conditioning, and containerized housing units, and proper shitters, and a MWR center with PlayStations and big-screen TVs, and a PX selling lame "Who's Your Bagh-Daddy?" T-shirts, and a Burger King. There would be internet terminals, and phone centers open 24/7, except when a soldier was killed, when they would be closed until the family was informed. There would be a concrete mortar bunker by the door of the conex, so that you didn't have to face them out in the open.

But he didn't care about the difficulties, not at first. You didn't sign up because you wanted to stay home and see out your time stateside. You signed up because you wanted to go to war, and what was it Secretary Rumsfeld said? You go to war with the army you have, not the army you wish you had. Then again, Secretary Rumsfeld still had all his limbs, last time he looked, so it was kind of easy for him to say.

He had some tattoos on his arms: stupid childish shit, but not gang related. He wasn't even sure that there were any gangs in Maine worth getting tattooed over, and even if there were, the tattoos wouldn't have meant much to real hard-asses like the Bloods and the Crips. The army would eventually add another tat of its own: his dog-tag information was etched on his side, his "meat tag," so even if he was blown to pieces and his dog tags lost or destroyed, his body would still bear his identity. A staff sergeant promised a waiver for the old tats when he enlisted, even offered to clear up any minor criminal stuff that might have been on his sheet, but he didn't have so much as a DUI to his name. He was guaranteed the good life: a signing bonus, paid leave, and a college education, if he wanted it, once he'd completed his time. He scored over 80 percent on the Vocational Aptitude Battery, the army's SATs, which made him eligible for a two-year enlistment, but he signed up for four. He didn't have a whole lot else going on anyway, and a four-year enlistment meant that he would be guaranteed a slot with a particular division, and he wanted to serve with other men from Maine, if that was possible. He'd enjoyed being a soldier. He was good at it. It was why he reenlisted. If he hadn't, then things would have been very different. The second time was the doozy. The second time was the killer.

But that was years away. First off, he was sent to Fort Benning for fourteen weeks of training, and he thought he was going to die on the second day. After basic, they gave him two weeks to kick around, then put him on the Hometown Recruiting Assistance Program where he was supposed to recruit his buddies in a Class A uniform, the army's equivalent of a pyramid selling scheme, but his buddies weren't buying. That was when he met Tobias. Even then, Tobias was an operator. He had a way of forming alliances, of cutting deals, of doing small favors that he could call in at a later date. Tobias took him under his wing.

"You don't know beans," Tobias told him. "You stick with me, and I'll educate you."

And he did. Tobias looked out for him, just as, in time, he himself had looked out for Damien Patchett, until the roles were reversed, and the bullets came, and he thought:

I am bait. I am a stalking goat.

I am going to die.

CHAPTER

V

I was back at Joel Tobias's place early the next morning. Instead of the Saturn, which, as on the night before, I sometimes used for surveillance, I'd been forced to drive the Mustang, just in case Tobias had any suspicions that he was being followed after our encounter the previous night. The Mustang wasn't exactly inconspicuous, but I'd parked behind a truck in the lot of the Big Sky Bread Company on the corner of Deering Avenue, and had angled myself so that I could just about see Tobias's house on Revere from where I was, but he would have trouble spotting me unless he came looking. His Silverado was still in the drive when I parked, and the drapes remained drawn at the upstairs window. Shortly after eight, Tobias appeared at the front door wearing a black T-shirt and black jeans. There was a tattoo on his left arm, but I couldn't tell what it was from a distance. He got in his truck and hung a right. Once he was out of sight, I went after him.

There was plenty of traffic on the streets, and I was able to stay well back from Tobias while still keeping him in sight. I nearly lost him at Bedford when the lights changed, but I caught up a couple of blocks later. Eventually, he pulled into a warehouse complex off the Franklin arterial. I drove by, then slipped into the lot next door, where I watched Tobias park by one of three big rigs parked close to a chain-link fence. He spent the next hour performing routine maintenance checks on his rig, then got back in the Silverado and returned to his house.

I filled up the Mustang's tank, bought a cup of coffee at Big Sky, and tried to figure out what I was supposed to be doing. All that I knew so far was that Tobias's finances didn't add up, and he might be having troubles with his girlfriend, as Bennett had suggested, but I couldn't help feeling that, in the end, little of this was any of my business. In theory, I could have stayed with him until he embarked on his planned run to Canada, followed him across the border, and then waited to see what transpired, but the chances of his not making me if I did follow him all the way up there were pretty slim. After all, if he was engaged in illegal activity, he was likely to be alert for any kind of surveillance, and a proper pursuit would require two, maybe three vehicles. I could have brought in Jackie Garner as the second driver, but Jackie didn't work for free, not unless he was guaranteed a little fun and the possibility of being able to hit someone without legal consequences, and following a truck up to Quebec hardly sounded like Jackie's idea of a good time. And if Tobias was smuggling, so what? I wasn't an arm of U.S. Customs.

The issue of whether or not he was hitting his girlfriend was another matter, but I couldn't see how my involvement was going to improve that situation. Bennett Patchett was in a better position to make a discreet approach to Karen Emory than I was, perhaps through one of her female colleagues at the diner, since a complete stranger coming up to her and asking if her boyfriend had beaten her up lately was unlikely to endear himself to her.

I called Bennett's cell phone. It went to voicemail, so I left a message. I tried the Downs, but he wasn't there, and the woman who answered the phone told me that she didn't expect him today. I hung up. My coffee was getting cold. I opened my window and poured it out, then tossed the paper cup in the back of the car. I was bored and frustrated. I took a James Lee Burke novel from the glove compartment, sat back in my seat, and started to read.

Three hours later, my ass was aching, and I had finished the book. The coffee had also made its way through my system. Like every good PI, I kept a plastic bottle in the car for just such an eventuality, but it hadn't reached that stage yet. I tried Bennett's cell phone again, and once more it went to voicemail. Twenty minutes later, Karen Emory's green Subaru appeared at the intersection, with Karen at the wheel. She was already wearing her blue Downs T-shirt. There appeared to be nobody else in the car with her. I let her go.

Half an hour later, Tobias's Silverado appeared and headed for the highway. I followed him to the Nickelodeon Theater on Temple, where he bought a ticket for a comedy. I waited for twenty minutes, but he didn't come out. For now, it seemed that Joel Tobias wasn't heading to Canada, at least not today. Even if he was preparing for a night run, there was little that I could do to follow him. I was also due at the Bear that night, and the next, and I couldn't let Dave Evans down. I felt that I had wasted a day, and Bennett wasn't going to get his money's worth out of me, not like this. It was now 5:00 P.M. I was due at the Bear by eight. I wanted to shower first, and I wanted to use the bathroom.

I drove back to Scarborough. It was a warm, close evening, with no breeze. By the time I had showered and changed, I had made a decision: I would charge Bennett for the hours I had put in so far, then give him back the rest of his money unless he could come up with a pressing reason why I should not. If he wanted me to, and he acted as an intermediary, I'd sit down with Karen Emory for free and advise her on her options if she was experiencing domestic abuse. As for Joel Tobias, assuming that he wasn't making up the shortfall in his finances through entirely legal means of which I had no knowledge, he could continue doing whatever it was he was doing until the cops, or customs, caught up with him. It wasn't an ideal compromise, but then compromises rarely were.

THE BEAR WAS BUZZING that night. There were some state cops drinking at the far end of the bar, away from the door. I considered it politic to avoid them, and Dave agreed. They had no love for me, and one of their number, a detective named Hansen, was still on medical leave after having involved himself in my affairs earlier in the year. It was no fault of mine, but I knew that his colleagues didn't see it that way. I spent the evening taking care of orders from the waitstaff, and left the two regular bartenders to look after those seated at the bar. The night passed quickly, and by midnight I was done. For the sake of it, I took another ride past Joel Tobias's place. The Silverado was still there, along with Karen Emory's car. When I went to the warehouse complex off Federal, Tobias's rig hadn't moved.

My phone rang as I was halfway home. The caller ID showed Bennett Patchett's number, so I pulled in at a Dunkin' Donuts and answered.

"Calling a little late, Mr. Patchett," I said.

"Figured you for a night owl, like myself," he replied. "Sorry for taking so long to return your call. I was tied up with legal business all day and, to tell you the truth, when I was done with it I didn't much feel like checking my messages. But I've had a nightcap, and I feel a bit more relaxed now. You find out anything worth mentioning?"

I told him that I hadn't, apart from the possibility that Joel Tobias's finances didn't quite add up, and Bennett had suspected as much already. I went over my concerns with him: how I believed that following Tobias would be difficult without additional manpower, and that perhaps there were better ways of dealing with the possibility that Karen Emory was a victim of domestic abuse.

"And my boy?" said Bennett. His voice cracked when he said it, and I wondered if he'd had more than a single nightcap. "What about my boy?"

I didn't know what to tell him. Your boy is gone, and this won't bring him back. Post-traumatic stress took him, not his involvement with whatever Joel Tobias might be doing under the guise of a legitimate trucking business.

"Look," said Bennett. "It may be that you think I'm a foolish old man who can't accept the circumstances of his son's death, and, you know, that's probably true. But I have a good sense for people, and Joel Tobias is crooked. I didn't like him when I first met him, and I wasn't happy about Damien getting involved in his affairs. I'm asking you to keep on this. It's not a question of money. Money I got. If you need to hire some help, then do it and I'll pay for that as well. What do you say?"

What was there to say? I said that I'd give it a few more days, even though I believed it was pointless. He thanked me, then hung up. I stared at the phone for a time before tossing it on the seat beside me.

That night, I dreamed of Joel Tobias's rig. It stood in a deserted lot, its container unlocked, and when I opened it there was only blackness, blackness that extended farther than the rear of the container, as though I were staring into a void. I felt a presence approaching fast from out of the darkness, rushing toward me from the abyss, and I woke to the first light of dawn and the sense that I was no longer quite alone.

The room smelled of my dead wife's perfume, and I knew that it was a warning.

VI

The mail boat was departing for its morning run as I parked at the Casco Bay terminal, a handful of passengers onboard, most of them tourists, watching as the wharf receded, taking in the bustle of the fishing boats and the ferries. The mail boat was an integral part of life on the bay, a twice-daily link between the mainland and the folks on Little Diamond and Great Diamond and Diamond Cove, on Long Island and Cliff Island and Peaks Island, on Great Chebeague, the largest of the islands on Casco Bay, and on Dutch Island, or Sanctuary as it was sometimes called, the most remote of the "Calendar Islands." The boat was a point of connection not only between those who lived by the sea and those who lived on the sea, but also between the inhabitants of the various outposts on Casco Bay.

The sight of the mail boat always brought with it a hint of nostalgia. It seemed to belong to another time, and it was impossible not to look upon it and imagine its earlier incarnations, the importance of that link when travel between the islands and the mainland was not so easy. The mail boat brought letters and packages and freight, but it also brought, and disseminated, news. My grandfather, my mother's father, took me on one of the mail boat's runs shortly after my mother and I returned to Maine in the aftermath of my father's death, as we fled north to escape the spreading stain of it. I wondered then if it might be possible for us to live on one of those islands, to leave the mainland behind forever, so that when the blood reached the limits of the coast it would drip slowly into the sea and be dispersed by the waves. Looking back, I realize that I was always running: from my father's legacy; from the deaths of Susan and Jennifer, my wife and child; and, ultimately, from my own nature.

But now I had stopped running.

THE SAILMAKER WAS, NOT to put too fine a point on it, a dump. It was one of the last of the old wharf bars in Portland, the ones that were built to cater to the needs of lobstermen, dock workers, and all those whose livelihood depended on the grittier aspects of Portland's working harbor. It was there long before anyone thought that tourists might want to spend time on the waterfront, and when the tourists did eventually appear they gave the Sailmaker a wide berth. It was like the dog on the street that snoozes in the yard, its fur pitted with the scars of old battles, its mouth, even in repose, always baring yellowed teeth, its eyes rheumy beneath half-closed lids, every aspect of it exuding restrained menace and promising the loss of a finger, or more, if a passing stranger were foolish enough to attempt a pat on the head. Even the name on the sign that hung outside the bar was barely legible, its paintwork ignored for years. Those who needed it knew where to find it, which was true of locals and a certain type of new arrival, the type that was not concerned with fine dining, and lighthouses, and nostalgic thoughts about mail boats and islanders. That kind sniffed out the Sailmaker and found their place in it, once they'd snapped at the other dogs, and taken their bites in return.

The Sailmaker was the only business still open on its wharf; around it, shuttered windows and padlocked doors secured premises that had nothing inside left to steal. Even to enter them would be to risk plummeting through the floor and into the cold waters beneath, for these buildings, like the wharf itself, were slowly rotting into the sea. It seemed a miracle that the whole structure had not collapsed many years before, and while the Sailmaker appeared to be more stable than its neighbors, it sat on the same uncertain pilings as they did.

So it was that drinking in the Sailmaker brought with it a sense of danger on a great many levels, the prospect of drowning in the bay due to stepping through a busted board being a relatively minor concern when compared with the more immediate threat of physical violence, serious or minor, from one or more of its customers. For the most part, even the lobstermen no longer frequented the Sailmaker, and the ones who did were less interested in fishing than in drinking steadily until fluid came out of their ears. They were lobstermen in name only, for those who ended up in the Sailmaker had resigned themselves to the fact that their days of being contributory members of society, of working hard for an honest wage, were long behind them. The Sailmaker was where you ended up when there was no-where else left to go, when the sole ending in sight was a funeral attended by people who knew you only by your seat at the bar and the drink that you ordered, and who would be mourning their own lives as much as yours as you were lowered into the ground. Every coastal town used to have a bar like the Sailmaker; in a way, the lost were more likely to be remembered in such places than they were among the remnants of their own family. In that sense, the Sailmaker was, nominally as well as figuratively, an apt venue in which to end one's days, for it was the sailmaker onboard ship who would sew the dead man up in his hammock, passing a final stitch through the nose of the departed to ensure that he was dead. At the Sailmaker, no such precautions were necessary: its patrons were drinking themselves to death, so when they stopped ordering drinks it was a pretty sure sign that they'd succeeded.

The Sailmaker was owned by a man named Jimmy Jewel, although I had never heard him called anything other than "Mr. Jewel" to his face. Jimmy Jewel owned a lot of places like the Sailmaker and the wharf upon which it stood: apartment buildings that barely came up to code; ruined structures on waterfronts and side streets in towns all the way from Kittery to Calais; and vacant lots that were used for nothing but storing filthy pools of stagnating rainwater, lots that were not for sale and bore no indication of ownership beyond a series of No Trespassing signs, some of them reasonably official in appearance, others just scrawled boards with increasingly varied and creative spellings of the word "Trespassing."

What these buildings and lots had in common was the possibility that they might, at some future date, be valuable to a developer. The wharf on which the Sailmaker sat was one of a number tipped to become part of the new Maine State Pier redevelopment, a $160 million effort to revitalize the commercial waterfront, involving a new hotel, soaring offices, and a cruise ship terminal that had since been dropped and now looked to be an increasingly distant prospect. The port was struggling. The International Marine Terminal that had once been filled with cargo containers waiting to be taken out on ships and barges, or transported inland by truck and train, was quieter than it had ever been. The number of fishing boats bringing their catches to the fish exchange on the Portland Fish Pier had fallen from 350 to 70 in the space of fifteen years, and the livelihoods of the fishermen were being threatened further by a reduction in their number of permitted fishing days. The high-speed Cat service between Portland and Nova Scotia was ending, taking with it much needed jobs and income for the port. Some were suggesting that the survival of the waterfront depended on increasing the number of bars and restaurants permitted on the wharfs, but the danger was that the port would then become little more than a theme park, with a handful of lobstermen left to eke out a meager living and provide some local color for the tourists, leaving Portland just a shadow of the great deep-water harbor that had defined the city's identity for three centuries.

And in the middle of all this uncertainty squatted Jimmy Jewel, sizing up the angles, his finger damp and raised to the wind. It wouldn't be true to say that Jimmy didn't care about Portland, or its piers, or its history. He just cared about money more.

But decaying buildings, although a significant part of his portfolio, did not represent the sum total of Jimmy's business interests. He had a slice of interstate and cross-border trucking, and he knew more about the smuggling of narcotics than almost anyone on the northeastern seaboard. Jimmy's main deal was pot, but he'd suffered a couple of serious hits in recent years, and now he was rumored to be taking a step back from the drug business in favor of more legitimate enterprises, or those enterprises that gave the appearance of legitimacy, which was not the same thing. Old habits died hard, and when it came to criminality Jimmy kept his hand in as much for the money as for the pleasure he got in breaking the law.

I didn't have to call ahead to make an appointment with him. The heart of Jimmy's empire was the Sailmaker. He had a small office in back, but it was used mainly for storage. Instead, Jimmy could always be found at the bar, reading newspapers, answering occasional calls on an ancient phone, and drinking endless cups of coffee. He was there when I entered that morning. There was nobody else with him, apart from a bartender in a stained white T-shirt who was hauling in crates of beer from the storeroom. The bartender's name was Earle Hanley, the same Earle Hanley who had tended bar at the Blue Moon on the night that Sally Cleaver was beaten to death by her boyfriend, for the owner of the Sailmaker and the Blue Moon were one and the same: Jimmy Jewel.

Earle looked up as I came in. If he liked what he saw, he made a manly effort to disguise the fact. His face creased, wrinkling like a ball of paper that had just been squeezed hard, and even in repose, Earle's face already resembled the last walnut in the bowl a week after Thanksgiving. He doubled as one of the guys who occasionally doled out beatings to recalcitrants who crossed Jimmy and incurred his displeasure. He appeared to have been constructed from a series of balls of encrusted lipids, the topmost fringed with greasy black hair. Even his thighs were circular. I could almost hear the fats sluicing around in his body as he moved.

Jimmy, meanwhile, wore a mortician's black suit over an open-collared blue shirt. He was thin, and his hair was varying shades of gray held in place with a pomade that smelled faintly of cloves. He was six feet tall, but slightly stooped, so that he seemed to be struggling under some burden invisible to all, but deeply oppressive to himself. The right-hand side of his mouth was permanently raised, as if life were some amusing comedy and he was merely a spectator. Jimmy wasn't a bad guy, as smugglers and drug dealers went. He'd knocked heads a couple of times with my grandfather, who was a state cop and knew Jimmy from way back, but they had respected each other. Jimmy had come to my grandfather's funeral, and the grief he had expressed to me was genuine. Since then, I had enjoyed few dealings with him, but our paths had crossed on occasion, and once or twice he'd been good enough to point me in the right direction when I had a question that needed to be answered, as long as nobody got hurt by it and the law didn't get involved.

He looked up from his newspaper, and that semi-smile flickered, like a lightbulb that has suffered a momentary disturbance to its power supply.

"Shouldn't you be wearing a mask?" he asked.

"Why? You got anything worth stealing?"

"No, but I thought all you avengers wore masks. That way people can say 'Who was that masked avenger?' as you vanish into the night.

Otherwise, you're just a guy who dresses too young for his age, sticking his nose where he's got no business sticking it, and looking surprised when it gets bloodied."

I took a stool across from him. He sighed and folded his newspaper.

"You think I dress too young for my age?" I said.

"You ask me, everybody dresses too young these days, when they get dressed at all. I can still remember a time when there were hookers in these bars, and even they wouldn't have dressed like some of the young girls I see passing by, summer and winter. I want to buy them all coats, make sure they wrap up warm. But what do I know from fashion? I think any suit that isn't black looks like something Liberace would wear." He stretched out a hand, and we shook. "How you doing, kid?"

"Pretty good."

"You still with that woman?" he asked. I didn't feel any urge to express surprise at his knowledge of my private life. Nobody survived for as long as Jimmy Jewel without keeping tabs on whoever crossed his path.

"No. We broke up. She's in Vermont."

"She take the kid with her?"

"Yes."

"I'm sorry to hear it."

This wasn't a topic of conversation I wanted to pursue. I sniffed warily at the air.

"Your bar stinks," I said.

"My bar smells fine," said Jimmy. "It's my clientele that stink, but to get rid of the stink I'd have to get rid of them, and then it would just be me and my ghosts. Oh, and Earle doesn't smell so good either, but that may be genetic."

Earle didn't reply, but just added a few more wrinkles to his expression and went back to rearranging the dirt.

"You want a drink? It's on the house."

"I don't think so. I hear you water your booze down to add taste."

"You got balls, coming in here and insulting my place."

"It's not a 'place,' it's a tax write-off. If it ever made any real money, your empire would collapse."

"I have an empire? I never knew. I did, I'd have dressed better, bought more expensive black suits."

"You have a guy who brings you coffee without being asked, and breaks heads on the same basis. I guess that counts for something."

"So, you want some coffee, then?" asked Jimmy.

"Is it as bad as everything else in here?"

"Worse, but I made it myself, so at least you know my hands are clean. Literally, not metaphorically."

"Coffee would be good, thanks. It's kind of early for me otherwise."

"Then you're in the wrong place. You think the windows are small because I couldn't afford the glass?"

The Sailmaker was always dark. Its customers didn't care to be reminded about the passage of time.

Jimmy raised a finger to Earle, who stood, retrieved a mug from somewhere, examined its insides to make sure that it wasn't too dirty, or was just dirty enough, and poured. When he put the mug down on the bar, coffee slopped over the sides and pooled on the wood. Earle looked at me, as though daring me to complain.

"He's dainty for a big man," I said.

"He doesn't like you," said Jimmy. "Don't take it personal, though: he doesn't like anyone. Sometimes, I think that he doesn't even like me, but I pay him so that buys me a degree of tolerance."

Jimmy passed me a silver jug of milk, not cream, and a bowl of sugar. Jimmy didn't like UHT milk, or cheap creamer, or sachets of sweetener. I took the milk, not the sugar.

"So, is this a social call, or have I done a great wrong that needs to be righted? Because I got to tell you, having you in my place makes me feel like checking my insurance."

"You think trouble follows me?"

"Jesus, Death himself probably sends you a fruit basket at Christmas, thanking you for the business."

"I have a question about trucking."

"Don't get into it, that's my advice. Long hours, no overtime. You'll sleep in a cab, eat bad food, and die at a rest stop. On the other hand, nobody will actively try to kill you, which seems to be one of the occupational hazards of your line of work, or the version of it that you pursue."

I ignored the career advice. "There's a guy, an independent. He's got payments to keep up on a nice rig, a mortgage, the usual stuff. I'd say, overall, his expenses come close to seventy grand a year, and that's not leading an extravagant lifestyle."

"That allowing for some massage on the figures?"

"Probably. You ever met an honest man?"

"Not when it comes to taxes. I did, I'd take him for every penny he was worth, just like the IRS, but not as vindictive. This guy, he do long haul?"

"Some Canadian stuff, but that's it, I think."

"Canada's a big place. How far are we talking?"

"Quebec, as far as I know."

"That's not long haul. He work a lot of hours?"

"Not enough, or that would be my take on it."

"So you figure he might be doing a little work on the side?"

"He's crossing the border. The thought had struck me. And, with respect, I don't think squirrels cross the border without you knowing it and taking ten percent of their nuts."

"Fifteen," said Jimmy. "And that's the friends' rate. This guy have a name?"

"Joel Tobias."

Jimmy looked away, and clicked his tongue.

"He's not one of mine."

"You know whose he might be?"

Jimmy didn't answer the question. Instead, he said: "What's your interest in him?"

On my way to Portland, I had debated how much I was prepared to tell Jimmy. In the end, I decided that I was going to have to tell him most of it, but I wanted to leave out Damien Patchett's death for now.

"He's got a girlfriend," I said. "A concerned citizen thinks he may not be treating her right, and that she'd be better off away from him."

"And what? You prove he's smuggling and she tosses him aside and dates a preacher instead? Either you're lying, and I don't believe you'd come in here and do that, or this concerned citizen needs a lesson in the ways of the world. Half the girls in this town will jump on a guy with a nickel in his pocket and wear him down to a stub, and they won't care where the money came from. In fact, you tell them you got it illegally, and some of them will call their sisters to join in as well."

"What about the other half?"

"They'll just steal his wallet. Short-term goals, short-term gains." He rubbed his face with his hand, and I heard the crackle of his stubble. "I know you're not the kind to take advice, but maybe you'll listen to me for the sake of your grandfather," he continued. "This one isn't worth it, not if it's just about some domestic situation that'll resolve itself one way or the other. Let it go. There's easier money out there."

I drank some coffee. It tasted like sump oil. If I hadn't watched him pour it, I'd have said that Earle had gone in back and dipped the mug in the bay before giving it to me. Then again, maybe he just kept a couple of really nasty mugs and glasses to one side, for special visitors.

"It doesn't work that way, Jimmy," I said.

"Yeah, I figured I was talking to the breeze."

"So you know about Tobias?"

"You first. This isn't just about a girl dating the wrong guy."

"I've been hired by someone who figures he's dirty, and may have a grudge against him."

"And you came to me because you suspect Tobias is augmenting his cargo illegally to make ends meet, and I'd know about it if he was."

"Jimmy, you know about stuff even God doesn't know about."

"That's because God is only interested in his own cut, and we all pay that, eventually, so God can afford to wait. I, on the other hand, am always seeking to expand."

"So, Joel Tobias."

Jimmy shrugged. "I don't have much to tell you about this guy, but what I do have you won't like. . . ."

Jimmy knew the ways of the border. He was familiar with every road, every inlet, every secluded cove in the state of Maine. He worked for himself largely in the sense that he was an agent for a number of criminal organizations who were often happy to remain at one remove from the illegal activities that funded them. Booze, drugs, people, money: whatever needed to be transported, Jimmy would find a way to do it. Long-standing bribes were in place, and there were men in uniform who knew when to look the other way. He used to say that he had more people on his payroll than the government, and his jobs were more secure.

The events of 9/11 changed things for Jimmy and others like him. Border security was tightened, and Jimmy was no longer able to guarantee deliveries without a hitch. The bribes grew larger, and some of his inside men quietly told Jimmy that they couldn't take the risk of working for him anymore. A couple of shipments were seized, and the people whose goods he was transporting weren't happy about it. Jimmy lost money, and clients. But the economic downturn had also helped some: cash was scarce, jobs were disappearing, and under those circumstances, smuggling seemed like a pretty good option to men who were struggling to weather hard times. But even though Jimmy was always in need of good help, he was careful about those whom he employed. He wanted people who could be trusted, who wouldn't show signs of panic when the dogs began sniffing around their trucks or their cars, who wouldn't decide to take a chance on ripping Jimmy off and making a run for it with the proceeds. Only newbies did stuff like that. The older ones knew better. Jimmy might have seemed like a genial guy, but Earle wasn't. Earle would break a kitten's legs for spilling its milk.

And if Earle couldn't handle the situation, which was rare, Jimmy had friends everywhere, the kind of friends who owed him and knew where to look for anyone dumb enough to cross Jimmy Jewel. And since newbies only got consignments to transport worth a low five-figure sum at most, there was a limit to how far any of them could run, assuming they could access the "traps," the hidden storage compartments, to begin with. Even those who did run inevitably ended up back where they came from, because Jimmy also made sure that he employed people who had friends and family within easy reach. Either the offending parties would return of their own volition, largely because they missed the company, or they would be encouraged to return in order to avoid trouble for those close to them. Then a beating would follow, and a sequestration of assets or, in the absence of any such assets, a couple of risky, dirty jobs done for little or no payment as a gesture of atonement. Jimmy resisted punishments that were terminal as they drew unwanted attention to his operations, but that wasn't to say that people had not died for crossing Jimmy Jewel. There were bodies buried in the Great North Woods, but Jimmy hadn't put them there. It was just that, sometimes, clients emerged who resented the disruption caused to their affairs by someone running off with their cash or their drugs, and who insisted upon an example being made *pour discourager les autres*, as some of his Quebecois contacts liked to put it. In such cases, Jimmy did his best to plead for leniency, but if his pleas fell on deaf ears, Jimmy had always made it clear that he wasn't about to cap anyone, because that wasn't the way he worked, and the finger on the trigger wouldn't belong to any of his people. Nobody ever complained about Jimmy's position on this matter, mainly because there were always men who were happy to dim some unfortunate's lights, if only to keep themselves fresh and in the game.

Jimmy never put pressure on anyone to work for him. He was content to make a delicate approach, sometimes through a third party, and, if that approach was rebuffed, to move on elsewhere. He was patient. Often, it was enough to sow the seed and wait for a change in financial circumstances to occur, at which point his offer might be reconsidered. But he kept tabs on the local truckers, and he was always listening for rumors of excessive cash being thrown around, or someone picking up a new rig when common sense would suggest that he should barely have been able to maintain the old one. If there was one thing Jimmy didn't care for, it was competition, or smart guys trying to run independent operations, however small in scale. There were some exceptions to that rule: he was rumored to have a sweet deal with the Mexicans, but he wasn't about to try to reason with the Dominicans, or the Colombians, or the bikers, or even the Mohawks. If they wanted to avail themselves of his services, as they sometimes did, that was fine, but if Jimmy Jewel started questioning their right to move product he and Earle would end up tied to chairs in the Sailmaker with pieces of themselves scattered by their feet, assuming their feet weren't among the scattered pieces, while the bar burned down around their ears, assuming they still had ears.

That was how Joel Tobias had come to Jimmy's attention. He had a new rig, a truck, a nice house, but he wasn't making the kind of runs that would enable him to keep them all for long. The figures didn't add up, and Jimmy had begun to make some gentle inquiries, because if Tobias was smuggling drugs then those drugs had both to come from somewhere and to go somewhere, once they'd crossed the border, and there were only a limited number of possible options in either case. Booze was unwieldy, and didn't bring in enough dough for the risk, and as far as Jimmy could tell Tobias was using the monitored crossings, which meant that he'd be subject to regular searches, and unless he was being provided with some very high-class documentation his career as a booze smuggler would be short. That left cash, but, again, large dollar amounts had to come from somewhere, and Jimmy had cornered the market in that particular specialty. Anyway, the actual physical movement of cash was also a very minor part of his operation, as there were easier ways to transport money from place to place than in the trunk of a car or the cab of a truck. So Jimmy was very curious indeed about Joel Tobias, which is why he decided to approach him directly one day when Tobias was drinking alone over at Three Dollar Dewey's after making a legitimate delivery to a warehouse on Commercial. It was four in the afternoon, so the evening rush hadn't yet hit Dewey's. Jimmy and Earle joined Tobias at the bar, one on either side of him, and asked if they could buy him a drink.

"I'm good," said Tobias, and went back to reading his magazine.

"Just trying to be friendly," said Jimmy.

Tobias had glanced at Earle in response. "Yeah? Your buddy has friendly written all over him." Earle had friendly written all over him the way that a plague rat had "Hug Me" emblazoned on its fur.

Tobias didn't appear disturbed, or frightened. He was a big guy; not as big as Earle, but better toned. Jimmy knew, from asking around, that Tobias was ex-military. He'd served in Iraq, and his left hand looked chewed up, missing the little finger and its nearest neighbor, but he was in good condition, so it appeared that he'd maintained the habits that he'd learned in the army. He'd also kept up with his old buddies, from what Jimmy could ascertain, which concerned him slightly. Whatever scam Tobias was running, he wasn't running it alone. Soldiers, former or otherwise, meant guns, and Jimmy didn't like guns.

"He's a pussycat," said Jimmy. "I'm the one you should be worried about."

"Look, I'm having a beer and reading. Why don't you take Igor here and go scare some kids? I've got nothing to talk to you about."

"You know who I am?" asked Jimmy.

Tobias took a sip of his beer, but didn't look at him. "Yeah, I know who you are."

"Then you know why I'm here."

"I don't need the work. I'm doing okay."

"Better than okay, from what I hear. You drive a sharp rig. You're making your payments, and you got enough left over to buy a beer at the end of a hard day's work. You ask me, you're rocking and rolling."

"Like you said, I work hard."

"Seems to me that you'd need thirty hours in the day to make the kind of money that you're pulling down in these difficult times. Independent operator, competing with the big guys. Hell, you mustn't ever sleep."

Tobias said nothing. He finished his beer, folded the magazine, and took most of his change from the bar, leaving a dollar tip.

"You need to let this go," he said.

"You need to show some respect," said Jimmy.

Tobias looked at him with a degree of amusement.

"Nice talking to you," he said as he got up. Earle reached for him to force him back down, but Tobias was too fast for him. He spun away from Earle, then kicked him hard in the side of the left knee. Earle's leg buckled, and Tobias grabbed Earle's hair as he went down and banged Earle's head hard against the bar. Earle slumped to the floor, stunned.

"You don't want to do this," said Tobias. "You mind your own business, and I'll mind mine."

Jimmy nodded, but it wasn't a conciliatory gesture, merely an indication that a suspicion had now been confirmed for him.

"Drive safely," he said.

Tobias backed out. Earle, who was nursing his knee but had recovered his composure, seemed inclined to take matters further when Jimmy put a hand on his shoulder to quieten him.

"Let him go," he said, as he watched Tobias depart. "This is just the beginning."

BACK IN THE SAILMAKER, Earle was doing a good job of pretending not to listen to our conversation.

"Tobias hurt his professional pride," said Jimmy.

"Yeah, well I'm all torn up about that."

"You should be. Earle doesn't forget a hurt."

I watched the big man cleaning the bar, even though there were no customers, and the Sailmaker wasn't about to get any cleaner without dousing its surfaces with acid. In that way, it had a lot in common with the Blue Moon.

"He didn't do a day's time for what happened to Sally Cleaver," I said. "Maybe a couple of years in the can might have made him a little less sensitive."

"He was younger then," said Jimmy. "He'd handle it differently now."

"Won't bring her back."

"No, it won't. You're a harsh judge, Charlie. People got the right to change, to learn from their mistakes."

He was right, and I wasn't in a position to point the finger, although I didn't like admitting it.

"Why do you let that place stand?" I said.

"The Moon? Sentimentality, maybe. It was my first bar. A shithole, but they're all shitholes. I know my place, and I know my customers."

"And?"

"It's a reminder. For me, for Earle. We take it away, and we start to forget."

"You know anything about Jandreau, the state trooper who died there?"

"No, and I already answered all the questions the cops had to throw at me about that. Last time I looked, you weren't wearing a badge, not unless it read 'Inquisitive Asshole.'"

"And Tobias?"

"It looks like he decided to keep a low profile after I spoke to him. He didn't make any runs outside the state for a month. Now he's started again."

"Any idea of destinations on the Canadian side?"

"All standard runs: some animal feed, paper products, machine parts. I could probably get you a list, but it wouldn't help. They're straight operations. Either I started asking questions too late, or these people are cleverer than they seem."

"People? We're talking associates?"

"Some army buddies. They've gone on runs with him. Shouldn't be hard for a man of your talents to find them." He picked up his newspaper and began reading. Our conversation had come to an end. "It was good talking to you again, Charlie. I'm sure you don't need Earle to show you out."

I stood up and put on my jacket.

"What's he moving, Jimmy?"

Jimmy's mouth creased, and the right side raised itself to mirror the left, forming a crocodile smile.

"That matter is in hand. Maybe I'll let you know how it works out. . . ."

VII

D id I trust Jimmy Jewel? I wasn't sure. My grandfather once described him as the kind of man who would lie through omission, but who preferred not to lie at all. Naturally, Jimmy made an exception for U.S. Customs and the forces of law and order in general, but even where they were concerned he tended to avoid confrontations whenever possible, thereby obviating the necessity for untruths.

But it was now clear, from what I had been told, that Joel Tobias was on Jimmy Jewel's radar, which was a little like being tracked by a military drone aircraft: it might just soar above you for the most part, but you never knew when it would call down vengeance upon your head.

After checking that Tobias's rig remained at the warehouse, and that his Silverado was still parked at his house, I stopped for a bowl of gumbo at the Bayou Kitchen on Deering. Jimmy had said that Joel Tobias was being helped by former soldiers, which brought with it a whole new set of problems. Maine was a veterans' state: there were more than 150,000 veterans living here, and that wasn't counting the ones who had been called up again to fight in Iraq and Afghanistan. Most of them lived away from the cities, holed up in rural areas like the county. In my experience, a lot of them didn't care much for talking to outsiders about their activities, legal or otherwise.

I made a call to Jackie Garner from my table, and told him that I had some work for him. Despite being well into his forties, Jackie still lived with his mom, who evinced a benign tolerance for her son's love of homemade explosives and other improvised munitions, although he was under strict instructions not to bring them into the house. Lately, a degree of tension had crept into this cozily Oedipal relationship, precipitated by the fact that Jackie had begun to date a woman named Lisa, who seemed very fond of her new beau, and was pressing him to move in with her, even if it wasn't yet clear how much she knew about the whole munitions business. Jackie's mother regarded the new arrival as unwanted competition for her son's affections, and had recently begun to play the frail, aging, "Who-will-look-after-me-when-you're-gone?" role, one into which she did not easily fit as there were great white sharks less well equipped for the solitary life than Mrs. Garner.

Thus it was that Jackie, caught between these twin poles of affection, like a condemned man whose arms have been attached to a pair of draft horses with a whip braced over their withers, seemed grateful for my call, and was more than willing to take on some otherwise dull surveillance work that did not involve dealing with the women in his life. I told him to stay with Joel Tobias, but if Tobias met up with anyone, then he was to follow the second party. In the meantime, I planned to talk with Ronald Straydeer, a Penobscot Indian who had his finger on veterans' affairs, and might be able to tell me a little more about Tobias.

But for now I had other obligations: Dave Evans had asked me to come in and cover for him for the weekly beer delivery at the Bear, and then act as bar manager for the rest of the day. It would be a long shift, but Dave was in a hole, so I put Ronald Straydeer off until the next day, then headed down to the Bear in time to meet the Nappi truck. And because the Bear was busy, afternoon slipped quickly into evening, and then into night, with barely a change to the bar's dimly lit interior, until at last it was after midnight, and I heard my bed calling.

THEY WERE WAITING FOR me in the parking lot. There were three of them, all wearing black ski masks and dark jackets. I caught a glimpse of one of them as I was opening my car door, but by then they were on top of me. I lashed out with my right hand, catching someone a glancing blow to the face with my elbow. I followed through with the car key, and felt it cut through the mask and tear the skin beneath. I heard swearing, and then I took a hard blow to the back of the head that sent me sprawling. A gun was placed against my temple, and a male voice said: "Enough." A car pulled up. Hands were placed beneath my armpits, dragging me to my feet. A sack was forced over my head, and I was pushed into the back of the car and made to lie flat on the floor. One booted foot was placed against the back of my neck. My hands were pulled behind my back, and seconds later I felt the plastic restraints tighten painfully against my skin. Gunmetal tapped me lightly on the same spot where I had earlier been struck, and sparks went off behind my eyes.

"Stay down, and stay quiet."

And with no further choice in the matter, I did as I was told.

WE HEADED SOUTH ON I-95. I could tell from the distance we traveled on Forest, and the turn we made onto the interstate. We drove for no more than fifteen minutes before pulling off to the left. I heard gravel crunch beneath the tires as we came to a halt, and then I was pulled from the car. My arms were forced high behind my back, almost to the point of dislocation, and I was made to walk bent over. Nobody spoke. A door opened. Through the sack I could smell old smoke, and urine. I was pushed inside, helped by a boot in the ass that sent me to the floor. Someone laughed. There were rough tiles beneath me, and the smell of human waste was nauseatingly strong. My captors took up positions around me. Their footsteps echoed. I was indoors, but the sound was wrong, and I had a sense of space above my head. In fact, I now had a pretty good idea of where I was. Even after all these years, the place still stank of burning. I was at the Blue Moon, and I understood that a connection had been made between Jimmy Jewel and me. Those who had brought me to this place knew about our meeting, and they had decided, wrongly, that I was in Jimmy's employ. A message was about to be sent to Jimmy through me, and even before they began communicating it I was certain that I would have preferred it to be delivered to Jimmy in person.

Someone knelt beside me, and the sack was pulled up as far as my nose.

"We don't want to hurt you." It was the same male voice that had spoken earlier. It was calm and measured, the voice of a younger man, and without animosity.

"Maybe you should have thought that one through before you knocked me down in the parking lot," I said.

"You were pretty fast with that key. Seemed like a good idea to quieten you down some. Anyway, enough with the pleasantries. Answer my questions, and you'll be back at your muscle car before the headache really starts to bite. You know what this is about."

"Do I?"

"Yes, you do. Why are you following Joel Tobias?"

"Who's Joel Tobias?"

There was silence for a time before the voice came again, closer now. I could smell mint on the man's breath.

"We know all about you. You're a big shot, running around with a gun, putting bad guys in the ground. Don't get me wrong: I admire you and what you've done. You're on the right side, and that counts for something. It's why you're still breathing instead of sinking into the marshes with a new hole in your head to let the water in. I'll ask you one more time: Why are you following Joel Tobias? Who hired you? Is Jimmy Jewel picking up the tab? Speak now, or you'll be forever holding your tongue."

My head ached, and my arms hurt. Something sharp was biting into my palm. I could just have told them that Bennett Patchett had hired me because he believed that Joel Tobias was abusing his girlfriend. I could have, but I didn't. It wasn't simply out of concern for Bennett's own safety; there was an element of stubbornness to it too. Then again, sometimes stubbornness and principle are almost indistinguishable from each other.

"Like I said, I don't know any Joel Tobias."

"Strip him," said another voice. "Strip him and cornhole him."

"You hear that?" said the first voice. "Some of my buddies here aren't as concerned about the niceties of conversation as I am. I could step outside to smoke a cigarette, and leave them to amuse themselves with you." A blade touched my buttocks, and glanced against my groin. Even through my trousers, I felt the keenness of its edge. "Is that what you want? You'll be a changed man after it, that's for sure. In fact, you'll be a bitch."

"You've made a mistake," I said, and I sounded braver than I felt.

"You're a fool, Mr. Parker. You're going to tell us the truth within the next minute. I guarantee you."

He let the sack drop down over my nose and mouth. Hands grabbed my legs, and I heard the sticky rasp of heavy-duty tape before it was wound tightly around my calves. The sack was twisted against my Adam's apple. Then I was lifted and carried across the room. I was turned so that I was facing up, and then my legs were raised higher than my head.

The voice spoke again.

"You're not going to like this," it said, "and I'd prefer not to have to do it, but needs must."

I could just about breathe through the material, but I was already hyperventilating. I tried to bring my breathing under control, counting slowly from one to ten in my head. I got as far as three before I smelled fetid water, and then I was plunged headfirst below its surface.

I tried to resist the urge to inhale, tried to hold my breath entirely, but a finger probed for my solar plexus and then began placing steady pressure on it. Water flooded into my nose and mouth. I started to choke. Then I began to drown. It wasn't just a sensation of drowning: my head was filling with water. When I inhaled, the cloth tightened against my face, and I took in fluid. When I tried to cough it away more water flooded my throat. I began to lose track of whether I was inhaling or exhaling, of what was up and what was down. I was certain that I was on the verge of blacking out when they pulled me out and laid me on the floor. The sack was yanked away from the lower half of my face. I was turned on my side and allowed to cough up water and phlegm.

"There's plenty more where that came from, Mr. Parker," said my interrogator, for that was what he was: my interrogator, and my torturer. "Who hired you? Why were you meeting with Jimmy Jewel?"

"I don't work for Jimmy Jewel." I gasped out the words.

"Then why did you go to his place today?"

"It was just a casual meeting. Look, I—"

The sack was pulled back down, the tape hanging loose now, and I was lifted and immersed, lifted and immersed, but there were no more questions, no opportunities to make it stop, and I believed that I was going to die. When I went down for the fourth time, I would have told them anything to bring it to an end, anything at all. I thought that I heard someone say, "You're killing him," but there was no anxiety about the fact. It was merely an observation.

I was raised from the water and lowered to the floor again, but I still felt as though I were drowning. The sack was pressed against my nose and mouth, and I couldn't breathe. I thrashed on my belly like a dying fish, trying to push the sack away, not caring as I scraped my face against the floor through the material. At last, mercifully, it was pulled up. I had to force myself to inhale, for my system seemed to have shut down in expectation of water, not air. Facedown, I felt hands pushing at my back, forcing the fluid from me. It seared my throat and nostrils as it emerged, as though it were acid, not filthy water.

"Jesus," said the same voice that had earlier commented on the possibility of my death, "he pretty much swallowed half the barrel."

The first man spoke again. "For the last time, Mr. Parker: who hired you to follow Joel Tobias?"

"No more," I said, and I hated the pleading tone of my voice. I was broken. "No more. . . ."

"Just be straight with us. But this is your last chance: the next time, we'll leave you to drown."

"Bennett Patchett," I said. I was ashamed at my weakness, but I didn't want to go under again. I didn't want to die that way. I coughed again, but less water emerged this time.

"Damien's father," came a third voice, one that I had not heard before. It was deeper than the rest, the voice of a black man. He sounded tired. "He's talking about Damien's father."

"Why?" said the first voice again. "Why did he hire you?"

"He employs Joel Tobias's girlfriend. He was concerned about her. He thought Tobias might be beating her."

"You're lying."

I felt him reach for the sack again, and I pulled away.

"No," I said. "It's the truth. Bennett's a good man. He was just worried about the girl."

"Shit," said the black man. "All this because Joel can't keep his old lady in line."

"Quiet! Did the girl say something to Patchett to make him think this?"

"No. They're his own suspicions, nothing more."

"There's more to it than that, though, isn't there? Tell me. We've come this far. It's nearly over now."

I had no dignity left. "He wants to know why his son died."

"Damien shot himself. The 'why' won't bring him back."

"I know. I told Bennett that, but it's hard for him to accept. He's lost his boy, his only son. He's hurting."

For a time, nothing else was said, and I experienced the first glimmer of hope that I might yet come out of this alive and, perhaps, that Bennett would not suffer for my weakness.

The interrogator leaned in close to me. His breath was warm against my cheek, and I felt the terrible intimacy that is part of the pact between the tormented and the tormentor. "Why did you follow Tobias to his rig?"

I swore. If Tobias had made that tail too, I was more out of practice than I thought. "Patchett doesn't like him, and he wanted evidence to present to the girl that might make her leave him. I thought that maybe he might be seeing someone else on the side. That was why I followed him."

"And Jimmy Jewel?"

"Tobias drives a truck. Jimmy Jewel knows the trucking business."

"Jimmy Jewel knows smuggling."

"He told me that he tried to recruit Tobias, but Tobias didn't bite. That's all I know."

He considered this. "It almost sounds plausible," he said. "Sleazy, but plausible. I'm tempted to give you the benefit of the doubt, except that I know you're an intelligent man. You're inquisitive. I'm pretty certain that Joel Tobias's sexual habits were not the only branch of his affairs that you might have been tempted to examine."

I could see his boots through the gap at the bottom of the sack. They were shiny and black. I watched as they moved away from me. A conversation was conducted nearby in tones too soft for me to pick up on what was being said. Instead, I concentrated on breathing. I was shaking, and my throat was raw. Eventually, I heard footsteps approaching, and those black boots appeared in my field of vision again.

"Now you listen, Mr. Parker. The girl's welfare isn't anything that you need to concern yourself with. She's in no danger, I guarantee you. There will be no further repercussions for you, or Mr. Patchett, as long as you both just walk away. I give you my word on that. Nobody is being hurt here, do you understand? Nobody. Whatever you suspect, or think you know, you're wrong."

"Your word as a soldier?" I said. I sensed him react, and braced myself for the blow, but none came.

"I guessed that you'd be a smart-ass," he said. "Don't get any ideas. I'm sure that you're all riled up, or you will be once we let you go, and you'll be tempted to come looking for payback, but I wouldn't if I were you. You come after us because of this, and we'll kill you. This is none of your concern. I repeat: this is *none* of your concern. I regret what had to be done here tonight, I truly do. We're not animals, and if you'd cooperated at the start then it wouldn't have been necessary. Consider it a lesson hard learned." He pulled the sack down. "We're done here. Take him back to his car, and treat him gently."

The tape was cut from my legs. I was helped to my feet and escorted to the car. I was disoriented and weak, and I had to stop halfway to throw up. Hands held me tight at the elbows, but at least I wasn't being made to walk bent over with my arms raised behind my back. This time, I was put in the trunk, not the back of the car. When we got to the Bear, I was laid facedown on the parking lot, and my restraints were removed. My car keys jangled as they landed beside me. The voice that had earlier spoken of Joel Tobias's old lady told me to keep my head covered for a count of ten. I remained where I was until the car pulled away, then raised myself slowly and stumbled to the edge of the lot. I could see the rear lights of a car racing away. Blue, I thought. Maybe a Ford. Too far to make out the plates.

The Bear was dark, and my car was the only vehicle still in the lot. I didn't call the cops. I didn't call anybody, not then. Instead, I drove home, fighting nausea all the way. My shirt and jeans were filthy and torn. I threw them in the trash as soon as I reached the house. I wanted to shower, to clean the dirt of the Blue Moon from my skin, but I elected simply to scrub myself in the sink. I wasn't ready for the sensation of water pouring on my face again.

That night, I woke up twice when the sheets touched my face, and I lashed out at them in panic. After the second time, I chose to sleep on top of, not under, them, and lay awake as my mind shuffled names like cards: Damien Patchett, Jimmy Jewel, Joel Tobias. I replayed in my head the voices I had heard, the sense of humiliation I had felt as they threatened me with rape, so that I would know them when I heard them again. I let anger course through me like an electrical charge.

You should have killed me. You should have left me to drown in that water. Because now I'm going to come after you, and I'm not going to do it alone. The men I'll bring with me will be worth a dozen of you, military training or not. Whatever you're doing, whatever operation you're running, I'm going to tear it apart and leave you to die in the wreckage.

For what you did to me, I'm going to kill you all.

CHAPTER

VIII

The body of Jeremiah Webber had been discovered by his beloved daughter after he failed to make a lunch appointment with her, a meeting dictated at least as much by the desire to hit on her old man for a few bucks and a good meal as the child's natural affection for her parent. Suzanne Webber loved her father, but he was a curious man, and her mother had hinted that his financial affairs did not bear close scrutiny. His shortcomings as a husband were merely one aspect of his flawed nature; as far as his first ex-wife was concerned, he could not be trusted to behave properly under any circumstances, with the exception of ensuring his daughter's well-being. In that, at least, she could be certain that he would act according to what passed for his better nature. And, as has been said before, she *liked* Jeremiah Webber. His second ex-wife, who had no residual affection for him whatsoever, regarded him as a reptile.

When his daughter found her father's body lying on the kitchen floor, her first thought was that there had been a robbery, or an assault. Then she saw the gun by his hand, and, given the implied precariousness of his financial circumstances, wondered if he had taken his own life. Although in shock, she had retained sufficient self-possession to use her cell phone to call the police, and not to touch anything in the room. She then spoke to her mother while she waited for the police to arrive. She sat outside, not inside. The smell in the house distressed her. It was the stink of her father's mortality, and something else, something that she could not quite place. Later, she would describe it to her mother as the lingering stench of matches that had been lit in an effort to disguise the aftermath of a bad trip to the restroom. She smoked a cigarette, and cried, and listened as her mother, through her own tears, denied the possibility that Webber had shot himself.

"He was selfish," she said, "but he wasn't *that* selfish."

It quickly became apparent to the investigating detectives that Jeremiah Webber had not, in fact, taken his own life, not unless he was a perfectionist who, having botched the first shot, had found the will and strength to pop a second one in his head in order to finish the job. Given the angle of entry, that would also have required him to be a contortionist, and possibly superhuman, considering the nature of the catastrophic injuries inflicted by the first bullet. So it looked like Jeremiah Webber had been murdered.

And yet, and yet . . .

There was powder residue on his hand. True, it might have been possible for his killer, or killers, to put the gun against his head and apply pressure to his finger in order to force him to pull the trigger, but that usually only happened in movies, and it was easier said than done. No professional was going to take the risk of putting a gun in the hands of someone who didn't want to die. At best, there was a chance that, before he was encouraged to plant one in his own head, he might fire a shot into the ceiling, or the floor, or someone else's head. In addition, there was no evidence of a struggle, and no marks on his body to indicate that Webber might have been restrained at some point.

So what if, suggested one of the detectives, he shot himself, botched it, and then someone else finished the job for him out of a sense of mercy? But who stands back and watches another man kill himself? Was Webber ill, or so overcome by difficulties, financial or otherwise, that he saw no way out of them but to take his own life? Had he then found someone loyal enough to stay by his side as he fired what was intended to be the fatal shot and then, having watched him fail, to deliver the coup de grace? It seemed unlikely. Better, then, to assume that the suicide was forced upon him, that the hands of another placed Webber's finger on the trigger and applied the pressure required to fire the first bullet into his brain, and that those same hands finished him off instead of leaving him to die in agony on his kitchen floor.

And yet, and yet . . .

Who tries to make a murder look like a suicide, and then undoes all that good work by firing a second shot?

An amateur, that's who; an amateur, or someone who just doesn't care about appearances. Then there was the matter of the wineglasses, three in all: one smashed on the floor, and the other two on the kitchen table. Both had been drunk from, and both had fingerprints upon them. No, that wasn't quite true. Both had Webber's fingerprints all over them, and the second glass had smears that were almost fingerprints, except that, when examined, they proved to be without whorls, or loops, or arches. They were entirely blank, leading to the suggestion that at least one other person in the room with Webber had been wearing gloves, or some form of patch to mask the prints, perhaps in an effort to put Webber at ease initially, for what kind of killer would choose to leave evidence upon a wineglass of his presence at a crime scene? The glass was sent for testing in the hope that DNA traces might be obtained from it. In time, that analysis would discover saliva that, when analyzed, revealed the presence of unusual chemical compounds: a drug of some kind. A clever lab technician, acting on little more than a hunch, separated the drug and its metabolites from the saliva using a metal-doped sol-gel immobilized in a glass capillary, and found it to be 5-fluoruoracil, or 5-FU, commonly used to treat solid tumors.

The second person in the room with Jeremiah Webber on the night that he died was thus shown to be a male on chemotherapy, which led to a possible resolution of the fingerprint issue: certain drugs used in the treatment of cancer, among them capecitabine, caused inflammation of the palms of the hands and the soles of the feet, leading to peeling and blistering of the skin and, over time, the loss of fingerprints. Unfortunately, by the time this was revealed, weeks had passed since the discovery of the body, and subsequent events had played themselves out to the end.

And so, on the day after the body was discovered, the police began investigating Webber's ex-wives, his daughter, and his business associates. In time, they would find more than one dead end, but the strangest of all was the correspondence in Webber's files relating to an institution described as the "Gutelieb Foundation," or, more often, merely "the Foundation," because the Foundation did not appear to exist. The lawyers who purported to represent it were shysters with holes in their shoes, and they claimed never to have encountered in person anyone from the Foundation. All bills were paid by money order, and all communication was carried out via Yahoo. The woman who took messages on the Foundation's behalf worked out of the back of a strip mall in Natick, sitting in a booth surrounded by five other women, all of them purporting to be secretaries and PAs for companies or businessmen whose offices were their cars, or their bedrooms, or a table in a coffee shop. The secretarial services company, SecServe (which the detectives investigating Webber's death felt was a name open to misinterpretation, particularly if spoken aloud), informed the police that all bills relating to the Foundation were paid, once again, by money order. SecServe had never raised any objection to this form of payment: after all, it was perfectly legitimate. Some of the company's other clients had been known to pay in bags of quarters, and in the current climate SecServe's boss, whose name was Obrad, was just relieved when people paid at all.

"What kind of name is Obrad anyway?" asked one of the detectives.

"It is Serbian," said Obrad. "It means 'to make happy.'"

He had even had it written on his business cards: OBRAD MAKE HAPPY. The cops were tempted to correct his grammar, and point out that statements like this, combined with the possibilities for misunderstanding inherent in his company name, were likely to get him into trouble at some point, but they did not. Obrad was helpful, and an enthusiast. They didn't want to hurt his feelings.

"And you never spoke to anyone connected with this 'Foundation'?"

Obrad shook his head. "Everything done on internet now. They fill out form, forward payment, and I make happy." Obrad did manage to produce a copy of the original contract form filled out over the Net. They traced it back to a cyber café in Providence, Rhode Island, and there the trail ended. The money orders came from a number of post offices all over New England. The same one was never used twice, and the transactions were untraceable since the U.S. Postal Service did not accept credit cards as payment for money orders. They set about seeking court orders to examine security footage from the post offices in question.

The existence of the Foundation troubled the investigating officers, but post offices and internet cafés were as close as they would ever get to it. As it happened, the Foundation was Herod, and it was only one of the names that he used to disguise his affairs. After Webber's death, the Foundation effectively ceased to exist. In time, Herod decided, he would reactivate it in another form. Webber had been punished, and the small community through which both men had briefly moved would be aware of the reason why. Herod was not worried about someone approaching the police. They all had something to hide, each and every one of them.

TWO NIGHTS AFTER WEBBER'S death, yellow tape still indicated the scene of the crime, but there was no longer a police presence at the house. The alarm system had been activated, and the local patrols made regular passes to discourage rubberneckers.

The alarm on the house went off at 12:50 A.M. The local police were at the door just as the clock tipped 1:10 A.M. The front door was closed, and all the windows appeared to be secure. At the back of the house, they found a crow with a broken neck. It appeared to have flown into the kitchen window, activating the alarm, although neither of the cops could remember ever seeing a crow in the dead of night.

The alarm went off again at 1:30 A.M., and a third time at 1:50 A.M. The alarm company's monitoring system indicated that, each time, the source was the kitchen window beneath which the dead crow had been found. They suspected a malfunction of some kind, which they would check in the morning. At the request of the police, the alarm was deactivated.

At 2:10 A.M., the kitchen window was opened from outside using a thin piece of metal, warped at the center so that its top half was perpendicular to its lower half, enabling it to be twisted in order to move the latch, unlocking the window. A man climbed through and alighted gently on the kitchen floor. He sniffed the air uncertainly, then lit a cigarette. Had the light been better, and had anyone been there to see him, he would have been revealed as a disheveled figure wearing an old black jacket and black trousers that nearly, but not quite, matched. His shirt might once have been white, but was now faded to a bone gray, its collar frayed. The man's hair was long, and slicked back, revealing a pronounced widow's peak. His teeth were yellow, as were his fingernails, all stained from decades of smoking. His movements were graceful, although it was the predatory grace of a mantis or a spider.

He reached into his jacket pocket and removed a Maglite. He pulled the drapes on the kitchen windows, twisted the top of the flashlight, and allowed its beam to play upon the table, the chairs, and the dried blood on the floor. He did not move, but simply followed the light, taking in all that it showed but touching nothing. When he had concluded his inspection of the kitchen, he progressed through the other rooms of the house, as before only looking, never touching. Finally, he returned to the kitchen, lit another cigarette from the first, and disposed of the remains of the latter in the sink. Then he retreated to the door connecting the kitchen to the hallway and leaned against the frame, trying to pinpoint the source of his unease.

The death of Webber had not come entirely as a surprise. The man in the kitchen kept a close eye on the activities of Webber and his kind. Their occasional lack of scruples did not surprise him. All collectors were the same: their desire would sometimes overcome their better natures. But Webber was not really a collector. True, he had kept some items for himself over the years, but he made his money as a middleman, a facilitator, a front for others. A certain degree of good faith was expected from such individuals. They might sometimes play one buyer off against another, but they rarely actively cheated. It was unwise to do so, for the short-term gain from a single deal handled dishonestly might well damage one's reputation. In Webber's case, the damage, revealed in a smear of blood and gray matter, had been fatal. The visitor took a long pull on his cigarette, his nostrils twitching. The smell that had so disturbed Webber's daughter and which, to her shame, she associated with the relaxation of her father's muscles after death, had faded, but the intruder's senses were intensely acute, and largely unaffected by his love of cigarettes. The smell bothered him. It did not belong. It was alien.

Behind him was the darkness of the hallway, but it was not empty. Forms moved in the gloom, gray figures with skin like withered fruit, shapes without substance.

Hollow men.

And though he felt them gathering, he did not turn around. They were his creatures, despite their hatred for him.

The man who stood in the kitchen called himself the Collector. He sometimes went by the name of Kushiel, the demon reputed to act as Hell's jailer, which might simply have been a dark joke on his part. He was not a collector in the manner of those for whom Webber solicited items. No, the Collector viewed himself more as a settler of debts, a striker of balances. There were some who might even have termed him a killer, for that, ultimately, was what he did, but it would have represented a misunderstanding of the work in which the Collector was engaged. Those whom he killed had, by their sins, forfeited the right to life. More to the point, their souls were forfeit, and without a soul a body was merely an empty vessel to be broken and discarded. From each one that he killed he took a token, often an item of particular sentimental value to the victim. It was his way of remembering, although he also took a considerable degree of pleasure from his collection.

And, my, how it had grown over the years.

Sometimes, those soulless beings lingered, and the Collector gave them a purpose, even if that purpose was only to add to their own number. Now, as they prowled back and forth behind him, he sensed a shift in their mood, if such lost, hopeless spirits could be said to retain even a semblance of real human emotion other than rage. They were frightened, but it was fear tempered by an edge of . . .

Was that expectation?

They were like a crowd of minor playground bullies, cowed by one stronger than them but now awaiting the approach of the big dog, the lead jock, the one who would put the usurper back in his rightful place.

The Collector rarely felt uncertain. He knew too much of the ways of this honeycomb world, and he hunted in its shadows. He was the one to be feared, the predator, the judge without mercy.

But here, in this expensively appointed kitchen of a house in a wealthy suburb, the Collector was nervous. He sniffed the air again, finding the taint that lingered. He walked to the window, reached for the drapes, then paused as though fearful of what he might see on the other side. Finally, he pulled them apart, stepping back as he did so, his right hand raised slightly to protect himself.

There was only his own reflection.

But something else had been here, and not the man who had delivered the shot that killed Webber, for the Collector knew all about him: Herod, always searching, never finding; Herod, who lived behind aliases and shell companies, who was so clever and so adept at concealment that even the Collector had failed to track him down. His time would come, eventually. After all, the Collector was engaged in God's work. He was God's murderer, and who could hope to hide from the Divine?

No, this was not Herod. This was another, and the Collector could smell him in his nostrils and taste him on his tongue, could almost see the faintest trace of his presence, like the condensation of a breath upon the glass. He had been here, watching as Webber died. Wait! The Collector's eyes widened as he made connections, speculation hardening into belief.

Not watching Webber as he died, but watching *Herod* as Webber died.

The Collector knew then why he had been drawn to this place, knew why Herod had been assembling his own private collection of arcane material, even if he believed that Herod did not yet himself fully understand the final purpose behind his efforts.

He was here. He had come at last: the Laughing Man, the Old Tempter.

The One Who Waits Behind the Glass.

IX

I woke feeling poorly rested, and with a deep ache in my throat, my nose, and my lungs. My right hand wouldn't stop shaking, and hot water spilled on my shirt when I tried to make a cup of coffee. In the end, it didn't matter about the coffee: it tasted of filthy water anyway. I sat in a chair looking over the marshes; my rage from the night before had departed, to be replaced by a lassitude that was not quite deep enough to block out my fear. I didn't want to think about Bennett Patchett and his dead son, or Joel Tobias, or containers filled with a rushing darkness. I'd experienced delayed shock before, but never like this. Added to the pain and the fear was the shame that I felt for naming Bennett Patchett. We'd all like to believe that, in order to protect another person, and to save a little something of ourselves, we might hold out against torture, but it's not true. Everybody breaks eventually, and to stop myself from being drowned in stagnant water I'd have told them anything that they wanted. I'd have confessed to crimes that I hadn't committed, and promised to commit crimes repugnant to my nature. I might even have betrayed my own child, and the knowledge of that made me curl in upon myself. They had unmanned me in the ruins of the Blue Moon.

After a time, I called Bennett Patchett. Before I could speak, he told me that Karen Emory hadn't shown up for work that day, and he hadn't been able to get a reply when he called the house. He was worried about her, he said, but I cut him off. I told him of what had happened the night before, and confessed what I had done. He didn't seem troubled, or even surprised.

"They were military?" he asked.

"Ex-military, I think, and they knew about Damien. For that reason, I want to believe that they're not going to cause you trouble, not if you just go back to mourning your son in silence."

"Is that what you'd do, Mr. Parker? Is that what you want me to do? Are you going to back away from all this?"

"I don't know, sir. Right now, I need some time."

"For what?" But he sounded resigned, as though no answer I could give would be good enough.

"To find my anger again," I said, and maybe, somehow, I gave him the one answer that sufficed.

"When you do, I'll be here," he said, and hung up.

I don't know how long I stayed in that chair, but eventually I forced myself to my feet. I had to do something, or else I would sink just as assuredly as if the men at the Blue Moon had released their grip and left me to fall headfirst to the bottom of a container of standing water.

I picked up the phone, and called New York. It was time to bring in some serious help. After that, I showered, and I made myself hold my face up to the falling water.

JACKIE GARNER CONTACTED ME an hour later.

"It looks like Tobias is moving out," he said. "He's got a bag packed, and he's out by his rig, giving it one last check."

It made sense. They probably figured that they'd scared me enough to proceed with whatever it was they were planning, and they might almost have been right.

"Stay with him for as long as you can," I said. "He's making a run to Canada. You have a passport?"

"It's at home. I'll call Mom. She can bring it to me. Even if Tobias gets on the road, I can stay with him until she catches up. Mom drives like a demon."

That I could believe.

"You okay?" said Jackie. "You sound sick."

I told him the basics of what had occurred the night before, and warned him about keeping his distance from Tobias. "When you figure out the route he's taking, you can pass him and wait for him over the border. Any sign of trouble, you let him go. These guys aren't screwing around."

"So you're not dropping this?"

"I guess not," I said. "In fact, company's coming."

"From New York?" asked Jackie, and he could barely keep the hope out of his voice.

"From New York."

"Man, wait until I tell the Fulcis," he said, and he sounded like a child at Christmas. "They'll be buzzed!"

I KNOCKED THREE TIMES, waiting a minute or two between each knock, before Karen Emory answered. She was wearing a robe and slippers, her hair was unkempt, and she looked as though she hadn't slept much. I knew how she felt. She had also been crying.

"Yes?" said Karen Emory. "What do you—?"

She stopped talking, and squinted. "You're the guy, the one who was at the restaurant," she said.

"That's right. My name is Charlie Parker. I'm a private investigator."

"Get lost."

She slammed the door closed, and my foot wasn't there to stop it. Sticking your foot in someone's door is a good way to get maimed, or have your toes broken. It's also trespassing, and I had enough of a reputation with the cops as it was. I was trying to keep my nose clean.

I knocked again, and kept knocking until Karen came back to the door.

"I'm going to call the cops if you don't leave me alone. I'm warning you."

"I don't think you're going to call the cops, Ms. Emory. Your boyfriend wouldn't like it."

It was a low blow, but like most low blows, it hit home. She bit her lip. "Please, just go away."

"I'd like to talk to you for a moment. Believe me, I'm taking more of a chance than you are. I'm not going to get you into any trouble. Just a few minutes of your time is all I ask, and then I'll be gone."

She looked past me, checking to make sure that there was nobody on the street, then stepped aside to let me in. The door opened directly into the living area, with a kitchen ahead and stairs to the right, and what looked like the entrance to a basement beneath them. She closed the front door behind me and stood with her arms folded, waiting for me to speak.

"Can we sit down?" I asked.

She seemed inclined to say no, then relented and led me to the kitchen. It was bright and cheerful, decorated in whites and yellows. It smelled of fresh paint. I took a seat at the table.

"You have a nice house," I said.

She nodded. "It's Joel's. He did all the work himself." She leaned against the sink, not sitting, keeping as much distance between us as possible. "You say you're a private detective? I suppose I should have asked for some ID before I let you in."

"It's usually a good idea," I said. I flipped open my wallet and showed my license to her. She examined it in a cursory way without touching it.

"I knew your mother a little," I said. "We went to the same high school."

"Oh. My mom lives in Wesley now."

"That's nice," I said, for want of something better to say.

"Not really. Her new husband is an asshole." She searched in the pocket of her robe and came out with a lighter and a pack of cigarettes. She lit one, then put the pack and the lighter back in her pocket. She didn't offer one to me. I didn't smoke, but it's always polite to ask.

"Joel says that Bennett Patchett hired you." I couldn't really deny it but, if nothing else, it confirmed that the men at the Blue Moon had spoken to Tobias after last night, and he, in turn, had spoken of it to his girlfriend.

"That's right."

She rolled her eyes in exasperation.

"He meant well," I said. "He was worried about you."

"Joel says that he doesn't think I should work there no more. He says I have to quit my job and find another. We had a fight about it."

She glared at me, the implication being that it was my fault.

"And what do you say?"

"I love him, and I love this house. If it comes down to it, there'll be other jobs, I guess, but I'd prefer to keep working for Mr. Patchett." Her eyes grew damp. A tear fell from her right eye, and she rubbed it away hurriedly.

This whole case was a mess. Sometimes, that's just the way things are. I wasn't even sure why I was here, apart from ensuring that Joel Tobias hadn't done to Karen Emory what, once upon a time, Cliffie Andreas had done to Sally Cleaver.

"Has Joel hit you, or abused you in any way, Ms. Emory?"

There was a long pause.

"No, not like you, or Mr. Patchett, think. We had a big argument a while back, and it got out of control, that's all."

I watched her closely. I didn't think it was the first time that she'd been hit by a boyfriend. The way she spoke suggested that she regarded the occasional slap as an occupational hazard, a downside of dating a particular type of man. If it happened often enough, a woman might start to believe that she was at fault, that something in her, a flaw in her psychological makeup, caused men to respond in a particular way. If Karen Emory wasn't already thinking along those lines, then she was close to it.

"Was it the first time that he'd hit you?"

She nodded. "It was—what do they say?—'out of character' for him. Joel's a good man." She stumbled a little on the last three words, as though she were trying to convince herself as well as me. "He's just under a lot of stress at the moment."

"Really? Why would that be?"

Karen shrugged and looked away. "It's hard, working for yourself."

"Does he talk to you about his work?"

She didn't reply.

"Is that what you were arguing about?"

Still no reply.

"Does he frighten you?"

She licked her lips.

"No." This time, it was a lie.

"And his friends, his army buddies? What about them?"

She stubbed out the half-smoked cigarette in an ashtray.

"You have to go now," she said. "You can tell Mr. Patchett that I'm fine. I'll give him my notice this week."

"Karen, you're not alone in this. If you need help, I can put you in touch with the right people. They're discreet, and they'll advise you on what you can do to protect yourself. You don't even have to mention Joel's name if you don't want to."

But even as I spoke, I could see that my words weren't going to have any effect. Karen Emory had hitched herself to Joel Tobias's star. If she left him, she'd have to go back to Bennett Patchett's dorms, and in time another man would come along, one who might be worse than Tobias, and she'd go with him just to escape. I waited for a moment, but it was clear that I was going to get no more out of her. She gestured to the door, and followed me down the hallway. As she opened the front door, and I slipped past her to stand on the porch, she spoke again.

"What would Joel do if he knew you'd been here?" she asked. She sounded like a mischievous child, but it was all bravado. Her eyes were bright with unshed tears.

"I don't know," I said, "but I think his friends might kill me. What are they doing, Karen? Why are they so worried about someone finding out?"

She swallowed hard, and her face crumpled.

"Because they're dying," she said. "They're all dying."

And the door closed in my face.

THE SAILMAKER WAS STILL barren of customers as I peered through the glass door, and Jimmy Jewel was still seated on the same stool at the bar, but there were now papers scattered before him, and he was checking figures on a desk calculator.

The light was constantly changing in the bar. Shards of sunlight broke the murk only to be swallowed up again by the movement of the clouds, like shoals of silver fish disappearing into the ocean's darkness. Although the Sailmaker should have been open for business by now, Jimmy had stopped Earle from unlocking the door. The Sailmaker had inherited some of the habits of the Blue Moon: it might be open before midday, or at five in the afternoon, but it might not. The regulars knew better than to go knocking on the door seeking entry. There'd be a place for them when Jimmy and Earle were ready, and once they were settled in nobody would bother them unless they fell on the floor and made a mess.

But I wasn't a regular, and so I knocked. Jimmy looked up, considered me for a time while he debated whether or not he could get away with telling me to go play with the white lines on I-95, then gestured to Earle to let me in. Earle did so, then went back to filling the coolers, which didn't present too much of a challenge since the bar didn't stock anything that might have counted as exotic when it came to beers. You could still order a Miller High Life at the Sailmaker, and PBR was drunk without a shot of irony on the side.

I took a seat at the bar, and Earle departed to grab a fresh pot of coffee for Jimmy. If I'd drunk as much coffee every day as Jimmy did, I wouldn't be able to write my name without trembling. On Jimmy, though, it seemed to have no effect. Maybe he had vast reservoirs of calm on which to draw.

"You know, it seems like only moments since you were last here," said Jimmy. "Either time is passing more quickly than it should, or you're just not giving me enough time to start missing you."

"Tobias is on the road again, as the song goes," I said.

Jimmy kept his eyes on his papers, adding figures and making notes in the margins. "Why is this such a beef with you? You work for the government now?"

"No, I prefer a private pension. As for why this is a beef, I made some new friends last night."

"Really? You must be pleased. Strikes me that you could use all the friends that you can get."

"These ones tried drowning me until I told them what they wanted to know. Friends like them I can do without."

Jimmy's pen stopped moving.

"And what did they want to know?"

"They were interested in why I was asking questions about Joel Tobias."

"And what did you tell them?"

"The truth."

"You didn't feel the urge to lie?"

"I was too busy trying not to die to make anything up."

"So you've already been warned off once, and not gently, and you're still asking questions?"

"That's the point. They weren't polite."

"Polite. What are you, a duchess?"

"There's also the matter of where they took me to ask their questions."

"Which was?"

"The Blue Moon, or what's left of it."

Jimmy pushed the calculator away. "I knew you'd bring bad luck with you. I knew it as soon as you walked in that first time."

"I think you might have helped by getting in Joel Tobias's face over in Dewey's, but, yeah, they connected me to you, or vice versa. Taking me to the Blue Moon was a way of warning us both, except you didn't get the business end of the message."

Earle had returned, and was now watching us. He didn't look happy at the return to the subject of the Blue Moon, but it was always hard to tell with Earle. He had a face like a bad tattoo. Jimmy, meanwhile, had gone somewhere else for a time. When he eventually spoke, he sounded tired and old.

"Maybe I should get out of this business," he said.

I didn't know if he was referring to the bar, or smuggling, or even life itself. He'd get out of them all eventually, if that was any consolation, but I didn't offer that thought. I just let him talk.

"You know, I have money tied up in this wharf. I thought it would pay dividends when they started developing it, but now it looks like the only cash I'll see out of it is the insurance money when it collapses into Casco Bay, and then this place will probably take me with it so I won't get to enjoy it."

Then he patted the bar softly and fondly, the way a man might stroke a beloved, if ornery, old dog.

"I always thought of myself as a gentleman trader," he continued. "It was a game, moving stuff over the border, trying to steal a nickel or two from Uncle Sam. People got hurt sometimes, but I did my best to make sure that didn't happen too often. I got into drugs kind of reluctantly, if that makes any sense to you, and I found ways to salve my conscience about it. Mostly, though, if I'm being honest, I don't think about it, and it doesn't bother me too much. Same with people, doesn't matter if they're Chinamen looking to work in the kitchen of some restaurant in Boston, or whores from Eastern Europe. I'm just the middleman." He turned to gauge my response. "I guess you think that I'm a hypocrite, or that I'm just fooling myself about all this."

"You know what you are," I said. "I'm not here to absolve you. I just want information."

"Cut to the chase, in other words."

"Yes."

Earle snapped into life and refreshed Jimmy's coffee, knowing instinctively that his boss now needed his gears oiled. He found a second mug and put it down beside me. I held my hand over it to indicate that I didn't want any, and thought for a moment that Earle might have been tempted to pour the hot coffee over my fingers, just to let me know that he could care less what I did or didn't want. In the end, he contented himself with turning his back on me and walking to the far end of the bar, where he retrieved a book from under the counter and began to read, or to pretend to read. It was a Penguin paperback, one of the old black-jacketed classics, although I couldn't see the name. I'd like to have said that I wasn't surprised, but I was. Earle didn't seem like the kind of guy who was big on self-improvement.

Jimmy followed the direction of my gaze.

"I'm getting old," he continued. "We all are. There was a time when Earle wouldn't have picked up a book, not unless it was a phone book and he was trying not to leave bruises on someone, but the years mellow us some, I suppose, in good ways and bad. There was also a time when Earle wouldn't have been taken so easily by someone like Joel Tobias either, but the guy managed him without blinking. He wanted to, he could have hurt Earle bad. I could see it in him."

"But he didn't."

"No. He really did just want us to leave him alone, but his needs are irrelevant, you might say. I want to know what he's doing. It's important to my business, but it's also crucial that the existing balance is maintained. The Mexicans, the Colombians, the Dominicans, the Russians, the cops, me, and just about anyone else with an interest in the movement of goods across the border, we all exist in a state of equilibrium. It's very fragile, and if someone who doesn't understand the rules starts screwing around with it, then it will all collapse and cause wicked amounts of trouble for everybody. I couldn't figure out Tobias's angle, and being out of the loop makes me nervous. So . . ."

"So?"

"So, I could have given customs a heads-up, but never ask a question to which you don't already know the answer when it comes to the law. If it suits me to feed Tobias to them, then I'll do it, but only when I know what he's carrying across the border. I've called in favors. Every time Joel Tobias gets a job, a copy of the paperwork comes to me. Lately, he's been working interstate in New England, and it all seems legit. This week, he has a job transporting feed from Canada, and that means a border crossing."

"And you have men on him."

Jimmy smiled. "Let's just say that I convinced some friends of mine to take a closer look at Joel Tobias."

And that was all I could get from Jimmy Jewel, barring the name of the company in Quebec that was supplying the feed, and the one in Maine that had ordered it, but I believed that it represented a great deal of what he knew about Joel Tobias. He was as much in the dark as I was.

I walked back to my car. The smell of fetid water was in my nostrils again, and on my clothes. I realized that it was coming from the Mustang, which had absorbed some of the stink of the Blue Moon. Then again, I might simply have been imagining it, one more facet of my response to what had taken place.

I drove out to the Blue Moon. I was always going to, eventually. There was an oil drum in the center of the floor, beneath what was left of the charred roof. Insects buzzed above the dark water inside it. I felt the urge to recoil at the sight of it, and I started to breathe faster as my system responded to the memories associated with the smell of this place. Instead, I took my little flashlight from my pocket and searched the ruin, but the men who had brought me there had left no trace of their presence.

Outside, I called Bennett Patchett, and asked him to put together a list of the names of those who had served alongside his son in Iraq and who were now back here, especially those who might have attended his funeral. He told me that he'd do it straightaway.

"So I guess you got your anger back?" he said.

"It seems I had untapped reserves," I replied, and hung up.

Psychological or not, the Mustang still smelled. I took it to a place in South Portland, Phil's One-Stop, that usually did a good job, hand washing it instead of using a hose, as a hose found every leak in the seals and made the upholstery so damp that the windows fogged up. They cleaned the Mustang inside and out while I drank a soda, even working at the dirt behind the fenders.

Which was how they found the device.

IN THE BEST POSSIBLE way, Phil Ducasse looked like the kind of guy who ran a one-stop valet and auto repair shop. I don't think he owned any clothing that didn't have an oil stain on it somewhere, he showed a five o'clock shadow by midday, and his hands appeared dirty even when they were clean. He was carrying a few pounds of burger weight, and his eyes held the weary impatience of one who would always know more about an engine's problems than the next guy, and who could fix everything quicker than anyone else if only he had enough time to fix everything, which he hadn't. Now he used a handheld lamp to point out an object around twelve inches long that was bound with black duct tape and attached to the inside of the fender with a pair of magnets.

"Ernesto thought it might be a bomb," said Phil, referring to the little Mexican who had been working on the car when the device was found. Ernesto was now standing some distance from the auto shop, along with most of the other employees, although nobody had yet called the cops.

"What do you think?"

Phil shrugged. "Could be."

"So how come we're standing here with our noses pressed against it?"

"Because it probably isn't."

"That 'probably' is reassuring."

"Why, you think it's a bomb?"

I looked more closely at the device. "From its shape, it seems to be mainly electronic components. I don't see anything that looks like explosives."

"You want to know what I think?" said Phil. "I think you've been tagged. It's a bug."

It made sense. It could have been placed on my car while I was being questioned at the Blue Moon.

"It's big," I said. "You couldn't call it inconspicuous."

"Inconspicuous enough not to be found unless someone went looking for it. You want to be certain, I can make a call."

"Who to?"

"Kid I know. He's a genius."

"Is he discreet?"

"You got a wallet?"

"Yes."

"Then he's discreet."

Twenty minutes later, a young man with bright yellow dreadlocks and a scrawny beard, and wearing a Rustic Overtones T-shirt, arrived on a red Yamaha Street Tracker bike.

"Seventy-seven," said Phil. He was beaming like a proud parent at graduation. "XS650, full restoration. I did most of that. The kid helped some, but I bled for that bike."

The kid's name was Mike. He was scrupulously polite, and insisted on calling me "sir," which made me feel I was representing the AARP.

"Wow, neat," he said, when he took his first look at the piece of equipment on my car. He carefully removed it and placed it on a workbench nearby. Using only his fingertips, he traced the outline of each piece of equipment under the tape. He then used a blade to make small incisions in the tape so he could examine what lay beneath. When he was done, he nodded approvingly.

"Well?" I said.

"It's a tracking device. Pretty sophisticated, although it may not look that way, what with all the tape wrapped around it. Some of this equipment, well, I'd guess that it's military grade. Could be that the government doesn't like you."

He looked at me hopefully, but I didn't bite.

"Anyway, whoever put it there probably didn't have a whole lot of time to work. If he had, he'd have used something smaller that could be hidden more easily, and run it off the car battery so it wouldn't need its own power supply. To do that, though, you'd need fifteen, twenty minutes to work undisturbed."

He used a screwdriver to point out a bulge at the center of the device. "That's a GPS receiver, just like the ones used in a regular sat-nav. It pinpoints the car's location so it can be checked on a PC. There are eight twelve-volt screw terminal batteries at the end providing the power. They'd have to be changed regularly, so if it was part of some long-term surveillance, it would make sense to come back and fit the smaller version to the car battery when the opportunity presented itself, but this baby would still do fine to be getting along with. The magnets wouldn't affect the reported position, and it would be easy to remove once it had done its job."

"Will whoever put it there know that it's been detached?"

"I don't think so. I deliberately didn't move it far from the car, and I don't believe the tracking is that sensitive."

I leaned back against the bench and swore. I should have been more careful. I had kept an eye on my mirrors when I was on my way to visit both Karen Emory and Jimmy Jewel, and had taken a circuitous route with dead ends and U-turns just in case, but had picked up no signs of anyone following me. Now I understood why. In addition, the men who had interrogated me at the Blue Moon now knew that I had been to see both Karen and Jimmy, which meant they were aware that their warnings to back off had fallen on deaf ears.

"You want me to put it back where you found it?" asked Mike.

"You serious?" said Phil. "Maybe he should just strap it to his chest so they can track him around the house as well."

"Uh, I don't think you want to do that, sir," said Mike. Sarcasm didn't seem to have much effect on him, which made me like him more.

I looked out at the lot. A big rig pulled in and flashed its lights for assistance. I thought of Joel Tobias. I wondered where he was now, and what he might be bringing over the border. The rig had Jersey plates. Jersey. Phil followed my gaze.

"Hey, I don't know the driver," he said. "Makes no difference to me."

Instead of sending the tracking device to Jersey, I told Mike to put the unit back where he'd found it after all. He seemed pleased that

I'd managed to catch up with his own thought processes at last: my knowledge of the unit's presence was a weapon that could be used against whoever put it there, if the right opportunity presented itself.

I paid Mike generously for his time, and he gave me his cell phone number in case I ever needed his help again.

"Good kid," I said, as Phil and I watched him go. "Smart too."

"My sister's boy," said Phil.

"He didn't call you 'Uncle Phil.'"

"I told you he was discreet."

I also tipped Ernesto. He thanked me, but clearly felt that the shock he'd received merited a bigger tip. Since he hadn't actually been blown up, I ignored his pained expression.

"You got any idea who put that thing on your car?" said Phil.

"I do."

"You figure they'll come at you?"

"Possibly."

"You got help?"

"It's on its way."

"It was me, and someone was putting military-grade surveillance packages on my car, I'd want the kind of help with a gun. Is it that kind of help?"

"No," I said. "It's the kind of help with *lots* of guns."

CHAPTER

They hijacked Tobias when he was only a few miles south of
Moosehorn on Route 27. A car had been behind him since he'd
crossed the border, but he'd paid it little heed. He'd made this
run so many times that he'd grown casual: his main concern was
the U.S. Customs post at Coburn Gore, and once he passed through
safely he tended to switch off. On this occasion, he was also frustrated: he was bringing back only a fraction of what he had anticipated, and he was tired of taking on the burden of these trips alone.
As the fatalities had mounted, their group had contracted to its core.
It meant more work, and more risk, for everybody, but the rewards
would be commensurately greater in the end.

There had been a problem at the warehouse that day. Canadian
cops had been crawling all over the neighboring complex as part of
a drug operation that was likely to be ongoing, and it seemed unwise
to begin moving items within a stone's throw of the law. Faced with
the choice of hanging around, or trying another run when everything
was quieter, Tobias had taken the second option. Later, though, he'd
berate himself for not being more wary on the journey home, but
he'd been assured that Parker had been taken care of, and the tracking device had confirmed that the detective had still been in Portland
when Tobias was an hour into his trip.

The detective concerned Tobias, but not as much as Jimmy Jewel did. He'd told the others about Jewel immediately after that first clumsy approach in Dewey's, and how it looked like he was getting curious about the economics of Tobias's operation, but they'd advised him to see how it played out. The best that he could do was to convince them to let the operation rest for a time, but as the days passed without incident they grew impatient, and soon he was back on the cross-border run, although for a while they kept tabs on Jimmy and the big elephant who watched his back, but it seemed like Jimmy had decided that Joel Tobias wasn't worth worrying about. Joel wasn't so sure, but the others had done their best to convince him otherwise. So with Jimmy apparently minding his own business, and no sign of anyone snooping around, Joel had begun to relax a little.

He was also tired: he was taking on more and more runs as the demand for what they were selling increased. They'd told him that this would happen just as soon as word got around about the quality, and rarity, of what was on offer. Until recently, they hadn't moved anything that wasn't already sold, but now Joel was transporting items in anticipation of the final big sale: the "fire sale," as they had begun to refer to it. They had always known that those initial "trickle" sales might raise warning flags somewhere, but they were necessary to bring in some funds and confirm the value, and extent, of what would ultimately become available. Now the big rewards were in sight, but Joel was the point man, and when Jewel and then the detective had come sniffing, he had been seriously unnerved. His advance payments had already increased substantially, but not as much as Joel would have liked, seeing as how he was taking all the risks. Words had been exchanged. On top of their initial casual approach to the Jewel business, it had made Joel resentful. He knew that a confrontation was coming. Maybe he should have kept his mouth shut, but deep down he felt that he was right, which was why he'd spoken up to begin with. It took a lot to make Joel mad. He was a simmerer, but when he did go off, then heaven help anyone who got caught by the blast.

He'd also been having more and more bad dreams, and the disruption of his sleep patterns had made him testier with Karen, and he hated that. She was a special girl, and he was lucky to be with her, but sometimes she just didn't know when to stop asking questions and stay quiet. Ever since Damien Patchett and the rest of them had died, she'd been different, perhaps fearful that the same fate might befall him, but Joel had no intention of taking his own life. Still, Damien's death had hit him harder than the earlier ones: three of them were dead now, three of his old squad, all by their own hands, but Damien had been the best of them. He always had been.

Damien and the others had started appearing to him in his dreams, bloody and ruined. They spoke to him, but not in English. He couldn't understand what they were saying. It was as if they had learned a new language on the other side of the grave. But even as he dreamed, he wondered if they were really his old brothers in arms that he was seeing. They scared him, and their eyes were wrong: they were black and filled with fluid, like oily water. Their bodies were warped, their backs hunched, their arms too long, the fingers thin and grasping . . .

Jesus, no wonder he was tense.

At least the border runs were coming to an end. He'd carefully cultivated the customs officials, and the goons from Homeland Security. His license plate holder identified him as a veteran, as did the stickers and decals in the cab. He wore an army baseball cap, and was careful to listen to the stories from the older veterans who now manned the border. He would slip them a pack of cigarettes occasionally, even playing on his injuries when necessary, and in return they smoothed the way for him. The others had no idea how hard he had worked on his image, and how much the success of their endeavor was dependent upon him.

With all this on his mind, he hadn't been paying as much attention as he should have to the car behind him. When it passed, he
was glad to see it go, but that was the rig driver's natural response to
any vehicle that got too close. Eventually, you knew that they were
going to try to pass, and you just had to hope that they did it sensibly.
Oh, there were truckers who liked playing around with impatient
motorists, and others who just took the view that they were the big-
gest, baddest sons of bitches on the road, and if you wanted to screw
around with them, then it was your funeral, sometimes literally. Joel
had never been that way, even before he'd started the border runs,
where drawing the attention of the law to himself by driving care-
lessly could see him end up in jail for a long time. Even though there
wasn't much room, and the trees were practically scratching at his
cab, he had pulled over slightly to let the car pass. It wasn't a smart
place to overtake as they were approaching a bend in the road, and if
someone else came at speed from the opposite direction then everyone involved would need as much blacktop as possible if they weren't
all to end up as roadkill. But the way ahead was clear, and he watched
the red lights disappear, leaving the road empty and dark.

Half a mile later, he saw the flashing lights, and someone waving
a pair of neon glowsticks. He hit the brakes as the beams of his truck
caught the yellow Plymouth that had overtaken him earlier. It was
sideways, bisected by the white line. Beside it was another car, the
one with the flashing red-and-blue lights. He couldn't make out any
markings on it, though, which was odd.

A figure in uniform approached him, its head slightly misshapen.
He rolled down the window.

"What seems to be the problem?" he asked, as a flashlight shone
in his face, forcing him to raise his hand to shield his eyes. In that
moment, the figure produced a gun, and two other men emerged
from the tree line, armed with semiautomatic weapons. Their faces
were hidden behind ghoulish masks, and now the man in uniform

was pulling a mask down on his face too, but not before Joel got a look at him and thought: Mexican. This was confirmed when the man spoke.

"Keep your hands where we can see them, *buey*," he said. "We don't want nobody to get hurt. We cool?"

Joel nodded. The fact that they were masked offered him some reassurance that he wasn't about to be killed. Killers on a lonely road don't need to worry about being identified by their victim.

"My friends here are going to get in that cab with you and tell you where to go. Just do as they say, and this will all be over and you can go home to your *novia, sí*?" Joel nodded again. So they knew that he had a girlfriend, which meant that they, or someone close to them, had been keeping tabs on him in Portland. He filed that particular piece of information away.

The cab doors weren't locked. Tobias kept his hands on the steering wheel as the two men climbed in. One slipped into the space behind the seat while the other stayed beside Joel, his body twisted slightly so that he was leaning against the door, the gun resting casually across his thigh. Casual seemed to be the order of the evening, thought Joel, although this changed when the radio of the uniformed man outside crackled into life.

"*Andale!*" he said, waving a hand first at the other vehicles, then at Joel. He pointed his gun at Joel through the windshield to make sure he got the message. "*Apurate!*" The Plymouth reversed a few feet before heading south. The second car killed its flashing lights as the uniformed man ran back to join it. It pulled over to one side to allow Joel to pass, then fell into place behind him, so that he was hemmed in by both cars.

"Where am I going?" he asked.

"Just watch the road, *buey*," came the reply.

Joel did as he was told, and remained silent. He could have asked them if they knew who they were screwing with, or made some threat of retribution if they didn't get their asses out of his cab right now and let him go about his business, but he didn't. All he wanted was to survive this in one piece, with his body and, with luck, his rig intact. Once he was safely back in Portland, he would start making calls, but he was already working on possibilities. If this was a standard hijacking, these guys had either picked the wrong truck or they'd been misinformed, which meant that they were going to score nothing more lucrative than a couple of grand's worth of dry animal feed. The other option was that this wasn't a standard hijacking, in which case they were very well informed indeed, and that could only mean trouble, and possibly pain, for Joel.

Ahead of him, the Plymouth began to signal right.

"Follow him," said the man behind him, and Joel began to slow down in order to make the turn. The road was narrow, and sloped slightly downhill.

"You want me to fit it through the eye of a needle while I'm at it?" he asked.

The machine pistol brushed the skin of his cheek lightly, its barrel icy cold.

"I can drive a truck," said a voice. It was so close to his ear he could feel the warmth of the man's breath on his skin. "You don't want to do it, then I will, but then we got no use for you, *mi hijo.*"

Joel figured the guy was bluffing, but he wasn't about to test his theory. He made the turn perfectly, and began following the lights of the Plymouth once again.

"Hey, you see what you can do with a little encouragement?" said the gunman.

The Plymouth flashed its warning lights as they pulled into a clearing before a ruined house, its stone chimney still standing intact beside its collapsed roof. There were two more men waiting beside a black SUV. Like the others, they wore masks, but instead of leather jackets they were dressed in suits. Cheap suits, but suits nonetheless. Joel hit the brakes.

"Get out," said the gunman.

Joel did as he was told. The brown car had joined them, and now he and his rig were lit by the headlights of three vehicles. One of the men in suits stepped forward. He was about a foot shorter than Joel, and stocky, but not fat. He stretched out a hand and, after a moment's hesitation, Joel shook it. The smaller man spoke English with hardly any hint of an accent.

"You can call me Raul," he said. "Let's make this as quick and easy as possible. What have you got in the truck?"

"Animal feed."

"Open it. Let me see."

With two guns trained on him, Joel unlocked the big double doors. Flashlights shone on the bags of feed, stacked on six wooden pallets. Raul pointed two fingers into the trailer, and two men climbed in with knives and began methodically tearing bags apart, scattering their contents inside the truck.

"I hope they're going to clean up after themselves," said Joel.

"Don't worry about it," said Raul. "I guarantee you that, if they don't find what they're looking for, you'll have more significant concerns."

"And what are they looking for: more protein in their diet? It's animal feed. You got the wrong rig, buddy."

Raul said nothing. He lit a cigarette and offered one to Joel, who declined. Together, the two men watched as the bags were cut and emptied, until the searchers were standing shin deep in the mess.

"It's a nice rig," said Raul. "It would be a shame to damage it."

"Look, I told you: you got the wrong shipment."

Raul shrugged. Joel heard movement from behind him. His arms were grasped tightly, and he was forced down on his knees. Raul lit a fresh cigarette and squatted so that he and Joel were face-to-face. He grabbed a handful of Joel's hair and placed the tip of the cigarette firmly against Joel's right cheek, just below the bone. There was no threat, no warning, just intense pain, the smell of burning flesh, and a low sizzling sound that was swamped by Joel's scream. After a couple of seconds, Raul withdrew the cigarette. The tip was still glowing faintly. Raul blew on it until it was entirely red once again.

"Listen to me," said Raul. "We could take your rig apart, piece by piece, and then set it alight before your eyes. We could even kill you, and bury you in the woods. We might not even go to the trouble of killing you before we bury you. All these options are open to us, but we don't want to do any of those things, because I don't yet have a problem with you personally. So here it is: I know you're smuggling. I want to know what you're smuggling, so you're going to show me the traps, and I am going to keep burning you until you do. Now, tell me."

After the third time, Joel did.

THEY LEFT HIM IN the clearing. Before he departed, Raul gave Joel a salve for his wounds. The burn on his face was bad; the two to his hands were worse. Raul had placed the cigarette to the skin between the thumb and forefinger on each hand. When that hadn't worked, he had threatened to put it out in Joel's right eye, and Joel had believed him. He told them where the trap was, but even after following his instructions they couldn't find it. It was a professional job, designed to pass undetected during anything but the most painstaking of searches. He was forced to show it to them, first explaining how the seat came apart so that the space, which ran the width of the cab, could be accessed. He then opened it by the careful application of pressure to its two lower corners.

The compartment was capable of being divided into smaller sections, depending upon what was being transported. On this occasion, there was a plastic tool box containing a dozen small cylindrical objects, similar in length to pieces of chalk, and wrapped in layers of cloth and plastic to protect them. The men in the cab handed one of them down to Raul, once it had been stripped of its protection. It was ornately carved, capped with gold at each end and inset with precious stones. Raul held it in the palm of his hand, testing its weight, then asked: "What is this?"

"I don't know," said Joel. "I'm just the transporter. I don't ask questions."

"It looks old, and valuable." Raul held out a hand, and a flashlight was placed in it. He used it to examine the stones more closely. "These are emeralds and rubies, and that's a diamond on the tip."

The seal in Raul's hand dated from 2100 B.C. It was an ancient bureaucratic device, used to verify business and legal transactions by impressing the seal into documents inscribed on clay tablets. By this point, Joel had seen enough of them to know, but he remained silent.

Carefully, Raul rewrapped the seal, and handed it to one of his men.

"Take them all," he said. "And handle them gently."

He lit another cigarette and smiled as he saw Joel wince involuntarily.

"So, you say that you just drive, and you know nothing about the items that you are paid to transport," said Raul. "I don't believe you, but that's of no consequence now. I'm going to ask around about those little cylinders, and if they're as valuable as they look I may hold on to some of them. You can tell your employers, if that's what they are, that they may consider it a penalty for attempting to run an operation like this without informing the proper authorities, and by that I don't mean U.S. Customs. If they want to continue transporting such items, then they should come talk to me, and we'll work something out."

"Why should they talk to you?" asked Joel. "Why not the Dominicans, or Jimmy Jewel?" He saw something flash in Raul's eyes, and knew that he'd hit a nerve.

"Because," said Raul, "we have the cylinders."

Then he walked away, leaving Joel to nurse his wounds, but not before stamping Joel's cell phone into pieces, and draining most of the fuel from his tanks, leaving him with just enough to get to a motel outside of Eustis. The burn to his face attracted a few glances when he entered the lobby, but nobody commented on it. He found the ice machine, then wrapped some of the ice in a towel from his room and used it to ease the pain in his hands and face before making the call from his room.

"There's been a problem," he said, when the phone was picked up. He gave a detailed account of all that had occurred, leaving out almost nothing

"We'll have to get them back," came the reply. "You say that this guy Raul wants to keep the seals as some kind of fine?"

"That's what he said."

"Jesus. You think he's going to use them to mark bags of coke?"

"I think he's going to try to sell them."

"We've succeeded so far because we've been careful. Those seals can't turn up on the open market."

Joel did his best to hide his irritation. Why, just because he drove a truck, was it assumed that he was some kind of moron? After all, he'd been there at every stage of the operation, right from the start. Without him, it would have fallen apart long before now.

"I'm aware of that," he said, and was unable to keep the edge from his voice.

"Don't get smart with me. I didn't lose the consignment."

"Yeah, well, I haven't seen enough cash to compensate me for the removal of an eye."

"You've seen more up front than anyone else. You don't like the arrangement, then walk away."

Joel stared at the wounds on his hands.

"That's not what I meant. Let's just get this mess fixed up."

"It won't take this Raul long to find out what he's got. After that, a child will be able to piece together what's happening. I'll start asking around, find out who he is."

"Jimmy Jewel knows."

"You sure?"

"Pretty sure. You ask me, I think the instruction to hit us came from him."

"Well, that's where we'll start, then. You say they took everything?"

"Yeah. They got it all."

"Go home. Get some sleep, and see to those burns. Call me tomorrow as soon as you've rested. This isn't the only mess that needs to be cleaned up."

Joel didn't ask for clarification on the final comment. He was too tired, and too sore. He hung up the phone and walked to the gas station across the road, where he bought a six-pack of beer to drink in his room, occasionally holding one of the cold bottles to his damaged cheek as he stared out of the window at the lights of passing cars, and the darkness of Flagstaff Lake. After two beers, he felt nauseated. It had been so long since he'd experienced shock that he'd almost forgotten the sensation, but what had been done to him in the clearing brought back other memories, other moments. He scratched absentmindedly at his left shin, feeling the scar tissue and the hollow in the muscle. He called Karen but she wasn't home, so he left a message on the machine telling her that he was tired and had decided to get a room for the night. He also told her that he loved her, and apologized for their fight that morning. The fight was all the detective's fault; his, and that meddling old bastard Patchett. Tobias knew enough about the detective from local gossip not to underestimate him, and he wasn't sure that threatening him was the way to deal with him, but he'd been angry as well as relieved when they'd come to him and told him that the detective had been hired to investigate him and his relationship, and not the larger operation.

He wanted to sleep. He popped some painkillers and sat on his bed, his legs stretched before him. He searched in his jacket pocket, and withdrew the two exquisitely carved gold loops. He had said that the Mexicans had taken everything, but he'd lied. He figured he was owed something for his pain, and for the fact that what he had already shipped was worth a fortune, a fortune of which he had yet to see more than a few bucks in real terms. He also wanted to make up to Karen for their fight.

He held the earrings up to the light, and even though in pain, he marveled at their beauty.

II

. . . I dream of horsemen in smoking hills, shadows on horseback, reed breastplates, quirts, half-breed moon. Some other war. Some other ancient war but this same place . . .

Richard Currey, *Crossing Over: The Vietnam Stories*

War smells. It smells of open sewers and excrement. It smells of garbage and rotting food and standing water. It smells of dog carcasses and human corpses. It smells of the homeless, and the dying, and the dead.

They were flown from McChord AFB to Rhein-Main AFB, then on to Kuwait. They traveled in full kit with their weapons, the bolts removed and kept in their pockets. In Kuwait, they filled sandbags to line the bottoms of their vehicles and absorb shrapnel. It was only a couple of days later that they were told they were heading into the box. The officers cheered: they wanted to earn their combat patches. The chill was intense as they moved north through the desert night. He had never been in the desert before, not unless you counted the Desert of Maine, and that was just a field with some sand in it. He hadn't expected the desert to be so cold, but then he knew about as much about deserts as he knew about Iraq. Before he was sent there, he couldn't even have found it on a map. He'd never had any intention of visiting, so why bother trying to look for it? But now he knew . . .

What did these people do? How did they live? There was nothing growing that he could see. The kids were barefoot, and lived in houses made of mud and brick. They were told not to trust anybody, but he still handed out candy and water to kids when he could. Most of the guys did, at the start, until the insurgency kicked in, and the rivers began filling up with bodies, and the haji started using children as lookouts, or human shields, or soldiers. After that, they stopped treating kids as kids. By then, he was scared most of the time, but he'd entered a place where the concept of fear had ceased to have any concrete meaning because fear was always present, either as a whisper or a scream.

Then there was the dust: it got everywhere. He tried to keep his M4 clean and well lubricated, but it didn't always help, and the gun sometimes jammed. There were those who said that the standard army cleaner wasn't worth a shit, and guys asked for commercial lubricants as part of their care packages from home. Later, he read that there was something about the Iraqi dust that was different from the dust used in the weapons tests stateside. It was smaller, and contained more salts and carbonates, which tended to corrode. It also reacted with some of the gun lubricants, creating bigger particles that blocked the chambers. It was as though the land itself was conspiring against the invaders.

This place was old. They didn't understand that. He didn't understand it either, not then. It was only after, when he began tracing its history, that he realized this was the cradle of civilization: the ancestors of these people peering at him fearfully from out of mud houses had created writing, philosophy, religion. This army of tanks and rockets and airplanes was following in the path of the Assyrians, the Babylonians, and the Mongols; of Alexander, and Julius Caesar, and Napoleon. This was once the greatest empire in the world. He struggled to grasp just how old it was, even as he read of Gilgamesh, and Mesopotamia, and the kings of Agade, and the Sumerians.

Then he came across the names, of Enlil and his wife, Ninlil, and the story of how Enlil took three forms and impregnated his wife three times, and from those three unions sprang Nergal, and Ninazu, and one other, one whose name was lost, rendered illegible by the damage to the old stones on which the story had been written. Three unions, three entities: things of the netherworld.

Demons.

And that was when he began to understand.

XI

Jackie Garner was all apologies when he called the next morning. He'd managed to stay with Joel Tobias as far as Blainville, Quebec, and had watched the loading of the animal feed. He hadn't noticed anything untoward, and then had stuck with Tobias until the border, where something about the way Jackie looked or, possibly, smelled had aroused suspicion. A chemical test had been run on his bag, and traces of explosives had been found. Given that this was Jackie Garner, the munitions king, it would have been a miracle if traces of explosives hadn't been found, but it meant that Jackie's car was searched, and he'd been forced to answer a lot of awkward questions about his hobbies before he was allowed to leave, by which time Joel Tobias had vanished.

"Don't worry about it, Jackie," I told him. "We'll find another way."

"You want me to go back to his house and wait for him?"

"Yeah, why not." It would make Jackie feel that he wasn't in trouble, if nothing else.

"Any word from New York?"

"They'll be here tonight."

"You won't tell them how I screwed up?"

"You didn't screw up, Jackie. You were just unlucky."

"I should be more careful," said Jackie, with regret. "But I do love explosives . . ."

Soon after, Bennett Patchett e-mailed me some names of veterans who had attended his son's funeral. The first two were Vernon and Pritchard. Both had a note beside them indicating that he wasn't sure of the spelling. He admitted that he couldn't remember the names of all those who had been there, because not everyone had signed the book of condolences, and not everyone had been introduced to him, but he thought that at least a dozen former soldiers had been present. He did recall a woman named Carrie Saunders, who had something to do with counseling veterans, but as far as he knew she'd had no formal contact with Damien before he died. There was also Bobby Jandreau, who was now in a wheelchair due to the injuries that he had suffered in Iraq. He was on my list of those to whom I wanted to talk, once the help from New York had arrived.

"Were any of those at the funeral black?"

"Vernon's a colored fella," he said. "Is that important?"

"Just curious."

I made a note to call Carrie Saunders, and to find out more about Bobby Jandreau, but first I took a trip out to Scarborough Downs, where Ronald Straydeer lived in a cabin within shouting distance of the racecourse. Ronald had served in the K9 corps during the Vietnam War, and was haunted as much by the loss of his dog, which he'd had to abandon as "surplus to requirements" during the fall of Saigon, as by the deaths of his comrades. Now his house was a kind of rest stop for veterans who happened to be passing through town and needed a place to sleep, somewhere they could have a beer and a toke without being bothered by foolish questions. I wasn't certain what Ronald did for a living, but it probably wasn't unconnected to the ready supply of weed that he always appeared to have close at hand.

Ronald had also recently begun to involve himself in the issue of rights for returning veterans. After all, he'd had firsthand experi-

ence of the problems that they faced upon his own return from
Vietnam and, especially after 9/11, he probably believed that he'd
seen the last of such ugliness. Instead, a whole new bag of ugly had
been opened on veterans, worse even than that faced by their Vietnam predecessors. Then it had been about returning soldiers being
blamed for an unpopular war, their critics inflamed by images of
kids dying on college campuses, or with burning napalm on their
skin as they ran across a Vietnamese bridge. Now that anger had
been replaced by ignorance of the consequences of combat, both
physical and psychological, for veterans, and the reluctance of those
who had been happy to send them to war to look after the injured
and battle scarred, whether those injuries were visible or not, once
they came home. I'd seen Ronald on local television a couple of
times, and he was often approached for comment by newspapers
in the state when the subject of disabled veterans was raised in
any form. He'd set up an informal organization called Concerned
Veterans of Maine, and for the first time since I'd known him he
seemed to have a real sense of purpose, a new battle to fight instead
of old ones to relive.

I saw a drape twitch when I arrived at his place. I knew that Ronald
had a sensor fitted at the end of the private drive that led up to his
house, and anything larger than a small mammal broke the beam.
He was smart enough not to keep too significant a stash at his home,
so that any raid would net possession, but not possession with intent
to supply. Then again, Ronald's activities were kind of an open secret
among certain branches of the local law enforcement community, but
they were content to let them slide because Ronald didn't sell to kids,
he didn't use violence, and he was helpful to the cops when the need
arose. It wasn't as if Ronald was operating a drugs empire anyway.
If he had been, he wouldn't have been living in a small cabin out by
Scarborough Downs.

He'd have been living in a big cabin out by Scarborough Downs.

Ronald came to the door as I stepped from the car. He was a large man, his black hair cut short and heavily streaked with silver. He wore tight-fitting jeans, and a checked shirt hung loosely over his belt. Around his neck hung a leather pouch.

"What is that?" I asked. "Big medicine?"

"Nope, I keep my small change in there."

His hand, tanned and corded with veins, gripped mine and swallowed it, like a gnarly old catfish consuming a minnow.

"You're the only Native American I know," I said, "and you don't do any of that proper Native American stuff."

"You disappointed?"

"Some. It just feels like you're not making the effort."

"I don't even want to be called a Native American. Indian does just fine."

"See? I bet I could have arrived here dressed as a cowboy and you wouldn't even have blinked an eye."

"Nope. I might've shot you, but I wouldn't have blinked an eye."

We sat at a table in his yard, and Ronald pulled a couple of sodas from a cooler. Music played softly from a boom box in the kitchen, a mix of Native American blues, folk, and Americana: Slidin' Clyde Roulette, Keith Secola, Butch Mudbone.

"Social call?" he asked.

"Sociable," I replied. "You remember a kid named Damien Patchett: local boy, served in Iraq with the infantry?"

Ronald nodded. "I went to his funeral."

I should have known. Whenever he could, Ronald attended the local funerals of veterans. His argument was that, in honoring one, he honored all. It was part of his ongoing personal duty to the fallen.

"Did you know him?"

"No, never met him."

"I hear that he may have taken his own life."

"Who told you that?"

"His father."

Ronald touched a small silver cross that hung from a leather strap around his wrist, a small gesture toward Bennett Patchett's grief. "It's happening again," he said. "You hope the brass and the politicians will learn, but they never do. War changes men and women, and some of them change so much that they don't know themselves anymore, and they hate what they've become. You ask me, we're just getting better at collating suicide figures, that's all. More Vietnam veterans have died by their own hands since the war than were killed in country, and more Iraq veterans will die by their own hands this year than will be killed in Iraq, judging by the way the figures are heading. The same dictum applies to both wars: poor treatment over there, poor treatment back home."

"What was the talk about Damien?"

"That he'd become isolated, that he was having trouble sleeping. A lot of guys have trouble sleeping when they get back. They have trouble doing a lot of stuff, but when you can't sleep, you know, your head gets messed up, and you start getting moody and depressed. Maybe you drink more than you should, or you take something to bring you down and then you start needing a little more of it every time. He'd been on Trazodone, but then he stopped."

"Why?"

"You'd have to ask someone who knew him better than I did. Some guys don't like taking sleep meds: they find they get a drug hangover from it when they wake up, and it screws up their REM sleep, but all I got was secondhand news about Damien. Did his father hire you to look into his death?"

"In a way."

"I didn't think that there was any doubt about how he died."

"There isn't, at least not about his final moments. It's what led him to do it that his father is curious to understand."

"So you're looking into post-traumatic stress disorder now?"

"In a way."

"I see that you're still having trouble answering straight questions."

"I like to think of it as circling."

"Yeah, like before a raid. Maybe you should have worn that cowboy hat after all."

He sipped his soda and looked away. It wasn't quite a huff, just the dignified Native American equivalent of one.

"Okay," I said. "I surrender. I'll give you a name: Joel Tobias."

Ronald had a good poker face. There was only the slightest flicker of his eyelids at the mention of Tobias's name, but it was enough to indicate that Ronald didn't care much for him.

"He was at the funeral too," he said. "A bunch of guys who served with Damien came to pay their respects, some from away. There was trouble at the cemetery, although they managed to keep the Patchetts from seeing any of it."

"Trouble?"

"A photographer was hanging around from a small newspaper, the *Sentinel-Eagle*. He was taking some shots, part of a photo essay he was putting together and hoping to sell to *The New York Times*: you know, the funeral of a fallen warrior, the grief, the release. Someone in the family—must have been Bennett—had told him that it would be okay. Well, it wasn't, not with everyone. A couple of Damien's old buddies had a word with him, and he went away. One of them was Tobias. He was introduced to me later, at a bar. By that time, we were down to the stragglers."

"Has Tobias come up on your radar?"

"Why would he?"

"There might be people who suspect he's smuggling."

"If he is, it's not pot. I'd know. You talk to Jimmy Jewel?"

"He doesn't know either."

"If Jimmy doesn't know, then I got no chance. You spend a dollar, that man hears the change hit the counter."

"But you're aware of Tobias?"

Ronald shifted in his seat. "Whispers, that's all."

"What kind?"

"That Tobias is working an angle. He's that kind of guy."

"Was he one of those who didn't want his picture taken?"

"There were four or five of them that spoke to the photographer, as far as I can remember. Tobias was among them. One of the others made the papers himself, a week or so later."

"How come?"

"His name was Brett Harlan, from Caratunk."

That name meant something. Harlan. Brett Harlan.

"Murder-suicide," I said. "Killed his wife, then himself."

"With an M9 bayonet. Those were hard deaths. Specialist Brett Harlan, Stryker C, Second Saber Brigade, Third Infantry. His wife was on leave from the One Hundred and Seventy-Second Military Intelligence Batallion."

"Damien Patchett served with the Second Saber Brigade."

"And so did Bernie Kramer."

"Who's Bernie Kramer?"

"Corporal Bernie Kramer. Hanged himself in a hotel room in Quebec three months ago."

I thought of what Karen Emory had said to me: *"They're all dying."*

"It's a cluster," I said. "A cluster of suicides."

"So it seems."

"Any reason why that might be?"

"I can give you general, but not specific. There's a woman out of Togus, ex-military. Her name is Carrie Saunders, and I think she'd met both Harlan and Kramer. You should talk to her. She's conducting research, and she came to me looking for some information: names of people who might be willing to be interviewed, both from my era and later. I gave her what I could."

"Bennett said that Carrie Saunders attended Damien's funeral."

"She might have been at the church. I didn't see her myself."

"What is she researching?"

Ronald finished his soda, crushed the can, and tossed it into a re-cycling bin.

"Post-traumatic stress disorder," he said. "Her specialty is suicides."

THE SUN ROSE HIGHER. It had turned into a beautiful summer's day, with clear blue skies and just the faintest of breezes, but Ronald and I were no longer outside. He had taken me into his small office, from which he was running Concerned Veterans of Maine. The walls were covered with clippings from newspapers, and tables of fatalities, and photographs. One, directly above Ronald's computer, depicted a woman helping her injured son from his bed. The picture had been taken from behind, so that only the mother's face was visible. It took me a moment to spot what was wrong with the photograph: almost half of the young man's head was missing, and what was left was a network of scars and crevasses, like the surface of the moon. His mother's face displayed a mixture of emotions too complex to interpret.

"Grenade," said Ronald. "He lost forty percent of his brain. He'll need constant care for the rest of his life. His mother, she doesn't look young, does she?" He said it as if noticing her for the first time, even though he must have stared at her every single day.

"No, she doesn't."

And I wondered what would be better: for him to die before his mother, so that his pain could come to an end, and hers could take another, perhaps less wrenching, form; or for him to outlive her, so that she could have her time with him, and be a mother to him as she was when he was an infant, when the possibility of a life like this could only have come to her in a nightmare. The former would be best, I thought, for if he lived too long then she would be gone, and eventually he would become a shadow in the corner of a room, a name without a past, forgotten by others and with no memories of his own.

Surrounded by all this, Ronald spoke to me of suicides and homelessness; of addiction and waking nightmares; of men left without limbs who were struggling to receive full disability from the military; of the backlog of claims, 400,000 and counting; and of those whose scars were not visible, who were damaged psychologically but not physically, and whose sacrifice was therefore not recognized as yet by their government, for they were denied a Purple Heart. And as he talked, his anger grew. He never raised his voice, never even clenched a fist, but I could feel it coming off him, like heat from a radiator.

"It's the hidden cost," he said at last. "Body armor protects the torso, and a helmet is better than no helmet. The medical responses are getting better, and faster. But one of those IEDs goes off beside you, or underneath your Hummer, and you can lose an arm or a leg, or take a piece of shrapnel in the back of your neck that leaves you paralyzed for life. Now you can survive with catastrophic injuries, but it might be that you'll wish you hadn't. You look at *The New York Times*, and you look at *USA Today*, and you see the death toll in Iraq and Afghanistan rising in that little box that they use for the bad news, but not as fast as it once did, not in Iraq anyway, and you think that maybe things are getting better. They are, if you're only counting the dead, but you need to multiply that figure by ten to count the injured, and even then there's no way to tell how many are seriously wounded. One in four of those who come home from Iraq and Afghanistan needs medical or mental health treatment. Sometimes, it's not available to them like it should be, and even if they're fortunate enough to get a little of what they need, the government tries to shortchange them at every turn. You got no idea how hard it is to get full disability, and then the same men who sent those soldiers over to fight tried to close Walter Reed to save a dollar. *Walter Reed.* They're fighting two wars, and they want to close the army's flagship medical center because they think it's costing too much money. This has got nothing to do with being for or against the wars. It's got nothing to do with liberalism, or conservatism, or any other label that you choose to throw at it. It's about doing what's right by those who fight, and they're not doing right by them. They never have. They never, ever have . . ."

His voice trailed off. When he spoke again, he sounded different.

"When the government won't do what it should, and the military can't take care of its own injured, then maybe it falls to others to try and do something about it. Joel Tobias is an angry man, and it could be that he's gathered others like him to his cause."

"His cause?"

"Whatever Tobias is doing, it grew out of good intentions. He knew men and women who were struggling. We all do. Promises were made. They would be helped."

"You're saying that the money from whatever they're moving across the border was meant for injured soldiers?"

"Some of it. Most of it. At first."

"What changed?"

"It's a lot of money. That's what I hear. The bigger the sum, the greater the greed."

Ronald stood. Our conversation was drawing to a close.

"You need to talk to someone else," he said.

"Give me a name."

"There was a fight at Sully's." Sully's was a notorious Portland dive bar. "It was after we buried the Patchett boy. A couple of us were in a corner, and Tobias and some others were at the bar. One of them was in a wheelchair, his trouser legs pinned up halfway to his groin. He'd had a lot to drink when he turned on Tobias. He accused him of reneging. He mentioned Damien, and the other guy, Kramer. There was a third name too, one that I didn't catch. It began with 'R': Rockham, something like that. Boy in the wheelchair said that Tobias was a liar, that he was stealing from the dead."

"What did Tobias do?"

Ronald's face creased with disgust.

"He pushed him toward the door. The guy in the wheelchair, there was nothing that he could do to stop it except put the brake on his chair. He almost fell to the floor, but Tobias held on to him. When he wouldn't lift the brake on his chair—and he struck out at them when they tried to force him—they just picked him up, chair and all, and put him out on the street. They stripped him of his dignity, just like that. They reminded him of how powerless he was. They didn't laugh after they did it, and one or two of them looked sickened, but it doesn't change what happened. That was a low thing that they did to that boy."

"Was his name Bobby Jandreau?"

"That's right. Seems that he served alongside Damien Patchett. He owed Damien his life, from what I hear. I went outside to make sure that he was okay, but he didn't want any help. He'd been humiliated enough. He *needs* help, though. I could see it in him. He was on the way down. So, now you know more than you did when you came here, right?"

"Yes. Thank you."

He nodded. "Part of me, it wanted them to succeed," he said. "Tobias, whoever else is helping him, I wanted them to make the score, whatever it is."

"And now?"

"It's gone bad. You should be careful, Charlie. They won't like you sticking your nose in their business."

"They already tried to warn me off by drowning me in an oil barrel."

"Yeah? So how's that working out for them?"

"Not so good. The one who did all the talking was soft-spoken, maybe with a hint of something southern in there. You get any ideas about who that might be, I'd like to hear them.'"

I TRIED TO REACH Carrie Saunders at the VA facility in Togus later that day, but the call went straight to her answering service. Then I called the *Sentinel-Eagle,* which was a weekly local paper in Orono, and from its news editor got a cell phone number for a photographer named George Eberly. He wasn't a staffer, but he did some freelance work for the paper. Eberly answered on the second ring, and when I told him what I wanted he seemed happy to talk.

"It was agreed with Bennett Patchett," he said. "He spoke to the rest of the family about what I wanted to do. It would be a memorial to his son, I told him, but also a way of connecting with other families who had lost sons and daughters, or fathers and mothers, to the war, and he understood that. I promised to be unobtrusive, and I was. I stayed in the background. Most people didn't even notice me, and then suddenly I was confronted by a bunch of goons."

"Did they tell you what their problem was?"

"They said it was a private ceremony. When I pointed out that I had the family's permission to take pictures, one of them tried to take my camera from me while the rest shielded him. I backed away, and a guy, a big guy with fingers missing, grabbed my arm and told me to delete any photographs that weren't of the family. He said that, if I didn't, he'd break the camera, and then, later, he and his buddies would find me and break something else of mine, something that didn't have a lens and couldn't be replaced."

"So you deleted the photos?"

"Like hell I did. I own a new Nikon. It's a complicated piece of machinery if you don't know what you're doing. I pressed a couple of buttons, locked the screen, and told him that I'd done what he asked. The big guy let me go, and that was it."

"Any chance that I could take a look at those photos?"

"Sure, I don't see why not." I gave him my email address, and he promised to send the photos as soon as he got back to his computer.

"You know," added Eberly, "there was a connection between Damien Patchett and a corporal named Bernie Kramer, who killed himself up in Canada."

"I know. They served together."

"Well, Kramer's family came from Orono. After he died we printed a piece that he'd written. His sister asked us to publish it. She still lives here in town. That's how I came to be interested in this whole photo project, to be honest. The article was a big deal around here, and it got the editor in trouble with the military."

"What did Kramer write about?"

"That PTSD thing. Post-traumatic stress. I'll forward the piece to you with the photos."

Eberly's material came in about two hours later, while I was cooking myself a steak for dinner. I took the pan from the heat and set it aside to cool.

Bernie Kramer's article was short, but intense. It spoke of his struggle with what he believed to be PTSD—his paranoia, his inability to trust, his moments of crippling fear and dread—and in particular his anger at the military's refusal to recognize PTSD as a combat injury instead of an ailment. Clearly, it had been written as an extended letter to the paper's editor, a letter never sent, but the editor had seen the potential in it and moved it to the op-ed page. Most affecting of all was a description of his time at the Warrior Transition Unit at Fort Bragg. Kramer implied that Fort Bragg was being used as a dumping ground for soldiers who were suffering from problems related to drug abuse, and that constant staff changes meant that awards, record recovery, and retirement ceremonies were being ignored. "By the time we came home," he concluded, "we were already being forgotten."

It wasn't hard to see how the army might have been unhappy with one of its ex-soldiers going on the record in this way, although worse had been written in soldiers' blogs and elsewhere. Nevertheless, a small local paper would have been easy meat for a military press officer with a point to prove to his superiors.

I printed out the article, and added it to those I had earlier collated regarding the deaths of Brett Harlan, and Margaret, his wife. I had also made notes for myself regarding PTSD and military suicides. Then I looked at the photos that Eberly had taken at Damien's funeral. Helpfully, he had circled the faces of the men who had confronted him, Joel Tobias's among them. I regarded the others carefully. Only one of them was black, so I figured that was Vernon. I checked the photographic printer to make sure that it had paper in it, then printed out duplicate copies of each of the best pictures. I wanted to know the names of the rest of these men. Ronald Straydeer might be able to help me. I had his email address, so I forwarded some of the images to him. Eberly had also given me the name and phone number for Bernie Kramer's sister, Lauren Fannan. I called her, and we spoke for a while. She told me that Bernie had come back "sick" from Iraq, and his condition had worsened in the months that followed. She was under the impression that pressure had been put on him not to talk about his problems, but she couldn't tell if that pressure had come from the military, or from his own buddies.

"Why would you say that?" I asked.

"There was a friend of his, Joel Tobias. He was Bernie's sergeant in Iraq. Tobias was the reason Bernie was up in Quebec to begin with. Bernie spoke fluent French, and he was doing some work for Tobias up there, something to do with shipping, and trucks. Bernie was taking medication to help him sleep, and Tobias told him to stop, because it was screwing with Bernie's ability to work."

If Joel Tobias had told Bernie Kramer to stop taking his medication because it was interfering with his assigned tasks, might he also have been responsible for Damien Patchett setting aside his Trazodone?

"Did Bernie seek professional help?"

"I got the impression that he was receiving some kind of help, because of the way he started talking about his condition, but he never said from whom. After Bernie died, I called Tobias and told him that he wouldn't be welcome at the funeral, so he stayed away. I haven't seen him since. I found the letter that Bernie had written about his post-traumatic stress among his private papers, and decided that it should be printed in the newspaper, because people should know how these men and women have been treated by their own government. Bernie was a lovely man, a gentle man. He didn't deserve to end his life that way."

"You mentioned Bernie's private papers, Mrs. Fannan. Do you still have them?"

"Some of them," she replied. "The rest I burned."

There was something here. "Why did you burn them?"

She had started to cry, and I had trouble understanding some of what she said next. "He'd written page after page of just . . . madness, about how he was hearing voices, and seeing things. I thought it was all part of his illness, but it was so disturbing, and so insane. I didn't want anyone else to read it, because if it got out I thought it would detract from the letter. He was talking about demons, and being haunted. None of it made any sense. None of it."

I thanked her, and let her go. A message had appeared in my mailbox. Ronald Straydeer had come through for me: he'd printed out one of the photographs, marked it, then scanned the image again and returned it. There was a short note above it.

After you left, I remembered something else about the funeral that struck me as odd. There was a veteran of the first Iraq war hanging around with Tobias and the others at Sully's. His name is Harold Proctor. As far as I can tell, he never gave a damn about anyone or anything, and there's no reason why he should be close to Tobias unless he's part of what's happening. He owns a rundown motel near Langdon, northwest of Rangeley. You don't need me to tell you how close that is to the Canadian border.

Proctor wasn't in any of the photographs. I knew that there was a system in place whereby veterans of former wars met returning soldiers, but I had no idea how to find out if Proctor had participated, or if he might have been among those who had met Damien Patchett when he got back home. But if Ronald was right in his assessment of Proctor, and I had no reason to doubt him, then the older man seemed an unlikely candidate for a meet and greet.

Ronald had given me two more names: Mallak and Bacci. Beside Mallak's name he'd written: "Unionville—but raised in Atlanta." He'd also formally identified the black man as Vernon, and a short, bearded man next to him as Pritchard. He'd put an X over the face of a tall man wearing glasses and had written "Harlan: deceased" next to it. Finally, barely visible in the distance to the left of the image, there was a muscular man in a wheelchair: Bobby Jandreau. Kyle Quinn's words returned to me, spoken as I looked at the photograph of Foster Jandreau in the newspaper.

A bad business.

I picked up my pen, and formally added Foster Jandreau's name to the list of the dead.

CHAPTER

XII

obias made the run to Harold Proctor's motel early the next
morning. He supposed that it was fate: he'd been on his way to
Proctor's place when the Mexicans had taken him, so it didn't
exactly throw him to be told to proceed there anyway, even without
a cargo to deposit. The reason for the trip was more unexpected,
although when he had time to think about it he believed that he had
foreseen just such an eventuality.

"Proctor's flaking on us," said the voice that morning on the other
end of the line. "He wants out. Take whatever is left there and pay
him off. It's mostly small stuff anyway."

"You certain he's not going to talk out of school?" said Tobias.

"He knows better than to do that."

Tobias wasn't so sure. He planned to have a few words with Proctor
when he saw him, just to make certain that he understood where his
obligations lay.

His face and hands were hurting. The ibuprofen that he'd taken
had dulled the pain somewhat, but not enough to help him sleep
properly. Lack of sleep was nothing new to him, though, not lately. In
Iraq, he'd slept through mortar fire, he'd been so tired all the time,
but ever since he'd returned home he'd been having trouble getting a
good night's rest, and when he did sleep he dreamed. They were bad

dreams, and recently they had begun to get worse. He thought that he could even trace the start of his problems to one of the runs that he'd made to Proctor's place a month or so ago. Ever since then, he hadn't been right.

Tobias wasn't much for hard liquor, but he could have used a serious drink right about now. Proctor would give him one, if he asked, but Tobias didn't intend to impose on Proctor's hospitality for that long. Anyway, the last thing Tobias wanted was to be stopped by the cops with booze on his breath while driving a rig: a rig, what's more, that would probably contain more potential wealth per square foot than any other that had ever previously been driven through the state.

As if to remind him of the wisdom of his decision to wait until he got back to Portland before slaking his thirst, a border patrol vehicle passed him on the road, heading east. Tobias raised a hand casually in greeting, and the gesture was returned. He watched the border cop in his mirrors until he was gone from sight, then breathed more easily. It would be just his luck to cross the cops after what had happened the night before. Proctor was simply the shitty icing on that particular turd cake.

Tobias didn't care much for the older man. Proctor was a lush, and he believed that the fact they had both served in the military meant that they were brothers deep inside, but Tobias didn't view the world in that way. They hadn't even served in the same war: their conflicts were separated by more than a decade. He and Proctor were on different paths. Proctor was drinking himself to death while Tobias was looking forward to making some money and improving his life. He thought that he might ask Karen to marry him, and once they were hitched they'd head south, get away from the damn Maine cold. The summers were better up here, not so humid as Florida or Louisiana, some August days excepted, but they weren't good enough to make up for the winters, not by a long shot.

He thought again about a drink. He'd settle for a couple of beers when he got back home. He hated himself when he got messy, and hated seeing others get messy too. He flashed to Bobby Jandreau in Sully's, Bobby shooting his mouth off and attracting attention, even in a place like Sully's where most people were too busy getting a drunk on to pay any mind to whatever might be going on around them. He pitied Bobby. Joel wasn't sure that he could have gone on living if he'd been wounded as badly as Bobby had. His own injuries were enough for him: he limped with every step, and he still experienced phantom pain where the tips of his missing fingers should have been. But Bobby's injuries didn't excuse him from getting loud and saying the things that he'd said. They'd promised him a cut, and Joel had been willing to keep to the deal, even after what was said at Sully's, but now Bobby didn't want it. He didn't want anything to do with them, and that worried Joel. It troubled the others too. They'd tried reasoning with Bobby, but it had done no good. Joel figured that his pride had been hurt by what they'd done with him at Sully's, but they'd had no choice.

Nobody gets hurt: that was the essence of the arrangement that they had. Do no harm. Unfortunately, that wasn't always possible in the real world, and the principle had been subtly altered to "Do no harm to our own." The detective, Parker, had asked for what had happened to him, and Foster Jandreau had too. Tobias might not have pulled the trigger on him, but he'd agreed on the necessity of it.

Tobias was already anticipating the sign for Proctor's Motel, giving him time to prepare for the turn. He was nervous. Again, there were few cops on this road—he could count on one hand the times that he'd encountered a uniform here, with fingers to spare, even allowing for the missing ones—but a rig turning into a disused motel was just the kind of action that attracted attention this close to the border. Tobias preferred those occasions when small items were being moved, and the exchange could be made at a gas station, or a diner. The movement of larger pieces, requiring him to come to the motel, always made him sweat, but there were only one or two more of those shipments to go, and he'd find some place near Portland to store them. After Kramer's death, a decision had been made that most of the larger items weren't worth the risk, presenting, as they did, all kinds of logistical difficulties. An alternative means of disposing of them would be found, even if it meant a smaller profit. After all, they'd gone to the trouble of transporting them as far as Canada, and damned if they were just going to dump them in a quarry somewhere, or bury them in a hole. Still, buyers had already been found for a number of statues, and it had fallen to Tobias to get them across the border. He'd driven the first shipment, certified as cheap stone garden ornaments for those with more money than taste, straight to a warehouse in Pennsylvania without a hitch. The second shipment had to be stored for a couple of weeks with Proctor, and moving it had taken four men, and five hours. All the time, Tobias had been waiting for the state police, or U.S. Customs, to come blazing in, and he could still recall his sense of relief when the work was completed and he was back on the road, heading for home, and Karen. He just needed to finish with Proctor this last time, then he would be done. If it was true that Proctor wanted out, so much the better. Tobias wouldn't miss him. He wouldn't miss him, or the stink of his cabin, or the sight of his lousy motel slowly sinking into the ground.

A man who couldn't hold his booze wasn't to be trusted. It was a sign of a deeper weakness. Tobias would bet a dollar to a dime that Proctor had come out of Iraq One a prime candidate for PTSD counseling, or whatever passed for it then. Instead, he'd retreated to a run-down motel at the edge of the woods and tried to fight his demons alone, aided only by the bottle and any food that came wrapped in plastic with a microwave time written on the side.

Tobias had never believed that he himself suffered from post-traumatic stress. Oh sure, he had trouble relaxing, and he still had to fight the urge to flinch at the sound of fireworks launching, or a car backfiring. There were days when he didn't want to get out of bed, and nights when he didn't want to get into bed, didn't want to close his eyes for fear of what might come, and that was even before the new nightmares. But post-traumatic stress? No, not him. Well, not the severe kind, not the kind where, just to get through the day, you had to be so doped up that it popped out of your pores like discolored sweat, not the kind where you wept for no reason, or you lashed out at your woman because she burned the bacon or spilled your beer.

No, not that kind.

Not yet, but it's started. You did lash out, didn't you?

He looked around the cab, certain that someone had spoken, the voice strangely familiar. The wheel twisted slightly so that he felt his heart skip a beat before he readjusted, fearful of sending the rig off the road and onto the slope, fearful of tumbling, of ending up trapped in his cab, trapped almost within sight of the old motel.

Not yet.

Where had that come from? And then he remembered: a warehouse, its walls cracked, its roof leaking, a consequence of the earlier bombing and the poor workmanship that had gone into its construction; a man, little more than a pile of bloodied cloth now, the life already leaving his eyes. Tobias was standing over him, the muzzle of his M4 carbine, the gun that had torn the man apart, pointing unwaveringly at the fighter's head, as though this bloodied rag doll could pose any threat to him now.

"Take it, take it all. It's yours." The fingers, stained red, indicated the crates and boxes, the shrouded statues, that filled the warehouse. Tobias was amazed that he could even speak. He must have taken four, five shots to the body. Now here he was, waving a hand in the flashlight's beam, as though any of this was his to give or to retain.

"Thanks," said Tobias, and he felt himself sneer as he spoke the word, and heard the sarcasm in his voice, and he was ashamed. He had belittled himself in front of the dying man. Tobias hated him, hated him as he hated all his kind. They were terrorists, haji: Sunni or Shia, foreign or Iraqi, they were all the same in the end. It didn't matter what they called themselves: al-Qaeda, or one of the bullshit names of convenience that they made up from their stock jumble of phrases, like those collections of magnetic words that you stuck to your fridge and used to create bad poetry: Victorious Martyrs of the Brigade of Jihad, Assassination Front of the Imam Resistance, all interchangeable, all alike. Haji. Terrorist.

Yet there was an intimacy to death in moments like this, in giving it and in receiving it, and he had just breached the protocol, answering like a surly teenager, not a man.

The haji smiled, and some white was still visible through the blood that had filled his mouth and stained his teeth.

"Don't thank me," he said. "Not yet . . ."

Not yet. That was the voice he heard, the voice of a man with the promised virgins waiting for him in the next world, the voice of a man who had fought to protect what was in that warehouse.

Fought, but not hard enough. That was what Damien had said to him: they fought, but not as hard as they should have.

Why?

The motel came into view. To his left, he saw the line of boarded-up rooms, and shivered. The place always gave him the creeps. No wonder Proctor had become what he was, holed up here with only the trunks of trees behind him and his bequest, this dump, before him. It was hard to look at those rooms and not imagine unseen guests, unwanted guests, moving behind the walls: guests who liked damp, and mold, and ivy curling around their beds; guests who were themselves in the process of decaying, malevolent shadows entwined on leaf-strewn beds, old ruined bodies moving rhythmically, dryly, passionlessly, the horns on their heads—

Tobias blinked hard. The images had been so vivid, so strong. They reminded him of some of the dreams he'd been having, except in those there had only been shadows moving, hidden things. Now they had shape, form.

Jesus, they had *horns*.

It was the shock, he decided, a delayed reaction to all that he had endured the evening before. He pulled up within sight of Proctor's cabin and waited for him to emerge, but there was no sign. Proctor's truck was parked over to the right. Under ordinary circumstances, Tobias would have hit the horn and rousted the old bastard, but it wouldn't have done to blast the woods, particularly not since Proctor had a neighbor who might be tempted to come and take a look at what all the noise was about.

Tobias killed the engine and climbed down from the cab. His burned hand felt damp beneath the bandages, and he knew that the wounds were seeping. The only consolation for the pain and humiliation was the knowledge that payback would not be long in coming. The wetbacks had crossed the wrong people.

He walked up to the cabin and called Proctor's name, but there was still no response from inside. He knocked on the door.

"Hey, Harold, wake up," he called. "It's Joel."

Only then did he try the door. Even so, he was careful, and slow. Proctor slept with a gun close by, and Tobias didn't want him coming out of a drunk's sleep and loosing a couple of shots at a suspected intruder.

It was empty. Even in the gloom created by the mismatched drapes, he could see that. He hit the light switch and took in the unmade bed, the wrecked television and the demolished phone, the laundry spilling from a basket in the corner, and the smell of neglect, of a man who had let himself go. To his right was the kitchen-cum-living room. Tobias saw what it contained and swore. Proctor had lost it, the asshole.

The remaining crates and boxes, the ones that were supposed to stay hidden in rooms 11, 12, 14, and 15, were stacked almost to the ceiling, visible to anyone who might just happen to stick their noses into Proctor's place to see what was going on. The crazy old bastard had hauled them up here by himself instead of waiting for Tobias to come and take them off his hands. He hadn't even bothered closing most of them. The stone face of a woman stared out of one; another contained more of the seals, their gemstones glittering as Tobias approached.

Worst of all, on the kitchen table, entirely unconcealed, stood a gold box, two feet long, two feet wide, and a foot deep, its lid comparatively plain apart from a series of concentric circles radiating from a small spike. There was Arabic lettering along the margins, and its sides were decorated with intertwined bodies: twisted, distended figures with horns protruding from their heads.

Just like the figures I imagined in the motel rooms, thought Tobias. He had helped to move the box on that first night, recalling how they had opened the lead casket in which it was contained, revealing it to the flashlights. The gold had gleamed dully; later, Bernie Kramer, who came from a family of jewelers, would tell him that the box had recently been cleaned. There were traces of paint still visible, as though it had once been disguised to hide its true value. He had barely glanced at it then, because there were so many other artifacts to take in, and adrenaline was still coursing through his body in the aftermath of the fight. He hadn't even seen the sides until now, just the top. There was no way that he could have known about the creatures carved into it, no way that he could have pictured them so clearly in his mind.

Warily, he approached the box. Three of its sides were sealed with twin locking devices shaped like spiders, with a single large spider lock on the front: seven locks in all. He heard that Kramer had tried to open it, but hadn't been able to figure out how the mechanisms worked. They had discussed the possibility of breaking the box open to see what it contained, but wiser counsel had prevailed. A bribe was paid, and the box was x-rayed. It was found to be not one box but a series of interconnected boxes, each of the interior boxes having only three sides, the fourth in every case being one of the walls of the larger box surrounding it, but every box still appeared to have seven locks, only the arrangement of them differing slightly, the locks themselves growing smaller and smaller. Seven boxes, seven locks on each, forty-nine locks in total. It was a puzzle contraption, and it was empty apart from what the radiographer identified as fragments of bone, wrapped in what appeared to be wire, each wire connected in turn to the locks on the boxes. It might have looked like a bomb on the X-ray, but the box, Kramer had suggested, was a reliquary of some kind. He had also translated the Arabic writing on the lid. *Ashrab min Damhum*: "I will drink their blood." It was decided that the box should remain intact, the locks unbroken.

Now they were so close, and Proctor had almost blown it for them. Well, Proctor could stay out here and drink himself to death as far as Tobias was concerned. He'd said that he didn't care about his cut of the final total, just wanted the stuff gone, and Tobias was happy to stick to that arrangement.

It took him an hour to get everything into the rig. Two of the pieces of statuary were particularly heavy. He had to use the dolly, and even then it was a struggle.

He left the gold box until last. As he was lifting it from the table, he thought that he felt something shift inside. Carefully, he tipped it, listening for any sign of movement, but there was nothing. The bone fragments, he knew, were slotted into holes carved in the metal and held in place with the wire. Anyway, what he had felt was not a piece of bone moving, but an identifiable change in the distribution of a weight from right to left, as though an animal were crawling inside.

Then it was gone, and the box felt normal again. Not empty, exactly, but not as though anything had come loose. He carried it to the rig and placed it beside a pair of wall carvings. The interior was a mess of animal feed and torn sacks, but he'd done his best to clean it up. Most of the sacks had been salvageable and they were now serving as additional packing for the artifacts. He'd have to come up with a story, and compensation, for the customer in South Portland, but he could manage both. He locked the box trailer and climbed into the cab. He backed the rig carefully toward the forest in order to turn back onto the road. He was now facing the motel. He wondered if Proctor was down there. After all, his truck wasn't gone, which meant that Proctor shouldn't have been gone either. Something might have happened to him. He could have taken a fall.

Then Tobias thought again of the treasures left in open view in Proctor's cabin, and the effort of moving them alone into the trailer, and the pain in his hands and face that had begun to return, and of Karen waiting for him back home, Karen with her smooth, unblemished skin, and her firm breasts, and her soft, red lips. The urge to see her, to take her, came to him so strongly that he almost wavered on his feet.

To hell with Proctor, he thought. Let him rot.

As he drove south, he felt no guilt at not searching the motel, at the possibility that he might have abandoned an injured man to death in a deserted motel, a veteran who had served his country just as he had served it. It did not strike him that such an action was not in his nature, for his thoughts and desires were elsewhere, and his nature was already changing. In truth, it had been changing ever since he had first set eyes on the box, and his willingness to countenance the killing of Jandreau and the torture of the detective was simply another aspect of it, but now the pace of that change was about to accelerate greatly. Only once, as he passed Augusta, did he feel discomfited. There was a sound in his head like waves breaking, as of the sea calling to the shore. It troubled him at first, but as the miles rolled by beneath him he began to find it soothing, even soporific. He no longer wanted that drink. He just wanted Karen. He would take her, and then he would sleep.

The road unspooled before him, and the sea sang softly in his head: breaking, hissing.

Whispering.

XIII

The Rojas warehouse stood on the northern outskirts of Lewiston. It had formerly been a bakery owned by the same family for half a century, and the family name, Bunder, was still visible, written in faded white paint, across the front of the building. The company's slogan—"Bunder—the Wonder Bread!"—used to run on local radio, sung to a tune not a million miles removed from that of the TV serial *Champion the Wonder Horse.* Franz Bunder, the father figure of the business in every way, had come up with the idea of using the tune himself, and neither he, nor the gentlemen responsible for creating the advert, bothered to concern themselves greatly with issues such as copyright or royalties. Given that the advert was heard only in eastern Maine, and no aggrieved fans of black-and-white horse dramas had ever complained, the tune remained in use until Bunder's Bakery eventually baked its last loaf, forced out of business by the big boys in the early eighties, long before people began to understand the value to a community of small, family-run operations.

Antonio Rojas, known to most of those in his ambit by his preferred pseudonym of "Raul," could never be accused of making a similar mistake, for his business was entirely dependent on family, near and extended, and he was acutely aware of his links to the larger community, since it bought pot, cocaine, heroin, and, more recently,

crystal meth from him, for which he was very grateful. Metham-
phetamine was the most widely abused narcotic in the state, both
as powder and "ice," and Rojas had been quick to realize its profit
potential, especially since its addictiveness guaranteed a greedy, and
constantly expanding, market. He was further aided by the popularity
of the Mexican variety of the drug, which meant that he was able to
tap into his own connections south of the border instead of relying on
local two-man meth labs which, even if they could source the raw materials, including ephedrine and pseudoephedrine, could rarely maintain the long-term consistency of supply that an operation like Rojas's
required. Instead, Rojas had it transported by road from Mexico, and
now supplied not only Maine but the adjacent New England states.
When necessary, he could call upon the smaller operations to boost
his own supply. He tolerated these labs as long as they didn't threaten
him, and he made sure that they were taxed accordingly.

Rojas was also careful not to alienate any of his competitors. The
Dominican cartels controlled the heroin trade in the state, and their
operation was the most professional, so Rojas was scrupulous and
bought wholesale from them whenever possible instead of cutting
them out entirely and risking reprisals. They also had their own meth
business, but Rojas had organized a sit-down years before with the
Dominicans, and together they had hammered out an agreement
about spheres of influence to which everyone had so far adhered. Cocaine was a relatively open market, and Rojas dealt mainly in crack,
which addicts preferred because it was simpler to use. Similarly, illegal pharmaceuticals from Canada represented pretty easy money, and
there was a ready market for Viagra, Percocet, Vicodin, and "kicker,"
or OxyContin. So coke and pharmaceuticals were in play for everyone, the Dominicans kept their heroin, Rojas looked after meth and
marijuana, and everyone was happy.

Well, nearly everyone. The motorcycle gangs were another matter.
Rojas tended to leave them alone. If they wanted to sell meth, or any-

thing else, then God bless them and *vaya con Díos, amigos.* In Maine, the bikers had a big cut of the marijuana market, so Rojas was careful to sell his product, mainly BC bud, out of state. Screwing with the bikers was time-consuming, dangerous, and ultimately counterproductive. As far as Rojas was concerned, the bikers were crazy, and the only people who argued with crazies were other crazies. Still, the bikers were a known quantity, and they could be factored into the overall equation so that equilibrium was maintained. Equilibrium was important, and in that he and Jimmy Jewel, whose transport links Rojas had long used, and who was a minority shareholder in some of Rojas's business ventures, were of one mind. Without it, there was the potential for bloodshed, and for attracting the attention of the law.

Recently, though, Rojas had become concerned about a number of issues, including the prospect of forces beyond his control impacting upon his business. Rojas was linked by blood to the small but ambitious La Familia cartel, and La Familia was currently engaged in an escalating war, not merely with its rival cartels, but with the Mexican government of President Felipe Calderón. It meant a definite end to what had been termed the "Pax Mafiosa," a gentleman's agreement between the government and the cartels to desist from actions against one another as long as movement of the product remained unaffected.

Rojas had not become a drug dealer in order to start an insurrection against anyone. He had become a drug dealer to get rich, and his ties by marriage to La Familia, and his status as a naturalized U.S. citizen thanks to his now deceased engineer father, had made him eminently suited for his present role. La Familia's main problem, as far as Rojas was concerned, was its spiritual leader, Nazario Moreno González, also known, with some justification, as El Más Loco, or the Craziest One. While quite content to accept some of El Más Loco's rulings, such as the ban on the sale of drugs within its home territory, which had no effect on his own operations, Rojas was of the opinion that spiritual leaders had no place in drug cartels. El Más Loco required his dealers and killers to refrain from alcohol, to the extent that he had set up a network of rehab centers from which La Familia actively recruited those who managed to abide by its rules. A couple of those converts had even been forced on Rojas, although he had managed to sideline them by sending them to BC to act as liaisons with the Canadian bud growers. Let the Canucks deal with them, and if the young killers suffered an unfortunate accident somewhere along the way, well, Rojas would smooth any ruffled feathers over a couple of beers, for Rojas liked his beer.

El Más Loco also seemed prepared to indulge, even encourage, what was, in Rojas's opinion, an unfortunate taste for the theatrical: in 2006, a member of La Familia had walked into a nightclub in Uruapan and dumped five severed heads on the dance floor. Rojas didn't approve of theatrics. He had learned from many years in the United States that the less attention one attracted, the easier it was to do business. Moreover, he regarded his cousins in the south as barbarians who had forgotten how to behave like ordinary men, if they had ever truly known how to conduct themselves with discretion. He did his best to avoid visiting Mexico unless it was absolutely necessary, preferring to leave such matters to one of his trusted underlings. By now, he found the sight of *los narcos* in their big hats and ostrich leather boots absurd, even comical, and their predilection for beheadings and torture belonged to another time. He was also under increasing pressure through his trucking connections to facilitate the movement of weapons, easily acquired in the gun stores of Texas and Arizona, across the border. As far as Rojas was concerned, it could only be a matter of time before he became a target for La Familia's rivals, or the DEA. Neither eventuality appealed to him.

Rojas's problems had been compounded by the global financial recession. He had squirreled away a considerable amount of money, both cash to which he was entitled by virtue of his role in La Familia's operations, and some to which he was not. Even in the early days, he had invested funds in shell banks in Montserrat, internationally notorious for being almost entirely fraudulent, and eminently willing to launder money. His "bankers" had operated out of a bar in Plymouth, until the FBI began putting pressure on Montserrat's government, and they had been forced to transfer their operations to Antigua. There it was business as usual under the two Bird administrations, father and son, until the U.S. government again began applying pressure. Unfortunately, Rojas had discovered too late one of the downsides of investing with fraudulent banks: they had a tendency to commit fraud, and their customers were usually the ones who suffered. Rojas's principal banker was currently languishing in a maximum security prison, and Rojas's investments, carefully funneled offshore over two decades, were now worth about 25 percent of what they should have been. He was looking for an out, before he ended up dead or in prison, which, for him, would be the same thing, as his life expectancy would be measured in hours once he was behind bars. If his rivals didn't get him, his own people would kill him to keep him quiet. He wanted to run, but he needed one big score before he could do so. Now, it seemed, Jimmy Jewel might just have given him that opportunity. He had already spoken with the old smuggler twice that day, initially to inform him of what had been found in the rig, and Rojas had sent him photographs of the items in question. Neither Rojas nor Jimmy trusted email, as they knew what the Feds were capable of when it came to surveillance. The solution they had come up with was to establish a free email account to which only they had the password. Emails would be written, but never sent. Instead, they were stored as drafts, where they could be read by one man or the other without ever attracting the attention of federal snoopers. After viewing the items, Jimmy had counseled caution until they evaluated precisely what they were dealing with. He would make inquiries, Jimmy told Rojas. Just keep the stuff safe.

Jimmy was as good as his word. He had contacts everywhere, and it didn't take long for the items to be identified as ancient cylinder seals from Mesopotamia. Rojas, who was not usually interested in such details, had listened in fascination as Jimmy told him that the seals in his possession dated from about 2500 B.C., or the Sumerian Early Dynastic period, whatever that was. They were used to authenticate documents, as testaments of ownership, and also as amulets of luck, healing, and power, which appealed to Rojas. Jimmy told him that the caps at the end appeared to be gold, and the precious stones inset on the caps were emeralds and rubies and diamonds, but Rojas hadn't needed Jimmy's help to figure out what gold and precious stones looked like.

In the course of their second conversation, which had just ended, Jimmy had also told Rojas that the gentleman with whom he had spoken had predicted huge interest among wealthy collectors for the seals, and furious bidding could be anticipated. The expert also believed that he knew the source of the items: similar seals had been among the treasures looted from the Iraq Museum in Baghdad shortly after the invasion, which offered some clue as to how they might have come to be in the possession of an ex-soldier turned truck driver. The problem for Jimmy and Rojas lay in getting rid of the seals that Rojas wanted to sell as his "tax" on the operation before the authorities realized that he had them and came knocking on his door.

But much as Rojas liked Jimmy Jewel, he was not about to trust him entirely. It was he, Rojas, who had taken the risk in hijacking the truck. He wanted to ensure that he was compensated appropriately for it, and he also wanted an independent assessment of the worth of the seals. He had already prized the gold and gemstones from two seals and had them valued: even allowing for the middleman, and the fact that they couldn't be disposed of on the open market, he was $200,000 in profit from taking down the truck driver. He had experienced only a slight pang of regret when Jimmy had told him that the seals were much more valuable intact, so that by destroying them he had sacrificed four or five times as much money again, at the very least. The destruction of such ancient artifacts did not disturb Rojas unduly, for he knew how to make money from gold and precious stones, while the market for old seals, however valuable, was significantly smaller and more specialized. Rojas was now wondering how many other such seals or similar items the driver named Tobias and his associates might have in their possession. He didn't like the idea that they might possibly have been running such valuable goods through what he regarded as his territory without anyone suspecting, at least not until Jimmy Jewel became involved.

The upper floor of the Bunder warehouse had been converted into a loft apartment by Rojas. He had kept the brick walls, and had furnished it in a determinedly masculine style: leather, dark woods, and handwoven rugs. There was a huge plasma screen TV in one corner, but Rojas rarely watched it. Neither did he entertain women here, preferring to use a bedroom in one of the houses nearby, all of which were owned by members of his family. Even meetings were conducted in venues other than his loft. This was his space, and he valued the solitude that it offered.

There were bunks on the floor below, and couches and chairs, and a TV that always seemed to be showing Mexican soap operas or soccer games. There was also a galley kitchen, and at any one time at least four armed men were in attendance. The floor of Rojas's loft had been soundproofed, so he was barely aware of their presence. Even so, his men tended to keep conversation to a minimum, and the volume on the TV low, in order not to disturb their leader.

Now, seated at a table, an anglepoise lamp adjusted so that it shone its light directly over his shoulder, Rojas examined one of the remaining seals, tracing the lettering carved upon it and allowing the rubies and emeralds embedded in it to reflect red and green shards of light upon his skin. He had no intention of handing all the undamaged seals back to Tobias and whoever else might be involved in their operation; he never had, and he already had plans for a number of the gemstones. For the first time, though, he considered holding on to some of the intact seals for himself, and not damaging them or selling them. Everything in his loft had been bought new, and although it was all beautiful, it was also anonymous. There was nothing distinctive about it, nothing that could not have been acquired by any man with a modicum of money and taste. But these, these were different. He looked to his left, where there was a fireplace topped by a stone mantel, and imagined the seals resting on the granite. He could have a stand made for them. No, better still, he could carve one himself, for he had always been skilled with his hands.

The mantel already housed a shrine to Jesús Malverde, the Mexican Robin Hood and patron saint of drug dealers. The statue of Malverde, with its mustache and white shirt, bore a certain resemblance to the Mexican matinee idol Pedro Infante, even though Malverde had been killed by police in 1909, thirty years before Pedro was born. Rojas believed that Jesús Malverde would approve of the seals being laid beside him, and might smile in turn upon Rojas's operations.

Thus "could" became "would," and the decision was made to keep the seals.

XIV

The room was almost entirely circular, as though set in a tower, and lined with books from floor to ceiling. It was perhaps forty feet in diameter, and dominated by an old banker's desk lit by a green-shaded lamp. Nearby was a more modern source of illumination, stainless steel and hinged, with a light source that could be adjusted to a pinpoint. Beside it lay a magnifying glass, and assorted tools: tiny blades, calipers, picks, and brushes. Reference volumes were piled one on top of another, their pages marked with lengths of colored ribbon. Photographs and drawings spilled from files. The floor itself was a maze of books and papers set in piles that seemed forever on the verge of collapsing, yet did not, a labyrinth of arcane knowledge through which only one man knew the true path.

The bookshelves, some of them seeming to bend slightly at the center beneath the weight of their volumes, had been pressed into service for other purposes as well. In front of the books, some leather-bound, some new, there were statues, ancient and pitted, and fragments of pottery, mostly Etruscan, although, curiously, no un-damaged items; Iron Age tools, and Bronze Age jewelry; and, littered among the other relics like curious bugs, dozens of Egyptian scarabs.

There was not a speck of dust to be found on anything in the room, and there were no windows to look out upon the old Massachusetts village below. The only light came from the lamps, and the walls absorbed all noise. Despite some modern appliances, among them a small laptop computer discreetly set on a side table, there was a timelessness about this place, a sense that, were one to open the single oak door that led from the study to elsewhere, one would be confronted with darkness and stars above and below, as though the room were suspended in space.

At the great desk sat Herod, a fragment of a clay tablet before him. Pressed to one eye was a jeweler's glass, through which Herod was examining a cuneiform symbol etched into the slab. It was the Sumerians who had first created and used the cuneiform writing system, which was soon adopted by neighboring tribes, most particularly the Akkadians, Semitic speakers who dwelled to the north of the Sumerians. With the ascendancy of the Akkadian dynasty in 2300 B.C., Sumerian went into decline, eventually becoming a dead language used only for literary purposes, while Akkadian continued to flourish for two thousand years, subsequently evolving into Babylonian and Assyrian.

Aside from the damage to the tablet over time, the difficulty facing Herod in determining the precise meaning of the logogram that he was examining lay in the difference between the Sumerian and Akkadian languages. Sumerian is agglutinative, which means that phonetically unchanging words and particles are joined together to form phrases. Akkadian, meanwhile, is inflectional, so that a basic root can be modified to create words with different, if related, meanings by adding vowels, suffixes, and prefixes. Thus Sumerian logographic signs, if used in Akkadian, would not convey the same exact meaning, while the same sign could, depending upon context, mean different words, a linguistic trait known as polyvalency. To avoid confusion, Akkadian used some signs for their phonetic values instead of their meanings in order to reproduce correct inflections. Akkadian also inherited homophony from Sumerian, the capacity of different signs to represent the same sound. Combined with a script that had between seven hundred and eight hundred signs, it meant that Akkadian was incredibly complex to translate. Clearly, the tablet was making reference to a god of the netherworld, but which god?

Herod loved such challenges. He was an extraordinary man. Largely self-educated, he had been fascinated by ancient things since childhood, with a preference for dead civilizations and near-forgotten languages. For many years, he had dabbled without purpose in such matters, a gifted amateur, until death changed him.

His death.

The computer beeped softly to Herod's right. Herod did not like to keep the laptop on his work desk. It seemed to him wrong to mix the ancient and the modern in this way, even if the computer made some of his tasks immeasurably easier than they might once have been. Herod still liked to work with paper and pen, with books and manuscripts. Whatever he needed to know was contained in one of the many volumes in this room, or stored somewhere in his mind, of which the library in which he toiled was a physical representation.

Under ordinary circumstances, Herod would not have abandoned such a delicate task to answer an email, but his system was set up to alert him to messages from a number of specific contacts, because access to Herod was carefully regulated. The message that had just arrived came from a most trusted source and had been sent to his priority box. Herod removed the eyeglass and tapped the Perspex lightly with the tip of a finger, like a player forced to leave the chessboard at a crucial moment, as if to say, "We are not done here. Eventually, you will yield to me." He stood and made his way carefully between the towers of paper and books until he reached the computer.

The message opened to reveal a series of high-resolution images depicting a cylindrical seal, its caps inset with precious stones. The seal had been laid upon a piece of black felt, then moved slightly for each photograph so that every part of it was revealed. Particular details—the jewels, a perfectly rendered carving of a king upon a throne—had been photographed in close-up.

Herod felt his heart beat faster. He drew nearer to the screen, squinting at what he saw, then printed off all the images and took them back to his desk, where he examined them again through a magnifying glass. When he was done, he made the call, although it was close to midnight. The woman answered almost immediately, as he knew she would, her voice cracked and old, a fitting instrument for the withered old hag that she was. Nevertheless, she had been in the antiques business for a long time, and had never yet led Herod astray. Their natures were also similar, although her malevolence was merely a dull echo of Herod's own capacities.

"Where did you get this?" he asked.

"I don't have it. It was brought to me, and I was asked to offer an opinion on its value."

"Who brought it to you?"

"A Mexican. He calls himself Raul, but his real name is Antonio Rojas. He works closely with a man named, ironically, Jimmy Jewel, who is based in Portland, Maine. Rojas told me that there were other seals; a number, regrettably, have been destroyed."

"Destroyed?"

"Taken apart for their gold and gemstones. The fragments, too, he showed to me. It was all that I could do not to cry."

Under ordinary circumstances, Herod would also have mourned the annihilation of such a beautiful object, but there were other seals, and such treasures were not unique. What he wished to find was immeasurably more valuable.

"And you believe that this is linked to what I seek?"

"According to the catalog, it was stored in Locker 5. Other, less valuable seals from Locker 5 were found at the scene of the warehouse killings, along with the lock from the lead storage box."

"Where did this Raul get the seals?" said Herod.

"He wouldn't say, but he is not a collector. He is a criminal, a drug dealer. I've facilitated him in the past with the sale of certain items, which is why he came to me. If he really has other seals, then my guess is that he stole them, or took them in payment of a debt. Either way, he has no idea of their true value."

"What did you tell him?"

"That I would make inquiries and get back to him. He gave me two days. Otherwise, he threatened to cut out the jewels on the remaining seals and sell them."

Despite his priorities, Herod hissed in disapproval, and he found himself already despising the man who had uttered the threat. So much the better. It would make what he would have to do next even easier.

"You've done very well," he said. "You'll be amply rewarded."

"Thank you. Do you want me to find out more about Raul?"

"Naturally, but be discreet."

Herod hung up the phone. His earlier tiredness began to fade. This was important. He had been searching for so long, and now it seemed that he might be closing in on that which he sought: myth given form.

He felt an old man's urge to visit the bathroom, so he left his library, breaking its bubble of solitude, and walked through the living room into his bedroom. He always used the master bath, never the main bathroom, because it was easier to clean. He stood over the toilet, his eyes closed, feeling the welcome release. Such a small pleasure, yet not one to be underestimated. His body was betraying him in so many ways that he felt a sense of elation at the minor triumph of an organ that functioned properly.

As the sound of the last trickle faded, Herod opened his eyes and regarded himself in the mirrored wall of the bathroom. The wound on his mouth tormented him. The physicians wanted to try again to remove the necrotic tissue, and he would have no choice but to acquiesce. Yet they had failed before, just as the chemotherapy had not arrested the metastasizing of his cells. He was being eaten alive, inside and out. A lesser man would have succumbed by now, would have chosen to end it all, but Herod had a purpose. He had been promised a reward: an end to his suffering, and a visitation of greater suffering on others in turn. That promise had been made to him when he died, and upon his return to this life he had commenced his great search, and his collection had begun to grow.

He buttoned himself up. No zippers for him: he was a man of older tastes. One of the buttons was giving him trouble, so he looked down as he struggled to slip it through its hole.

When he glanced back at the mirror, he had no eyes.

HEROD HAD DIED ON September 14, 2003. His heart had stopped during an operation to remove a diseased kidney, the first of the fruitless attempts to stall the progress of his cancers. Later, the surgeons would describe the occurrence as extraordinary, even inexplicable. Herod's heart should not have ceased beating, yet it did. They had fought to save him, to bring him back, and they had succeeded. A chaplain visited him while he was recovering in the ICU, inquiring if Herod wanted to talk, or to pray. Herod shook his head.

"They tell me that your heart stopped on the operating table," said the priest. He was in his fifties, overweight and red-faced, with kind, twinkling eyes. "You've died and returned. Not many men can say they've done that."

He smiled, but Herod did not smile back. His voice was weak, and his chest hurt as he spoke.

"Are you trying to find out what's beyond the grave, priest?" he said, and even in the man's weakened state, the chaplain detected the hostility in his voice. "It was like dark water closing over my head, like a pillow suffocating me. I felt it coming, and I knew. There is nothing beyond this life. Nothing. Are you happy now?"

The priest stood.

"I'll leave you to rest," he said. He was untroubled by the man's venom. He had heard worse before, and his faith was strong. Strangely, too, he had the sense that the patient, Herod—and from where did such a name originate, or was it chosen as some bleak joke?—was lying. It was most peculiar, yet with it came another realization. If Herod was lying, the priest did not want to know the truth. Not that truth. Not Herod's truth.

Herod watched the priest go, then closed his eyes and prepared to relive the moment of his own death.

THERE WAS LIGHT. IT shone red against his eyelids. He opened his eyes.

He was lying on the operating table. There was an open wound in his side, but it gave him no pain. He touched his fingers to it, and they came away bloody. He looked around, but the theater was empty. No, not merely empty: it was abandoned, and had been for some time. From where he lay, he could see rust upon the instruments, and dust and filth upon the tiles and the steel trays. A clicking noise came from his right, and he watched as a cockroach skittered into hiding. He was lying in a pool of light that came from the great lamp that burned above the table, but a gentler illumination rippled around the walls of the theater, although he could not detect its source.

He sat up, then placed his feet on the floor. There was a bad smell, the stink of decay. He felt the dust between his toes, and looked down. There were no other footprints to be seen. He saw that the sinks to his right were stained brown with dried blood. He turned the faucet. No water came, but he heard sounds coming from the pipes.

They echoed around the room, making him uneasy. He turned the faucet back to its previous position, and the sounds ceased.

Only when the noise from the pipes disturbed the quiet did he realize just how deep was the silence. He pushed through the theater doors, barely pausing to take in the deserted prep area. Here, too, the sinks were stained with blood, though it had also splashed on the floor and the walls, a great gusher that seemed to have come from the sinks themselves, as though the pipes had spit back all the fluids that had been washed into them over time. The mirrors above the sinks were almost entirely obscured by the dried blood, though he caught a glimpse of himself in a dusty but otherwise unmarked spot. He looked pale, and there were yellow stains around his mouth but, the hole in his side apart, he appeared well. He still could not understand why there was no pain.

There should be pain. I *want* pain. Pain will confirm that I am alive and not . . .

Dead? Is this death?

He walked on. The corridor beyond the theater was empty but for a pair of wheelchairs, and the nurses' station was deserted. Each ward room that he passed contained an unmade bed, filthy sheets tossed aside or trailing across the floor, pulled from beneath the mattress where—

Where the patients had resisted being dragged away, he thought, clinging to the sheets in a last effort to prevent what was about to occur. It resembled a hospital evacuated during wartime and never reoccupied, or perhaps one that had been in the process of moving its patients when the opposing forces had arrived, and the slaughter had begun. But if that was so, where were the bodies? Herod thought of the images from old news footage of World War Two, of villages purged by the Nazis, littered with the scattered remains of the dead, like broken crows dotting a highway on a warm, still day; of pale forms in camp pits lying on top of one another like figures from the nightmares of Bosch.

Bodies. Where were the bodies?

He turned a corner. A pair of elevator doors stood open, the shaft gaping emptily. He peered down cautiously, holding on to the wall for support. He could see nothing for a moment, only blackness, but as he prepared to withdraw he was certain that, far below, there was movement. The faintest scratching carried up to him, and there was a smear of gray in the dark, like a brushstroke on a black canvas. He tried to speak, to call for help, but no sound came from his lips. He was mute, struck dumb, and yet, in the depths of the elevator shaft, the presence below arrested its progress, and he felt its regard as an itch upon his face.

Softly, quietly, he stepped back, as behind him the lights in the corridor extinguished themselves, throwing the path that he had followed into shadow. What did it matter? he thought. What was there to go back to? He should continue searching. Yet even as he made the decision, the lights to his rear continued to go out, forcing him to go forward if he were not to find himself trapped in the gloom, and as he walked, the darkness pressed against his back, urging him on. He thought that he heard movement behind him, but he did not look over his shoulder for fear that those gray smears might assume a more concrete form of tooth and claw.

The environs of the hospital grew older as he walked. The institutional paint faded and began flaking, until only bare walls remained. Tiles became wood. There was no longer glass in the doors. Instruments glimpsed in treatment rooms appeared cruder, more primitive. Operating tables were reduced to blocks of scarred and pitted wood, buckets of stinking water at their feet to sluice the blood from them. All that he saw spoke of pain both ancient and eternal, testament to the fragility of the body and the limits of its endurance.

At last he came to a pair of large wooden doors that stood open to admit him. Inside was a light, slight and flickering. Behind him, the darkness encroached, and all that it contained.

He stepped through the doors.

The room, or what he could see of it, was empty of furniture. Its walls and ceiling were invisible to him, lost in shadow, but he imagined his surroundings as impossibly high and immeasurably wide. Still, he felt claustrophobic and constrained. He wanted to go back, to leave this place, but there was nowhere to return to. The doors behind him had closed, and he could no longer see them. There was only the light: a hurricane lamp, placed on the dirt floor, in which a flame burned faintly.

The light, and what was illuminated by it.

At first he thought it a shapeless mass, an accumulation of detritus brushed into a pile and forgotten. Then, as he drew closer, he saw that it was covered in cobwebs, the threads so old that they were coated in dust, forming a blanket of strands that almost entirely obscured what lay beneath. It was much larger than a man, although it shared a man's form. Herod could discern the muscles in its legs and the curvature of its spine, although its face was hidden from him, sunk deep into its chest, its arms flung over its head in an effort to shield itself from some impending hurt.

Then, as though slowly becoming aware of his presence, the figure moved, like an insect in its pupal shell, the arms lowering, the head beginning to turn. Herod's senses were suddenly flooded with words and images—

books, statues, drawings

(a box)

—and in that moment his purpose became clear.

Suddenly, Herod's body arched as the wound in his side was violated. It was followed by a convulsion. He saw

light

and heard

voices.

Before him, the patina of cobwebs was broken, and a thin finger emerged, topped by a sharp nail ingrained with dirt. The shock came again, longer now, more painful. His eyes were open, and there was something plastic in his mouth. There were masked faces above him, only the eyes visible. There were hands on his heart, and a voice was speaking to him, softly and insistently, talking of grave secrets, of things that must be done, and before his resurrection it spoke his name and told him that it would find him again, and he would know it when it came.

Now, as he stepped back from the bathroom mirror, the reflection remained in place, a featureless, eyeless mask hanging behind the glass, before it found its place above the collar of an old checked suit like a fairground barker's, a red bow tie knotted tightly at the neck of a yellow shirt decorated with balloons.

Herod gazed, and he knew, and he was not afraid.

"Oh Captain!" he whispered. "Oh Captain! my Captain . . ."

XV

The city was changing, but then it was in the nature of cities to change; perhaps it was just that I was getting older, and had already seen too much fall away to be entirely comfortable with the closure of restaurants and stores that I had known. The transformation of Portland from a city that was struggling not to drop into Casco Bay and sink to the bottom, into one that was now thriving, artistic, and safe, had begun in earnest at the start of the 1970s, funded largely with federal money through the kind of pork-barrel appropriations that are frowned upon by pretty much everyone except those profiting from them. Congress Street got brick sidewalks, the Old Port was rejuvenated, and the Municipal Airport became the International Jetport, which at least had the benefit of sounding futuristic, even if, for most of the last decade, you couldn't fly direct to Canada from Portland, let alone anywhere that wasn't part of the contiguous land mass, making the "International" part largely superfluous.

Some of the gloss had gone from the Old Port in recent years. Exchange Street, one of the loveliest streets in the city, was in transition: Books Etc. was gone, Emerson Books was about to close due to the retirement of its owners, and soon only Longfellow Books would be left in the Old Port. Walter's restaurant, where I had eaten with both

Susan, my late wife, and Rachel, the mother of my second child, had shut its doors in preparation for a move to Union Street.

But Congress Street was still flying the flag for weirdness and eccentricity, like a little fragment of Austin, Texas, transported to the northeast. There was now a decent pizzeria, Otto, offering slices late into the night, and the various galleries and used bookstores, vinyl outlets and fossil stores had been augmented by a comic book emporium and a new bookstore, Green Hand, that boasted a museum of cryptozoology in its back room, which was enough to gladden the heart of anybody with a taste for the bizarre.

Well, nearly anybody.

"What the fuck is cryptozoology?" asked Louis as we sat in Monument Square, drinking wine and watching the world go by. Today, Louis was wearing Dolce & Gabbana: a black three-button suit, white shirt, no tie. Even though his voice was not loud, an elderly woman eating soup outside the restaurant to our left looked at Louis disapprovingly. I had to admire her courage. Most people tended not to give Louis looks of any kind other than fear or envy. He was tall, and black, and quite lethal.

"My apologies," said Louis, nodding to her. "I didn't mean to use inappropriate words." He turned back to me, then said: "What the fuck is whatever it was you said?"

"Cryptozoology," I explained. "It's the science of creatures that may or may not exist, like Bigfoot, or the Loch Ness monster."

"The Loch Ness monster is dead," said Angel.

Today, Angel was wearing tattered jeans, no-name sneakers in red and silver, and a virulently green T-shirt promoting a bar that had closed down sometime during the Kennedy era. Unlike his partner in love and life, Angel tended to provoke responses that varied between bemusement and outright concern that he might be color blind. Angel was also lethal, although not quite as lethal as Louis. But then, that was true of most people, as well as most varieties of poisonous snake.

"I read it somewhere," Angel continued. "This expert who was looking for it for years and years, he decided that it had died."

"Yeah, like two hundred and fifty million years ago," said Louis. "Course it's dead. The fuck else would it be?"

Angel shook his head in the manner of one faced with a child who can't grasp a simple concept. "No, it died *recently*. Until then, it was still alive."

Louis stared hard at his partner for a long time, then said: "You know, I think we need to set a limit on the conversations you can join in on."

"Like in a churrascaria," I offered. "We could turn up a green symbol when you can speak, and a red one when you have to sit quietly and digest whatever it is you've just heard."

"I hate you guys," said Angel.

"No, you don't."

"I do," he confirmed. "You don't respect me."

"Well, that is true," I admitted. "But, then, we really have no reason to."

Angel thought about this, before conceding that I had a point. We moved on to the subject of my sex life, which, although apparently endlessly entertaining to Angel, didn't detain us for long.

"What about that cop, the one who'd started coming into the Bear? Cagney?"

"Macy."

"Yeah, her."

Sharon Macy was pretty and dark, and she'd certainly been sending out signals of interest, but I had still been trying to figure out how to deal with the fact that Rachel and our daughter were now going to be living in Vermont, and that my relationship with Rachel was effectively over.

"It was too soon," I said.

"There's no such thing as 'too soon,'" said Louis. "There's just 'too late,' and then there's 'dead.'"

A trio of young men in loose-fitting jeans, oversize T-shirts, and fresh-out-of-the-box sneakers oozed along Congress like algae on the surface of a pond, heading for the bars on Fore Street. They had "out of town" written all over them—or written anywhere that wasn't already occupied by a brand logo, or the name of a rapper. One, God help us, even wore a retro Black Power T-shirt, complete with clenched fist, even though they were all so white they made Pee Wee Herman look like Malcolm X.

Beside us, two men were eating burgers and minding their own business. One of them wore a discreet rainbow triangle on the collar of his jacket, and a "Vote No on 1" badge beneath it, a reference to the impending proposition intended to overturn the possibility of gay marriage in the state.

"You gonna marry him, bitch?" said one of the passing strangers, and his friends laughed.

The two men tried to get on with their meal.

"Fags," said the same guy, clearly on a roll. He was small, but muscled up. He leaned over and took a French fry from the plate of the man with the badges, who responded with an aggrieved "Hey!"

"I ain't gonna eat it, man," said their tormentor. "Never know what I might catch from you."

"Burn, Rod!" said one of his buddies, and they high-fived.

Rod tossed the fry on the ground, then turned his attention to Angel and Louis, who were watching them without expression.

"What you looking at?" said Rod. "You faggots too?"

"No," said Angel. "I'm an undercover heterosexual."

"And I'm really white," said Louis.

"He is really white," I confirmed. "Takes him hours to put on his makeup before he can leave the house."

Rod looked confused. His face fell into the appropriate expression without too much effort, so it probably wasn't the first time.

"So I'm just like you," continued Louis, "because you're not really black either. Here's something for you to think about: all those bands on your shirts, they only tolerate you because you put money in their pockets. They're hardcore, and they're talking to, and about, black people. In an ideal world, they wouldn't need you, and you'd just have to go back to listening to Bread, or Coldplay, or some other maudlin shit that white boys are humming to these days. But, for now, those guys will take your money, and if you ever wander into any of the 'hoods they emerged from, you'll get stomped and someone will take the rest of your money as well, and maybe your sneakers too. You want me to, I can draw you a map, and you can go express your solidarity with them, see how that works out for you. Otherwise, you run along, and take Curly and Larry there with you. Go on, now: bust a move, or whatever it is you homeboys do to help you perambulate."

"Bread?" I said. "You're a little out of touch with popular culture, aren't you?"

"All that shit sounds the same," said Louis. "I'm down with the kids."

"Yeah, the kids from the nineteenth century."

"I could kick your ass," said Rod, feeling the urge to contribute something to the conversation. He might have been dumb enough to believe it, but the two guys behind him were smarter, which wasn't exactly something worth putting on their business cards. Already, they were trying to move Rod along.

"Yes, you could," said Louis. "Feel better now?"

"By the way," said Angel. "I lied. I'm not really heterosexual, although he still really isn't black."

I looked at Angel in surprise. "Hey, you never told me you were gay. I knew that, I'd never have let you adopt those children."

"Too late now," said Angel. "The girls are all wearing comfortable shoes, and the boys are singing show tunes."

"Oh, you gays and your cunning ways. You could run the world if you weren't so busy just making things prettier."

Rod seemed about to say something else when Louis moved. He didn't get up from his chair, and there was nothing obviously threatening about what he did, but it was the equivalent of a dozing rattlesnake adjusting its coils in preparation for a strike, or a spider tensing in the corner of its web as it watches the fly alight. Even through his fog of alcohol and stupidity, Rod glimpsed the possibility of serious suffering at some point in the near future: not here, perhaps, on a busy street with cop cars cruising by, but later, maybe in a bar, or a restroom, or a parking lot, and it would mark him for the rest of his life.

Without another word, the three young men slipped away, and they did not look back.

"Nicely done," I said to Louis. "What are you going to do for an encore: scowl at a puppy?"

"Might steal a toy from a kitten," said Louis. "Put it on a high shelf."

"Well, you struck a blow for something there. I'm just not sure what it was."

"Quality of life," said Louis.

"I guess." Beside us, the two men abandoned their burgers, left a twenty and a ten on the table, and hurried away without saying a word. "You even frighten your own people. You probably convinced that guy to vote Yes on Prop One just in case you decide to move here."

"With that in mind, remind us why we're here again," said Angel. They had arrived barely an hour before, and their bags were still in the trunk of their car. Louis and Angel only took planes when it was absolutely necessary to do so, as airlines tended to frown on the tools of their trade. I told them everything, from my first meeting with

Bennett Patchett, through the discovery of the tracking device on my car, and finished with my conversation with Ronald Straydeer and the sending of the photographs from Damien Patchett's funeral.

"So they know that you haven't dropped the case?" said Angel.

"If the GPS tracker was working, yes. They also know that I visited Karen Emory, which may not be good for her."

"You warn her?"

"I left a message on her cell phone. Another call in person might just have compounded the problem."

"You think they'll come at you again?" asked Louis.

"Wouldn't you?"

"I'd have killed you the first time," said Louis. "If they figured you for the kind of guy who walks away after some amateur waterboarding, they got you all wrong."

"Straydeer said that they'd started out with the intention of helping wounded soldiers. It may be that killing is a last resort. The one who interrogated me said that nobody was going to be hurt by what they were doing."

"But he made an exception for you. Funny how folks do that where you're concerned."

"Which brings us back to why you're here."

"And why we're meeting in public, on a bright summer evening. If they're watching, you want them to know that you're not alone."

"I need a couple of days. If I can get them to keep their distance, it will make life that much easier."

"And if they don't keep their distance?"

"Then you can hurt them," I said.

Louis raised his glass, and drank.

"Well, here's to not keeping one's distance," he said.

We paid our check, and headed to the Grill Room on Exchange for steak, for the prospect of hurting someone always made Louis hungry.

XVI

Jimmy Jewel sat in his usual seat as Earle finished locking up. It was close to midnight, and the bar had been quiet all evening: a few rummies looking for a straightener after the previous night's excesses, yet without the stamina or the funds to embark on another bender; and a pair of Masshole tourists who had taken a wrong turn and then decided to order a couple of beers while congratulating themselves on the authentic squalor of their surroundings. Unfortunately, Earle didn't take kindly to people making unkind remarks about his working environment, especially not urban preppies who, in the good old days, would have been kissing the lid of a trash can in a back alley as atonement for their bad manners. The Massholes' attempt to order a second round was met by a blank stare and the suggestion that they should take their business elsewhere, preferably somewhere over the state line, or even over multiple state lines.

"You got a way with people," Jimmy told Earle. "You ought to be with the UN, helping in trouble spots."

"You wanted them to stay, you should have said," Earle replied. His face was guileless. There were times when even Jimmy didn't know if Earle was being sincere or not. Still waters, and all that, thought Jimmy. Occasionally, Earle would pass a remark, or make an observation, and Jimmy would stop whatever he was doing as his brain struggled to process what he had just heard, forcing him to reassess Earle just when he believed that he had him figured out. Lately, it was Earle's choice of reading material that was throwing him: he seemed to be playing catch-up with classic literature, and not just Tom Sawyer and Huckleberry Finn either. Earlier that evening, Earle had been reading a collection by Tolstoy, *Master and Man and Other Stories*. When Jimmy had questioned him about it, Earle had described the plot of the title story, something about a wealthy guy who shields his serf after they both become lost in a winter storm, so that the serf lives and the wealthy guy dies. The wealthy guy made it to heaven as a consequence, though, so that was all right.

"Is there supposed to be a message in that?" Jimmy had asked.

"For whom?"

"For whom," like Earle was John Houseman now.

"I don't know," said Jimmy. "For wealthy guys with bad consciences."

"I'm not a wealthy guy," said Earle.

"So you're like the other guy?"

"I guess. I mean, I didn't take it that way. You don't have to be one or the other. It's just a story."

"If we get caught in a blizzard, and one of us is going to die, you think I'm not going to use you like a blanket to keep warm? You think I'd take a hit for you?"

Earle had considered the question. "Yeah," he said. "I think you would take a hit for me. Wouldn't be the first time, either."

And Jimmy knew that Earle was referring to Sally Cleaver, because he had sensed it playing on Earle's conscience ever since the detective's first visit. Jimmy knew Earle well enough by now to recognize when that particular ghost had chosen to whisper in Earle's ear.

"You're out of your mind," said Jimmy.

"Maybe," said Earle. "Thing of it is, I wouldn't let you take that hit, Mr. Jewel. I'd keep you alive, even if I had to smother you to do it."

That sounded to Jimmy like a contradiction in terms, and he was also mildly disturbed by the image of his slender frame lost in the folds of Earle's fleshy body. He decided that this was a conversation that they didn't need to have again. With no further customers likely to trouble them, and with other, more pressing matters on his mind, Jimmy had told Earle to lock the door for the night.

Now the floor was swept, the glasses were clean, and the night's meager takings were safely locked up in the safe in Jimmy's office. A newspaper lay, half read, by Jimmy's left hand. This was unusual, thought Earle. By now, Jimmy would usually have dispensed with the paper entirely, even down to the crossword, but today he had seemed distracted, and he was currently staring at the pencil that lay on the bar before him, as though expecting it to move of its own volition and provide him with the answers that he sought.

Jimmy was right about Earle. Despite his bulk, and the impression he gave that his family tree still had members hanging from it making "ook-ook" noises, Earle was not an insensitive man. The routine of the bar gave an order to his life that allowed him to function with the minimum of unwanted complexities, but also gave him time to think. His role was to lift, carry, threaten, and guard, and he performed all these tasks willingly and without complaint. He was paid relatively well for what he did, but he was also loyal to Jimmy. Jimmy looked out for him, and he, in turn, looked out for Jimmy.

But, as his boss had guessed, Earle had been brooding in recent days. He didn't like being reminded about Sally Cleaver. Earle was sorry for what had happened to her, and he felt that he should have acted to prevent it, but it wasn't like it was the first domestic that had ever broken out in the Blue Moon, and Earle was smart enough to know that the best course of action on such occasions was simply not to get involved but to move the feuding parties off the premises and let them sort everything out in the privacy of their own home. It was only when Cliffie Andreas had come back into the bar with blood on his fists and face that Earle had begun to realize his attitude amounted to an "abdication of responsibility," as one of the detectives had later put it, indicating that, in a just world, Earle would have spent some time behind bars alongside Cliffie for what had happened. Deep down, which was deeper than even Jimmy might have allowed, Earle knew that the cop was right, and so every year, on the anniversary of Sally Cleaver's death, Earle would leave a bouquet of flowers in the garbage-strewn, weed-caked lot of the Blue Moon, and apologize to the shade of the dead girl.

But Jimmy had never ascribed even partial blame to Earle for what had occurred, even though it had led to the closure of the Blue Moon. He made sure that Earle had the best legal representation close by when there was talk of charging him as an accessory to the crime. They had only discussed Earle's feelings about those events on one occasion, and that was on the day that Jimmy had told Earle he was not going to reopen the bar. Earle had assumed that this meant he would be looking for employment elsewhere, and that Jimmy was washing his hands of him, just like a lot of people said he should, because around town Earle's name wasn't worth the spittle it would take to say it. Earle had begun to apologize again for allowing Sally Cleaver to die, and as he did so, he found that his voice was breaking. He kept trying to form coherent sentences, but they wouldn't come. Jimmy had sat him down and listened as Earle described going outside and seeing Sally Cleaver's ruined face, and how he had knelt beside her as her lips moved and she spoke the last words that anyone would ever hear her speak.

"I'm sorry," she whispered, as Earle, not knowing what else to do, laid one of his huge hands on her forehead and gently brushed her bloodstained hair from her eyes. At night, Earle told Jimmy, he saw Sally Cleaver's face, and his hand would reach out automatically to brush her hair from her eyes. Every night, Earle said. I see her every night, just before I fall asleep. And Jimmy had told him that it was a crying shame, and all he could do to make up for it was ensure that it never happened to another woman, either on his beat or off it, not if he could do anything to prevent it. The next day, Earle had started working at the Sailmaker, even though there was already barely enough customers for old Vern Sutcliffe, the regular bartender. When Vern died a year later, Earle became the sole bartender at the Sailmaker, and thus it had remained ever since.

Now, after ruminating for hours on how he might broach the subject, Earle had come to a conclusion. He placed the last bottles of beer in the cooler, collapsed the box, then made his way tentatively to where Jimmy was sitting. He laid his fists on the bar and said: "Anything wrong, Mr. Jewel?"

Jimmy emerged from his reverie, looking slightly shocked.

"What did you say?"

"I said, 'Anything wrong, Mr. Jewel?'"

Jimmy smiled. In all the years that he had known him, Earle had probably asked no more than two or three questions of a remotely personal nature. Now here he was, his face filled with concern, and only minutes after indicating that he'd lay down his life for his employer. If things went any further, they'd be booking a church for the wedding and moving to Ogunquit, or Hallowell, or somewhere else with too many rainbow flags hanging from the windows.

"Thank you for asking, Earle. Everything is fine. I'm just mulling over how to handle a certain matter. When I've figured it out though, I may ask for your help."

Earle looked relieved. He'd already come as close as he had ever done to expressing his affection for Mr. Jewel, and he wasn't sure that he could cope with any further intimacy. He lumbered away to add the crushed box to the recycling pile, leaving Jimmy alone. Jimmy took a series of photographs from beneath the newspaper, and examined once again the images of the jeweled seals. The gems alone were worth a fortune, but combined with the artifacts themselves, well,

Jimmy had no concept of how much the right person might pay for such an item.

Now Jimmy knew that Tobias and his comrades were not smuggling drugs; they were smuggling antiquities. Jimmy wondered what else in a similar vein they might have in their possession. He had spent a day trying to work out the angles, figuring out a way that he could profit from what he had learned, and at the same time expand his knowledge. His only regret was that Rojas was involved. Rojas had let slip that he had begun trying to sell some of the gems and gold, promising Jimmy a cut of 20 percent as a "finder's fee," as though Jimmy were just some rube to be palmed off with a chump's cut. Rojas couldn't see the big picture. The trouble was, neither could Jimmy, but unlike him, Rojas wasn't prepared to wait until it was revealed.

Jimmy twisted the saucer with his finger, causing the cold coffee in the cup to ripple slightly. He wasn't hurting for money, but he could always do with more. The downturn in the economy, and the hiatus in the development of the waterfront, meant that he had cash tied up in buildings that were depreciating with every passing day. The market would bounce back—it always did—but Jimmy wasn't getting any younger. He didn't want it to bounce back just in time to provide him with a bigger headstone.

He shivered. There was an unseasonably cool breeze coming in off the water, and Jimmy was highly susceptible to cold. Even in the height of summer he wore a jacket. He had always been that way, ever since he was a little kid. There just wasn't enough meat on his bones to keep him warm.

"Hey, Earle!" he called. "Close the goddamn door."

There was no reply. Jimmy swore. He walked through the office and past the storeroom to where a door opened on to the bar's small parking lot. He stepped outside. There was no sign of Earle. Jimmy called his name again, suddenly uneasy.

His foot slipped as he stepped into the lot. He looked down and saw the dark, spreading stain. To his left was Earle's truck. The blood was coming from beneath it. Jimmy squatted so that he could see under the truck, and looked into Earle's dead eyes. The big man was lying on his belly on the far side of the vehicle between the passenger door and the garbage cans by the wall, his mouth open, his face frozen in a final grimace of pain.

Jimmy stood, and felt the gun nudge his skull, like death's first tentative touch.

"Inside," said a voice. Jimmy couldn't hide his surprise at the sound of it, but he did as he was told. He glanced at the truck as he rose, and caught a glimpse of a masked figure reflected in the window. Then the blows rained down on him for having the temerity to look. Kicks followed, driving him along the hallway and into the storeroom. The assault ceased as Jimmy crawled over to the liquor shelves, looking for some kind of purchase so he could raise himself. He could taste blood in his mouth, and he had trouble seeing out of his left eye. He tried to speak, but the words came out as hoarse whispers. Still, it was clear that he was begging: for time to recover, for the blows to stop.

For more life.

One of the kicks had broken a rib, and he could feel it grinding as he moved. He slumped against the shelves, drawing ragged breaths. He raised his right hand in a placatory gesture.

"You killed a man for a hundred and fifty dollars and change," said Jimmy. "You hear me?"

"No, I killed him for much more than that."

And Jimmy knew for sure that this wasn't about the money in the safe. It was about Rojas, and the seal, and Jimmy Jewel understood that he was about to die as the black mouth of the suppressor gaped like the void into which Jimmy would soon pass.

He gave away everything after the first shot, but his interrogator had fired two more anyway, just to be sure that he wasn't holding anything back.

"No more," said Jimmy, "no more," his wounds bleeding onto the floor, and it was both a plea and an admission, a rejection of further pain and an acceptance that all was about to come to an end.

His interrogator nodded.

"Oh my God," whispered Jimmy, "I am heartily sorry—"

The final bullet came. He did not hear it, but only felt the mercy of it.

IT WOULD BE DAYS before his body, and that of Earle, were found. Summer rains came that night and washed away Earle's blood, sending it flowing across the sloped surface of the lot, through the wooden pilings that supported the old pier, and into the sea, salt to salt. Earle's truck was left at the Maine Mall, and when it was still there after two days mall security took an interest, and subsequently the police arrived, for by then it was clear that Jimmy Jewel had fallen off the radar. Calls were going unanswered, and beer could not be delivered to the Sailmaker, and the drunks who worshipped there missed its cloisters.

Jimmy was discovered in the storeroom. He had been shot through both feet, and one knee, by which point he had presumably told all that he knew, and therefore the fourth shot had taken him through the heart. Earle lay at Jimmy's ruined feet, like a faithful hound dispatched to keep its master company in the afterlife. It was only later that someone noticed the correspondence of dates: Earle and Jimmy had died on June 2, ten years to the day since Sally Cleaver had breathed her last at the back of the Blue Moon.

And old men shrugged, and said that they were not surprised.

XVII

Karen Emory woke to find Joel gone from their bed. She listened for a time, but could hear no sound. Beside her, the clock on the night table read 4:03 A.M.

She had been dreaming, and now, as she lay awake, trying to discern some indication of his presence in the house, she felt a kind of gratitude that she was no longer sleeping. It was foolish, of course. In less than three hours she would have to get up and get dressed for work. She had decided that she would keep working for Mr. Patchett for the moment, and had told Joel so when she came home and found him returned from his trip, a dressing on his face that he wouldn't explain.

He hadn't objected, which had surprised her, but maybe her arguments had made sense to him, or so she thought at first: that work was hard to come by; that she couldn't just sit around at home or she'd go crazy; that she'd give Mr. Patchett no further cause to go looking into her affairs, or Joel's.

She needed to sleep. Soon, her legs and feet would be aching from hours of service, but then her feet always hurt. Even with the best shoes in the world, which she couldn't have afforded anyway, not on her pay, she still would have experienced the ache in her heels and the balls of her feet that came from standing for eight hours a day.

Mr. Patchett was a better boss than most, though, better, in fact, than any boss she'd ever had before, which was one of the reasons that she wanted to remain at the Downs Diner. She'd worked for enough sleazebags in her time to recognize a good soul when she encountered one, and she was grateful for the hours that he gave her. The diner could easily get by with one less waitress, and as one of the most recent employees she would be among the first to be shown the door, but he continued to put regular work her way. He was looking out for her, the way he looked out for all the people who worked for him, and at a time when businesses were letting staff go left and right, there was something to be said for a man who was prepared to shuck a little profit in order to let people live.

But Mr. Patchett's concern for her was a problem, especially since the private detective had started "nosing around," as Joel put it. She'd have to be careful what she said to Mr. Patchett, just as she'd tried to be careful when the detective came to the house, even though she'd ended up saying more than she should have.

It was Joel who had first spotted the detective. Joel had a kind of sixth sense about these things. For a man, he was very perceptive. He could tell when she was sad, or when there was something preying on her mind, just by looking at her, and she had never encountered a man like that before. Maybe she'd just been unlucky with her choices before Joel came along, and most men were as attuned to the women they were with, but she doubted it. Joel was unusual in that way, and in others.

And yet Karen hadn't wanted to tell Joel about the detective's visit. She couldn't have said why, exactly, not at first, except for a vague sense that Joel wasn't being straight with her about parts of his life, and because of her own fears for his safety, which was why she'd let some stuff slip to the detective when he came by. She had watched how the deaths of Joel's friends had affected him: he was frightened, even though he didn't want to show it. Then he had come home yesterday evening with the Band-Aid on his face and the wounds on his hands and wouldn't speak of how he'd hurt himself. Instead, he'd retired to the basement, moving stuff in boxes down there from the truck, wincing sometimes when a box touched his injuries.

And when he eventually came to bed . . .

Well, that hadn't been so good.

She sighed, and stretched. The clock had moved up two digits. There was still no sound, no flushing of the toilet or closing of the refrigerator door. She wondered what Joel was doing, but she was afraid to go looking for him after what had happened earlier. Karen wondered if he had been hiding that aspect of himself all along, and if she had been mistaken in her assessment of him. No, not mistaken. Misled. Taken for a fool. Manipulated, and abused, by a man she hardly knew.

She had been looking to get away from the Patchett dorms. Oh, she'd been grateful for the room, and the company of the other women, but such places were always meant to be temporary stops, she felt, even though one of the waitresses, Eileen, had been living there for fifteen years now. That wasn't going to happen to Karen, living like a spinster according to Mr. Patchett's old-fashioned rules about not keeping male company in the dorm house. First, it had seemed like Damien might have provided an escape, but he had no interest in her. She thought that he might even have been gay, but Eileen assured her that he was not. He'd had a fling with the previous hostess in between deployments, and it had seemed like they might get together permanently, but she hadn't wanted to become an army wife or, worse, an army widow, and it had fizzled out. Karen thought that Mr. Patchett might have liked it if she and Damien had become an item, and when Damien returned home permanently his father had done everything to steer the two of them together, inviting Karen to have dinner with them, or sending her off with Damien to buy produce and talk to suppliers. But by then she'd already begun seeing Joel,

whom she'd met through Damien. When she had eventually allowed
Joel to pick her up from work for the first time, she'd seen the disap-
pointment in Mr. Patchett's face. He hadn't said anything, but it was
there, and he'd never been quite as easy with her after that. When his
son died, the possibility struck her that he might believe she was in
some way to blame for what happened, that if Damien had someone
to care for, and who cared for him, then he wouldn't have taken his
own life. Maybe that was what lay behind the hiring of the detective:
Mr. Patchett was angry with her for dating Joel, but he was taking it
out on Joel, not her.

Joel made good money driving his truck, more money than she
thought an independent truck driver could, or should, make. Most of
his work involved him moving back and forth across the border with
Canada. She'd tried to find out about it from him, and he'd told her
that he hauled whatever needed to be hauled, but the way he said it
left her under no illusions that this was a discussion he neither wel-
comed nor wanted to continue, and she'd dropped the subject. Still,
she wondered . . .

But she loved Joel. She had decided that within a couple of weeks
of meeting him. She just knew. He was strong, he was good to her,
and he was older than she, so he understood more about the world,
which made her feel secure. He had a place of his own, and when he
asked her to move in with him he'd barely had time to finish the sentence before she'd said yes. It was a house, too, not some apartment
where they'd be bumping into the walls and getting on each other's
nerves. There was plenty of space: two bedrooms upstairs, and a den;
a big living area and a nice kitchen; and a basement where he kept
his tools. He was clean, too, cleaner than most of the men that she'd
known before. Oh, the bathroom had needed a good scrub, and the
kitchen too, but they weren't filthy, just untidy. She'd been happy to
do it. She was proud of their house. That was how she thought of it:
"their" house. Not just his, not anymore. Slowly, she was imposing

elements of her own personality upon it, and he seemed content to let her do so. There were flowers in vases, and more books than there had been before. She'd even picked up some pictures for the walls. When she'd asked him if he liked them, he'd said, "Sure," and made an effort to examine each one, as though he were appraising them for a sale at some later date. She knew that he was just doing it to please her, though. He was a man largely unconcerned with trimmings, and she doubted if he would even have noticed the paintings if she hadn't pointed them out to him, but she appreciated the fact that he'd made the effort to seem interested.

Was he a good man? She didn't know. She'd thought so at the start, but he'd changed so much in recent weeks. Then again, she supposed that all men changed, once they got what they wanted. They stopped being quite as caring as before, as solicitous. It was as if they put up a front to attract women, and then slowly shed it once that was achieved. Some dispensed with it more quickly than others, and Lord knows she'd seen men switch from lambs to wolves with the flip of a coin or with one last drink for the road, but his change had appeared more gradual, and was somehow more disturbing because of that. At first, he'd just been distracted. He didn't talk as much to her, and he sometimes snapped at her when she persisted in trying to have a conversation. She thought that it might have been something to do with his injuries. Sometimes, his hand hurt. He'd lost a fistful of muscle from his leg, and his hearing wasn't so good in his left ear. He'd been lucky. The other guys hit by the IED hadn't made it. He rarely talked about what had happened, but she knew enough. He was away a lot, driving his truck, and then there were his army buddies, the ones who used to come to the house but didn't anymore. They never said much to her, and one of them, Bacci, gave her the creeps, the way his eyes wandered over her body, lingering on her breasts, her crotch. When they arrived, Joel would close the living room door, and she would hear the steady buzz of their soft tones through the walls, like insects trapped in the cavities.

"Joel?"

There was no reply. She wanted to go and find him, but she was frightened. She was frightened because he had hit her again. It had come as she tried to question him about his wounds, after she opened the bathroom door and saw him applying salve to the burns on his hands, and the terrible one on his face. He had answered her question with one of his own.

"Why didn't you tell me about your visitor?" he said, and it took her a moment to realize that he was referring to Parker, the detective. After all, how could he have known? She was still trying to come up with a suitable reply when his right hand had shot out and caught her. Not hard, and he'd seemed almost as shocked by what he'd done as she was, but it had been a strike nonetheless, catching her on the left cheek and causing her to stumble backward against the wall. It was different from the first time: that had been an accident. She was sure of it. This one had power and venom behind it. He'd apologized as soon as it happened, but she was already running to the bedroom, and it was a couple of minutes before he followed her. He kept trying to talk to her, but she wouldn't listen. She *couldn't* listen, she was crying so hard. Eventually, he just held her, and she felt him fall asleep against her, and in time she fell asleep too, because it was an escape from thinking about what he had just done. He woke her during the night to say sorry again, and his lips had brushed hers, his hands searching her body, and they had made up.

But, no, they hadn't, not really. She had done it for him, not for herself. She hadn't wanted him to feel bad, and she hadn't wanted him to . . .

hurt her

Yes, that was it. That was the horror of it.

Now, as she lay in the darkness, she realized that her view of him had changed as much as he had. She'd wanted him to be a good man, or at least a better man than some of those she'd dated before him, but deep down she thought now that he wasn't, not really, not if he could hit her like that, not if he was changing so dramatically. Sex was no longer gentle. He'd actually hurt her some when he'd woken her earlier, and when she'd asked him to be more tender with her he'd simply finished and turned away from her, leaving her staring at his bare back.

"I'm talking to you," she'd said, and had tugged at his shoulder, trying to get him to look at her. She'd felt him tense up, and then he had turned, and the expression on his face, even in the darkness, had caused her to let her hand fall, and she had moved as far away from him as she could in their bed. For a moment, she had been certain that he was going to hit her again, but he had not.

"Leave me alone," he had said, and there was something in his eyes that might almost have been fear, and she'd had the sense that he might have been talking both to her and to someone else, an unseen entity of whom only he was aware. Then she had dozed, and the dream had come. She couldn't call it a nightmare, not really, although it made her uneasy. In it, she was trapped in a small space, almost like a coffin, but it was simultaneously larger and smaller than that, which made no sense to her. She was struggling for breath, and her mouth and nostrils were filling with dust.

But worst of all, she wasn't alone. There was a presence in there with her, and it was whispering. She couldn't understand what it was saying, and she wasn't even sure that the words were meant for her anyway, but it never stopped speaking.

A noise came from downstairs, an unfamiliar sound that did not belong in the darkness of their home. It was a giggle, quickly stifled. There was something childlike about it, yet also unpleasant. It was a spontaneous eruption of mirth at a word or act that was more shocking than funny. It was laughter at a thing that should not be laughed at.

Carefully, she pushed back the blankets and put her feet to the floor. The boards did not creak. Joel had done much of the work on the house himself, and was proud of its solidity. She padded across the carpet and opened the door wider. Now she heard whispering, but it was his voice, not the voice of the others, the ones in her dream. *Others.* She had not recognized that before. It was not one, but more than one. There were many voices, all speaking in the same tongue, but using different words.

She moved to the top of the stairs, then knelt down and peered through the banisters. Joel was sitting cross-legged on the floor by the cellar door, his hands in his lap, tugging at his fingers. He reminded her of a small boy, and she almost smiled at the sight of him.

Almost.

He was carrying on a conversation with someone on the other side of the basement door. He always kept that door locked. It didn't concern her unduly, not at first. She'd gone down there with him to help him bring up some paint during the first week after she'd moved in, and it had seemed to her just the usual clutter of boxes, junk, and old machinery. Since then, she had rarely gone down there, and always with Joel. He hadn't forbidden her from entering the basement. He was smarter than that and, anyway, she had no cause to do so. In addition, she had never liked dark spaces, which was probably why her dream was troubling her so much.

She held her breath as she peered down, straining to hear what he was saying. He was whispering, but she could hear no response to his words. Instead, he would speak for a moment, then listen before responding. Sometimes, he would nod his head silently, as though following the course of an argument that only he could hear.

He giggled again, and as he did so he put his hands to his mouth, smothering the sound. He glanced up instinctively as he did so, but she was hidden in the shadows.

"That's bad," he said. "You're naughty."

Then he seemed to listen once more. "I've tried," he said. "I can't do it. I don't know how."

He was silent again. His face grew serious. She heard him swallow hard, and thought that she could sense his fear, even from her perch above him.

"No," he said, determinedly. "No, I won't do that." He shook his head. "No, please. I won't. You can't ask me to do that. You can't."

He put his hands to his ears, trying to block out the voice that only he could hear. He stood up, keeping his hands in place.

"Leave me alone," he said, his voice rising. "Stop it. Stop whispering. You have to stop whispering."

He banged against the wall as he began to climb the stairs.

"Stop it," he said, and she could hear in his voice that he had begun to cry. "Stop, stop, *stop!*"

She slipped back into the bedroom, and pulled the sheets around her seconds before he opened the door and stepped inside. He did it so noisily that she couldn't help but react, but she did her best to sound sleepy and surprised.

"Honey," she said, lifting her head from the pillow. "Are you okay?"

He didn't answer her.

"Joel?" she said. "What's the matter?"

She saw him move toward her, and she was frightened. He sat down on the edge of the bed, and touched his hand to her hair.

"I'm sorry I hit you," he said. "But I'd never hurt you bad. Not really." She felt her stomach contract so hard that she was sure she'd have to run to the bathroom to avoid soiling herself. It was those last two words. *Not really:* as if it was somehow okay to hurt someone a little now and again, but only when it was deserved, only when a nosy little bitch asked questions that she shouldn't, or entertained snoops in the kitchen. Only then. And the punishment would fit the crime, and later she could spread herself for him and they'd make up, and it would be all right because he loved her, and that was what people who loved each other did.

"When I hit you," he continued, "that wasn't me. It was something else. It was like I was a puppet, and someone pulled my string. I don't want to hurt you. I love you."

"I know," she replied, trying to keep the tremor from her voice, and only partly succeeding. "Honey, what's wrong?"

He leaned into her, and she felt his tears as he put his cheek against hers. She wrapped her arms around him.

"I had a bad dream," he said, and she heard the child in him. Even as she did so, she looked down and saw him staring up at her, and for an instant his eyes were cold and suspicious and even, she thought, amused, as though they were both playing a game here, but only he knew the rules. Then it was gone, his eyes closing as he nuzzled against her breasts. She held him tightly even as she felt the urge to cast him aside, to run from that house and never, ever return.

*S*tress damages the mind: that was what they didn't understand, the people back home, the ones who hadn't been there. Even the army didn't understand that, not until it was too late. Take a little R & R, they said. Hang out with the family. Make love to your girlfriend. Occupy yourself. Get a job, find a routine, embrace normality.

But he couldn't have done that, even if his legs didn't end halfway down his thighs, because stress is like a poison, a toxin working its way through the system, except that it affects only one vital organ: the brain. He remembered how he'd been in an automobile accident out on Route 1 when he was thirteen, shortly before his dad died. It hadn't been a bad smash: a truck had run a red light, and had hit the passenger side of their car. He'd been in the back, on the driver's side. It was pure dumb luck: there was an automobile dealership on that part of the road, and it always had some cool old cars lined up outside if the weather was good. He liked looking at them, imagining himself behind the wheel of the best of them. At any other time, he'd have been on the passenger side so that he could talk to his dad, and who knows what might have happened then. Instead, they'd both been shaken up pretty badly, and he'd been cut some by the glass. Afterward, when the tow truck had gone and the Scarborough cops had given them a ride home, he'd gone pale and started shaking before puking up his breakfast.

That was what stress did. It made you ill, physically and mentally. And if you kept encountering stressful situations day after day, broken up by periods of tedium, of hanging around playing games, or eating, or catching some rack, or writing the compulsory monthly card home to let your nearest and dearest know that you weren't dead yet, with no end in sight because your deployment kept being extended, then your neurons became so polluted that they couldn't recover, and your brain began to rewire itself, altering its modes of operation. The nerve cell extensions in the hippocampus, which deals with learning and long-term memory, started to rot. The response capacity of the amygdala, which governs social behavior and emotional memory, changed. The medial prefrontal cortex, which is involved in establishing feelings of fear and remorse, and enables us to interpret what is real and unreal, altered. Similar frazzling of the wiring could be found in schizophrenics, sociopaths, drug addicts, and long-term prisoners. You became like them, like the dregs, and it wasn't your fault, because you hadn't done anything wrong. You'd simply done your duty.

During the Civil War, they called it "irritable heart." For the soldiers of the Great War, it was "shell shock," and in World War Two it was "battle fatigue," or "war neurosis." Then it became "post-Vietnam syndrome," and now it was PTSD. He sometimes wondered if the Romans had a word for it, and the Greeks. He had read the Iliad upon his return, part of his attempt to understand war through its literature, and believed that he saw, in the grief of Achilles for his friend Patroclus, and in the rage that followed, something of his own grief for the comrades that he had lost, Damien most of all.

They left you this way. Your emotions are no longer under control. You are no longer under your own control. You become depressed, paranoid, removed from those who care about you. You believe that you are still at war. You fight your bedclothes at night. You become estranged from your loved ones, and they leave you.

And maybe, just maybe, you start believing that you are haunted, that demons speak to you from boxes, and when you can't satisfy them, when you can't do what they want you to do, they turn you against yourself, and they punish you for your failings.

And maybe, just maybe, that moment of obliteration comes as a relief.

XVIII

Herod arrived in Portland by train at 11:30 A.M., carrying only a black garment bag, the leather old but undamaged, a testament to the quality of its manufacture. He was not averse to flying, and rarely felt the necessity to carry anything that might make a bag search at an airport awkward, if not actively unwelcome, but where possible he preferred to travel by train. It reminded him of a more civilized era, when the pace of life was slower and people had more time for small courtesies. In addition, his debilitated condition meant that he found driving for long distances to be uncomfortable and a chore, as well as potentially hazardous, for the medication that he took to control his pain often led to drowsiness. Unfortunately, this was not a particular problem at present: he had reduced the dosage to keep his head clear, and consequently he was suffering. On a train, he could get up and prowl the carriage, or stand in the café car sipping a drink, anything to distract himself from the torments of the body. He had taken a seat in a quiet car at Penn Station, a contented smile on his face as the train emerged from belowground into hazy sunshine. The blue surgical mask hid his mouth, and attracted only one or two glances from those who passed him.

He became aware of the Captain's presence just as the Manhattan skyline vanished from view. The Captain was sitting in the seat directly across the aisle from Herod, visible only in the window glass, and then only partially: he was a smear, a blur, a moving figure captured by a camera lens when all around him was otherwise still. Herod found it easier to see him when he did not look directly at him.

The Captain was dressed as a clown. Say what you wanted about the Captain, Herod thought, but he had a fondness for the old reliables. The Captain wore a jacket of white and red stripes, and a small bowler hat from beneath which sections of a bedraggled red wig sprouted. There were cobwebs in the artificial hairs, and Herod thought that he could make out the shapes of spiders moving through them. The Captain's pants were baggy and patched. His forearms were extended along the armrests of his seat, and his hands were mostly hidden by stained white gloves, except at the fingertips where sharp, blackened nails had erupted through the material. The forefinger of his right hand tapped rhythmically, slowly raising itself and then falling, like a mechanical device winding up and then releasing, over and over. The Captain's face was thick with white pancake makeup. The mouth was large and red, and painted as a frown. There were blots of rouge on each cheek, but the eye sockets were empty and black. The Captain stared fixedly ahead, and only his finger moved.

The car was full, but the Captain's seat, while apparently unoccupied, remained empty, as did the seat next to Herod's, as though something of the Captain's aura had extended across the aisle. The woman seated by the window next to the Captain was old, and Herod watched her discomfort grow as the journey progressed. She shifted in her seat. She tried to put her arm on the shared armrest, but she would only allow it to remain in place for a second or two before she withdrew it and rubbed her skin in distress. Sometimes her nose wrinkled, her face crinkling in disgust. She began to brush at her hair and face, and when Herod looked at her reflection he could see that some of the Captain's spiders had begun to colonize her gray strands. Eventually, she picked up her coat and bag and left for another car.

New passengers passed through the car after each regional station stop, and although a number paused at the two empty seats, some atavistic instinct caused them to move on.

And all the time the Captain sat, and his finger went *tap-tap-tap* . . .

HEROD ALIGHTED AT PORTLAND'S new transport terminal. He could still recall the old Union Station, where the service from Boston had once terminated. He had last taken it—when? 1964, he thought. Yes, certainly it was '64. He could almost picture the big silver car with its interlinked blue B and white M. The fact that there was now a train, once again, between Boston and Maine, even if it meant switching stations in Boston, pleased him.

He took a cab to the airport in order to pick up a rental car. Like his train ticket, the reservation was not in his own name. Instead, he was traveling under the name Uccello. Herod always used the name of a Renaissance artist when he was obliged to show identification. He had drivers' licenses and passports in the name of Dürer, Brueghel, and Bellini, but he had a special fondness for Uccello, one of the first artists to use perspective in his paintings. Herod liked to think that he, too, had an awareness of perspective.

The Captain was no longer with him. The Captain was . . . *elsewhere*. Herod drove into Portland, and found the bar owned by the man named Jimmy Jewel. He parked behind the building opposite, and slipped his gun into the pocket of his overcoat before making his way to the other side of the wharf. The bar appeared to be closed, and he could see no signs of life inside. As he stared through the glass, the Captain returned, a bright reflected figure. He stood for a moment, that red frown fixed on his face, then turned and walked to the back of the bar. Herod followed, the Captain's progress visible in the panes of the windows, like the frames of a film being projected too slowly. At the rear door, Herod knelt and examined the step. He touched his fingers to the spots of blood, then stared at the door for a moment before nodding to himself and turning away.

He was back at the car, and about to start the engine, when he felt a coldness at his shoulder. He looked to the right and saw the Captain's image in the passenger window, the Captain's left hand holding him in place. The Captain's attention was fixed upon the bar. There was a man at the main door, his actions mirroring Herod's own earlier attempts to see inside. He was about five-ten in height, his hair graying at the temples. Herod watched him curiously. There was a sense of threat to the new arrival: it was in the way that he held himself, a kind of grim self-possession. But there was an "otherness" to him too, and Herod, aided by the Captain, recognized one like himself, a man who spanned two worlds. He wondered what it was that had opened the fissure, that had enabled this one to see as Herod saw. Pain? Yes, inevitably so, but not merely physical, not where this man was concerned. Herod picked up grief, and rage, and guilt, the Captain acting like a transmitter, pulses of emotion coursing through him.

As if responding to Herod's interest, the man turned. He stared at Herod. He frowned. The grip tightened on Herod's arm and Herod understood the Captain's desire to leave. He started the engine and pulled away, passing two other men as he turned right: a black man, exquisitely attired, and a smaller white man who appeared to have dressed in a hurry from his laundry basket. He saw them watching him in his rearview mirror, and then they were gone, and so too was the Captain.

"You see that guy in the car?" I asked Louis.

"Yeah, the one with the mask. Didn't get a good look at him, but I'd guess that he's ailing for something."

"Was he alone?"

"Alone?"

"Yes, was there someone else in the passenger seat beside him?"

Louis appeared puzzled. "No, it was just him. Why?"

"Nothing, it must have been the sunlight on his window. No sign of Jimmy Jewel. I'll try again later. Let's go . . ."

HEROD DROVE TO WALDOBORO, because that was where his contact lived, the old woman who ran the antiques store. He ordered coffee and a sandwich in a diner, and made a call from a pay phone while he waited for his food to arrive. Only a handful of other customers were present, none of them nearby, so he had no fear of being overheard.

"Where do we stand?" he said, when the call was answered.

"He lives above a warehouse in Lewiston. An old bakery."

Herod listened as the location was described to him in detail.

"Does he keep company with his kind?" he asked.

"Some."

"And the items?"

"It appears that some interested parties have already emerged, but they remain in his possession."

Herod grimaced. "How did the other parties come to hear of them?"

"He is a careless man. Word has spread."

"I am on my way. Make contact with him. Tell him I'd like to talk."

"I'll tell Mr. Rojas that I may have a buyer, and that he should take no further action until we meet. As you know, he is not unaware of the value of the objects. It could be an expensive business."

"I'm sure that I can convince the seller to be reasonable, especially since I have no interest in what he is selling, merely in the source."

"Nevertheless, he is not a reasonable man."

"Really?" said Herod. "How unfortunate."

"Neither is he unintelligent."

"Intelligent *and* unreasonable. One would have assumed such qualities were mutually contradictory."

"I have a photograph of him, if that might help. I printed it from the surveillance camera in my store."

Herod described his car, and where it was parked. He told the woman that it was unlocked, and she should leave whatever material she had under the passenger seat. It was better, he felt, if they did not meet. The woman did her best not to sound disappointed at the news.

He hung up. His food had arrived. He ate it slowly, and in a corner far from the other customers. He knew that his appearance had a way of putting people off their food, but equally he found eating under such scrutiny to be unpleasant. Eating was hard enough for him as it was: his appetite was minimal at best, but he had to consume to keep up his strength. That was more important now than ever before. As he ate, he thought about the man at the door of the bar, and the Captain's reaction to his presence.

There was a mirror on the wall opposite his booth. It reflected the road, where a little girl in a torn blue dress, her back to the diner, held a red balloon and watched the cars and trucks going by. A big Mack rig was heading her way, but she did not move, and the driver, high in his cab, did not appear to see her. Herod turned from the mirror as the truck hit the girl, driving straight over her. Herod almost cried out, and when the truck had passed, the girl was gone. There was no sign that she had ever been there.

Slowly, Herod looked back at the mirror, and the girl was where she had always been, except now she was facing the diner, and Herod. She seemed to smile at him, even as the dark hollows of her eyes mocked the light. Gradually, she faded from sight and, in the reflected world, her balloon floated up toward gray-black clouds streaked with purple and red, like wounds torn in the heavens. Then the sky cleared, and the mirror was merely a reflection of this dull world, not a window into another.

When Herod had eaten as much as he was able, he lingered over his coffee. After all, he had plenty of time. It would be some time before darkness fell, and Herod worked best in the dark. Then he would pay a visit to Mr. Rojas. Herod had no intention of waiting until the next day to begin negotiations.

In fact, Herod had no intention of negotiating at all.

Far away, in an apartment on the Rue du Seine in Paris, just above the sales rooms of the esteemed ancient art dealers Rochman et Fils, a deal was about to be concluded. Emmanuel Rochman, the latest in a long line of Rochmans to make a very comfortable living from the sale of the rarest of antiquities, waited for the Iranian businessman seated across from him to cease prevaricating and announce the decision that they both knew he had already reached. After all, this face-to-face meeting in the presence of the ancient artifacts was but the final step in a lengthy negotiation that had begun many weeks before, and items as rare and beautiful as those currently before him were never likely to be offered to him again: two delicate ivories from the tombs of the Assyrian queens at Nimrud, and a pair of exquisite lapis lazuli cylindrical seals, 5,500 years old and, therefore, the oldest such items that Rochman had ever been able to offer for sale.

The Iranian sighed and shuffled on his seat. Rochman liked dealing with Iranians. The Iranians had been particularly keen pursuers of the stolen items from the Iraq Museum that had so far made it on to the market, even if they, like the Jordanians, had ultimately been forced to relinquish most of the loot that had come their way. While many thousands of items remained missing, the most valuable of them had largely been recovered. Opportunities to acquire Iraqi treasures were growing increasingly rare, and the amount that collectors were willing to pay had increased accordingly. Although Rochman had not encountered this particular buyer before, he came strongly recommended by two former clients who had spent a great deal of money with Monsieur Rochman without troubling themselves unduly about matters of provenance and paperwork.

"Will there be more?" asked the Iranian. He called himself Mr. Abbas, "the Lion," which was clearly a pseudonym, but his good-will deposit of $2 million had cleared without a hitch, and those who vouched for him had assured Rochman that $2 million barely represented a day's earnings for Mr. Abbas. Nevertheless, Rochman was starting to grow weary of this particular lion hunt. Come, he thought, I know you're going to buy them. Just say yes, and we can be done.

"Not like these," said Rochman, then reconsidered. Who knew how much extra revenue a little patience might generate? "The ivories, or others even half as beautiful as them, are unlikely ever to resurface. If you decline, they will disappear. The seals—" He tipped his right hand back and forth in the universal gesture of possibility, erring on the side of the negative. "But if you are satisfied with this particular purchase, artifacts of a similar quality may be made available to you."

"And provenance?"

"The House of Rochman stands behind everything that it sells," said Rochman. "Naturally, were any legal issues to materialize, the buyer would be the first to know, but I am confident that no such difficulties will arise in this particular instance."

It was a standard line on the rare occasions when Rochman truly breached the boundaries of legality. Oh, there were often gray areas when it came to ancient treasures, but this was not one of them. Both he and Abbas knew the source of the ivories and the seals. It did not need to be spoken aloud, and no receipts would accompany this particular sale.

Abbas nodded in apparent contentment. "Well, I am satisfied," he said. "Let us proceed."

He reached into his pocket and removed a gold pen, pressing the top to make the nib appear.

"You won't need a pen, Monsieur Abbas," Rochman began to say, which is when the door burst open, and armed police appeared, and Mr. Abbas smiled at him and said, "The name is Al-Daini, Monsieur Rochman. My colleagues and I have some questions for you . . ."

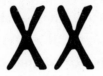

Angel and Louis had stayed with me at my house, and I suspected that neither of them had slept simultaneously that night, conscious that a move might be made against us at any time. The next morning, I spent an hour with them going back over everything that I knew about Joel Tobias. He was the principal link, and it was a useful exercise. The fact that he had served in the military helped, since it meant the existence of an official paper trail for a big chunk of his life. It all seemed pretty straightforward. He had signed up in 1990, straight out of high school in Bangor, and had trained as a truck driver. He'd been invalided out early in 2007 after an IED exploded while he was escorting medical supplies to the Green Zone in Baghdad, removing part of his left calf and two fingers on his left hand. When he returned to Maine later that year, he applied for a Maine commercial driver's license after passing the written exam, eye exam, and road exam. He had also received a HazMat endorsement after putting his fingerprints on record and passing the requisite Transportation Safety Administration background check. So far, his license was clean.

I found an obituary notice for his mother in the *Bangor Daily News* of July 19, 1998, and another for his father, who had served in Vietnam, in April 2007. It mentioned that his son, Joel, was also serving in the military, and was recuperating after being injured in the line of duty. There was even a picture of Tobias at the graveside. He was in full dress uniform, and was supporting himself on crutches. There were no siblings. Joel Tobias was an only child.

I felt an unwelcome pang, the guilt of someone who had not made sacrifices for his country now faced with someone who had. It seemed, on the surface, that Tobias had served honorably, and had suffered for it. I had never even considered the military as an option when I left school, but I respected those who had. I wondered what had made Tobias sign up. Was it family history, a belief that he should follow in his father's footsteps? Then again, his father had not been a career soldier. The obit made it clear that he had been drafted. A lot of guys had come back from Vietnam with a burning desire to ensure that their kids didn't have to go through what they had. I supposed that, since Tobias had signed up willingly, he was either rebelling against his old man, or seeking his approval.

I then opened up the file on Bobby Jandreau, who had gone to the same high school in Bangor as Tobias, although more than a decade separated them. During Jandreau's final tour in Iraq, he'd been seriously injured in a gun battle in Gazaliya. The first bullet had hit him in the upper thigh, and while he was lying in the dirt the Shia militiamen who had attacked his convoy continued to fire shots at his legs in an effort to draw his comrades into a rescue and inflict further injuries on the squad. Jandreau had eventually been pulled to safety, but his legs were ruined. Amputation had been judged the only option.

I knew all this because his name had been mentioned in a newspaper article on wounded Maine veterans who were trying to cope with life outside the military. Damien Patchett was named as the fellow soldier who had saved Jandreau's life, but if Damien had been asked to comment, he had declined. In the course of the article, Jandreau admitted that he was struggling. He spoke of an addiction to prescription medication, which he was overcoming with the help of his girlfriend. As the reporter noted: "Jandreau stares out of the window of his Bangor home, his hands clutching the arms of his wheelchair. 'I never really thought I'd end up like this,' he says. 'Like most guys, I knew that there was a chance that it could happen, but I always believed that it would be someone else who'd get hurt, not me. I'm trying to find some positive aspect to it, but there isn't one, not that I can see. It just sucks.' His girlfriend, Mel Nelson, strokes his hair tenderly. There are tears in her eyes, but Jandreau's are dry. It is as if he is still in shock, or as if he has no more tears left to shed."

"Tough break," said Angel. Louis, who was also reading from the screen, said nothing.

I couldn't find an address for a Bobby Jandreau in Bangor, but the newspaper article had mentioned that Mel Nelson worked as an office manager in her father's lumber company in Veazie. She was at her desk when I called, and we had a long conversation. Sometimes, people are just waiting for the right call. It turned out that she was no longer Bobby's girlfriend, and she wasn't happy about the situation. She cared about him, and she loved him, but he had driven her away and she couldn't understand why. When I hung up, I had Bobby Jandreau's address and phone number, and a sense of admiration for Mel Nelson.

Carrie Saunders called while we were eating breakfast. It would be untrue to say that she sounded enthused at the prospect of meeting me, but I had learned not to take that kind of response personally. I told her that I was working for Bennett Patchett, Damien's father, and she simply confirmed an appointment at her office in the Togus VA Medical Center up in Augusta at midday before hanging up. Louis and Angel shadowed me all the way up to Augusta. I was interested to see what might emerge as we drove north, but they detected no sign of pursuit.

CHAPTER

XXI

arrie Saunders's office was located close to the Mental Health Service. Her name—simply "Dr. Saunders"—was etched on a plastic plate by her door, and when I knocked the door was opened by a woman in her mid-thirties, with short blond hair and the build of a lightweight boxer. She was wearing a dark T-shirt over black business slacks, and the muscles on her forearms and shoulders were clearly defined. She was about five-seven, and sallow skinned. Her office was small, and maximum use had been made of all available space: there were three filing cabinets to my right, and to my left there were bookshelves lined with assorted medical texts and cardboard document storage boxes. On the walls was framed evidence of qualification from the Uniformed Services University of the Health Sciences in Bethesda, Maryland, and from Walter Reed. One impressive piece of paper indicated a specialization in disaster psychiatry. The floor was covered in hard-wearing gray carpet. Her desk was neat and functional. There was a disposable coffee cup beside the phone, and the remains of a bagel.

"I eat when I can," she said, clearing away what was left of her lunch. "If you're hungry, we can get something at the canteen."

I told her that I was fine. She gestured to the plastic chair at the opposite side of her desk, and waited for me to sit before doing so herself.

"How can I help you, Mr. Parker?"

"I understand that you're conducting research into post-traumatic stress disorder."

"That's right."

"With a particular emphasis on suicide."

"On suicide prevention," she corrected. "May I ask who told you about me?"

It was probably my natural antipathy toward authority, especially the kind of authority represented by the military, but it seemed a good idea to keep Ronald Straydeer out of this for now.

"I'd prefer not to say," I replied. "Is that a problem?"

"No, just curious. I don't often get private detectives requesting to see me."

"I noticed that you didn't ask what this was about when we spoke on the phone."

"I did some checking up on you. You've got quite the reputation. I could hardly turn down the prospect of meeting you."

"My reputation is inflated. I wouldn't believe everything that you read in the papers."

She smiled. "I didn't read about you in the papers. I prefer to deal with people."

"Then we have that in common."

"It may be the only thing. Tell me, Mr. Parker, have you ever been in therapy?"

"No."

"Grief counseling?"

"No. Are you hustling for business?"

"As you noted, I'm interested in post-traumatic stress."

"And I seem like a candidate."

"Well, wouldn't you agree? I know about what happened to your wife and child. It was appalling, almost beyond countenance. I say 'almost' because I served my country in Iraq, and what I saw there, what I endured there, changed me. Every day, I deal with the consequences of violence. You might say that I have a context into which to place what you've gone through, and what you may still be going through."

"Is this relevant?"

"It is if you're here to talk about post-traumatic stress. Whatever you learn today will be dependent on your understanding of the concept. That understanding may be commensurately greater if you can relate to it personally, however peripherally. Are we clear so far?"

Her smile hadn't gone away. It managed to stay just the right side of patronizing, but it was a close-run thing.

"Very."

"Good. My research here is part of an ongoing effort on the part of the military to deal with the psychological effects of combat, both on those who have served and have been invalided out, and on those who have left for reasons unrelated to injury. That's one aspect of it. The other relates to preempting trauma. At the moment, we are phasing in emotional resiliency programs designed to improve combat performance and minimize mental heath difficulties, including PTSD, anger, depression, and suicide. These symptoms have become increasingly recognizable as soldiers undertake repeated deployments.

"Not every soldier who experiences trauma will suffer from post-traumatic stress, just as individuals in civilian life react differently to, say, assault, rape, natural disasters, or the violent death of a loved one. There will be a stress response, but PTSD is not an automatic consequence. Psychology, genetics, physical condition, and social factors all play a part. An individual with a good support structure—family, friends, professional intervention—may be less likely to develop PTSD than, say, a loner. On the other hand, the longer the delay in developing PTSD, then arguably the more severely it will be experienced. Immediate post-traumatic stress usually begins to improve after three to four months. Delayed PTSD may be more long term, up to a decade or more, and is therefore harder to treat." She paused. "Okay, that's the lecture part over with for now. Any questions?"

"None. Yet."

"Good. Now you get to participate."

"And if I don't?"

"Then you can leave. This is a trade-off, Mr. Parker. You want my help. I'm prepared to give it, but only in return for something. In this case, it's your willingness to acknowledge when, and if, any of the symptoms I'm about to detail are familiar to you. You need answer only in the most general of terms. There are no records of this conversation being kept. If, at some point in the future, you would consider offering some deeper insights into what you've been through, then I would be grateful. You might even find it beneficial, or therapeutic. In any event, it goes back to what I said at the start. You're here to find out about PTSD. This is your chance."

I had to admire her. I could leave, but I would have learned nothing, except not to underestimate women who look like boxers, and I'd figured that out long before I met Carrie Saunders.

"Go ahead," I said. I tried to keep the resignation out of my voice. I don't think that I succeeded.

"There are three main categories of post-traumatic stress disorder. The first involves flashbacks, the reexperiencing of the event that may have sparked the disorder or, less severely, and more commonly, a series of unwanted, intrusive thoughts that may feel like flashbacks, but aren't. We're talking about dreams and bad memories on one level, or making associations with the event from unrelated situations: you'd be surprised by how many soldiers dislike fireworks, and I've seen traumatized men hit the deck at the sound of a door banging, even a child shooting a toy gun. But on another level there may be an actual reliving of what occurred, to the extent that it feels real enough to disrupt ordinary, day-to-day functioning. One of my colleagues calls it 'ghosting.' I don't like the term myself, but I've spoken to sufferers who've seized on the concept."

There was silence in the room. A bird flew by the window, and the sunlight caused its shadow to flit across the room: an unseen thing, separated from us by glass and brick, by the solidity of the actual, making its presence felt to us.

"There were flashbacks, intrusive thoughts, or whatever you want to call them," I said at last.

"Severe?"

"Yes."

"Frequent?"

"Yes."

"What would bring them on?"

"Blood. The sight of a child—a girl—on the street, with her mother or alone. Simple things. A chair. A blade. Advertisements for kitchens. Certain shapes, angled shapes. I don't know why. As time went on, the images that would cause problems for me became fewer."

"And now?"

"They're rare. I still have bad dreams, but not so often."

"Why do you think that is?"

I was conscious of trying not to pause too long before my replies, of not giving the impression to Saunders that she might have hit on an interesting avenue to explore. The possibility that I believed myself to have been haunted by my wife and child, or some dark version of them that had since been replaced by forms less threatening but equally unknowable, would have qualified as an interesting avenue even if I'd been in group therapy with Hitler, Napoleon, and Jim Jones. Under the circumstances, I was pleased that my reply to her last question was virtually instantaneous.

"I don't know. Time?"

"It doesn't heal all wounds. That's a myth."

"Maybe you just get used to the pain."

She nodded. "You might even miss it when it's gone."

"You think so?"

"You might if it gave you purpose."

If she wanted another response, she wasn't going to get it. She seemed to realize it, because she moved on.

"Then there are avoidance symptoms: numbness, detachment, social isolation."

"Not leaving the house?"

"It may not be that literal. It could be just staying away from people or places associated with the incident: family, friends, former colleagues. Sufferers find it hard to care about anything. They may feel that there's no point, that they have no future."

"There was some detachment," I admitted. "I didn't feel part of ordinary life. There was no such thing. There was just chaos, waiting to break through."

"And colleagues?"

"I avoided them, and they avoided me."

"Friends?"

I thought of Angel and Louis, waiting outside in their car. "Some of them didn't want to be avoided."

"Were you angry at them for that?"

"No."

"Why not?"

"Because they were like me. They shared my purpose."

"Which was?"

"To find the man who killed my wife and child. To find him, and to tear him apart."

The answers were coming more quickly now. I was surprised, even angry at myself for letting this stranger get beneath my skin, but there was a pleasure in it too, a kind of release. Perhaps I was a narcissist, or I had simply not been so clinically incisive with myself in a very long time, if ever.

"Did you feel that you had a future?"

"An immediate one."

"That lay in killing this man."

"Yes."

She was leaning forward slightly now, a white light in her eyes. I couldn't figure out where it was coming from, until I realized that I was seeing my own face reflected in the depths of her pupils.

"Arousal symptoms," she said. "Difficulty concentrating."

"No."

"Exaggerated responses to startling stimuli."

"Like gunshots?"

"Perhaps."

"No, my responses to gunshots weren't exaggerated."

"Anger. Irritability."

"Yes."

"Sleeping difficulties."

"Yes."

"Hypervigilance."

"Justified. A lot of people seemed to want me dead."

"Physical symptoms: fever, headache, dizziness."

"No, or not excessively so."

She sat back. We were nearly done.

"Survivor guilt," she said softly.

"Yes," I said.

Yes, all the time.

CARRIE SAUNDERS STEPPED FROM her office and came back with two cups of coffee. She took some sachets of sugar and creamer from her pocket and laid them on the desk.

"You don't need me to tell you, do you?" she said, as she filled her cup with enough sugar to make the spoon stand upright without a hand to support it.

"No, but then you're not the first one to try."

I sipped the coffee. It was strong, and tasted bitter. I could see why she was adding so much sugar to it.

"How are you doing now?" she asked.

"I'm doing okay."

"Without treatment?"

"I found an outlet for my anger. It's ongoing, and therapeutic."

"You hunt people down. And, sometimes, you kill them."

I didn't reply. Instead, I asked: "Where did you serve?"

"In Baghdad. I was a major, initially attached to Task Force Iron-horse at Camp Boom in Ba Qubah."

"Camp Boom?"

"Because there were so many explosions. It's called Camp Gabe now, after a sapper, Dan Gabrielson, who was killed at Ba Qubah in 2003. It was basic as anything when I got there: no plumbing, no A/C, nothing. By the time I left, there were CHEWS, central water for the showers and latrines, a new power grid, and they'd begun training the Iraqi National Guard there."

"Chews?" I said. I felt as though I were listening to someone speaking pidgin English.

"Containerized housing units. Big boxes to you."

"Must have been hard, being a female soldier out there."

"It was. This is a new war. In the past, female soldiers didn't live and fight alongside men, not the way they do now. It's brought its own problems. Technically, we're barred from joining combat units, so instead we're 'attached' to them. In the end, we still fight, and we still die, just like men. Maybe not in the same numbers, but over a hundred women have died in Iraq and Afghanistan, and hundreds more have been injured. But we're still called bitches and dykes and sluts. We're still open to harassment and assault by our own men. We're still advised to walk in pairs around our own bases to avoid rape. But I don't regret serving, not for one minute. That's why I'm here: there are a lot of soldiers who are still owed something."

"You said you started at Camp Boom. What about after that?"

"I was seconded to Camp Warhorse, and then to Abu Ghraib as part of the restructuring of the prison."

"You mind if I ask what your duties there involved?"

"Initially, I dealt with prisoners. We wanted information, and they were naturally hostile to us, especially after what happened in the prison in the early days. We needed to find other ways to get them to talk."

"When you say 'other ways' . . ."

"You saw the photographs: humiliation, torture—simulated and otherwise. That didn't help our cause. Those idiots on talk radio who laughed about it had no understanding of the impact it had. It gave the Iraqis another reason to hate us, and they took it out on the military. American soldiers died because of Abu Ghraib."

"Just a few bad apples getting out of line."

"Nothing happened in Abu Ghraib that wasn't sanctioned from above, in general if not in detail."

"And then you arrived with a new approach."

"I, and others. Our maxim was simple: don't torture. Torture a man or woman for long enough, and you'll be told exactly what you want to hear. In the end, all they want is for the torture to stop."

She must have seen something in my face, because she stopped talking and eyed me intently over her coffee. "You've been hurt in that way?"

I didn't answer.

"I'll take that as a 'yes,'" she said. "Even moderate pressure, and by that I mean physical pain that doesn't leave one in fear of death, is scarring. In my view, someone who has endured torture is never quite the same again. It removes a part of oneself, excises it entirely. Call it what you will: peace of mind, dignity. Sometimes, I wonder if it even has a name. Anyway, in the short term it has a profoundly destabilizing affect on the personality."

"And in the long term?"

"Well, in your case, how long has it been?"

"Since the last time?"

"There's been more than one?"

"Yes."

"Jesus. If I was dealing with a soldier in your position, I'd be making sure that he was undergoing intensive therapy."

"That's reassuring to know. To get back to you . . ."

"After my time in Abu Ghraib, I moved into counseling and therapy. It became clear at a very early stage that there were problems with stress levels, and those increased when the military instituted repeated deployments, stop-loss, and began calling up weekend warriors. I became part of a mental health team working out of the Green Zone, but with particular responsibility for two FOBs: Arrowhead and Warhorse."

"Arrowhead. That's where the Third Infantry is based, right?"

"Some brigades, yes."

"You ever encounter anyone from a Stryker unit while you were there?"

She set her cup aside. Her expression changed.

"Is that why you're here, to talk about the men of Stryker C?"

"I didn't mention Stryker C."

"You didn't have to."

She waited for me to proceed.

"From what I can tell, three members of Stryker C, all known to one another, have died at their own hands," I said. "One of them took his wife with him. That sounds like a suicide cluster to me, which would probably be of interest to you."

"It is."

"Did you speak to any of those men before they died?"

"I spoke to all of them, but Damien Patchett only informally. The first was Brett Harlan. He'd been attending the Veterans Outreach Center in Bangor. He was also a drug addict. For him, it helped that the needle exchange program was based next to a veterans center."

I couldn't tell if she was joking.

"What did he tell you?"

"That's confidential."

"He's dead. He doesn't care any longer."

"I'm still not going to reveal the substance of my discussions with him, but clearly you can take it that he was suffering from post-traumatic stress disorder, although—"

She stopped. I waited.

"He was experiencing auditory phenomena," she added, slightly reluctantly.

"So he was hearing voices?"

"But that doesn't fit with the diagnosis criteria for PTSD. That's closer to schizophrenia."

"Did you investigate further?"

"He discontinued treatment. And then he died."

"Was there a specific event that triggered his problem?"

She looked away. "It was . . . nonspecific, as far as I could ascertain."

"What does that mean?"

"There were nightmares, and he was having trouble sleeping, but he couldn't relate it to a specific occurrence. That's all I'm prepared to say."

"Was there any indication that he might have been about to murder his wife?"

"None. Do you seriously think that we wouldn't have intervened if we thought that there was such a risk? Come on."

"Is it possible that the same stimulus could have led all three to act as they did?"

"I'm not sure what you mean."

"Could something have happened in Iraq that led to a form of . . . collective trauma?"

Her mouth twitched slightly in amusement. "Are you making up psychiatric terms, Mr. Parker?"

"It sounded right. I couldn't think of any other way to explain what I meant."

"Well, it's not a bad effort. I dealt with Bernie Kramer twice, shortly after he returned. He displayed mild stress symptoms at the time, similar to those being experienced by Brett Harlan, but neither referred to any common traumatic occurrence in Iraq. Kramer declined to continue treatment. Damien Patchett I encountered briefly after Bernie Kramer died, as part of my research, and, again, he spoke of nothing that might correspond to what you're suggesting."

"His father didn't mention that he was receiving counseling."

"That's because he wasn't. We talked for a time after Kramer's funeral and subsequently talked on one further occasion, but there was no formal therapy. Actually, I'd have said that Damien appeared very well adjusted, apart from some insomnia."

"Did you prescribe drugs for any of those men?"

"It's part of my job, when necessary. I'm not a fan of heavily medicating troubled individuals. It just helps to mask the pain, without dealing with the underlying problem."

"But you did prescribe drugs."

"Trazodone."

"For Damien Patchett?"

"No, just for Kramer and Harlan. I advised Damien to consult his own physician if he was having trouble sleeping."

"But that wasn't the limit of his problems."

"Apparently not. It may be that Kramer's death was the catalyst for the emergence of Damien's own difficulties. To be honest, I was surprised when Damien took his life. But I approached a number of Kramer's former comrades at the funeral, Damien included, and offered to help facilitate counseling services for them, if they chose to avail themselves of them."

"With you?"

"Yes."

"Because it would have helped with your research."

For the first time, she got angry. "No, because it would have helped *them.* This isn't some merely academic exercise, Mr. Parker. It's about saving lives."

"It doesn't seem to be working out so well for the Stryker C," I said. I was goading her, and I didn't know why. I suspected that it was resentment at myself for opening up to her that I was now trying to throw back. Whatever the reason, I needed to stop. She precipitated it by standing, indicating that our time together was over. I stood and thanked her for her input, then turned to leave.

"Oh, one last thing," I said as she began to open folders on her desk and return to her work.

"Yes," she said. She didn't look up.

"You attended Damien Patchett's funeral?"

"Yes. Well, I went to the church. I would have gone to the cemetery too, but I didn't."

"Can I ask why?"

"It was communicated to me that I wouldn't be welcome."

"By whom?"

"That's none of your business."

"Joel Tobias?"

Her hand froze for an instant, and then continued turning a page.

"Good-bye, Mr. Parker," she said. "If you'll take some professional advice, you still have a lot of issues to work out. I'd speak to someone about them, if I were you. Someone other than myself," she added.

"Does that mean you don't want me to be part of your research?"

Now she looked up. "I think I've learned enough about you," she said. "Please close the door on your way out."

CHAPTER

XXII

Bobby Jandreau still lived in Bangor, a little over an hour north of Augusta, in a house at the top of Palm Street, just off Stillwater Avenue. Once again, Angel and Louis stayed with me all the way there, but we reached Jandreau's place without incident. It didn't look like much from the outside: single story, paintwork that flaked like bad skin, a lawn that was trying its best to pretend that it wouldn't soon be overrun by weeds. The best that could be said about the exterior was that it didn't raise any expectations that the interior of the house couldn't live up to. Jandreau answered the door in his wheelchair. He was dressed in gray sweatpants pinned at the thighs, and a matching T-shirt, both of which were stained. He was building up a gut that the shirt didn't even attempt to conceal. His hair was shaved close to his skull, but he was growing a rough beard. The house smelled stale: in the kitchen behind him, I could see dishes piled up in the sink, and pizza boxes lying on the floor by the trash can.

"Help you?" he said.

I showed him my ID. He took it from me and held it on his lap, staring at it the way someone might examine the photograph of a missing child that had been presented to him by the cops, as though by gazing at it for long enough he might remember where he'd seen the kid. When he had finished examining it, he returned it and let his hands fall between his thighs, where they worried at each other like small animals fighting.

"Did she send you?"

"Did who send me?"

"Mel."

"No." I wanted to ask him why she might have wanted to send a private detective to his home, because she'd given no indication of that level of trouble when we talked, but it wasn't the time for that, not yet. Instead, I said: "I was hoping to talk to you about your army service."

I waited for him to ask me why, but he didn't. He just wheeled his chair backward and invited me inside. There was a wariness to him, a consciousness, perhaps, of his own vulnerability and the fact that, until he died, he would always be destined to look up at others. His upper arms were still strong and muscular, and when we went into the living room I saw a rack of dumbbells over by the window. He saw where I was looking, and said, "Just because my legs don't work no more doesn't mean I have to give up on the rest of me." There was no belligerence or defensiveness to his words. It was simply a statement of fact.

"The arms are easy. The rest"—he patted his belly—"is harder."

I didn't know what to say, so I said nothing.

"You want a soda? I don't have anything stronger. I've decided that it's not good for me to have certain temptations around."

"I'm fine. You mind if I sit down?"

He pointed at a chair. I saw that my first impressions about the interior had been wrong, or at least unfair. This room was clean, if a little dusty. There were books—mainly science fiction, but history books too, most of them relating to Vietnam and World War Two, from what I could see, but also some books on Sumerian and Babylonian mythology—and today's newspapers, the *Bangor Daily News* and *The Boston Globe.* But there was a mark on the carpet where something had splattered recently and had been imperfectly cleaned up, and another on the wall and floor between the living room and the kitchen. I got the sense that Jandreau was trying his best to keep things together, but there was only so much that a man in a wheelchair could do about a stain on the carpet, not unless he was going to tip himself out of his chair to deal with it.

Jandreau was watching me carefully, gauging my reactions to his living space.

"My mom comes around a couple of times a week to help me with the stuff I can't do for myself. She'd be around here every day if I let her, but she fusses. You know how they can be."

I nodded. "What happened to Mel?"

"You know her?"

I didn't want to tell him that I'd spoken with her until I was ready. "I read the interview with you in the newspaper last year. I saw her picture."

"She went away."

"Can I ask why?"

"Because I was an asshole. Because she couldn't deal with this." He patted his legs, then reconsidered: "No: because *I* couldn't deal with this."

"Why would she hire a detective?"

"What?"

"You asked if Mel had sent me. I'm just wondering why you might have thought that."

"We had an argument before she left, a disagreement about money, about ownership of some stuff. I figured maybe she'd hired you to take it further."

Mel had mentioned some of this in our conversation. The house was in both their names, but she hadn't made any effort yet to seek legal advice about her position. The breakup was still new, and she hoped that they might yet be reconciled. Still, something in Jandreau's tone gave the lie to what he had just said, as though he had greater concerns than domestic issues.

"And you trusted me when I told you that she hadn't sent me?"

"Yeah, I guess. You don't seem like the kind of man who'd try to beat up on a cripple. And if you were, well—"

His right hand moved very fast. The gun was a Beretta, hidden in a makeshift holster attached to the underside of the chair. He held it upright for a couple of seconds, the muzzle pointing to the ceiling, before he restored it to its hiding place.

"Are you worried about something?" I asked, even if it seemed like a redundant question when faced by a man with a gun in his hand.

"I'm worried about lots of stuff: falling over while using the john, how I'm going to manage when winter comes around. You name it, I've got a worry for it. But I don't like the idea of someone finding me an easy mark. That, at least, I can do something about. Now, Mr. Parker, how about you tell me why you're interested in me."

"Not you," I said. "Joel Tobias."

"Suppose I told you that I don't know any Joel Tobias."

"Then I'd have to assume that you were lying, since you served together in Iraq, and he was your sergeant in Stryker C. You were both at the funeral of Damien Patchett, and later you got into a fight with Tobias in Sully's. So you still want to tell me that you don't know any Joel Tobias?"

Jandreau looked away. I could see him sizing up his options, debating whether to talk to me or simply send me on my way. I could almost feel the suppressed anger rolling off him, waves of it breaking on me, on the furniture, on the stained walls, the spume of it splashing back on his own maimed body. Anger, grief, loss. His fingers created intricate patterns from themselves, interweaving and then coming apart, forming constructions that only he could understand.

"So I know Joel Tobias," he said at last. "But we're not close. Never were."

"Why is that?"

"Joel's old man was a soldier, so Joel had it in his blood. He liked the discipline, liked being the alpha dog. The army was just an extension of his nature."

"And you?"

He squinted at me. "How old are you?"

"Forties."

"They ever try to recruit you?"

"No more than they tried to recruit anyone else. They came to my high school, but I didn't bite. But it wasn't the same then. We weren't at war."

"Yeah, well, we are now, and I bit. They promised me cash, money for college. Promised me the sun, the moon, and the stars." He smiled sadly. "The sun part was true. Saw a lot of that. Sun, and dust. I've started working for Veterans for Peace now. I'm a counter-recruiter."

I didn't know what that was, so I asked him.

"Army recruiters are trained only to answer the right question," he said. "You don't ask the right question, then you don't get the right answer. And if you're a seventeen- or eighteen-year-old kid with poor prospects, faced with a guy in uniform who's so slick you could skate on him, then you're going to believe what you're told, and you're not going to examine the small print. We point out the small print."

"Such as?"

"Such as that your college fees aren't guaranteed, that the army owes you nothing, that less than ten percent of recruits get the full amount of bonuses or fees that they were promised. Look, don't get me wrong here: it's honorable to serve your country, and a lot of these kids wouldn't have any kind of career at all if it wasn't for the army. I was one of them. My family was poor, and I'm still poor, but I'm proud that I served. I'd have preferred not to end up in a wheelchair, but I knew the risks. I just think the recruiters should be more up-front with the kids about what they're getting themselves into. It's the draft in all but name: you target the poor, the ones who got no job, no prospects, the ones who don't know any better. You think Rumsfeld didn't know that when he inserted a recruiter provision into the No Child Left Behind Act? You think he made it compulsory for public schools to provide the military with all their student details because it would help the kids read better? There are quotas to be filled. You gotta plug the gaps in the ranks somehow."

"But if the recruiters were completely honest, then who'd join up?"

"Shit, I'd *still* have signed on the dotted line. I'd have done anything to get away from my family, and this place. All that was here for me was a minimum-wage job and beers after work on Friday. And Mel." That gave him pause. "I guess I still got the minimum-wage job: four hundred dollars a month, but at least they threw in health care, and I saw most of my bonus." He grimaced. "Lot of contradictions, huh?"

"Was that why you fought with Joel Tobias, because of your work with Veterans for Peace?"

Jandreau looked away. "No, it wasn't. He tried to buy me a beer to quiet me down, but I didn't want to drink on his dime."

"Again: why?"

But Jandreau skirted the question. As he himself had said, he was a man of contradictions. He wanted to talk, but only about what interested him. He appeared polite, but there was ferocity beneath the veneer. I knew now what Ronald Straydeer meant when he said that Jandreau was a man who looked like he was on the way down. If he didn't use that gun on someone else, there was a chance that he might use it on himself, just like some of his buddies.

"What's your interest in Joel Tobias anyway?" he asked.

"I was hired to find out why Damien Patchett killed himself. I heard about the altercation at the funeral. I wanted to know if there was any connection."

"Between a bar fight and a suicide? You're full of shit."

"That, or a really bad detective."

There was a pause and then, for the first time, Jandreau laughed.

"At least you're honest." The laughter ceased, and the smile that followed was sad. "Damien shouldn't have killed himself. I don't mean that in a religious way, or a moral way, or because it was a waste of a life. I mean that he wasn't the kind. He left his grief in Iraq, or most of it. He wasn't traumatized, or suffering."

"I spoke to a shrink in Togus who said the same thing."

"Yeah? Who was that?"

"Carrie Saunders."

"Saunders? Give me a break. She's got more questions than Alex Trebek, but none of the answers."

"You've met her?"

"She interviewed me as part of her study. Didn't impress me at all. As for Damien, I served with him. I loved him. He was a good kid. I always thought of him like that, as a kid. He was intelligent, but he had no smarts. I tried to look out for him, but he ended up taking care of me in the end. Saved my life." His fist tightened on the arm of his chair. "Fuckin' Joel Tobias," he whispered, and it sounded like a shout.

"Tell me," I said.

"I'm angry with Tobias. Doesn't mean I'm going to rat him out, him or anyone else."

"I know that he's running an operation. He's smuggling, and I think he might have promised some of the proceeds to you. You, and men and women like you."

Jandreau turned away and wheeled himself to the window.

"Who are the guys outside?" he asked.

"Friends."

"Your friends don't look like the friendly type."

"I felt like I needed some protection. If they looked too inviting, it would defeat the purpose."

"Protection? Who from?"

"Maybe from the same people who've given you cause to carry that gun: your old buddies, led by Joel Tobias." He still hadn't turned back to me, but I could see his reflection in the glass.

"Why would I be frightened of Joel Tobias?"

Frightened: it was an interesting choice of words. Its very use was an admission of sorts.

"Because you're worried that they think you're a weak link."

"Me? I'm a regular stand-up guy." He laughed again, and it was a terrible sound.

"I think you were worried about Damien Patchett. You owed him, and you didn't want anything to happen to him. Maybe he was in too deep, or he didn't listen, but when he died, you decided to take action. Or perhaps you had to wait for what happened with Brett Harlan and his wife before you began to discern a pattern."

"I don't know what you're talking about."

"I think you spoke to your cousin. You called Foster Jandreau, because he was a cop, but a cop that you could trust, because he was family. You probably fed him a little, and hoped that he'd find out the rest for himself. When he started making inquiries, they killed him, and now you believe that's it's just a matter of time before they come for you. Does that sound about right?"

He spun the chair quickly, and the gun was back in his hand.

"You don't know that. You don't know *anything*."

"This has to be stopped, Bobby. Whatever's happening, people have begun to die, and no amount of money can be worth that, unless your conscience is up for bids."

"Get out of my house!" he shouted. "Get out!"

Behind him, I could see Angel and Louis starting to run as they heard the noise from the house. If I didn't defuse the situation, Bobby Jandreau's door would be lying in his hallway, and he might have cause to use that gun, if he was fast enough.

I made my way to the door, opened it, and let Angel and Louis see that I was okay, but Bobby Jandreau chose that moment to wheel himself, one-handed, into the hallway. For a moment, I was trapped between three guns.

"Take it easy! Everyone! Easy!" Slowly, I dipped two fingers into my jacket pocket and removed one of my cards. I placed it on the table next to the door.

"You owed Damien Patchett, Bobby," I said. "He's gone, but your debt's still in play. Now his father's holding it. You think about that."

"Get lost," he said, but the anger was already disappearing, and he just managed to sound tired. His voice quavered on the word "lost," a recognition that he was the one who was drifting on dark, unknown seas.

"And one more thing," I said, following up my advantage on a crippled veteran. "Go make up with your girlfriend. I think you forced her away because you're scared of what's coming, and you didn't want her to be hurt if they did come after you. She still loves you, and you need someone like her in your life. You know it, and she knows it. You have my card, you need any more counseling."

I walked away, Angel and Louis still watching my back. I heard the door close, and then they were beside me.

"Let me get this straight," said Louis, as we reached the cars. "Man pulls a gun on you, and you give him relationship advice?"

"Somebody had to."

"Yeah, but you? Dodo eggs got laid more recently than you."

I ignored him. As I got in my car, I saw Bobby Jandreau at his window, watching me.

"You think he'll come around?" asked Angel.

"About his girlfriend, or Tobias?"

"Both."

"He has to, on both. If he doesn't, he's dead. Without her, he's dying already. He just hasn't admitted it yet. Tobias and the others will just finish what he's started himself."

"Wow," said Angel. "You think there's a Hallmark card for that: 'Shape Up or Die'?"

We drove away, Angel and Louis behind me, but only as far as the next street. They looked puzzled when I pulled over and then walked back to them.

"I want you to stay here," I said.

"Why?" asked Angel.

"Because they're going to come for Bobby Jandreau."

"You seem pretty sure of that."

I walked to the Mustang, and pointed out the GPS tracker on the rear fender.

"This will bring them. That's why it's staying here with you while I take your car."

"Your car stays here," said Louis, "and they'll think Jandreau is giving you chapter and verse, so they'll try to take you both out."

"Except they won't," I said, "because you're going to kill them when they move on Jandreau."

"And then Jandreau will talk."

"That's the plan."

"And where are you going to be?" asked Angel.

"Over by Rangeley."

"What's in Rangeley?"

"A motel."

"So we skulk in the bushes while you stay in a motel?"

"Something like that."

"Yeah, good deal."

We switched cars, but not before Louis and Angel emptied the rest of their toys from the compartment in the trunk. As it turned out, they'd traveled light, for them: two Glocks, a couple of knives, a pair of semiautomatic machine pistols, and some spare clips. Louis found a position in the woods with a clear view of Jandreau's house, and they settled in to wait.

"You got any questions you want us to ask before we kill them?" asked Louis. "Assuming we got to kill them."

I thought of the barrel of water in the Blue Moon, and the feel of the sack pressed hard against my nose and mouth. "If you don't have to, then don't, but I don't much care either way. As for questions, you can ask them what you want."

"What would we have to ask them?" asked Angel.

Louis thought about the question.

"Eyes open, or eyes closed?" he said.

ALL WAS MOVEMENT. THE pieces were on the board, and that night the game would reach its conclusion.

From her bedroom window, Karen Emory watched Joel leave. He had said a cursory good-bye to her, and kissed her with dry lips upon the cheek. She had held him tightly, even as she felt him pull away from her, and before she let him go, her fingertips touched against the gun at his back.

Joel did not look back at her. He took the Silverado and drove north, but only as far as Falmouth, where the others were waiting with the van and two motorcycles: Vernon and Pritchard, the ex-marines, who constituted the main sniper team; and Mallak and Bacci. Vernon and Pritchard were both big men, and even though the former was black, and the latter white, they were brothers beneath the skin. Tobias didn't care much for either of them, but that was at least as much about the mutual antipathy that existed between soldiers and Marines as it was about Vernon's seeming inability to open his mouth without asking a question, and loading it with attitude.

Vernon and Pritchard were elite scout snipers, or HOGs, in the language of their trade: hunters of gunmen. They were veterans of the sniper battles in Baghdad, a largely hidden conflict that had escalated after the loss of two marine sniper teams, a total of ten men lost to the hajis. They had played cat-and-mouse games with the near mythical "Juba" an anonymous sniper variously believed to be a Chechen, or even a collective name for a cell of snipers, armed with Iraqi-produced "Tabuk" rifles, a Kalashnikov variant. Juba was disciplined, waiting for soldiers to stand up in, or dismount from, vehicles, looking for the gaps in the body armor, never firing more than one shot before melting away. Vernon and Pritchard differed on whether or not Juba was one man, or many, but in the end both men had been targeted by him and lived. Like their fellow soldiers, they had become adept at "cutting squares": zigzagging, ducking, moving back and forth, and bobbing their heads in order to provide a more difficult target to hit. Pritchard called it the "Battlefield Boogie"; Vernon the "Jihad Jitterbug." What was odd was that neither man could dance to save his life on a regular dance floor, but threatened by an expert killer they had moved like Gene Kelly and Fred Astaire.

Vernon and Pritchard had known the four men from Echo Company who had died in Ramadi in 2004. Three of them had been shot in the head, a fourth virtually torn apart by bullets. In addition, one marine's throat had been slit. The attack had happened in broad daylight, within eight hundred yards of the command post. Later they learned that a four-man "hit" team had probably been responsible, and that the marines had been targeted for some time, but the killings had marked the beginning of Vernon and Pritchard's disillusionment with the nature of the conflict in Iraq. Only one of the dead men had been a trained sniper. The others had been grunts, and that wasn't the way the system was supposed to work. No fewer than two trained snipers on any team—that was the golden rule. When the six-man sniper team of the Reserve Third Batallion died in Hadithah a year later, and the remaining snipers were forced to operate according to ever more restrictive rules of engagement, Vernon and Pritchard decided that the marines could go screw themselves, subsequently aided by an explosion that had detached the retina in Vernon's right eye, leading to permanent vision loss.

After he was injured, Vernon was shipped home, and Pritchard had left the military shortly after. By then, they were both tied in with Tobias and the operation. They may not have liked Tobias, but they did like the idea of being wealthy.

"Where are Twizell and Greenham?" asked Vernon, referring to the second sniper team.

"They'll join us later," said Tobias. "They have something else to do first."

"Shit," said Vernon in reply. "Don't suppose you feel like sharing the details with the troops?"

"No," said Tobias, and held Vernon's gaze until the other looked away.

Mallak and Bacci, who had served in Tobias's squad in Iraq, exchanged a glance, but didn't intervene. They knew better than to take sides in the ongoing pissing competition between Vernon and the sarge. Mallak had come home a corporal, and never questioned orders, even though he recognized that there was now a growing distance between Tobias and him. Tobias had grown strange in recent weeks, and pragmatic to the point of cruelty. It was Tobias who had suggested that the detective, Parker, should be disposed of entirely, and not simply questioned to find out what he knew. Mallak had argued for discretion, and had subsequently taken responsibility for the detective's interrogation. He wasn't in the business of killing Americans on home soil, or anywhere else. The climbdown over Parker was a small victory, and nothing more: Mallak had decided to pretend that he knew nothing about the death of Foster Jandreau, or any other hostile actions that had been taken.

Bacci, meanwhile, was a bald thug who just wanted his money, and was lucky that Tobias had not yet punched his lights out for the way he looked at Karen Emory.

We're just one big happy family, thought Mallak, and the sooner all this is over, the better.

"All right," said Tobias. "Let's move out."

MEANWHILE, TWO MEN HEADED north in an anonymous brown sedan, passing Lewiston and Augusta and Waterville, Bangor slowly drawing nearer. One of them, the passenger, had a computer on his lap. Occasionally, he would refresh the map screen, but the blinking dot never moved.

"That thing still working?" asked Twizell.

"Looks like it," said Greenham. He kept his eye on the dot. It stayed close to the intersection of Palm and Stillwater, not far from the home of Bobby Jandreau. "We've got a sitting target," he confirmed, and Twizell grunted in satisfaction.

AS GREENHAM AND TWIZELL passed Lewiston, Rojas, still a little fuzzy from some recently administered dental anesthetic, and his teeth now aching, was sitting at a table working on the slab of red oak that would serve as a platform for the ornate seals. They lay beside him on a piece of black cloth as he worked, their presence a source of comfort to him, a reminder of the potential for beauty in this world.

And Herod drove north, drawing closer and closer to Rojas, grateful for the Captain's absence, grateful that his pain was tolerable, for now. And as he went, another closed in on him.

The Collector, too, was on the move.

III

Q. What were you firing at?
A: At the enemy, sir.
Q: At people?
A: At the enemy, sir.
Q: They weren't even human beings?
A: Yes, sir.
Q: Were they men?
A: I don't know, sir . . .

Testimony of Lieutenant William Calley,
the My Lai Courts-Martial, 1970

CHAPTER

XXIII

The Rangeley Lakes region of the state, northwest of Portland, east of the New Hampshire state line and just south of the Canadian border, was not one with which I was very familiar. It was best known as a sportsman's paradise, and had been since the nineteenth century. I had never had much cause to go there, although I had a vague recollection of passing through it as a boy, my parents in the front seats of my father's beloved LeSabre, on our way to somewhere else: Canada, perhaps, because I can't imagine my father going all that way to visit eastern New Hampshire. He always regarded New Hampshire as suspect, for some reason that I never fully grasped, but it is so long ago now, and my parents are no longer around to ask.

I did have one other memory of Rangeley, and that came from a man named Phineas Arbogast, who was a friend of my grandfather and sometimes hunted in the woods around Rangeley, where his family had a cabin and, it seems, had always had a cabin, for Phineas Arbogast was "Old Maine" and could probably have traced his ancestry back to the nomads who crossed from Asia into North America 11,000 years before over the spit of land that is now the Bering Islands, or at least to some pigheaded pilgrim who had headed north to escape the worst rigors of Puritanism. As a boy, I had found his speech almost unintelligible, for Phineas could have drawled for his country. He could even find ways to lengthen a word that didn't have any vowels to lengthen. He could have drawled in Polish.

My grandfather was fond of Phineas who, if he could be pinned down, and understood, was a mine of historical and geographical knowledge. As he grew older, some of that knowledge inevitably began to leach from his brain, and he tried to put it down in a book before it all trickled away, but he didn't have the patience for the task. He was part of an older, oral tradition: he told his stories aloud so that others might remember them and pass them on in turn, but eventually the only ones who would listen to him were people nearly as old as he was. Young people didn't want to hear Phineas's stories, not then, and by the time some people from one of the universities came looking for people like him to record their tales, Phineas was telling his stories late at night to his neighbors in the churchyard.

So the memory I have is of Phineas and my grandfather sitting by the fire, Phineas talking, my grandfather listening. My father was dead by then, my mother elsewhere that night, so it was we three only, warming ourselves by the winter logs. My grandfather had asked Phineas why he didn't go to his cabin so much anymore, and Phineas had paused before answering. It wasn't his usual pause, a moment to draw breath and compose his thoughts before starting out along a rambling anecdotal path. No, there was uncertainty and—could it be?—an unwillingness to proceed. So my grandfather waited, curious, and so did I, and eventually Phineas Arbogast told us why he no longer went to his cabin in the woods near Rangeley.

He had been hunting squirrel with his dog, Misty, a mutt whose ancestry was as complex as that of some royal families, and who duly carried herself like a bastard princess. Phineas had no use for the squirrels that he shot: he just didn't care much for squirrels. Misty, as usual, had gone racing ahead, and after a time Phineas could no longer see or hear her. He whistled for her, but she didn't return, and Misty, despite her airs, was an obedient dog. So Phineas went searching for her, moving deeper and deeper into the woods, and farther and farther from his cabin. It began to grow dark, and still he searched, for he was not going to leave her alone in the forest. He called her name, over and over, to no reply. He began to fear that a bear might have taken her, or a lynx or bobcat, until at last he thought that he heard Misty whining, and he followed the sound, grateful that he still had most of his hearing and more of his eyesight, even at seventy-three.

He came to a clearing, and there was Misty, now barely visible as the moon appeared in the sky. Briars had wound themselves around her legs and her muzzle, and as she had struggled against them the briars had tightened on her, so that all she could do was whimper softly. Phineas drew his knife, preparing to free her, when there was movement to his right, and he turned his flashlight in that direction.

A little girl of perhaps six or seven stood at the edge of the clearing. Her hair was dark, and she was very pale. She wore a black dress of coarse cloth, and simple black shoes on her feet. She didn't blink in the strong beam of the flashlight, nor did she raise her hands to shield her eyes. In fact, Phineas thought, the light seemed to make no difference to her whatsoever; it was as if she merely absorbed it into her skin, for she appeared to glow whitely from within.

"Honey," said Phineas, "what are you doing way out here?"

"I'm lost," said the girl. "Help me."

Her voice sounded strange, as though it were coming from inside a cave, or the hollowed-out trunk of a tree. It echoed when it should not have done so.

Phineas moved toward her, already shrugging his coat off to put it over her shoulders, when he saw Misty tugging at the briars again, her tail now wedged between her back legs. The effort clearly caused her pain, but still she was determined to break free. When her attempt continued to prove fruitless, she faced the girl and growled. Phineas could see the dog trembling in the moonlight, and the hackles on her neck were raised. When he looked back, the girl had retreated a couple of feet, moving a little deeper into the woods.

"Help me," she repeated. "I'm lost, and I'm lonely."

Phineas was wary now, although he could not have said why, beyond the girl's pallor and the affect her presence was having on his dog, yet still he walked toward her, and as he did so she moved a little farther away, until at last the clearing was at his back, and there was only forest before him: forest, and the dim form of the girl among the trees. Phineas lowered his torch, but the girl did not fade into the shadows of the forest. Instead, she continued to luminesce faintly, and although Phineas could see his own breath pluming thickly before him, no such cloud emerged from the girl's mouth, not even as she spoke again.

"Please, I'm lonely and I'm scared," she said. "Come with me."

Now she raised her hand, beckoning to him, and he saw the dirt beneath her fingernails, as though she had clawed her way out of some dark spot, a hiding place of earth, and worms, and scuttling bugs.

"No, honey," said Phineas. "I don't think I'll be going anywhere with you."

Without taking his eyes from her, he backed away until he was beside Misty, and then he squatted and began to hack at the briars. They came away reluctantly, and they were sticky to the touch. Even as he cut at them, he thought that he felt others begin to curl around his boots, but later he told himself that it was probably just his mind playing tricks on him, as if that one small detail might make up for the far greater trick of a girl glowing in the depths, asking an old man to join her in her forest bower. He felt her anger, and her frustration, and, yes, her sadness, because she *was* lonely, and she *was* scared, but she didn't want to be saved. She wanted to visit her loneliness and fear on another, and Phineas didn't know what would be worse: to die in the woods with the girl for company, until eventually the world faded to black; or to die and then wake up to find himself like her, wandering the woods looking for others to share his misery.

At last, Misty was freed. The dog shot away, then paused to make sure that her master was following her, for even in her relief to be free she would not abandon him in this place, just as he had not abandoned her. Slowly, Phineas went after her, his eyes fixed on the little girl, keeping her in sight for as long as he could, until she was visible no longer and he found himself once again on familiar ground.

And that was why Phineas Arbogast stopped going to his cabin in the Rangeley woods, where the ruins of it may still be visible somewhere between Rangeley and Langdon, bound with sticky briars as nature claims it as her own.

Nature, and a little girl with pale, glowing skin, seeking in vain for a playmate to join her in her games.

I STILL HAD AN old edition of a brochure called *Maine Invites You* given to me by Phineas. It was published by the Maine Publicity Bureau sometime in the late 1930s or early 1940s, as the letter of greeting inside the front cover was written by Governor Lewis O. Barrows, who was in office from 1937 until 1941. Barrows was an old-school Republican of the stripe that some of his more rabid descendants would cross the street to avoid: he balanced the budget, improved state school funding, and reinstated old-age benefits payments, all while reducing the state deficit. Rush Limbaugh would have called him a socialist.

The brochure was a touching tribute to a bygone era, when you could rent a high-end cabin for $30 per week and eat a chicken dinner for a dollar. Most of the places mentioned in it are long gone—the Lafayette Hotel in Portland, the Willows and the Checkley out at Prout's Neck—and the writers managed to find something kind to say about almost everywhere, even those towns whose own residents had trouble figuring out why they'd stayed in them, never mind why anyone else might want to travel there on vacation.

The town of Langdon, midway between Rangeley and Stratton, had a page all to itself, and it was interesting to note how many times the name Proctor appeared on the advertisements: among others, there was a Proctor's Camp; and the Bald Mountain diner, run by E. and A. Proctor; and R. H. Proctor's Lakeview Fine Dining Restaurant. Clearly, the Proctors had Langdon pretty much all sewn up back in the day, and the town was enough of a draw for tourists—or the Proctors felt that it might be—to justify taking out a series of top-end ads, each one adorned with a photograph of the establishment in question.

Whatever appeal Langdon might once have had for visitors was no longer apparent, if it had ever been anything more than a figment of the Proctors' own ambitions to begin with. It was now merely a strip of decrepit houses and struggling businesses, closer to the New Hampshire border than the Canadian, but easily accessible from either. The Bald Mountain diner was still there, but it looked like it hadn't served a meal for at least a decade. The town's only store bore a sign announcing that it was closed due to a bereavement and would reopen in a week's time. The notice was dated "October 10, 2005," which suggested the kind of mourning period usually associated with the deaths of kings. Apart from that, there was a hairdresser's, a taxidermist's, and a bar named the Belle Dam, which might have been a clever pun on Rangeley's own dams or, as seemed more likely on closer inspection, the result of the loss of the letter *e* from the sign. There was nobody on the streets, although a couple of cars were parked along it. Ironically, only the taxidermy showed any signs of life. The front door was open, and a man in overalls came out to watch me as I took in the bright lights of Langdon. I figured him for sixty or more, but he might just as easily have been older and holding off the predations of the years. Maybe it had something to do with all of the preservatives with which he worked.

"Quiet," I said.

"I guess," he replied, in the manner of one who wasn't entirely convinced that this was the case and, even if it was, he sort of liked it that way.

I looked around again. It didn't seem like there was much room for argument, but maybe he knew something that I didn't about what was going on behind all those closed doors.

"Hotter than a Methodist hell, and all," he added. He was right. I hadn't noticed while I was in the car, but I had begun to perspire as soon as I stepped from it. The taxidermist, meanwhile, wasn't so much sweating as self-basting. No-see-ums hovered around us both.

"Your name wouldn't be Proctor, by any chance?" I asked him.

"No, I'm Stunden."

"You mind if I ask you some questions, Mr. Stunden?"

"You already are, far as I can tell."

He was grinning crookedly, but there was no malice in it. He was just breaking the monotony of daily life in Langdon. He detached himself from the frame of his door and indicated with a nod of his head that I should follow him inside. The interior was dark. Antlers, tagged and numbered, lay on the floor or hung from the old rafters. A recently stuffed and mounted large-mouth bass was propped on top of a freezer to my left, and to the right were shelves lined with jars of chemicals, paint, and assorted glass eyes. Blood had dripped down the side of the freezer, hardening and then corroding the metal. The room was dominated by a steel workbench upon which currently lay a deer hide and a round-bladed shaver. Piles of discarded meat lay on the floor beneath the bench. I could see that he knew his business: he was being careful to scrape the hide down to the dermis, leaving no trace of fat that might turn to acid and cause the hide to smell, or the hair to fall out. Nearby was a foam mannequin of a deer head, waiting for the skin to be applied to it. The whole place stank of dead flesh. I couldn't help but wrinkle my nose.

"Sorry about the smell," he said. "I don't notice it anymore. I'd talk to you outside, but I got this deer hide to finish, and I'm working on a couple of ducks for the same guy."

He pointed at two clear containers of ground corncob, in which he was degreasing the duck carcasses. "Can't shave a duck," he said. "The skin won't take it."

Since shaving a duck had never struck me as something I'd feel the inclination to do, I contented myself with observing that it wasn't yet hunting season.

"This deer died of natural causes," said Stunden. "Tripped and fell on a bullet."

"And the ducks?"

"They drowned."

As he worked the shaver, he began to sweat even more.

"Looks like a hard grind," I said.

Stunden shrugged. "Deer are hard. Waterfowl, not so much. I can take care of a duck in a couple of hours, and I get to indulge my artistic side. You have to be careful with the colors, else it won't look right. I'll get five hundred dollars for those ones. I know the guy will pay, too, and that's not always the case. Times are hard. I take deposits now, and I never had to do that before."

He continued shaving the deer. The sound was faintly unpleasant. "So, what brings you to Langdon?"

"I'm looking for a man named Harold Proctor."

"He in trouble?"

"Why do you ask?"

"No disrespect, but al'st I know is that you look like the kind of man calls about trouble."

"My name's Charlie Parker. I'm a private investigator."

"Doesn't answer my question. Is Harold in trouble?"

"He might be, but not from me."

"He coming into money?"

"Again, he might be, but not from me."

Stunden glanced up from his work. "He lives out by the family motel, about a mile west of here. Hard as a snow snake to find, though, if you don't know the road."

"The motel still in business?"

"The only thing still in business here is me, and I don't know how much longer I'll be able to say that. The motel's been closed for a decade or so now. Before that, it was a camp, but motels seemed to be the way to go, or so the Proctors thought. Harold's momma and poppa used to run it, but they died, and the motel closed. Never made much money anyway. Poor location out in the williwigs for a motel. Harold's the last of the Proctors. Hard to believe. They used to run half this town, and the other half paid them rent, but they weren't big breeders, the Proctors; or lookers, come to think of it, which might have something to do with it. The Proctor creatures were kind of homely, I seem to recall."

"And the men?"

"Well, I wasn't looking at the men, so I can't rightly say." His eyes twinkled in the gloom, and I guessed that Mr. Stunden might have been quite the heartbreaker in his time, had there been anyone apart from homely Proctor women on whom to test his charms. "When they started dying out, the town died with them. Now we get by on what we can make from Rangeley's overflow, which ain't much."

I waited as he completed his work on the hide. He switched off the shaver, and used dish soap to clean the grease from his hands.

"I ought to tell you that Harold's not too sociable," he said. "He was never what you might call outgoing, but he came back from Iraq—the first war, not this one—with a troubled disposition. He keeps himself to himself out there, mostly. I pass him on the road from time to time, and I see him at Our Lady of the Lakes in Oquossoc on Sundays, but that's it. Best I can get out of him now is a nod. Like I said, he's never been exactly friendly, but until recently he'd always give you the time of day, and a word or two on the weather. He used to come into the Belle Dam, and if he was in the mood we'd talk." He pronounced it "Belle Dayme." "In case you're wondering, I own that too. During hunting season, I make a few bucks on it. The rest of the year, it's just something to do in the evenings."

"Did he talk to you about his time in Iraq?"

"Generally he preferred to drink alone. He'd buy his liquor in New Hampshire, or over the border in Canada, and bring it back to his place, but once a week he'd come out of the woods and relax some. He hated it over there. Said he spent most of his time either bored or scared shitless. But, you know—"

He stopped speaking, but continued drying his hands as he sized me up. "Why don't you tell me your interest in Harold before I go any further?"

"You seem protective of him."

"This is a small town, and barely that. If we don't look out for one another, who will?"

"And yet you're worried enough about Harold to talk with a stranger."

"Who says I'm worried?"

"You wouldn't be talking to me otherwise, and I can see it in your eyes. I told you, I don't mean him any harm. For what it's worth, I'm working for the father of a former soldier who served in Iraq this time round. His son committed suicide after he returned home. It seems that the boy's behavior had changed in the weeks before his death, and his father wants to know what might have brought that on. Harold knew the boy some, I think, because he attended the funeral. I just want to ask him some questions."

Stunden shook his head in sadness. "That's a hard burden to bear. You got kids?"

That question always gave me pause. Yes, I have a daughter. And, once, I had another.

"One," I said. "A girl."

"I got two boys, fourteen and seventeen." He must have seen something in my face, because he said: "I married late in life. Too late, I think. I was set in my ways, and I never could get my head around girlin'. My boys live with their mother down in Skowhegan now. I wouldn't want them to join the military. If one of my sons wanted to join up, then I'd let him know how I felt about it but I wouldn't try to stop him. Still, if I had a boy over in Iraq or Afghanistan, I'd spend every hour just praying for him to be safe. I think it would cost me some of the years left to me."

He leaned back against his workbench.

"Like I said, Harold's changed," he said. "I don't mean just because of the war, and his injury. I think he's sick, inside." He tapped the side of his head, just in case I was under any illusions about the nature of Proctor's troubles. "The last time he came into the bar, which was, oh, must be two weeks ago, he looked different, like he wasn't sleeping right. I'd have said that he was frightened. I had to ask him what was wrong, it was so obvious to me."

"What did he say?"

"Well, he'd had a skinful by then, and that was before he even got as far as the Dame, but he told me that he was being haunted." He let the word hang in the air for a moment, waiting for the dead flesh and old hides to cover it and give it form. "He said that he was hearing voices, that they were keeping him from his sleep. I told him he should go see a military doctor, that maybe he was suffering from that stress thing. Post-traumatic whatever."

"What were these voices saying?"

"He couldn't understand them. They didn't speak English. That was when I became sure that it was something to do with what happened to him over there. We talked about it some more, and he said that he might give someone a call."

"And did he?"

"I don't know. That was the last time he came into the bar. But I was concerned about him, so a week after that I took a ride out to his place to see how he was. There was a car parked outside his cabin, so I figured that he had visitors and decided not to disturb him. As I was reversing back down the hill, the cabin door opened, and four men came out. Harold was one of them. I didn't recognize the other three. They just watched me go. But later, the three visitors came here, and stood where you're standing now. They asked me what I was doing out at Harold's place. The colored one who did most of the talking was real polite about it, but I could tell he didn't like the fact that I'd driven out there. I told them the truth: that I was a friend of Harold's, and I was worried about him, that he hadn't seemed himself of late. That seemed to satisfy him. He told me they were old army buddies of Harold's, and that Harold was doing just fine."

"You had no cause to disbelieve them?"

"They were military men for sure. They had that bearing about them. The other one limped some, and was missing fingers from here." Stunden held up his left hand. "I took it for a war wound."

Joel Tobias.

"And the third?"

"He didn't say much. Big guy, bald head. I didn't care for him."

That was Bacci, I thought, remembering Ronald Straydeer's annotated photograph. Karen Emory didn't like him either. I wondered if he was the one who had first suggested raping me at the Blue Moon.

"Anyway, the bald guy asked if I'd be able to preserve a person, and made some joke about trophies for his wall," said Stundem. " 'Haji,' that's the word that he used: haji trophies for his wall. I guess he meant terrorists. The other guy, his friend with the damaged hand, told him to shut his mouth."

"And you haven't spoken to Harold since that night at the bar?"

"No. Seen him once or twice in passing, but he hasn't been back at the Dame."

Stunden had nothing more to add. I thanked him for his time. He asked me not to tell Harold Proctor that we'd spoken, and I gave him that promise. As we walked to the door, Stunden said: "This boy, the one who killed himself, you say his father thought that he'd changed before he died?"

"That's right."

"Changed how, you mind me asking?"

"Cut himself off from his friends. Became paranoid. Had trouble sleeping."

"Like Harold."

"Yes, like Harold."

"Maybe, after you've talked to him, I'll go out there and see how he's doing. Could be I can convince him to see someone before—"

He trailed off. I shook his hand.

"I think that would be a good thing to do, Mr. Stunden. I'll try to call by before I leave, let you know how it all went."

"I'd appreciate that," he said.

He gave me directions to Proctor's place, then raised a hand in farewell as I drove away. I did the same, and the fragrance from the soap that Stunden had used to clean himself, and which had passed to me from his hand, wafted through the car. It was strong, but not strong enough, for underlying it was an animal smell of flesh and burned hair. I opened the window, despite the heat and the bugs, but it would not disperse. It was on my skin, and it stayed with me all the way to the Proctor motel.

CHAPTER

XXIV

Despite Stunden's directions, I still managed to miss the turn for the motel on my first pass. He had told me that the remains of a big sign were just about visible across from the entrance road, but the forest had grown thickly around it, and it was only by chance on the return run that I caught a glimpse of it through the foliage. Some faded red letters were barely discernible on the rotting wood, along with what might have been deer antlers, but a green arrow that would once have stood out against the white of the sign was now merely another shade in summer's paint box.

Its origins as a camp were clear, as it lay at the top of a curving trail that ran west through thick woods. The trail was pitted, and the undergrowth had not been cut back for so long that it scraped at the side of my car, but I spotted broken branches and crushed vegetation in places, and the tracks of a heavy vehicle were clear in the dirt, like the slowly fossilizing footprints of a dinosaur.

Eventually, I emerged into a clearing. To my right was a small cabin, its doors and windows firmly closed despite the heat. It was probably a relic of the original camp. It certainly looked old enough. I could see part of what appeared to be a more modern extension at the back, where the cabin's living area had been expanded for long-term habitation. Between the cabin and where I was parked stood a red Dodge truck.

Another dirt track led from the cabin to the motel. It was a standard L-shaped structure, with the office at the angle where the two arms met and a vertical neon motel sign, long out of use, pointing at the sky. I wondered if it had even been visible from the road, since the motel was located in a kind of natural hollow. Maybe the cabins had proved too difficult to maintain, and the Proctors believed that their customers would remain loyal to them even after they went with the times and changed to a motel, but it was clear that Stunden had been right: nothing about the Proctor motel suggested that it had ever been a good idea to build it. Now the doors and windows of every unit were boarded up, the grass had grown through the cracked stone of the parking lot, and ivy was creeping up the walls and along the flat roof. If it stayed standing for long enough, it would join the ranks of the other phantom towns and abandoned dwellings that were so much a part of this state.

I sounded the horn and waited. Nobody emerged from the cabin or the surrounding woods. I recalled what Stunden had said about Proctor. A veteran living out here in the wild was likely to have a gun, and if Proctor was as disturbed as Stunden had intimated then I didn't want him taking me for a threat. His truck was still there, so he couldn't have gone far. I hit the horn again, then left the car and began to walk to the cabin. As I did so, I glanced into the cab of the truck. An open pack of doughnuts lay on the passenger seat. It was crawling with ants.

I knocked on the cabin door and called Proctor's name, but there was no reply. I peered through a window. The television lay busted on the floor, and I could see pieces of a phone scattered beside it. The bed was unmade, yellowed sheet coiled upon the floor like melted ice cream.

I returned to the door, half-expecting to see an irate Proctor emerge from the woods, waving a gun and muttering about ghosts, then tried the handle. It opened easily. Flies buzzed, and there were more ants moving in columns across the linoleum floor. The whole place stank of cigarette smoke. I checked the refrigerator. The milk was still in date, but it was as close as Proctor was likely to come to a healthy diet, because otherwise the refrigerator was filled with the kind of food that would sap a dietician's will to live: cheap ready meals, microwavable burgers, processed meats. There was no sign of fruit or vegetables, and at least half of the storage space was devoted to bottles of regular cola. The trash bag in the corner was packed with discarded French fry cartons, chicken buckets, burger wrappers from fast food joints, crushed Red Bull cans, and empty bottles of Vicks Nyquil. Apart from soups, and beans, Proctor's kitchen shelves held mainly candy and cookies. I also found a couple of big jars of coffee, and half a dozen bottles of cheap gin and vodka. The sleeping area contained more bottles of Nyquil, a bunch of antihistamines, and some Sominex. Proctor was living on stimulants—sugar, energy drinks, caffeine, nicotine—and then using mostly over-the-counter medicines to help him sleep. There was also an empty package of clozapine, recently prescribed by a local physician, which meant that Proctor had been desperate enough to seek professional help. Clozapine was an antipsychotic used as a sedative, and also as a means of treating schizophrenia. I thought back to my conversation with Bernie Kramer's sister, and her belief that Kramer had been hearing voices before he took his own life. I wondered what voices Harold Proctor was hearing.

On the bed lay the keys to the truck, and an empty holster.

I continued searching the place, which was how I found the envelope of cash. It had been placed beneath the mattress, unsealed, and contained $2,500 in twenties and fifties, all neatly arranged face up. Even out here, it didn't make much sense for a man to leave money like that under his mattress, but then none of this made any sense. Proctor clearly hadn't been in his cabin, or his truck, for some time.

If he'd intended to leave, he'd have taken the money, and the truck. If there was a problem with his truck, he'd still have taken the money. I looked at the envelope again. It was clean and new. It hadn't been under the mattress for very long.

I put the money back where I found it and walked down to the motel. Only the office was not boarded up. The door was unlocked, so I took a look inside. Proctor had clearly been using it for storage: there were cans of food stacked in one corner—beans, chili, and stews, mostly—along with big packs of toilet paper and some old window screens A faint whirring sound was coming from somewhere. Behind the reception desk was a closed door, presumably leading into a back room. I lifted the hatch on the counter and stepped inside. The sound was louder now. I pushed the door open with my foot.

Before me was a wooden console, with sixteen small bulbs arrayed in lines of four, each marked with a number. The sound was coming from a speaker beside the console. I guessed that it was an old intercom system, enabling guests to communicate with the front desk without using a phone. I'd never seen anything like it before, but it might be that the Proctors hadn't bothered with phones in all the rooms when the motel opened, or they had first opted for a quainter system and then retained it as a conversation piece. The console didn't have a maker's name on it, and I thought that it might have been hand built by the Proctors. Clearly, though, there was still power running in the motel.

The sound was making me uneasy. It might simply have been a malfunction, but why now? Anyway, power or no power, the system shouldn't even have been working after all these years. Then again, they used to build things to last, and it was depressing how easily we were surprised by good workmanship these days. I checked the console, tapping the bulbs as I went.

When I tapped the bulb for room 15, it began to blink redly.

I drew my gun and went back outside, following the doors along the right. When I came to room 14, I saw that the screws had been removed from the board on its door, and the board itself now simply lay against the frame. When I reached room 15, though, its board was still firmly in place. Nevertheless, I could hear an echo of the intercom buzzer from inside.

I leaned against the wall between the two rooms and called out.

"Mr. Proctor? You in there?"

There was no reply. Quickly, I pushed away the board from in front of room 14. The door behind it was closed. I tried the handle, and it opened easily. Daylight shone on the frame of a bare bed that had been pushed upright against the wall, leaving the floor space largely clear. Two bedside lockers had been stacked in a corner. Otherwise, the room was unfurnished. There were white strands on the carpet, which smelled of mold. I picked up one of the strands and held it to the light: it was a wood shaving. Beside the lockers lay a couple of foam chips. I ran my hand across the carpet, and felt the marks left by boxes of some kind. Carefully, I approached the small bathroom at the back, but it was empty. There was no connecting door between rooms 14 and 15.

I was about to leave when I noticed marks on the wall. I had to use my flashlight to see them properly. They looked like handprints, but they seemed to have been burned into the paintwork. Ash and blistered paint fell away when I touched my fingers to them. I had an uncomfortable sense of contamination, and although the bed was bare, and the room was damp, I felt that it had been occupied recently, so recently that I could almost hear the fading echo of a conversation, albeit a disagreeable one.

I went outside again, and examined the boarded-up entrance to room 15. It should have been held in place by screws, just like the other doors that I had passed, but no heads were visible. With no great expectation of success, I managed to slip my fingers into the gap between the board and the door frame, and tugged.

The board came away easily, almost knocking me backward as it did. I saw that it had been held loosely in place by a single long screw drilled through the frame into the board. The screw had been driven in from inside, not out. This time, when I tried the door handle, it did not open. I kicked at it, but it was sealed tight. I went back to my car and retrieved a crowbar from the trunk, but even with it I had no luck. The door had been firmly secured from within. Instead, I began to work on the board covering the window. That was easier, as it had been nailed, not screwed, into the frame. When it came away it revealed filthy, thick glass, cracked, but not shattered, by a pair of bullet holes. The drapes were drawn inside the room.

It took a little effort, but I managed to smash the glass pane with the crowbar, shielding myself with the wall just in case whoever was in there was still together enough to take a shot at me, but no sound came. As soon as I smelled the odor coming from inside, I knew why. I pushed the drapes aside and climbed into the room.

The bed had been broken up, and its boards nailed to the door frame, sealing it shut. More long nails had been driven through the door and into the frame at an angle, although some of them had come away, either partially or entirely, as though whoever had put them in place had then reconsidered and begun removing them again; that, or they were so long that they'd penetrated right through, and someone from outside had started hammering them back, although I could see no damage to the ends.

There was more furniture in this room than in its neighbor: a long chest and a TV stand in addition to twin beds and two bedside lockers. It had all been stacked in one corner, the way a child might have constructed a fortress at home. I moved closer. A man lay slumped in the corner behind the furniture, his head resting against the intercom button on the wall. There was a cloud of blood and bone behind his head, and a Browning hung loosely from his right hand. The man's body was swollen, and so colonized by maggots and insects that they gave it the impression of movement and life. They had quarried in his eyes, leaving them hollow. I covered my mouth with my hand, but the smell was too strong. I leaned out of the window, gasping, and tried not to throw up. Once I'd recovered, I took off my jacket and pressed it against my face, then made a cursory examination of the room. There was a tool kit beside the body, along with a nail gun. There was no sign of food or water. I ran my fingers over the metal backing of the door and felt the marks of five bullet holes. I turned the flashlight on them and picked out more in the walls. I counted twelve in all. The Browning's magazine held thirteen. He had saved the last one for himself.

There was a bottle of water in the Lexus. I used it to wash the taste of decay from my mouth, but I could still smell it on my clothes. I now stank of soap, and dead deer, and dead men.

I called 911 and waited for the police to come.

The names still haunted him. There was Gazaliya, just about the most dangerous neighborhood in Baghdad, where it had all come to an end; and Dora; and Sadiya, places where they killed the trash collectors so that the streets piled up with filth and it became impossible to live there. There was the Umm al-Qura mosque in western Baghdad, headquarters of the Sunni insurgency, which, in an ideal world, they would simply have wiped off the face of the earth. There was the Amiriya racetrack, where kidnap victims were bought and sold. From the racetrack, a road led straight to Garma, controlled by the insurgents. Once you were taken to Garma, you were gone.

In Al-Adhamiya, the Sunni stronghold in Baghdad, close to the Tigris River, the Shia death squads dressed as policemen and set up false checkpoints to catch their Sunni neighbors. The Shias were supposed to be on our side, but nobody was really on our side. As far as he could tell, the only difference between the Sunnis and the Shias lay in the way that they killed. The Sunnis beheaded: one evening, he and a couple of the others had watched a beheading on a DVD given to them by their interpreter. They'd all wanted to see it, but he'd regretted asking as soon as it started. There was the man, cowering: not an American, because they didn't want to watch one of their own die, but some poor bastard Shia who'd chosen the wrong turn, or stopped when he should have put the *foot down and taken his chances with the bullets. What struck him was how matter-of-fact the executioner had been, how seemingly removed from the task at hand: the cutting had been methodical, grim, practical, like the ritualistic killing of an animal; an appalling death, but one without sadism beyond the actual act of killing itself. Afterward, they had all said the same thing: don't let them take me. If there's a chance of it, and you see it happening, kill me. Kill us all.*

The Shias, meanwhile, tortured. They had a particular fondness for the electric drill: knees, elbows, groin, eyes. That was it: Sunnis behead, Shias torment, and they all worship the same god, except there was some dispute about who should have taken over the religion after the prophet Mohammed died, and that was why they were now hacking heads and drilling bones. It was all about qisas: *revenge. It didn't surprise him the first time the interpreter told him that, according to the Islamic calendar, it was still only the fifteenth century: 1424, or something like it, when he arrived in Iraq. That made a kind of sense to him, because these people were still behaving like it was the Middle Ages.*

But now they were part of a modern war, a war fought with night-vision lenses, and heavy weapons. They responded with RPGs, and mortars, and bombs hidden inside dead dogs. When they didn't have those, they retaliated with stones, and blades. They answered the new with the old; old weapons, and old names: Nergal, and Ninazu, and the one whose name was lost. They set the trap, and waited for them to come.

XXV

The first to arrive at the Proctor place were two state troopers out of Skowhegan. I'd never met them before, but one of them knew my name. After some cursory questioning, they let me sit in the Lexus while we waited for the detectives to arrive. The cops made small talk between themselves but left me alone until, after about an hour, the detectives showed up. By then, the sun was setting, and they broke out the flashlights for the examination.

As it turned out, I'd met one of them before. His name was Gordon Walsh, and he looked like a real bruiser as he stepped from his car, his big sunglasses giving the impression that a large bug had evolved to the point that it could wear a suit. He was a former college football player, and he'd kept in shape. He had four or five inches on me, and a good forty pounds. A scar ran across his chin where someone had had the temerity to slash him with a bottle when he was still a trooper. I hated to think of what might have happened to the assailant. They were probably still trying to extract the bottle surgically from wherever Walsh had stuck it.

Beside him was a smaller, younger detective whom I didn't recognize. He had that rookie look to him, a veneer of severity that couldn't quite disguise his uncertainty, like a young colt trying to keep up with the stallion that had sired it. Walsh glanced up at me but said nothing, then followed one of the troopers down to the room in which Proctor's body lay. Before he entered, he smeared some Vicks VapoRub under his nose, but he still didn't stay in there for long, and he took some deep breaths when he emerged. Then he and his partner went up to the cabin and spent some time poking around inside. After that, they examined the truck, all the while studiously ignoring me. Walsh had obviously found the keys, and reached in to turn on the ignition. The truck started the first time. He killed the engine, then said something to his partner before both of them at last decided to pass the time of day with me.

Walsh sucked on one arm of his shades and tut-tutted as he approached me.

"Charlie Parker," he said. "As soon as I heard your name, I knew my day was about to get more entertaining."

"Detective Walsh," I replied. "I saw evildoers tremble and knew that you were near. I see you're still subsisting on raw meat."

"*Mens sana, in corpore sano.* And vice versa. That's Latin. Benefits of a Catholic education. This is my partner, Detective Soames."

Soames nodded, but didn't say anything. His mouth was rigid, and his jaw jutted in a Dudley Do-Right manner. I bet he ground his teeth at night.

"Did you kill him?" asked Walsh.

"No, I didn't kill him."

"Damn, I was hoping we could get this thing all tied up by midnight if you confessed. I'd probably be given a medal for putting you behind bars at last."

"And I thought you liked me, Detective."

"I do like you. Imagine what the ones who don't like you say about you. So, if you're not prepared to break down and confess, you want to tell me something useful?" said Walsh.

"His name is Harold Proctor, or I assume that's who he is, or was," I said. "I've never met him, so I can't say for sure."

"What brings you to his neck of the woods?"

"I'm looking into the suicide of a young man down in Portland, a former soldier."

"Who for?"

"The boy's father."

"What's his name?"

"The father's name is Bennett Patchett. He owns the Downs Diner in Scarborough."

"Where did Proctor fit in?"

"Damien Patchett, the son, might have met him at some point. Proctor attended Patchett's funeral. I thought he might have some insights into Damien's frame of mind before he took his own life."

"Insights, huh? You do talk nice, I'll give you that. Any doubts about how this Patchett boy died?"

"None that I can tell. He shot himself out in the woods near Cape Elizabeth."

"So how come his father is paying you good money to investigate his death?"

"He wants to know what made his son kill himself. Is that so difficult to understand?"

Behind us, the forensics unit appeared, picking its way up the trail. Walsh tapped his partner on the arm.

"Elliot, go give them a heads-up, point them in the right direction."

Soames did as he was told, but not before a slight crease of unhappiness furrowed his otherwise unlined brow at being shooed away while the grown-ups talked. Maybe he wasn't as wet as he appeared.

"New boy?" I said.

"He's good. Ambitious. Wants to solve crimes."

"You remember when you were young like that?"

"I was never good, and if I was ambitious I'd be somewhere else by now. Still like to solve crimes, though. Gives me a sense of purpose. Otherwise, I don't feel like I'm earning my wage, and a man should earn his wage. Kind of brings us back to this Patchett thing." He took a look over his shoulder to where Soames was talking to a man who was pulling on a white protective suit. "My partner likes things to be official," he said. "He types reports neatly as he goes along." He turned back to me. "I, on the other hand, type like one of Bob Newhart's monkeys, and I prefer to write my report at the end, not the beginning. So it seems to me, unofficially, that you're looking into the suicide of a veteran, and it brings you out here where you find another veteran who also appears to be the victim of a self-inflicted gunshot wound, except before he killed himself he managed to loose off most of a mag at someone outside before popping one more into his own skull. Am I reading this right?"

Outside. That word gave me pause. If the threat was outside, why had Proctor been firing at the walls of the room? He was ex-military, so poor shooting couldn't have been the excuse. But the room was sealed up from the inside, so the threat couldn't have been in there with him.

Could it?

I kept those thoughts to myself, and contented myself with: "So far."

"How old was the Patchett boy?"

"Twenty-seven."

"And Proctor?"

"Fifties, I'd say. Early fifties. He served in the first Iraq war."

"He a sociable man, would you have said?"

"I never had the pleasure."

"But he lived up here, and Patchett lived in Portland?"

"Scarborough."

"Lot of miles between here and there."

"I suppose. Is this an interrogation, Detective?"

"Interrogations involve bright lights, and sweaty men in shirt-sleeves, and people trying to lawyer up. This is a conversation. My point is: how did Proctor and Patchett come to be acquainted?"

"Does it matter so much?"

"It matters because you're here, and because they're both dead. Come on, Parker, give a guy a break."

There wasn't much point in holding back all that I knew, but I decided to keep some of it, for luck.

"At first, I thought Proctor might have been one of the veterans assigned to meet soldiers when they return from active duty, and he and Patchett might have met up that way, but now I think Patchett and Proctor may have been involved in a business venture together."

"Patchett and Proctor. Sounds like a firm of lawyers. What kind of business venture?"

"I don't know for sure, but this place is near the border, and it's been used for storage recently. There are wood shavings and foam pellets in the room next to the body, and marks on the floor that look like they could have been left by packing cases. Might be worth getting a sniffer dog in there."

"You figure drugs?"

"It's possible."

"You take a look inside his cabin?"

"Just to see if he was there."

"You search it?"

"That would be illegal."

"That's not answering the question, but I'll assume that you did. I would have, and you're at least as unscrupulous as I am. And since you're good at what you do, you'd have found an envelope filled with cash under the mattress."

"Would I? How interesting."

Walsh leaned against my car and looked from the cabin to the truck, then to the motel and back again. His face grew serious.

"So he's got cash, food in the refrigerator, enough booze and candy to stock a convenience store, and his truck appears to be running fine. Yet somehow he ends up barricading himself inside a motel room, firing shots off at the door and window, before sticking the gun in his own mouth and pulling the trigger."

"His phone, TV, and radio were all broken up," I said.

"I saw that. By him, or by someone else?"

"The trailer wasn't trashed. All the books were on the shelves, his clothes were still in his closet, and the mattress was still on the bed. If someone was serious about taking the place apart, then they'd have found the money."

"Assuming they wanted it to begin with."

"I spoke to a man named Stunden down in Langdon. He's the taxi-dermist, but he also runs the local bar."

"You gotta love small towns," said Walsh. "If he could add under-taker to his list of accomplishments, he'd be indispensable."

"Stunden told me that Proctor was troubled. He felt that he was being haunted."

"Haunted?"

"That was the word he used to Stunden, but Stunden seemed to think that it might be a symptom of post-traumatic stress as a con-sequence of his time in Iraq. He wouldn't be the first soldier to come back with mental as well as physical scars."

"Like your client's son? Two suicides, each known to the other. That strike you as odd?"

I didn't reply. I wondered how long it would take Walsh to con-nect the deaths of Proctor and Damien with the earlier suicide of Bernie Kramer up in Quebec, and the murder-suicide involving Brett Harlan. Once he did so, he'd probably come up with Joel Tobias as well. I made a mental note to ask Bennett Patchett to keep Tobias's name out of any conversations he might have with the state police, at least for now.

Four soldiers, three from the same squad and one peripher-ally connected to the others, all dead from what appeared to be self-inflicted wounds, along with a wife who had been unfortunate enough to encounter her husband with a bayonet in his hand. I'd gone back to the newspaper reports on the killings, and it wasn't hard to read between the lines and figure that both Brett and Margaret Harlan had met terrible ends.

Increasingly, I was starting to believe that something very bad had occurred over in Iraq, an experience that the men of Stryker C had shared and brought back with them, even if Carrie Saunders had nixed that idea. I still couldn't grasp how it might tie in with what Jimmy Jewel suspected of Joel Tobias: that he was running a smuggling operation via his trucking business. But there were the marks on the floor of room 14 to consider, and the traces of packing materials alongside them, and the fact that, if Stunden was right, then Proctor had apparently been visited by some of the men from Stryker C before he died. Then there was the cash under the mattress, which suggested that Proctor had recently been paid for something: storage facilities, I guessed, which raised the question of what was being stored. Drugs still seemed the likeliest option, but Jimmy Jewel hadn't been convinced, and it would have taken a lot of very heavy drugs to leave those marks on the carpet. Anyway, from what I knew of the international drug trade, Afghanistan was more likely to provide a source of wholesale drugs than Iraq, and Tobias's squad hadn't served in Afghanistan.

Soames called to Walsh, and he left me to my thoughts. I wondered what was happening over in Bangor. If Bobby Jandreau didn't see the wisdom of talking soon, it would be time at last to put significant pressure on Joel Tobias.

Darkness closed in, but the air did not cool. Insects bit, and I heard movement in the undergrowth of the forest as the night creatures came out to feed, and to hunt. The medical examiner arrived, and klieg lights illuminated the motel as Harold Proctor's body was removed, ready to be taken to the Maine medical examiner's office down in Augusta. His would be the sole body down there, but not for long. Soon, he would have plenty of company.

XXVI

They came at nightfall. A soft breeze brought movement to the woods, hiding their approach, but Angel and Louis had been waiting for them, knowing that they would come. They had exchanged positions every hour to keep each other alert, and it was Angel who was watching the Mustang when the figures appeared, his sharp eyes picking up the slight change in the shadows cast by the swaying trees. He touched his partner's sleeve, and Louis turned his attention from the house to the car. Silently, they watched the two men descend, their arms unnaturally extended by the guns in their hands, the suppressors like swollen tissue about to burst.

They were good: that was Louis's first thought. There must be a vehicle nearby, but he hadn't heard it, and Angel hadn't picked them up until they were almost on top of the car. Anyone in the Mustang would have been dead before he realized what was happening. The two men melted back into the shadows again as they realized the Mustang was unoccupied, and even Louis had to strain to follow their progress. They wore no masks, which meant that they weren't concerned about witnesses, because they would only be seen by whoever was in the house, and then for only as long as it took their victims to die.

Victims: that was the other matter. The situation at Bobby Jandreau's house had been complicated by the arrival of Mel Nelson, his estranged girlfriend, two hours earlier. Incredible as it seemed, the spontaneous relationship advice offered that afternoon seemed to have made an impression. Louis had regarded the couple impassively as they talked in the living room for a time before Mel walked slowly over to Bobby, then knelt before him and embraced him. After that, they had retired to what Louis presumed was the bedroom, and they had not been seen since.

More distorted shadows. The gunmen were at the rear of the house now, where there was no chance of being seen by a neighbor at a window, or by someone taking a dog for a bedtime walk. One at either side of the door. A nod. Breaking glass. A figure poised to provide cover, the gun raised, as the other reached in through the hole to open the lock. Movement inside the house in response to the intrusion. A scream. The slamming closed of a bedroom door.

Louis took the first man with two shots to the back and a third, the killing shot, to the base of the skull. There was no warning, no invitation to turn with his hands held high, no chance to surrender. Such gestures were for the good guys in westerns, the ones who wore white hats and got the girl at the end. In real life, good guys who give chances to killers end up dead, and Louis, who had no idea if he was truly good or not, and could not have cared less, had no intention of dying for a romantic ideal. As the slain man fell, Louis's gun was already swinging right. The second of the would-be killers was struggling to drag his hand back through the broken pane, his sleeve snagged on a jagged edge, his own body preventing him from responding to the approaching threat. But now there were two guns on him, and he froze for an instant as he acknowledged the impossibility of his own survival. There was sudden pain and then, fast upon it, sound, and he slumped against the wood, his left arm still hanging above his head, the glass erupting through the material of his jacket. He had just enough strength left to raise his gun, but it was pointing at nothing, and then nothing was all that there was.

The bedroom door remained closed. Angel called out to Jandreau as Louis began to detach the impaled man from the door.

"Bobby Jandreau, can you hear me?" he said. "My name is Angel. My partner and I were here earlier with Charlie Parker."

"I hear you," said Jandreau. "I have a gun."

"Well, that's great," said Angel. "Good for you. In the meantime, we got two bodies out here, and you and your girlfriend are only alive because of us. So do whatever you have to do, because we're moving you out."

There was the sound of whispered conversation from inside. Moments later, the door opened and Bobby Jandreau appeared in the gap, seated in his wheelchair and wearing only a pair of boxer shorts, his Beretta held uncertainly before him. He looked at Louis, who was dragging in the first of the bodies while Angel kept watch. It left a bloody trail along the pine floor.

"We need trash bags and duct tape," said Louis. "A mop and water too, unless you think red goes well with the walls."

Mel peered around the door. She seemed to be naked, apart from a strategically placed towel.

"Ma'am," said Angel, nodding his head in acknowledgment of her. "You might want to put some clothes on. Playtime's over . . ."

BY THE TIME JANDREAU and his girlfriend were dressed, and had packed some clothes and toiletries into a bag, the two bodies were trussed in black garbage sacks and wrapped with tape. Jandreau stared at them from his chair. He had identified them instantly, even as death wrought its changes on them: Twizell and Greenham, both ex-Marines.

"They were STA," he said. "Surveillance and Target Acquisition, 8451 military occupational specialty."

Angel stared at him blankly.

"Scout snipers," explained Louis. "They were slumming it tonight."

"They were one of two marine sniper teams that we inserted into Al-Adhamiya," continued Jandreau. "It was just before—"

Well, that was it. That was the story. Bobby Jandreau wanted to talk now. He wanted to tell it all because his buddies had turned on him at last, but Angel told him to save it for later. Mel Nelson drove a big old truck with a cabin back, so they had her bring it around behind the house and they threw the bodies inside. Then they put Jandreau and Mel into the Mustang, first taking care to remove and disable the GPS, and Angel drove them to a motel just outside Bucksport while Louis, following Jandreau's directions, took the truck to a disused granite quarry near Frankfort. There, using rope and chains from Jandreau's garage, he weighted the bodies and dropped them into dark water. He was about to dump the GPS tracker in the Penobscot when he reconsidered. It really was a neat piece of gear, better than he could have constructed himself. He tossed it in the back of Mel's truck and joined the others back at the motel.

And there, for want of anything better to do, they let Bobby Jandreau begin to tell his tale.

Walsh kept me sitting around until Proctor's body had been taken away. I think he was punishing me for not being more forthcoming, but at least he was talking to me and hadn't come up with some obscure legal reason to put me in a cell for the night. Since it would take me almost three hours to get to Portland, and I was tired and wanted to shower, I decided to find a place nearby to stay. The decision wasn't entirely mine to make. Forensics wanted to wait until morning to make a full sweep of the property, and the sniffer dogs would arrive soon after. Walsh had suggested that, in a spirit of goodwill and cooperation, I might like to remain in the vicinity, just in case a question occurred to him the next day, or even during the night.

"I keep a notepad beside my bed expressly for that purpose," he said as he leaned his considerable bulk against the car.

"Really?" I said. "Just in case you can come up with awkward questions to ask me?"

"That's right. You'd be surprised by how many cops might say the same thing."

"You know, I wouldn't be."

He shook his head in a despairing way, like a dog trainer faced with a recalcitrant animal that refuses to give up its ball. Some distance away, Soames was watching us unhappily. Once again, he clearly very much wanted to be part of the conversation, but Walsh was deliberately excluding him. It was interesting. I predicted tensions in their relationship. Had they been a couple, Walsh would have been sleeping in the spare room that night.

"Some might say that we underpaid state cops have a legitimate beef against you, given what happened to Hansen," he continued, and I instantly recalled Hansen, a detective with the Maine State Police, standing in the deserted house in Brooklyn in which my wife and child had been killed. He had followed me there out of some misguided missionary zeal, and he had been punished for it: not by me, but by another, a killer to whom Hansen was inconsequential and for whom I was the true prize.

"It doesn't look like he's ever going to work again," said Walsh, "and it's never been clear just what he was doing in your house on the night that he was hurt."

"Are you asking me to tell you about that night?"

"No, because I know that you won't, and anyway, I read the official version. It had more holes in it than a hobo's drawers. If you did tell me anything, it would be a lie, or a partial truth, like all that you've told me so far this evening."

"And yet here we are, taking in the night air and being civil to each other."

"Indeed. I bet you're curious as to why that might be."

"Go on, I'll bite."

Walsh hoisted himself from off my car, found his cigarettes, and lit up.

"Because even though you're a jerk, and you think you believe better than everyone else, despite overwhelming evidence to the contrary, I think you're fighting the good fight. We'll talk tomorrow, just in case I've scribbled something brilliant and incisive in my notebook overnight, or in case forensics has a question about some part of the crime scene that you've contaminated, but after that you can go about your business. What I expect in return is that, at some point in the near future, I'll receive a call from you, and you'll feel compelled to unburden yourself of what you know, or what you've learned. After that, if it's not too late to do anything other than view a body, given your previous form, I'll have an answer to what happened here, and I may even get a promotion by wrapping it all up. How does that sound?"

"That sounds reasonable."

"I'd like to think so. Now you can get in your fancy Lexus and drive out of here. Some of us have overtime to earn. Incidentally, I never took you for a Lexus guy. Last I heard, you were driving a Mustang, like you're Steve McQueen."

"The Mustang's in the shop," I lied. "This is a loaner."

"A loaner from New York? Nice. Don't give me a reason to run those plates. Well, if you can't find a room in Rangeley, you can just sleep in that car. It's big enough. Drive safely now."

I headed back to Rangeley and sought out a room at the Rangeley Inn. The main building, its lobby decorated with deer heads and a stuffed bear, wasn't yet open for the season, so I was given a motel room in the lodge at the rear. There were a couple of other cars parked nearby, one of them with a map of the area on its passenger seat, and a decal for a TV station out of Bangor on the dashboard, to which had been appended a handwritten sign pleading "Do Not Tow!" I showered, and changed my shirt for a T-shirt I had picked up at a gas station. The smell of Proctor's decay was still with me afterward, but it was mostly remembered, not actual. More troubling to me was the sense of unease that I had experienced in the room adjoining Proctor's body. It felt as though I had wandered in at the tail end of an argument in time to hear only the echo of the final words, all venom and malice. I wondered if they were the same words that Harold Proctor heard before he died.

I walked over to Sarge's bar to get something to eat. It wasn't a hard choice, since it was the only place nearby that seemed to be open. Sarge's had a long, curving counter with TVs showing four different sports and, in the case of the final screen behind the bar, a local news show. The volume on the sports screens had been turned down, and a group of men was watching the news in silence. Proctor's death had made the lead, as much for the oddness of his passing as for the fact that it was a slow news night. Suicides didn't usually merit that kind of coverage, and the local news stations generally tended to be pretty sensitive to the feelings of the relatives of the deceased, but some of the details of Proctor's death had clearly caught their attention: a man sealed up from the inside in a room of a disused motel, his life ended by an apparently self-inflicted wound. The report didn't mention the shots that he had fired at someone outside the room before he killed himself.

I heard muttered words as I took a seat away from the bar, and a couple of heads turned in my direction. One of them belonged to Stunden, the taxidermist. I ordered a burger and a glass of wine from the waitress. The wine arrived quickly, closely followed by Stunden. I cursed myself quietly. I had forgotten all about my earlier promise to him. The least I had owed him, both for the information he had provided and because of his concern for Harold Proctor, was a personal visit, and some clarification of what had occurred.

Those who had stayed in their seats were all looking in my direction. Stunden smiled apologetically, and shot a quick look at the men behind him, as if to say, well, you know how small towns are. To their credit, those at the bar were clearly trying to balance embarrassment with curiosity, but curiosity was ahead by a neck.

"Sorry to bother you, Mr. Parker, but we hear that it was you who found Harold."

I gestured to the seat across from me, and he sat. "There's no apology necessary, Mr. Stunden. I should have paid a courtesy call to you after the police let me go, but it had been a long day, and I forgot. I'm sorry for that."

Stunden's eyes looked red. He'd been drinking some, but I thought that he might also have been crying.

"I understand. It was a shock for all of us. I couldn't open the bar, not after what happened. That's why I'm here. I thought somebody might know more than I did, and then you came in, and, well . . ."

"I can't tell you much," I said, and he was smart enough to pick up on the dual meaning of the words.

"If you'd just tell me what you can, that would be enough. Is what they're saying about him true?"

"Is what who's saying true?"

Stunden shrugged. "The TV people. Nobody here has heard anything official from the detectives. Closest thing we have is the border patrol. The story is that Harold committed suicide."

"It looks that way."

If there had been a cap in Stunden's hand, he would have twisted it awkwardly.

"One of the border cops told Ben here"—he jerked a thumb at an overweight man in a camo shirt, his belt so weighted with keys, knives, phones, and flashlights that his pants were almost around his thighs—"that there was something hinky about Harold's death, but he wouldn't say what it was."

There was that word again: hinky. Joel Tobias was hinky. Harold Proctor's death was hinky. It was all hinky.

Ben, and two other men from the bar, drawn by the prospect of some enlightenment, had gravitated toward us. I weighed up my options before I spoke, and saw that there was no benefit to me in holding anything back from them. Everything would emerge eventually, if not later tonight when some off-duty border cop came in for a drink, then tomorrow at the latest when the town's own information-gathering resources began to kick into gear. But I also knew that while there might be aspects of Harold Proctor's death about which they did not know, then equally there would be parts of his life about which I had no knowledge, and they did. Stunden had been helpful. Some of these men might be helpful too.

"He fired all the bullets in his gun before he died," I said. "He saved the last one for himself."

Everyone probably came up with the same question at the same time, but it was Stunden who asked it first.

"What was he firing at?"

"Something outside," I said, again pushing to the back of my mind the spread of the bullet holes in the room.

"You think he was chased in there?" asked Proctor.

"Hard to see how a man being chased would have time to nail himself up in a room," I replied.

"Hell, Harold was crazy," said Ben. "He never was the same after he came back from Iraq."

There were general nods of agreement. If they had their way, it would be carved on his headstone: "Harold Proctor. Somewhat Missed. Was Crazy."

"Well," I said, "you now know as much as I do."

They began to drift away. Only Stunden remained. He was the only one of the men who appeared genuinely distressed at the circumstances of Harold's death.

"You okay?" I asked him.

"No, not really. I guess I wasn't as close to Harold in recent times as I once was, but I was still his friend. It troubles me to think of him being so . . ."

He couldn't find the word.

"Frightened?" I said.

"Yeah, frightened, and alone. To die that way, I mean, it just doesn't seem right."

The waitress came by with my burger, and I ordered myself another glass of wine. I pointed at Stunden's glass.

"Bushmills," he said. "No water. Thanks."

I waited until the drinks appeared, and the waitress was gone. Stunden took a long sip of his drink as I ate my food.

"And I suppose I feel guilty," he said. "Does that make sense? I feel like, had I done more to stay in touch with him, to bring him out of his shell, to ask him about his problems, then none of this would have happened."

I could have lied to him. I could have said that Proctor's death had nothing to do with him, that Proctor had been set on a different path, a path that led ultimately to a lonely, terrified death in a sealed room, but I didn't. It would have belittled the man before me, a man who was decent and honorable.

"I can't say if that's true or not," I told him. "But Harold got himself involved in something odd, and that wasn't your fault. In the end, that's probably what got him killed."

"Odd?" he said. "What do you mean by odd?"

"Did you ever see trucks go in and out of Harold's place?" I asked. "Big rigs, possibly on the way down from Canada."

"Jeez, I wouldn't know. If the truck came up from Portland or Augusta, maybe, but if they came through Coburn Gore then they'd get to Harold's place before they reached Langdon."

"Is there someone who would know?"

"I can ask around."

"I don't have that kind of time, Mr. Stunden. Look, I'm not the police, and you have no obligation to provide me with information, but do you remember what I told you earlier today?"

Stunden nodded. "About the boy who killed himself."

"That's right. And now Harold Proctor is dead, and it looks like another suicide."

I could have mentioned Kramer in Quebec, and Brett Harlan and his wife, to clinch the deal, but if I did, then it would become part of the bar conversation, and that, in turn, would get back to the cops eventually. There were any number of reasons why I didn't want that to happen. I'd only just got my license back, and despite vague assurances that it was in no danger of immediate revocation again, I didn't need to give the state police any excuse to go after me. At the very least, I'd incur the displeasure of Walsh, and I kind of liked him, although if we were ever jailed together I wouldn't want to share a cell with him.

But, more than all that, I recognized the old hunger. I wanted to explore what was happening, to uncover the deeper connections between the deaths of Harold Proctor, Damien Patchett, and the others. I knew now that I was a private investigator in name only, that the mundane stuff of false insurance claims, cheating spouses, and thieving employees might be enough to pay my bills, but it was no more than that. I had come to realize that my desire to join the police and my short, less than illustrious career in the NYPD were not solely about making recompense for my father's perceived failings. He had killed two young people before taking his own life, and his actions had tainted the memory of him, and marked me. I was a bad cop—not corrupt, not violent, not inept, but still bad—for I lacked the discipline and patience, and maybe the absence of ego, that the job required. The acquisition of a private investigator's license had seemed like a compromise that I could live with, a means of fulfilling some vague sense of purpose by acquiring the trappings of legality. I knew that I could never be a cop again, but I still had the instincts required, and the sense of purpose, of vocation, that marked out the ones who didn't do it solely for the benefits, or the camaraderie, or the promise of cashing out in twenty and opening a bar in Boca Raton.

So I could have handed over everything that I knew or suspected to Walsh, and walked away. After all, his resources were greater than mine, and I had no reason to believe that his sense of purpose was inferior to my own. But I *wanted* this. Without it, what was I? So I would take my chances; I would trade when I had to trade, and hoard what I could. At some point, you have to trust your instincts, and yourself. I had learned something in the years since my wife and child were taken from me, and I had hunted down the one responsible: I was good at what I did.

Why?

Because I had nothing else.

Now I watched Stunden as he considered the two suicides. I didn't speak for a while. I just let the possibility of a connection dangle itself before him like a brightly colored fly while I waited for him to bite.

"There's a guy name of Geagan, Edward Geagan," said Stunden. "He lives up behind Harold's place. You wouldn't know it, not unless you were looking for him, but he's up there all right. Like a lot of people around here, like Harold did, he keeps himself to himself, but he's not weird or nothing. He's just quiet. If anyone would know, Edward would."

"I want to talk to him before the cops do. He have a phone?"

"Edward? I said he was quiet, I didn't say he was a primitive. He does something with the internet. Marketing, I think. I don't even know what 'marketing' means, but he's got more computers up there than NASA. *And* a phone," he added.

"Call him."

"Can I promise that you'll buy him a drink?"

"You know those old Westerns, where the hero tells the bartender to leave the bottle?"

Stunden blinked.

"I'll call Edward."

EDWARD GEAGAN TURNED OUT to be from geek central casting. He was in his mid-thirties, tall and pale and thin, with long, sandy hair and rimless glasses, dressed in brown polyester pants, cheap brown shoes, and a light tan shirt. He looked like someone had put a wig on a giraffe and run it through the local Target.

"This is Mr. Parker, the man I told you about," said Stunden. "He has some questions he'd like to ask you." He spoke as though he were talking to a child. Geagan cocked an eyebrow at him.

"Stunds, why do you insist on talking to me like I'm a moron?" he said, but there was no hint of unfriendliness to his voice, only vague amusement tinged with a little impatience.

"Because you look like you belong at MIT, not in the woods in Franklin County," said Stunden. "I feel like I should look out for you."

Geagan grinned at him, and Stunden, for the first time that evening, grinned back.

"Asshole."

"Rube."

As it turned out, the bartender declined to leave us with the bottle, but he was prepared to keep refilling the glasses as long as Stunden and Geagan could keep ordering without slurring their words. Unfortunately for me, their tolerance for alcohol was at least as great as their tolerance for each other. Sarge's began to empty at about the same pace as the bottle behind the bar, until pretty soon we were the only people left. We spent some time making small talk, and Geagan told me how he'd ended up in Franklin County, having tired of city life down in Boston.

"The first winter was hard," he said. "I thought Boston sucked when it snowed, but up here, well, you might as well be at the bottom of an avalanche." He grimaced. "I miss women too. You know, female company. These small towns, man. The ones who aren't married have left. It's like being in the Foreign Legion."

"It gets better when the tourists come," said Stunden. "Not much, but some."

"Damn, I might be dead of frustration by then."

They both stared into the bottom of their glasses, as though hoping a mermaid might pop her head out of the booze and flick her tail invitingly at them.

"About Harold Proctor," I said, trying to move the conversation along.

"I was surprised when I heard," said Geagan. "He wasn't the kind."

That phrase was starting to recur a little too often. Bennett Patchett had used it about his son, and Carrie Saunders had said much the same thing about both Damien Patchett and Brett Harlan. If they were all correct, then there were a lot of dead people who had no business being dead.

"Why do you say that?"

"He was hard. He had no regrets about anything that he'd done over there, and he'd done some pretty hardcore stuff, or so he said. Well, I thought it was hardcore, but then I've never killed anyone. Never will, I hope."

"You got along with him?"

"I drank with him a couple of times during the winter, and he helped me when my generator gave out. We were neighborly without being close. That's the way of things up here. Then Harold grew different. I talked to Stunds here about it, and he said the same. Harold started keeping his own counsel more than before, and he was never what you might call a chatterbox. I'd hear his truck starting up at odd times: after dark, sometimes well after midnight. Then the rig started arriving. A big truck—red, I think—hauling a trailer."

A red truck, just like Joel Tobias's.

"Did you get a plate number?"

Geagan recited it from memory. It was Tobias all right. "I've got a photographic memory," he said. "Helps with what I do."

"When did this happen?"

"Four or five times that I can recall: twice last month, once this month, the last time just yesterday."

I leaned forward. "The truck came through yesterday?"

Geagan looked flustered, as though fearful that he'd made a mistake. I could see him counting back the days. "Yep, yesterday morning. I saw it coming out as I was heading back to my place from town, so I don't know what time it went in."

I knew from the little that Walsh had told me that Proctor had probably been dead for two or three days. It was hard to tell given the heat in the room, and the consequent speed of putrefaction. Now it seemed that Tobias had been at the motel since Proctor had died, but hadn't taken the trouble to look for him; that, or he knew Proctor was dead, but said nothing, which sounded unlikely. Whoever Proctor had been firing at, it wasn't Joel Tobias.

"And it was definitely the same truck as before?"

"Yeah, I told you: I've seen it a few times. Harold and the other guy, the driver—no, wait, there was one time when I thought there might have been three of them—would unload stuff from the back, and the truck would drive away again."

"Did you ever mention this to Harold?"

"No."

"Why not?"

"It wasn't bothering me, and I didn't think Harold would appreciate me asking. He must have known that I might hear or see them, but up here it doesn't pay to question other people about their business."

"Didn't you wonder what he was doing?"

Geagan looked uneasy. "I thought he might be considering reopening the motel. He talked about it sometimes, but he didn't have the money he needed to restore it."

Geagan's eyes wouldn't meet my face.

"And?" I said.

"Harold liked to smoke a little pot. So do I. He knew where to get it, and I'd pay him for it. Not much, just enough to keep me going through the long winter months."

"Was Harold dealing?"

"No, I don't believe so. He just had a supplier."

"But you thought he might have been storing drugs in the motel, right?"

"It would make sense, especially if he was looking to make some money to reopen the place."

"Were you tempted to take a look?"

Geagan looked uneasy. "I might have been, once, when Harold wasn't around."

"What did you see?"

"The rooms were all blocked up, but I could tell that some had been opened recently. There were wood chips on the ground, and the dirt was all torn up. There were grooves in the earth, like they'd wheeled something heavy inside."

"You never saw what they were bringing in when you looked out of your window?"

"The front of the truck was always facing me. If they were unloading anything, then it was easiest to keep the back of the truck to the motel. I could never quite see what they were moving."

Never "quite" see. "But you think that you might have spotted something, right?"

"It's going to sound strange."

"Believe me, you don't know from strange."

"Well, it was a statue, I guess. Like one of those Greek ones, y'know, white, and from a museum. I thought it was a body at first, but it had no arms: like the *Venus de Milo*, but male."

"Damn," I said softly. Not drugs: antiquities. Joel Tobias was just full of surprises. "Have you talked to the police yet?"

"No. I don't think they even know I'm up there."

"Talk to them in the morning, but leave it till late. Tell them what you told me. Last thing: the police think Harold killed himself three days ago, give or take. Did you hear any shots during that time?"

"No, I was down in Boston visiting my folks until the day before yesterday. I guess Harold killed himself while I was away. He *did* kill himself, didn't he?"

"I believe he did."

"Then why did he lock himself up in that room to do it? What was he shooting at before he died?"

"I don't know."

I waved at the bartender for the tab. I heard the door open behind me, but I didn't turn around. Stunden and Geagan looked up, and their faces changed, brightening after the darkness of our conversation.

"Looks like somebody's luck may be about to change," said Geagan, straightening his hair, "and I sure hope it's mine."

As casually as I could, I tried to glance over my shoulder, but the woman was already by my right hand.

"Buy you a drink, Mr. Parker?" asked Carrie Saunders.

Geagan and Stunden rose to their feet and prepared to leave.

"Looks like I'm shit out of luck. Again," said Geagan. "Beg pardon, miss," he added.

"No apology necessary," said Saunders. "And this is professional, not personal."

"Does that mean I still have a chance?" asked Geagan.

"No."

Geagan gave an exaggerated sigh. Stunden patted him on the back.

"Come on, let's leave them to it. I'm sure I got a bottle somewhere at home that could help you with your troubles."

"Whiskey?" said Geagan.

"No," said Stunden. "Ethyl alcohol. You might need to cut it with something, though . . ."

They made their excuses and left, although not before Geagan cast a final lingering glance in Saunders's direction. The guy had clearly spent too long in the woods: if he didn't get some action soon, even moose would be in danger from him.

"Your fan club?" asked Saunders, once the waitress had brought her a Mich Ultra.

"Some of it."

"It's bigger than I expected."

"I like to think of it as small but stable, unlike your patient base, which seems to be dwindling by the day. Maybe you should consider an alternative profession, or cut a deal with a mortuary."

She scowled. Score one for the guy with the chip on his shoulder.

"Harold Proctor wasn't one of my patients. It looks like a local physician was prescribing his meds. I contacted him in an effort to have him participate in my study, but he didn't want to cooperate, and he didn't ask for my professional help. And I don't appreciate your flippant attitude toward what I do, or toward the former servicemen who've died."

"Get off your soapbox, Dr. Saunders. You were in no hurry to offer me help the last time we met, when I was under the misguided impression that we wanted the same thing."

"Which was?"

"To find out why a small group of men, all of whom knew one another, were dying by their own hands. Instead, I got the party line and some cheap analysis."

"That wasn't what you wanted to find out."

"No? They teach you telepathy at head school too, or is that something you've been working on when you get tired of being supercilious?"

She gave me the hard stare. "Anything else?"

"Yeah, why don't you order a real drink? You're embarrassing me."

She broke. She had a nice smile, but she'd fallen out of the habit of using it.

"A real drink: like a glass of red wine?" she said. "This isn't a church social. I'm surprised the bartender didn't take you outside and beat you with a stick."

I sat back and raised a hand in surrender. She put the Mich aside and signaled the waitress. "I'll have what he's having."

"It'll look like we're on a date," I said.

"Only to a blind man, and then he'd probably have to be deaf as well."

Saunders was certainly a looker, but anyone seriously considering engaging with her on an intimate level would need to wear body
armor to counter the spikes. Her wine arrived. She sipped it, didn't
appear to actively disapprove, and sipped again.

"How did you find me?" I asked.

"The cops told me that you were in Rangeley. One of them, Detective Walsh, even described your car for me. He told me that I should
slash your tires when I found it, just to make sure you stayed put. Oh,
and for the sake of it."

"The decision to stay was kind of forced upon me."

"By the cops? They must really love you."

"It's tentative, but mutual. How did you find out about Harold
Proctor?" I asked.

"The cops found my card in his cabin, and it seems that his physician is on vacation in the Bahamas."

"It's a long way to drive for a man that you didn't know well."

"He was a soldier, and another suicide. This is my work. The cops
thought I might be able to shed some light on the circumstances of
his death."

"And could you?"

"Only what I could tell from my sole visit to his home before tonight. He lived alone, drank too much, smoked some pot, judging by
the smell in his cabin, and he had little or no support structure."

"So he was a prime candidate for suicide?"

"He was vulnerable, that's all."

"Why now, though? He'd been out of the military for fifteen years
or more. You told me that post-traumatic stress could take as long
as a decade to undo, but fifteen years seems like a long time for it to
begin in the first place."

"That I can't explain."

"How did you come to find him?"

"As I interviewed former soldiers, I asked them to suggest others who might be willing to participate, or those whom they felt were vulnerable and could use an informal approach. Someone suggested Harold."

"Do you remember who it was?"

"No. I'd have to check my notes. It might have been Damien Patchett, but I couldn't say for sure."

"It wouldn't have been Joel Tobias, would it?"

She scowled. "Joel Tobias doesn't hold with psychiatrists."

"So you tried?"

"He conducted the last of his physical therapy at Togus, but there was a psychological component as well. He was assigned to me, but our progress was limited." She examined me steadily over the lip of her glass. "You don't like him, do you?"

"I've barely met him, but I don't like what I've found out about him so far. Joel Tobias drives a big rig with a bigger trailer. There's a lot of space to hide something in a box that size."

Her eyes didn't even flicker.

"You seem very convinced that there *is* something to hide."

"The day after I began looking into Joel Tobias, I was worked over very professionally: no bones broken, no visible marks."

"It might not have been connected to Tobias," she interrupted.

"Listen, I appreciate that there may be people out there who don't like me, but most of them aren't very smart, and if they arranged a beating for me they'd be sure to claim a little credit. They're not the anonymous-donor type. These guys used water, and a sack. It was made clear that I should stay out of Joel Tobias's business and, by extension, theirs."

"From what I hear, most of the people who might have had real difficulties with you are no longer in a position to arrange beatings, not unless they can contract out from the grave."

I looked away. "You'd be surprised," I said, but she didn't seem to hear. She was lost in her own thoughts.

"The reason why I declined to help you when we first met was because I didn't believe that you wanted what I wanted. My role is to help these men and women where I can. Some of them, like Harold Proctor and Joel Tobias, don't want my help. They may need it, but they consider it a sign of weakness to confess their fears to a shrink, even an ex-army shrink who spent time in the same dust bowl that they did. There's been a lot written in the newspapers about suicide rates among military personnel, about how physically and psychologically damaged men and women have been abandoned by their government, about how they may even be a threat to national security. They've been fighting an unpopular war, and, okay, it's not quite Vietnam, either in terms of casualties over there or in the animosity toward veterans back home, but you can't blame the military for being defensive. When you came along, I thought you might just be another jackass trying to prove a point."

"And now?"

"I still think you're a jackass, and that detective out at the Proctor place clearly concurs, but maybe our ultimate aims aren't so different. We both want to find out why these men are dying at their own hands."

She took another sip of wine. "Look, I take this seriously. That's why I'm engaged in this research. My study is part of a joint initiative with the National Institute of Mental Health to try to come up with some answers, and some solutions. We're looking at the role that combat, and multiple deployments, play in suicide. We know that two-thirds of suicides take place during or after a deployment: that's fifteen months in a war zone, with barely enough time to decompress afterward before exhausted men and women are sent back into the field again.

"It's clear that our soldiers need help, but they're afraid to ask for it in case it's recorded and the jacket follows them. But the military also needs to change its attitude toward its troops: mental health screening is poor, and commanders are reluctant to allow military personnel to gain access to civilian therapists. They're hiring more general practitioners, which is a start, and more mental-health care providers, but the focus is on troops in combat. What happens when they come home? Of the sixty soldiers who killed themselves between January and August 2008, thirty-nine of them did so *after* they returned to this country. We're letting these men and women down. They're wounded, but the wounds don't show in some cases until it's too late. Something has to be done for them. Someone has to take responsibility."

She sat back. Some of the hardness fell away from her, and she just looked tired. Tired, and somehow younger than she was, as though her distress at the deaths was both professional yet also almost childlike in its purity.

"Do you understand now why I was wary when a private investigator, and one, with respect, whose reputation for violence precedes him, began asking about the deaths of veterans by their own hands?"

It was a rhetorical question or, if it wasn't, then I chose to consider it as such. I signaled for another round. We didn't speak again until it arrived, and she had poured the remainder of her first glass into her second.

"And you?" I asked. "How does it affect you?"

"I don't understand the question," she said.

"I mean that it must be hard, listening to all those stories of pain and injury and death, seeing those damaged men and women week after week. It must take its toll."

She pushed her glass around the table, watching the patterns that it formed: circles upon circles, like Venn diagrams.

"That's why I left the military and became a civilian consultant," she said. "I still experience guilt about it, but over there I sometimes felt like King Canute, trying to hold back the tide alone. In Iraq, I could still be overruled by a commander who needed soldiers in the field. The needs of the many outweighed the needs of the few, and for the most part all I could do was offer tips on how to cope, as if that could help soldiers who had already gone far beyond the possibility of coping. In Togus, I feel like I'm part of a strategy, an attempt to see the bigger picture, even if the bigger picture is thirty-five thousand soldiers already diagnosed with PTSD, and more to come."

"That isn't answering the question," I said.

"No, it isn't, is it? The name for what you're implying is secondary trauma, or 'contact distress': the more deeply therapists involve themselves with victims, the more likely they are to experience some of their trauma. At the moment, mental health evaluations of therapists are practically nonexistent. It's self-evaluation, and nothing more. You know you're broken only when you break."

She drank half of her wine.

"Now, tell me about Harold Proctor, and what you saw out there," she said.

I told her most of it, leaving out only a little of what Edward Geagan had revealed, and the money that was discovered in Proctor's cabin. When I was finished, she didn't speak, but maintained eye contact. If it was some kind of psychiatric ruse designed to wear me down and blurt out everything that I'd kept hidden since childhood, it wasn't working. I'd already given away more than I wanted about myself to her, and I wasn't about to do it again. I had a vision of myself closing a stable door while a horse disappeared over the horizon.

"What about the money?" she said. "Or did you just forget to mention it?"

Clearly, the state cops were more susceptible to her wiles than I was. When next we met, I'd have a word with Walsh about maintaining some backbone and not coming over all giggly when a good-looking woman patted his arm and complimented him on his weapon.

"I haven't figured that part out yet," I said.

"You're not dumb, Mr. Parker, so don't assume that I am. Let me suggest what conclusions I think you may have come to, and you can disagree with me when I'm done. You believe that Proctor was storing items in his motel, possibly, even probably, drugs. You believe that the cash in his cabin was a payment for his services. You believe that some, or all, of the men who have died might also have been involved in this same operation. Joel Tobias makes runs in his truck back and forth across the Canadian border, so you believe that he's the likeliest transport link. Am I wrong?"

I didn't respond, so she continued talking.

"And yet I don't think you've told the police all of this. I wonder why. Is it because you feel some loyalty to Bennett Patchett, and you don't want to besmirch his son's reputation unless you absolutely have to do so? I think that may be part of it. You're a romantic, Mr. Parker, but sometimes, like all romantics, you confuse it with sentimentality. That explains why you're cynical about the motives of others.

"But you're also a crusader, and that fits in with your romantic streak. That crusading impulse is essentially selfish: you're a crusader because it gives you a sense of purpose, not because it serves the larger requirements of justice or society. In fact, when your own needs and the greater collective need have come into conflict, I suspect that you've usually chosen the former over the latter. That doesn't make you a bad person, just an unreliable one. So, how'd I do?"

"Close on Proctor and Tobias. I can't comment on the second bout of free analysis."

"It's not free. You're going to pay for my drinks. What have I missed about Proctor and Tobias?"

"I don't think it's drugs."

"Why not?"

"I talked to someone who'd know if there was an attempt to increase the local supply, or to use the state as a staging post. It would involve squaring things with the Dominicans, and probably the Mexicans too. The gentleman to whom I spoke would also look for his cut."

"And if the new players just decided to dispense with the niceties?"

"Then some men with guns might be tempted to dispense with *them*. There's also the question of supply. Unless they're growing bud themselves across the border, or are importing heroin straight from the source in Asia, they'd have to deal with the current suppliers somewhere along the line. It's hard to keep those kinds of negotiations quiet, especially when they might threaten the status quo."

"If not drugs, then what?"

"There might be something in their military records," I said, avoiding the question.

"I've looked into the records of the deceased. There's nothing."

"Look closer."

"I'll ask you again: what are they smuggling? I think you know."

"I'll tell you when I'm sure. Go back to the records. There must be something. If you're concerned about the reputation of the military, then having the cops uncover a smuggling operation involving veterans isn't going to help. It would be better if the military could be the instigators of any action against them."

"And in the meantime, what are you going to do?"

"There's always a weak link. I'm going to find it."

I PAID THE TAB, on the assumption that I could run it past the IRS as a justifiable expense if I claimed not to have enjoyed myself, which was only partly true.

"Are you driving back to Augusta tonight?" I asked Saunders.

"No, I'm staying in the same place that you are," she said.

I walked with her across the road to the motel.

"Where'd you park?"

"On the street," she said. "I'd ask you in for a nightcap, but I have no booze. Oh, and I don't want to. There's that too."

"I won't take it personally."

"I really wish that you would," she said, and then she was gone.

BACK IN MY ROOM, I checked my cell phone. There was one message: it was from Louis, giving me the number of a motel, and the room in which he was staying. I used the room phone to call him. The main building was locked up for the night, and I wasn't worried about anyone listening it. Nevertheless, we kept the conversation as circumspect as possible, just in case.

"We had company," he said after Angel passed him the phone. "Two for dinner."

"They make it to the main course?"

"Didn't even last until the appetizers."

"And after?"

"They went swimming."

"Well, at least they did it on an empty stomach."

"Yeah, can't be too careful. Now it's just the four of us."

"Four?"

"Seems like you have a new career in relationship counseling."

"I'm not sure my skills are up to helping you with yours."

"We find ourselves in that much trouble, we'll make a suicide pact first. In the meantime, you need to get over here. Our friend has turned out to be quite the conversationalist."

"I promised the state cops I'd hang around until morning."

"Well, they'll miss you, but I think you need to hear this more."

I told him it would take me a few hours to get there, and he said that they weren't planning on going anywhere. As I drove out of the lot, a light still burned in Carrie Saunders's room, but I didn't think that it burned for me.

IV

Menelaus: We were swindled by the gods. We
had our hands upon an idol of the clouds.
Messenger: You mean it was for a cloud,
for nothing, we did all that work?

Euripides, *Helen*, ll

He'd spent too long in just about every vehicle the army had to offer, and knew their strengths and shortcomings, but he was eventually brought in to fill a vacant spot on Tobias's Stryker squad.

There had been a lot of crap tossed at the Stryker, usually by the kind of shitheads who subscribed to gun magazines and wrote letters to them about the "warrior class," but soldiers liked the Stryker. The seat cushions sucked, the A/C was like the beating of fly wings, and there weren't enough outlets to run DVD players or iPods for an entire squad, but it was superior to the Humvees, even the up-armored ones. The Stryker offered integral 14.5-millimeter protection from anything the haji could throw at it, with additional cover from RPGs provided by a cage of armor eighteen inches from the main body. It had the M240 at the rear, and a .50 cal that rocked. By comparison, the Humvee was like wrapping yourself in tissue and waving a .22.

And that kind of stuff mattered, because against every rule that he had ever been taught about urban warfare, the army had them marking the same patrol routes at the same times every day, so the haji could set their clocks and, by extension, their IEDs, by them. By this point, it wasn't a matter of if they were going to be hit on a given day, but when. The upside was that, following a hit, the vehicle was automatically returned to base for repairs, so the squad could rest up for the remainder of the day.

The transfer to the Stryker squad had been Tobias's doing; Tobias, and the man named Roddam. Tobias had earned his sergeant's stripes and was squad leader. He wasn't a jerk, though: he even scored them some beers, and getting busted for drinking was a serious offense. You might pull an Article 15 for a fistfight, or borrowing a vehicle without permission, but alcohol and drugs merited judicial punishment. Tobias's own neck was on the line over the beer, but he trusted them. By then, though, he had become familiar with the way Tobias operated, and he knew that the beers were a way of softening them up. Tobias had his own unique spin on Newton's third law of motion: for every action, there was an equal or greater reaction expected. They would pay for those beers, one way or another, and Roddam was the one who was going to extract the payment.

Roddam was a spook of some kind. Baghdad was overrun with them, both genuine and charlatans, and Roddam was a little of both. He was private, not CIA, and he didn't talk much about what he did, like any good spook. He said that he worked for a small outfit called Information Retrieval & Interpretation Services, or IRIS, but Tobias let it slip that it was basically a one-man operation. IRIS's logo, not unexpectedly, was an eye, with the world as its pupil. Roddam's cards boasted offices in Concord, New Hampshire, and Pont-Rouge, Canada, but the Pont-Rouge office turned out to be little more than a tax scam with proximity to an airfield, and the Concord office was a telephone and an answering machine.

Roddam was ex-agency, though: he had contacts, and he had influence. Part of his role in Baghdad was to act as the middleman between the army and the smaller contractors, the ones who didn't have their own transport networks and were trying to keep their costs down so that they could bank a bigger share of whatever they were overcharging Uncle Sam to begin with. Roddam arranged for the transportation of anything on which the big boys like Halliburton didn't already have first dibs, from a box of obscure screws to weapons that were required, for whatever reason, to bypass the regular transport channels.

That paid his bills, and more, but it wasn't his main area of expertise: Roddam, as it turned out, was an expert in interrogation and information analysis, which explained the origins of the name IRIS. There were too many Iraqis in custody for the regular intelligence guys to process, so the little fish were thrown to Roddam. If you got enough little fish, and cross-referenced whatever information could be gleaned from them, then it was possible that a bigger picture might be constructed from the individual pieces. Roddam was some kind of genius at analyzing the information coaxed from prisoners, sometimes without them even knowing that they'd revealed anything crucial. Roddam would occasionally deal with prisoners himself, usually in an effort to clarify a point, or in an effort to make a solid connection between two apparently random pieces of information. He wasn't a thumbscrew and waterboarding kind of guy. He was patient, and soft-spoken, and careful. Everything he learned went into a computer program that he had created, and for which Iraq was to be the testing ground: it collated key phrases, minor operational details, even turns of phrase, and cross-referenced them in the hope of establishing patterns. Army intelligence and the agency would feed him their scraps too so that, over time, Roddam came to know more about the day-to-day operation of the insurgency than just about anyone else on the ground. He was the go-to guy, trusted as a virtual oracle. In return, what Roddam wanted, Roddam got.

He never learned how Roddam and Tobias managed to hook up. He supposed that men like them just inevitably found each other. So, when Tobias brought the beer, Roddam came with him. In fact, it was probably Roddam who had sourced the beer in the first place.

By that time, the squad had taken some hits: Lattner was dead, and Cole. Edwards and Martinez were injured, and had been replaced by Harlan and Kramer, and it looked like Hale, who'd been hit by a sniper, *wasn't going to pull through. He'd taken one in the head, and it would be a mercy if he died. The squad had been marked for Force Protection duties until it could be restored to full strength: no patrols, just guard shifts in the tower, which meant hour after hour of radio checks with Front Line Yankee, and replies of "Lima Charlie—Loud and Clear," and maybe ducking occasionally when someone in the darkness decided to lob a mortar, or send in an RPG, or just fire off a couple of rounds to keep them from getting bored.*

That night, Tobias—or Roddam—had swung it so that they were relieved of FP, so there were eight of them in Tobias's CHEW: him, Tobias, Roddam, Kramer, Harlan, Mallak, Patchett, and Bacci. After a couple of beers to soften them up, Tobias began to speak. He told them about Hale, and how the rest of his life was going to be a struggle at best. He spoke of other guys that they knew. He told of how men were finding it tough to get money under Section 8, welfare, the VA, anything; of how the VA had denied Keys, the assistant gunner that Patchett had replaced, a claim for his leg, informing him that he rated only 60 percent disabled. Keys had gone to the press, and his rating got bumped up, but only to keep him quiet. He'd been lucky, but there were a lot of other injured men out there who weren't so lucky, or who didn't have a sympathetic newspaper to take up their cause. Tobias said that Roddam had a proposition for them, and if they went along with it they'd be able to help some of their injured brothers and sisters, and make life more comfortable for themselves once they got back home. He told them to listen up, and they did.

Roddam was fifty, balding, overweight. He always wore short-sleeved shirts and a tie. His glasses had black frames. He looked like a science teacher. Roddam said that he'd come by some information. He told them about the looting of the Iraq Museum in Baghdad in 2003, and Patchett interrupted and said that he'd been there in the aftermath, and Roddam seemed interested. Later, he would take Patchett aside to talk with him, but for now Roddam simply filed this fact away and con-

tinued with his story. He spoke of gold, and statues, and ancient seals. Kramer scoffed some. Joe Radio, the army rumor mill, occasionally threw up tales of Saddam's hidden treasures, or of gold bars buried in gardens, tales usually originating with shadowy Iraqis who were looking for dollars to grease palms but who would disappear into the night, never to be seen again, if someone were dumb enough to pay them anything. Tobias told Kramer to shut his mouth and listen, and Kramer did.

By the time Roddam had finished speaking, they were convinced, all of them, even Kramer, because Roddam had a quiet, serious way about him. They told him they were in, and Roddam left to arrange the details. They were his creatures now.

He had forgotten what it was like to be drunk. Back home, a six-pack would barely have helped him to get a buzz on but here, cut off from alcohol for months, his mouth always dry, his body always warm, it was as if he had knocked back a week's worth of production from the Coors brewery. His head hurt the next day, but he was still aware of the promise that they'd made. He was just glad that they were going out in the Stryker and not in some makeweight meat wagon, even as he began to have doubts about what it was they were doing. The night before, with a couple of beers under his belt, and not enough food in his belly, he'd been all gung ho like the others, but now the reality of their situation was impacting upon him. On a regular "movement to contact" mission, the new, kinder name for "search and destroy," the little FBCB2 screen behind the TC's hatch would start displaying red triangles once the enemy was located, and that bitch's voice, both lovely and appalling, would kick in to announce that there was an enemy in the area, but they'd be flying blind and alone on this one.

Tobias treated it like a regular patrol: he patted each of them down to make sure that they all had a CamelBak of water; gloves; pads; a clean, oiled weapon; and fresh batteries in the NODs, the night vision goggles.

They'd all carried out their own pre-combat inspection, and they had the OP order in their heads, but, whatever his flaws, Tobias was a stickler for ensuring that everybody knew his appointed task, and had the proper equipment to carry it out. Roddam watched without speaking, uncomfortable in his Kevlar. He was nervous, and kept looking at his watch. Tobias checked the extra ammo for the .50 cal strapped to the right side of the Stryker. It was hard to get to in a firefight, but there was nowhere else to put it, and better to have it out there than not to have it at all. After the check, they performed their own intimate motions, touching medals, crosses, pictures of their families. Whatever routines had kept them alive in the past, they made sure to maintain. All soldiers were superstitious. It came with the territory.

It was Sunday evening, and the sun was going down, when they rolled out. They all had good food in their bellies, because the best food was always served on Sundays, but they'd skipped the coffee. There was enough adrenaline coursing before a raid. He remembered the sound his boots made on the dust, the grains of sand compacting beneath the soles, the solidity of the ground and the power of his legs, and then the hollow echo from the floor of the Stryker as he stepped to his seat. Such a simple act, the placing of one foot before the other. Gone now. All gone.

The warehouse was in Al-Adhamiya, the old quarter of Baghdad, a Sunni stronghold. They rolled down narrow alleyways custom built for ambushes, kerosene lamps burning in the windows of the houses as they passed, but not a single figure to be seen on the streets. Two blocks from the target, all lights disappeared, and there was only a half moon above them to gild the buildings with silver and differentiate their lineaments from the blackness above and below.

They advanced the last one hundred feet on foot. There were two entrances to the warehouse, which looked more modern than the buildings that surrounded it and was entirely dark inside: one door to the south, at the rear, and the other on the western wall. There were two small windows at ground level, protected by bars, and so thick with dust and *grime that it was impossible to see through the glass. The doors were reinforced steel, but they blew the locks with C_4 and came in hard and fast. Through the NODs, he saw figures moving, weapons being raised, and even as he fired he thought: something about this is not right. How can we have taken them by surprise? If a fly lands in Al-Adhamiya, someone runs to tell a spider.*

One down. Two. He heard a cry of "Get some!" to his left, a voice that he both recognized and did not recognize, a voice transformed by the fury and confusion of combat. A television blared, its screen almost blindingly bright through the goggles, and then the screen exploded and went dark. He heard Tobias shouting "Cease fire!" and it was over. Over almost as soon as it had begun.

They searched the building, and found no other haji. Three were dead, and one was dying. Tobias stood over him while the perimeter was secured, and he thought that he heard words exchanged between them. The squad flipped their goggles as flashlights bounced around the walls, revealing crates and cardboard boxes and odd shapes wrapped in linen. The dying haji's pupils were dilated, and he was smiling and singing softly to himself.

"He's high," said Tobias. "Artane, probably."

Artane was an antipsychotic used to treat Parkinson's disease, but was popular with the younger insurgents. In Baghdad, it was part of the pharmacopia available at places like the Babb al-Sharq, the Eastern Gate. It left the user with a feeling of euphoria and a sense of invulnerability. The haji's voice rose in prayer, and then there was a single shot as Tobias finished him off. There would be no policing of the dead tonight, no bagging of the bodies to be dropped off at the nearest police station. They would stay where they had fallen.

The dead haji all wore black headbands, the mark of shaheed, of martyrs. He mentioned it to Tobias, but Tobias did not appear interested.

"So what?" he said. "If they wanted to be martyrs, then they got their wish."

Tobias didn't understand. They were waiting for us, he wanted to say, but they barely fought back. If they'd wanted to, they could have taken us in the street, where we were vulnerable, but they didn't. They let us come to them, and then they let us kill them.

Roddam joined them, speaking on a satellite phone. Minutes later, they saw lights, and a Buffalo armored vehicle appeared outside. Lord knew how they'd managed to get it down those streets, but somehow they had. It was closely followed by a single Humvee. He didn't recognize the four men who drove the vehicles. Later, he would learn that they were National Guardsmen, two from Calais, the other two from somewhere in the ass end of the county. More Mainers, more men who owed Tobias a favor. Three never made it home. The fourth was still trying to make his new arms work.

They rolled two pneumatic lifters out of the Buffalo, and started moving the heavier crates out of the warehouse. Tobias formed four of the squad into a line, and they piled the smaller items in the Hummer, and the larger ones into the Buffalo. It took four hours. In all that time, nobody approached the warehouse, and they were allowed to depart Al-Adhamiya unhindered. Along the way, they picked up two teams of snipers. It wasn't unusual: that was how the system worked. Snipers—Delta, Blackwater, Rangers, SEALS, Marines—would be attached to an infantry unit on a cordon-and-search mission. When the unit left, the snipers would stay and go to ground. Later, a unit would return and pick up the snipers. In this case, he knew that the snipers' mission had been arranged by Roddam, and only to provide cover for the raid on the warehouse, because their squad had dropped off both teams earlier in the week.

There should have been gunfire, he whispered to himself. They should have been challenged. It made no sense. None of it made any sense.

But it didn't have to, because they were rich.

Even now, the scale of what Roddam managed to pull off astonished him, but then Roddam was smart: he knew how to exploit the chaos of war, and Iraq was chaos squared. What mattered was what was being brought into the country, not what was being shipped out: half of what they had seized at the warehouse was flown to Canada, sometimes via the United States, in otherwise empty planes returning to stock up on more overpriced equipment for the war effort. Larger items were shipped through Jordan, and onward by sea. Where necessary, bribes were paid, but not in the States or Canada. Even without Roddam's CIA contacts to smooth the way, Iraq was a gold mine for contractors. Equipment was needed yesterday, at any price, and nobody wanted to be accused of interfering with the war effort by quibbling about paperwork.

Over the months that followed, they all began to drift home, some more intact than others. They handed over their weapons, filled out their medical questionnaires on PalmPilots, none of them 'fessing up to any psychological issues, not then, which made the army happy. They all listened to the same speech from the batallion commander, advising them not to hit their wives and girlfriends when they got home, or words to that effect, and about how the army would welcome them back with open arms, a bunch of flowers, and forty virgins from the southern states should they choose to return.

Or words to that effect.

Then Kuwait, then Frankfurt, passing over Bangor, Maine, on their way to McCord AFB, then back to Bangor again, and home.

All except him, because by then his legs were ruined. He took a different route: a Black Hawk medevac to the "Cash" in the Green Zone, where he was stabilized before transfer to the trauma center at Landstuhl Regional Medical Center near Frankfurt, where they performed the amputations. Landstuhl to Ramstein, Ramstein to Andrews AFB on a C-141 Starlifter, men stacked like kindling in the center of the plane, like captives on a slave ship, six inches separating each man from the man above him, the smell of blood and urine sickening, even through the fog of medication, the noise of the aircraft deafening despite the earplugs. Andrews to Walter Reed. The hell of occupational therapy; the attempts to fit prostheses, ultimately abandoned because of the pain they caused him, and he'd had enough of pain.

Then the return to Maine, and the arguments with Tobias. He'd be looked after, Tobias told him; all he had to do was keep his mouth shut. But he wasn't concerned solely about himself. There had been an agreement: the money would be used to help their brothers- and sisters-in-arms, the ones who were injured, the ones who had lost so much. Tobias said that had changed. He wasn't going to police the consciences of others. They could give what they wanted. They all could. It was complicated. They had to be careful. Jandreau didn't understand.

But he did understand. He understood a lot more than Tobias was willing to give him credit for. The hajis were bad guys, of that there was no doubt, and he didn't regret their deaths. Okay, maybe the mission didn't qualify as a military engagement in the strictest sense, and if the brass discovered what they had done then they'd spend a long time behind bars, but he could square it with his conscience if the money—or most of it, at least—was used for some good. Otherwise, they were all just thieves and criminals, and they'd killed not for their country, or for an ideal, or to reduce the number of their enemies, but because someone had waved the promise of wealth at them, and they'd bitten. That wasn't why he'd joined up, and it demeaned his own sacrifice. He was in a chair, and he was hurting, but he wanted to be able to say that he'd served with honor, that whatever he had done in uniform had contributed to the greater good.

He had tried to speak of this with Damien, but by then Damien had fallen under Tobias's influence with a vengeance. He was reluctant to talk to his old buddy, reluctant to listen to anything that might undermine his confidence in the operation, and in Tobias. Damien wasn't the same guy at all; in fact, none of the others were as he remembered them, if the truth were to be told. Not Kramer, who had become skittish as hell; not Harlan, who had always used drugs but now seemed to be high more often than not, and when he wasn't high he was picking holes in his own skin and worrying that his wife was screwing around with half the U.S. military; not even Tobias, for whom pragmatism had warped into ruthlessness. It was as though they'd all drunk the same Kool-Aid, and it had poisoned their souls. Maybe he felt a little of it in himself too, a memory of voices that called to him in his sleep, telling him that he was useless, that he was barely a man anymore, that he should end it with a bullet because it would be easier and quicker that way. Hey, and while he was about it, and just in case he got a little lonely on the other side, he might consider taking his girlfriend along with him for the ride. He would wake with the memory of the voices, and the sense of what they were telling him to do, while realizing at the same time that their words were unintelligible to him. He felt himself slipping into madness, but he fought it, and he wondered if what he had endured had somehow made him stronger than the others, if something of what was tormenting him was also hurting them, but they were unable to ignore its call. He still felt a loyalty to them, and he told himself that this was one of the reasons why he wasn't going to go straight to the cops or the Feds or the military with what he knew, as much as his own fear of being a prisoner in a wheelchair, serving hard time for what he had done.

And suddenly they started dying. It was Kramer who told him about the box, Kramer who discussed the nightmares he was having, Kramer who led him to delve into the dark corners of Sumerian mythology, but it wasn't until just after Damien Patchett died that he found out the truth about Roddam. Roddam was dead. He had been found in the IRIS office in Concord one week after Tobias and Bacci returned home, the first of the men involved in the Al-Adhamiya raid to do so. It had passed the rest of them by, if any of them had even cared, because Roddam wasn't his real name: it was Nailon, Jack Nailon. He'd fallen asleep on the couch in his office with a lit cigar in an ashtray on the couch arm, and with too much whiskey in his system and on his clothes. He had burned to death, they said.

Except that Roddam, or Nailon, or whatever his real name was, didn't drink. That was what he remembered from the beer night at the base, when he and Roddam had exchanged a couple of words after he had offered Roddam a beer. Roddam was a diabetic, and suffered from high blood pressure. He couldn't drink alcohol, and he didn't smoke. He didn't know why that hadn't come up during the investigation into Roddam's death. Maybe, like everything else about Roddam, his medical history was uncertain, hidden. But then he recalled some of the things that Tobias had begun to say about Roddam before Tobias went home: Roddam was unreliable. Roddam wasn't one of us. Roddam was causing trouble in Quebec. Roddam wanted a bigger cut. As though he were preparing the way for Roddam's removal.

He'd brought up Roddam's death after Damien's funeral. He'd brought up lots of stuff because he was sad, and he was drunk, and he missed Mel, and he was sure as hell going to miss Damien. If Roddam wasn't in charge, then who was? Tobias was classic NCO material. He didn't originate ideas; he just put them into action, and this was a complicated operation.

And Tobias had told him to keep quiet, to mind his own business, because a man in a wheelchair was vulnerable, and cripples had accidents all the time.

After that, he'd started carrying the gun under his chair.

CHAPTER

XXIX

The Collector was now only steps behind Herod. He felt himself drawing closer to him, and as he did so his fears increased.

Herod was an unusual case. The Collector might even have viewed him simply as an interesting challenge, like a hunter who finds that the animal he is pursuing has displayed unexpected depths of cunning, had he not become increasingly concerned about the man's ultimate purpose, and the imminence of its fulfillment. Herod had concealed himself well, and the Collector had only been able to find traces of him: deals, and threats, made; lives ruined, and bodies left unburied; items purchased, or taken from the dead. It was the nature of these artifacts—occult, arcane—that had first drawn the Collector's attention. Carefully, he had tried to discern a pattern. There seemed to be no distinct historical period to which Herod was attracted, and the items themselves were baffling in their variety and relative value. The Collector had only the peculiar sense that this was the reflection of a consciousness, as though Herod were furnishing a room in preparation for the arrival of an honored guest, so that the visitor might be surrounded by treasures and curios that were familiar or of interest to him; or preparing a museum display that would only come together for the viewer when the main exhibit was finally put in place.

The Collector had come close to confronting Herod on a number of occasions, but the man had always slipped away. It was as though he had been forewarned about the Collector's approach, and had found ways to avoid him, even if it meant sacrificing an item that he desired, for the Collector had made certain to bait his traps well. The Collector had already decided to dispose of Herod some years before. Herod had killed a child, a young boy, whose father had reneged on a deal, and in the Collector's mind Herod had damned himself by that action. It was one of Herod's apparent peculiarities that he seemed to regard himself, and those with whom he dealt, as being bound by some twisted notion of honor, the rules of which appeared to be set by Herod, and Herod alone.

But if the Collector had experienced any doubts about the legitimacy of killing Herod, they had been swept away when he began to learn of Herod's inquiries into the treasures looted from the Iraq Museum. That had given the Collector his first real inkling of what was being sought. He had heard rumors about the box, but had disregarded them. There were so many such tales, going right back to the original legend of Pandora, yet this one was different, because Herod was interested in it, and Herod did not embark on fruitless searches. Herod had an end in sight, and everything that he did served it.

Herod had been in contact with Rochman in Paris, anxious to establish the source of the seals that he had acquired. Rochman had proved uncooperative, for Herod did not have the funds necessary to engage in a serious bid for the items, even had Herod been interested in purchasing them, which he was not. Herod, in turn, had seemed oddly reluctant to threaten Rochman in order to force the information from him. The Collector had noted that Herod used violence only against the weak, like a playground bully. The House of Rochman was well established, and had influence. If Herod crossed it, he would risk alienating a clique of unscrupulous and wealthy dealers who would, at best, ostracize him, or, as was more likely, move against him. The Collector did not doubt that anyone getting into a conflict with Herod would suffer for it along the way, but a battle with men seeking to protect a billion-dollar industry dependent on the secret movement of stolen antiquities could only end with Herod's annihilation.

So Herod had backed off, biding his time. Now a number of seals had appeared in a town in Maine, for as soon as Rojas began seeking ways to turn gold and jewels into hard cash, rumors had spread. It was not only the dealers, and Herod, who would be drawn by them. The federal government was already taking an interest, for Rochman had begun to talk in an effort to save himself and his business. The seals in his possession had come from Locker 5 in the basement of the Iraq Museum, as had the seals currently available for sale in Maine. Rochman's seals were a down payment for his advice on valuations, and for his help in sourcing buyers. In time, he would give all that he knew to the investigators, and it would only be a matter of days before they would start to close in on all involved.

The Collector knew of Dr. Al-Daini, and he believed that the Iraqi was ultimately seeking the box, even as he set about recovering the other treasures lost in 2003. The Collector had made inquiries, and had learned that Al-Daini was now on his way to the United States. He would fly into Boston, and be taken straight from there to a disused motel in the town of Langdon, Maine.

The men who were transporting the stolen artifacts from the motel had been careless. A pair of small alabaster figures had been found lying in the long grass, and had quickly been identified as part of a hoard discovered at Tell es Sawwan, on the left bank of the Tigris, in 1964, and subsequently looted from the Iraq Museum. The body of a man had also been discovered at the motel, sealed into a room from the inside, dead from a self-inflicted gunshot wound after having first apparently fired at some unknown threat.

The body had been discovered by the detective, Charlie Parker.

There were no coincidences, the Collector knew, not where Parker was concerned. He was part of something that he did not understand; that, in truth, the Collector did not fully understand either. Now, once again, he and Parker were circling the same quarry, like twin moons orbiting a dark, unknown planet.

The Collector made a telephone call to his lawyer. He wanted to know where Parker was. His lawyer, an ancient man who disdained computers, and cell phones, and most of the significant technical innovations of recent years, made a call in turn to a gentleman who specialized in matters of triangulation, and Parker's cell phone was traced to a motel near Bucksport.

Bucksport was an hour away.

The Collector began to drive.

Herod stood by his car and gazed upon the Rojas warehouse. Lights burned on both floors, and he could see figures moving behind glass on the lower level. There were vehicles parked in the front lot: Rojas Brothers trucks, a couple of cars, and a white SUV.

Herod needed his medication, and in serious doses. The pain had grown worse as the day proceeded, and now he wanted all this to be over with so that he could rest for a while.

There came a prickling at the base of his neck. At first, he barely noticed it against the shrillness of his agony; it was like trying to pick out a melody from the cacophony of an orchestra tuning its instruments. The wound on his mouth throbbed in the warm night air, and the insects were feeding on him.

I reek of decay, he thought. Were I to lie down and wait for death to take my breath, they would plant their eggs in my flesh before I passed over. There might even be some relief in it. He imagined the maggots emerging from the eggs and feasting on his tumors, consuming the rotting tissue and leaving the rest to regenerate, except that there was no good flesh left, and so they would devour him entirely. He might have embraced such an end, once upon a time, for at least it would have been faster, and more natural, than the manner in which his body was cannibalizing itself. Instead, he had found another outlet for his pain. If this was a visitation from the Divine, a punishment for his sins—for Herod had sinned, and taken joy in his transgressions—then Herod would inflict punishment on others in turn. The Captain had given him the means, had endowed him with a purpose beyond the simple infliction of hurt in revenge for his own torments. The Captain had promised him that the world would mourn because of Herod. Before he was pulled back from the darkness—back, perhaps, from one hell of another's making to the hell of his body's own capacities—the Captain had flashed images in his mind: the image of a black angel hidden behind a wall, a presence trapped within it; bodies slowly fading but never dying, each with something of the Captain within itself . . .

And the box. The Captain had shown him the box. But by then it was already missing, and so the search had commenced.

The tingling continued. He rubbed at his neck, expecting to feel a blood-gorged creature pop beneath his fingers, but there was nothing. An open field lay between Herod and the warehouse. At its closest border was a pool of standing water, cloudy with bugs. Herod drew closer to it, until he could stare at his reflection: his own, and that of another. Behind him stood a tall scarecrow in a black suit, wearing a black top hat with a busted crown on its head. Its face was a sack in which two eyeholes had been crudely cut, and it had no mouth. The scarecrow was unsupported. There was no wooden cross upon which it might rest.

The Captain had returned.

VERNON AND PRITCHARD LAY on a slight rise, their position concealed by briars and low-hanging branches. They had a clear line of sight to the houses adjoining the Rojas warehouse. Both were entirely still; even up close, they seemed barely to be breathing. Pritchard's right eye was close to the night sight of the M40. The rifle was accurate up to 1,000 yards, and Pritchard was barely 800 yards distant from the targets. Beside him, Vernon tracked doors and windows through an ATN Night Spirit monocular.

In a sense, history was repeating itself for them. Both men had been present on the night that the warehouse in Al-Adhamiya was raided. They were Team 1, covering the southern approaches. Twiz-ell and Greenham were Team 2, covering the north. Nobody had questioned the purpose of the mission: it was in the nature of sniper units that they planned and executed their own operations, and they had announced their insertion into the area days earlier so that units on patrol could work around them. Only Tobias and Roddam knew exactly where they would be. In the end, they had not been required to fire a single shot on the night of the raid, which had disappointed them. Tonight would be different.

Both men were quiet, patient, reclusive, as individuals of their calling needed to be. They were without remorse. When asked if he experienced regret at the lives that he took, Pritchard would reply that all he ever felt was the recoil. This was not entirely true: killing gave him a rush that was better than sex, yet he was also a moral and courageous man who believed that his vocation was noble, and he was intelligent enough to recognize the tension implicit in the desire to take lives in a moral fashion while simultaneously experiencing pleasure in the performance of the act.

He and Vernon wore homemade ghillie suits, with holes in the back for ventilation. They had doused themselves with mud and water from a nearby creek and, as it was a moonlit night, their hats bore netting to break up the shape of the human face. They were not using laser range finders. Instead, both men automatically performed all the necessary calculations in their heads: range, angle to the targets, air density, wind speed and direction, humidity, even adding in the temperature of the propellant in the cartridge, for a cartridge that is twenty degrees warmer than another will strike a target twenty inches higher at a thousand meters. In the past, they had used data books, calculators loaded with ballistics software, and data tables glued to rifle stocks. Now, they knew such details by heart.

The slant angle was slightly downhill. Pritchard figured that he'd be aiming fifteen feet above the target, and to the left, to allow for bullet drop. All was set. The only problem was Twizell and Greenham. They weren't in position. Pritchard had no idea where they were. Both he and Vernon continued to be troubled by the fact that Tobias had sent the others somewhere in advance, but hadn't bothered to run it by them first. Vernon had been a staff sergeant, an E-6, the highest ranking of the four snipers, and he and Tobias still butted heads when it came to operational matters. He and Pritchard should have been consulted. Now they were down a team, and that wasn't good.

THE VAN WAS PARKED in a copse some four hundred feet from the back of the Rojas warehouse. The driver's door was open. Tobias, concealed by a black ski mask and black fatigues, was scanning the warehouse and surrounding buildings through a pair of night vision lenses. He started as a noise came from nearby, and then there was a low whistle and a figure emerged from the bushes before him.

"Four, plus Rojas," said Mallak. "Three with MP5s, one with a big-ass pump action. Mossberg Roadblocker, most likely. Two Glock nines in shoulder rigs, one with the shotgun, the other with the MP5 nearest the door. No alcohol that I can see. TV is on, but not too loud. Remains of food on the table."

Tobias nodded. That was good. Men were more sluggish after food.

"What about Rojas?"

"There's a stairway against the western wall, enclosed, no turns. Ends at a steel door, slightly open. My guess is that it can be sealed at the first sign of trouble. Windows are thickened glass on the first floor, so no reason to think Rojas's level is any different. There's no outside stairwell, but there is a weight-activated ladder on the southern exterior wall, accessible from the window above."

"Surrounding houses?"

"Two families at A and B," said Mallak, using his fingers to indicate the buildings in question. "Two female juveniles, one adult female, two adult males in A: one Glock, belt. Two adult females, one male juvenile, one adult male in B: one Glock, belt. Three males in C: two AK-47s; one Glock, shoulder. Vernon and Pritchard have the intel, but we're still a team down."

Tobias took one more look at the target through the lenses, then tossed them on the driver's seat. They could wait for Greenham and Twizell, or proceed. The longer they stayed in position, though, the more likely it was that they would be discovered. He leaned over the seat and looked into the interior of the van. Bacci gazed back at him, his mask rolled up to his forehead in the heat of the van, his face damp with sweat.

"All right," said Tobias, as Mallak slouched against the side of the van, "listen up . . ."

HEROD WAS UNARMED. HIS gun was in the car. He carried only a pair of manila envelopes. The first contained a piece of paper on which a figure was typed. This represented the sum of money that Herod was prepared to transfer to any account nominated by Rojas in return for information on how, and from whom, he had obtained the seals. If Rojas refused to provide such information, then Herod knew where Rojas's American mistress lived, along with Rojas's illegitimate five-year-old son. Herod would take them both. If necessary, he would kill the woman first, to indicate his seriousness to Rojas, but he did not believe that such action would be required, especially not after Rojas looked in the second envelope containing photographs of those who had crossed Herod in the past, for Herod had a particular way with women. His understanding of their bodies might even have made him a gifted lover, but Herod was a sexless being. Neither was he cruel. Pain and suffering were, for him, a means to an end, and he gained no particular pleasure from their infliction. Herod was not without empathy, and his own sufferings had made him reluctant to prolong the pain of others. For this reason, he hoped that Rojas would take the money.

He looked again at the Captain's reflection. He felt no unease. He liked being in the Captain's presence. He wondered if the Captain would come with him to the Rojas warehouse. He was preparing to find out when, on the surface of the pond, the Captain moved. His fingers were made from twigs, and they rustled slightly as he raised his hand and placed it on the shoulder of Herod's reflection. Herod himself shivered involuntarily at the pressure, and the chill, of the Captain's touch, feeling it as surely as he felt the warmth of the night air, and the biting of the insects, but he stayed as he was, and together they kept watch on the building before them.

ONE SIDE OF THE first floor of the Rojas warehouse was lined from floor to ceiling with crates of Rojas Brothers Fuego Sagrado hot sauce. If anyone took the trouble to inquire, then the importation and distribution of the sauce was the reason for the warehouse's existence, and one of the means whereby Antonio Rojas made his living. Rojas had lost count of the number of times the trucks transporting the sauce had been searched by local and federal law enforcement, but he didn't mind. It distracted them from all the other trucks and cars transporting far more valuable cargo, although, if Rojas were to be honest, he made a very respectable living from the sauce too, even if there were those on the other side of the border who regarded the name, and the packaging, as almost blasphemous. It had a distinctive label, a red fiery cross on a jet-black background, and it was marketed as a premium product to gourmet food stores, and the better Mexican restaurants, across New England. The markup was nearly as high as on pot or cocaine, and Rojas was careful to declare all income derived from it to the IRS. With the help of a creative accountant, it appeared as though Antonio Rojas was making a reasonable, if not excessive, profit as a purveyor of quality hot sauce.

It was the sound of one of those hot sauce bottles breaking that alerted Rojas. He looked up from the papers on his desk, and his hand drifted to the gun that was never far away. The door to his living quarters was slightly ajar, otherwise the insulation on the floor would have masked all the noises from below: glass shattering, a chair scraping, something heavy yet soft falling to the floor.

Rojas stood and made a lunge for the door, but he was seconds too late. The muzzle of a weapon was thrust through the opening, and there was a burst of muffled gunfire that took him across the thighs, almost cutting his legs from his torso. He collapsed as the door opened fully, but even as he fell he had time to squeeze off two shots that hit the dark-garbed figure in the chest. The Kevlar vest absorbed the impact, rocking the man on his heels. Rojas's third shot was higher, and a messy splash of blood burst forth from the back of the man's head, the aftermath of a pebble dropped in a red pool. Rojas barely had time to register it before there was more gunfire, and he felt the hot punches as the shots tore through his back. He lay unmoving, and yet he did not die. His eyes took in the shiny black boots that surrounded him, and registered some of the words that he heard: "shoot"; "question"; "no choice"; and, "dead, he's dead." Rojas chuckled wetly.

More footsteps, receding then drawing nearer once again. Black knees by his face. Fingers in his hair, raising his head. The bag of seals, held in gloved hands, the display stand that he had been making for them tossed aside, splintering on the tiled floor. Pink lips moving in the gap of the mask. White teeth, clean and even.

"Where are the rest of them?"

"*No comprendo.*"

A knife appeared. "I can still hurt you."

"No, you can't," said Rojas, and he smiled as he died, revealing twin rows of ancient gold and precious stones newly embedded in his teeth.

A BURST OF GUNFIRE was carried from the Rojas warehouse to the hide site, but it was not followed by a second.

"Shit," said Vernon. He'd known that they were unlikely to get in and out of the warehouse entirely without trouble, but he had been hoping for the best. "Okay, ready up."

Slowly, he moved the monocular across the three houses, designated Curly, Larry, and Moe. "Moe. Doorway, bearing right," he said, picking out the figure of a man carrying an AK-47.

"I see him."

Breathe. Exhale. Take up trigger slack. Exhale.

Pressure.

Fire.

Vernon watched as the target threw his hands in the air, the final wave, then fell.

"Hit," he said. "Curly. Door. Range seven hundred and fifty yards. Zero wind. No correction. Come up seven and two." This time, the gunman was staying inside, using the frame of the door for cover as he tried to figure out where the shot had come from.

"Shooter up."

"Spotter up. Send it."

Pritchard fired again. There was an explosion of wood chips from the door, and the target ducked back inside.

"Uh, miss, I think," said Vernon. "It should keep him pinned, though."

Momentarily, he shifted his sight to the Rojas warehouse, from which two of their men were emerging, carrying a third between them.

"Okay, they're on the move, but they've got a casualty. Let's—"

There was a burst of white flame from the nearest right-side window of Curly. "Curly. Door."

Pritchard fired, and Vernon saw the shooter leap into the air as the shot took him in the head, causing his legs to spasm. "Hit," said Vernon.

There was more firing from Moe. Vernon shifted the monocular just in time to see a second man of the assault team fall to the ground.

"Ah, hell," said Vernon. "Second man down."

Pritchard adjusted himself as quickly as possible and began pumping shots through the window of the house in a "spray and pray," concerned only with providing cover while the injured were taken to safety, but now there were shouts, and lights were going on in the other houses. Vernon could see the last man on his feet—he thought it might be Tobias—carry one of his fallen team back to the van in a fireman's lift and lay him as gently as possible on the floor. He then went back for the second man.

"Let's go," said Pritchard.

They picked up the "kill brass" and ran to where a pair of Harleys were parked by the side of a rutted track. On the ground behind them, they left a muddied denim jacket taken from a biker in Canada, a drug mule targeted by Vernon and Pritchard and left for dead at Lac-Baker. It was a crude piece of framing, but they didn't think the Mexicans would be concerned with the niceties of a formal investigation. They would want vengeance, and the jacket, combined with the roar of the departing bikes, might be enough to throw them off the scent for a couple of days.

———

TOBIAS GOT BEHIND THE wheel of the van and pulled out. In his side mirrors, the Rojas warehouse was a dark mass against the night sky, the dancing shadows of approaching men visible at either side. He was the only one left alive. Mallak had died at the warehouse, and Bacci had taken a bullet to the base of his neck as they carried Mallak's body away. It was a mess that could have been avoided if Greenham and Twizell had been there, but he'd made the call, and he'd have to live with it. Maybe if fucking Pritchard had been faster off the mark . . .

The explosion wasn't loud, the noise dampened by the thick brick walls of the old building, but the purpose of the thermite device, 25 percent aluminum to 75 percent iron oxide, was not to blow apart the warehouse itself but to burn everything within, leaving the minimum of evidence. It would also serve to distract his pursuers: with Mallak and Bacci dead, there was no one left to provide covering fire, so it would be a matter of hitting the highway and keeping his foot down all the way. Vernon and Pritchard would take another route to the rendezvous, but Tobias would have words with them when next they met, if only to preempt the snipers' inevitable anger.

There was a message on his phone. He listened as he drove, and learned that something had gone wrong in Bangor. Greenham and Twizell had not reported back, and it had to be presumed that the Jandreau situation was unresolved. The GPS tracking device in the detective's car was no longer responding, and the detective was still alive. It was a mess, but at least he now had the missing seals. He also had, in his pocket, as many of Rojas's teeth as he could knock from his mouth in the time available. It was time to get rid of what they had, make as much money as they could as quickly as possible, and then disappear.

He did not notice Herod's car, its lights extinguished, idling on a side road. Moments later, Herod was following the van.

XXXI

It was quiet in the motel room. Mel and Bobby sat together on one bed, she holding him and stroking his face, as though rewarding him for the fact that he had unburdened himself at last of all that he knew. Angel was by the window, watching the lot. I sat on the second bed, and tried to take in all that I had learned. Tobias and his crew were smuggling antiquities, but if Bobby was to be believed, they'd brought something else over with them, something that was never meant to be discovered, and never meant to be opened. It had been part of the bait, like a dose of poison contained in meat. I wanted to believe that Jandreau was wrong, that it was guilt and stress that was leading these men to take their lives and the lives of others, including Brett Harlan's wife, and Foster Jandreau, for Bobby confirmed that he had approached his cousin about his concerns, and that he believed Foster's unofficial inquiries had led to his murder. It was just a question of who had pulled the trigger. My money was on Tobias initially, but Bobby was less sure: he had warned his cousin about Joel Tobias, and he couldn't see Foster agreeing to meet up with him in the darkened lot of a ruined bar with no witnesses. It was then that he told me of his sessions with Carrie Saunders, and of how he had discussed some of his concerns with her.

Carrie Saunders. It wasn't Tobias alone who connected all these

men to one another, it was Saunders. She had been at Abu Ghraib, as
had the mysterious Roddam, or Nailon. She'd been in contact with
all the dead men at one point or another, and had a reason to move
between them. Jandreau wouldn't have agreed to meet a potentially
dangerous ex-military man like Tobias in a deserted lot, but he might
have agreed to meet a woman. I called Gordon Walsh, and I told him
everything that I knew, leaving out only Tobias. Tobias was mine. He
said that he'd pick up Saunders himself and see what came of it.

IT WAS LOUIS, SLOUCHED low in the Lexus so that he could watch the
approaches to the room, who spotted him. The raggedy figure strolled
across the parking lot, a cigarette dangling from his right hand, his
left empty. He wore a black coat over a black suit, his shirt wrinkled
and open at the neck, the jacket and pants bearing the marks of cheap
cloth, ill used. His hair was slicked back from his skull, and too long
at the back, hanging in greasy strands over his collar. He seemed
simply to have materialized, as though atoms had been pulled from
the air, their constituent parts altered as he reconstructed himself in
this place. Louis had been watching the mirrors as well as the expanse
of motel visible through the windshield. He should have seen him
coming, but he had not.

And Louis knew him for who, and for what, he was: this was the
Collector. The man might have been dressed in thrift store clothes,
his appearance that of one who has been poorly served by life, and
has chosen to respond in kind, but it was all a veneer. Louis had met
dangerous men before, and some had died at his hand, but the man
now walking toward the door to 112 exuded menace the way other
people sweated from their pores. Louis could almost smell it off him
as he slipped from the car and moved in; that, and something more:
a hint of burned offerings, of blood and charnel houses. Though Louis's approach was silent, the Collector raised his hands without turn-

ing while Louis was still fifteen feet away. The cigarette had burned down as far as the yellowed skin on the Collector's fingers, but if it hurt him then he did not show it.

"You can drop that, if it's bothering you," said Louis.

The Collector let the cigarette slip from his fingers. "A shame. There was another pull left on it."

"They'll kill you."

"So I've been told."

"Maybe I'll kill you first."

"And we haven't even been formally introduced, although I do feel that I know you. You might say that I've watched you from afar, you and your partner. I've admired your work, especially since you appear to have developed a conscience."

"I guess I should be flattered, huh?"

"No, you should simply be grateful that I haven't had cause to come after you. You were on the verge of damnation for a time. Now, you are making recompense for your sins. If you continue on that path, you might yet be saved."

"Are you saved? If you are, I'm not sure I want to be keeping that kind of company."

The Collector expelled a breath through his nose, the closest he had come to laughter in an eternity.

"No, I exist between salvation and damnation. Suspended, if you will: a dangling man."

"Kneel," said Louis. "Put your hands on your head and keep them there."

The Collector did as he was told. Louis advanced on him quickly, placed the gun to his head, and knocked hard on the door. Up close, the smell of nicotine made his eyes water, but it served to mask the other smells.

"Me," said Louis. "I got company. An old friend of yours."

The door opened, and the Collector looked up at me.

———

HE SAT IN A chair by the door. Louis had frisked him, but the Collector was unarmed. He examined the No Smoking sign by the television, and frowned as he knitted his fingers across his stomach. Bobby Jandreau stared at him the way one might stare, upon waking, at a spider suspended above one's face. Mel had retreated, and was sitting in a corner behind Angel, her eyes fixed on the stranger, waiting for him to pounce.

"Why are you here?" I asked.

"I came looking for you. It seems that we are working toward similar ends."

"Which would be?"

A thin finger, the nail the color of rust, extended itself and pointed to Jandreau.

"Let me guess the story so far," said the Collector. "Soldiers; treasure; a falling out among thieves."

Jandreau looked as though he might have been about to dispute the use of the word "thieves," but the Collector turned his mocking gaze in the direction of his finger, and Jandreau remained silent.

"Except they didn't know what they were stealing," the Collector continued. "They were indiscriminate. They took all that they could, without wondering why it had been made so easy for them. But you paid a high price for it, didn't you, Mr. Jandreau? You're all paying a high price for your sins."

Jandreau started. "How do you know my name?"

"Names are my business. There was a box, was there not? A gold box. They left it for you to find. It was probably in a lead receptacle, for they couldn't be too careful, but they left it where it wouldn't be ignored. Tell me, Mr. Jandreau. I'm right, am I not?"

Jandreau just nodded.

"I want the box," said the Collector. "That's why I'm here."

"For your collection?" I said. "I thought someone had to die before you got to claim one of their possessions."

"Oh, someone will die, if I have my way, and my collection will increase greatly as a consequence, but the box will not be part of it. It does not belong to me. It does not belong to anyone. It is dangerous. Someone is looking for it, a man named Herod, and it is essential that he not be allowed to find it. If he does, he will open it. He has the patience, and the skill. The one with him has the knowledge."

"What's in it?" asked Angel.

"Three entities," said the Collector simply. "Old demons, if you prefer. The box is the latest in a series of attempts to contain them, but its construction was flawed by the vanity of its creator, who forgot that he was forging a prison. Gold is such soft metal. Over the years, gaps appeared. Something of what was contained inside found a way to reach out, to poison the minds of those who came into contact with it. The lead box was an effort to counteract that threat: crude, but effective. Like the dull paint used to cover the gold, it also served to conceal what was inside."

"Why didn't they just dump it in the ocean, or bury it somewhere?"

"Because the only thing worse than knowing where it might be is not knowing. The box was watched. It had always been watched, the knowledge of it transferred from one generation to the next. In the end, it was hidden away among a jumble of worthless artifacts in a museum basement in Baghdad, and then the war came, and the museum was looted. The box disappeared, along with much else that was of value, but somehow an understanding of its nature, however incomplete, reached those who had seized it. It may even have been that they knew exactly what they had from the moment it appeared, for looting is a relative term. The items stolen from the Iraq Museum were carefully chosen, for the most part. Do you know that seventeen thousand items were stolen from the museum over those April days; that four hundred and fifty of four hundred and fifty-one cases were emptied, but only twenty-eight of those cases were broken? The rest were simply opened, which means that those who stole from them had keys. Astonishing, don't you think? One of the greatest museum thefts in history, one of the greatest sackings since the time of the Mongols, and it may have been an inside job.

"But no matter. When Mr. Jandreau and his friends came looking for treasure, the box was passed on to them, perhaps in the hope that they would do exactly what they did: transport it back to this country, the country of the enemy, where it would be opened. Now you know what it is. In return, tell me where to find it."

His eyes scanned every face in the room, as though the knowledge that he sought might somehow be read in them, before he fixed on mine.

"Why should we trust you?" I said. "You manipulate truth for your own ends. You're just a killer slaughtering under some divine flag of convenience, and nothing more."

A light flared in the Collector's eyes, like twin torches being ignited in an abyss. "No, I am no mere killer: I am an instrument of the Divine. I am God's murderer. Not all of His work is beautiful . . ."

He looked disgusted, both with me and, I believed, at some level kept hidden even from his own conscience, with himself.

"You must set aside your qualms, just as I must set aside mine," he said, after a moment. "If I trouble you, then you disturb me. I dislike being near you. You are part of a plan of which I have no knowledge. You are bound for a reckoning that will be the death of you, and of all who stand alongside you. Your days are numbered, and I do not wish to be close to you when you fall."

He raised his palms to me, and there was a plea in his voice. "So let us do this one thing, for as bad as you may believe me to be, the man named Herod is worse, and he is himself being shadowed by an entity, one that he believes he understands, one that will have promised him a reward for his service. It has many names, but he will know it by only one, the one that it gave him when first it found a way to worm itself into his consciousness."

"And what do you call it?" I asked.

"I call it nothing but what it is," said the Collector. "It is the Darkness: evil incarnate. It is the One Who Waits Behind the Glass."

XXXII

Herod put his hands beneath the faucet and let the flow of water wash the blood away. He watched the patterns that it made, the crimson vortex that swirled against the stainless steel like the arms of a distant nebula spiraling into collapse. A bead of sweat dripped from his nose and was lost. He closed his eyes. His fingers hurt, and his head ached, but at least it was pain of a different kind, the pain of hard labor. Torturing another human being was a wearying business. He looked up at his reflection and saw, in the glass, the man slumped in the chair, his hands bound behind his back. Herod had removed the rag from his mouth so that he could hear what he had to say. He had not bothered to replace it when the man had finished talking. There was no need. He barely had the strength to breathe, and soon even that would be gone.

Behind the slouched man stood another figure, its hands resting lightly on the back of the chair. Once again, the Captain had taken the form of the little girl in the blue dress, her hair long and worn in braids that hung between her breasts. As before, the girl could not have been more than nine or ten, but her breasts were surprisingly well developed; obscenely so, thought Herod. Her face was startlingly pale, but unfinished. Her eyes and mouth were black ovals, blurred at the edges as though a dirty eraser had smeared the marks made by a thick pencil. She stood very still, her head almost on a level with that of the seated man.

The Captain was waiting for Joel Tobias to die.

It would not have been true to say that Herod was an immoral man. Neither was he amoral, for he admitted the distinction between moral and immoral behavior, and was conscious of the necessity for fairness and honesty in all his dealings. He required it of others, and demanded it of himself. But there existed in Herod an emptiness, like the hollow at the center of certain fruits once the pit has been removed, speeding their decay, and out of that emptiness came the capacity for certain types of behavior. He had taken no pleasure in hurting the man who was now dying on the chair, and as soon as Herod had learned all that he wished to know he had ceased working on the interior of the man's body, although the damage that had been inflicted was so great that the suffering had continued despite the cessation of violent, invasive actions. Now, as the last of the blood was washed away, Herod felt compelled to bring those sufferings to a close.

"Mr. Tobias," he said, "I believe we've reached the end."

He picked up his gun from beside the sink, and prepared to turn away from the glass.

As he was about to do so, the figure of the girl moved. She shifted position so that she was slightly to his right. One filthy hand reached out and stroked Tobias's face. Tobias opened his eyes at the touch. He looked confused. He could feel fingers on his skin, and yet he could see nothing. The girl leaned closer. From out of the dark orb of her mouth a tongue appeared, long and thick, and lapped at the blood around the dying man's mouth. Now he tried to turn his head away, but the girl responded to the movement, clinging to his clothing, her legs between his, her body pressing against him. Something in the way that Tobias's position had changed allowed him to see his own reflection in the smoked glass of an oven door: his reflection, and the nature of the being that was forcing itself upon him. He whimpered in fear.

Herod walked over to the chair, placed the gun against Tobias's head, and pulled the trigger. The Captain disappeared, and all movement ceased.

Herod took a step away. He was aware of the Captain's presence somewhere nearby. He felt his rage. He risked a glance at the oven door, but could see nothing.

"It was not necessary," he said to the listening dark. "He had suffered enough."

Enough? Enough for whom? For him, yes, but for the Captain, there could never be sufficient suffering. Herod's shoulders sank. With no other option, he was compelled to look again at the window.

The Captain was directly behind him, but no longer was he a little girl. Instead, he was a sexless form in a long, gray coat. His face was a blur, a constantly altering series of visages, and in them Herod saw everyone for whom he had ever cared: his mother and his sister, now gone; his grandmother, adored and long buried; friends and lovers, living and dead. Each of them was in agony, their faces contorted in torment and despair. And, finally, Herod's face appeared among them, and he understood.

This was how it could be. Cross the Captain again, and this was what would come to pass.

The Captain departed, leaving Herod alone with the body. He restored the gun to the holster beneath his shoulder, and took one last look at the dead man. He wondered how long it would be before his friends discovered him, or how many of them might even be left. It hardly mattered. Herod now knew who had the box, but he had to move fast. The Captain had warned him: the Collector was coming.

Herod had heard stories of the Collector long before the man's pursuit of him had commenced, of the strange, tattered individual who believed himself to be a harvester of souls, and hoarded souvenirs of his victims. From the Captain, he had learned yet more. The Collector would want the box for himself. That was what the Captain said, and Herod believed him. Herod had been careful to hide himself well, operating under a variety of aliases, using shell companies, and lawyers untroubled by scruples, and shadowy transporters who cared little for paperwork and customs documents as long as the money was right. But the uniqueness of some of his purchases, and the inquiries he had made in the course of his searches, however discreet, had inevitably drawn the Collector's interest to him. Now it was crucial that he remain at one remove from him, for it would take time to figure out the intricacies of the box's locks. Once the box was opened, there would be nothing that the Collector, or anyone else, could do. The Captain's triumph would be Herod's revenge, and he could die at last and claim his reward in the next world.

Herod left the house, walking past the bodies of Pritchard and Vernon where they lay in the yard, and got into his car. There were sirens in the distance, moving closer. As he put the key in the ignition, he heard the sound of banging from the trunk, until it was lost in the roar of the engine.

CHAPTER

XXXIII

When Karen Emory was a little girl, and had only just begun sleeping in her own room, albeit with the door open and her mother's bedroom in clear view, a man had broken into their house shortly after midnight. Karen had woken to find the intruder standing in the corner of her bedroom, wreathed in darkness, watching her. He was completely silent—she could not even hear his breathing—yet his presence had pulled her from her rest, a primitive awareness that all was not as it should be, and a threat was near. She had been unable to scream as she looked at him, so terrified was she. Decades later, she could still recall the dryness in her mouth, the asthmatic sound that her breath had made as she tried to summon help, the sense that some great weight was holding her down on the bed, preventing her from moving. They were trapped in a stasis, these two strangers: one unmoving, one incapable of movement.

Suddenly, the man had shifted his weight, as though preparing to leap at her, his gloved hands reaching for her, and the spell was broken. She had screamed then, so loudly that for days after her throat hurt, and the intruder had bolted for the stairs. Her mother came out of her bedroom in time to see a figure open the front door and disappear. After checking on her daughter, she called 911. Cars descended on the neighborhood, and a search began. Eventually, a drifter named Clarence Buttle was picked up as he hid in an alleyway behind a Dumpster. Karen had told the policemen that she didn't get a good look at the man in her room, and couldn't recall anything about him. Her mother, too, claimed only to have seen the man's back in the darkness, and had been too tired and shocked to notice anything that might have distinguished it from any number of other backs that she had seen. The intruder had entered their home through a window, but had left no prints. Buttle protested his innocence loudly, claiming that he had only hidden in the alley because he was frightened of the police and didn't want to be blamed for something that he hadn't done. He spoke like a child, and seemed reluctant to meet the eyes of the detectives who questioned him.

They kept him for twenty-four hours. He did not ask to see a lawyer as he had not been charged with the commission of any crime. He gave them his name, and told them that he was originally from Montgomery, Alabama, but had been on the road for almost twelve years. He wasn't sure about his age, but he thought he might have been thirty-three, "like Our Lord, Jesus Christ."

During the period of his incarceration, a piece of cloth was found on a nail by Karen's window. It matched perfectly a hole in Clarence Buttle's coat. He was charged with forcible entry, trespass, and possession of a deadly weapon: a shiv found tucked into the lining of his coat. He was taken to the county jail to await trial, and was still there when his fingerprints produced an AFIS match. A year earlier, a nine-year-old girl named Franny Keaton had been abducted from her parents' home in Winnetka, Illinois. After a weeklong search, her body was found in a storm drain. She had been strangled, but there was no sign of sexual assault, although the girl's clothing had been removed. The fingerprint that matched Clarence Buttle's had come from the left eye of the doll found alongside Franny Keaton's body.

When asked about Winnetka, Clarence Buttle had smiled slyly and said, "I've been a bad, *bad* boy."

As the years went by, Karen Emory would still wake at least once every month, convinced that Clarence Buttle, that bad, bad boy, had come back to take her down to a storm drain and ask her to play with him.

But now other nightmares had taken the place of those concerning Clarence Buttle. She had heard the voices whispering again in their strange tongue, but this time she believed that they were not trying to communicate with her. In fact, she sensed their complete disregard, even contempt, for her. Instead, they were anticipating the arrival of another, one who would respond to their entreaties. They had been waiting a long time, and they were growing impatient. In her dream, she saw Joel entering the basement, stepping into the darkness, and the voices rose in a crescendo of welcome . . .

But Joel was not here. Before he had departed, he had put a small box on the pillow beside her.

"I was going to keep them for your birthday," he said. "Then I thought, why wait?"

It was an apology, she supposed, an apology for striking her, and hurting her. She had opened the box. The earrings were dull gold, but intricately carved, and so delicate that they seemed more like lace than metal. She knew before she touched them that they were old; old, and valuable.

"Where did you get them?" she asked, and as soon as the words were out of her mouth she knew that she had reacted wrongly, that her tone was doubtful and not filled with the wonder and gratitude Joel had anticipated. She thought that he might snatch the box away from her, or explode into another fit of rage, but instead he just looked hurt.

"They're a gift," he said. "I thought you'd like them."

"I do," she said, her voice trembling. She reached out and lifted them from the box. They were heavier than she had anticipated. "They're beautiful." She smiled, trying to rescue the situation. "They're really beautiful. Thank you."

He nodded. "Well, okay then," he said.

He watched as she put them on, but his response as she turned her head to let them catch the sunlight filtering through the drapes was distracted. She had disappointed him. Worse, she felt that, by her actions, she had confirmed a suspicion he had of her. When she was sure that he was gone, she took off the earrings and put them back in the box, then pulled the sheet over her head and prayed for sleep to come. She so wanted to rest, and not to dream. Eventually, she took half an Ambien, and sleep came, and with it the voices.

It was late afternoon when she woke. Her head felt fuzzy, and she was disoriented. She was about to call out for Joel, and as she recalled his absence she wished, even amid their troubles, that she was not alone, and that he was near. He said that he would be gone overnight, perhaps even for two nights. He had promised to let her know. A big deal was about to come good for him, he said, and they could look for a better place. They might even head off somewhere for a while, somewhere pretty and quiet. She told him that she'd like to go away with him, but she was happy too just to stay where they were. She'd be happy anywhere, she said, as long as he was beside her, and as long as he was content. Tobias said that that was one of the reasons why he liked her so much, because she didn't go asking for expensive things, because she had simple tastes. But that wasn't what she had meant at all, and it annoyed her that he'd misunderstood her. He had patronized her, and she hated being patronized, just as she hated the stupid secrets he now kept in his basement, and the fact that he wasn't telling her everything about the trips he took in his truck, and the goods that he delivered.

And then there were the earrings. She rolled over on the bed and opened the box. They *were* beautiful. Antiques, too. No, older even than that. Antiques were like furniture or jewelry from the 1800s, or so she had always thought. These earrings, though, were *ancient*. She could almost feel their age when she had first touched them.

She got up and ran a bath. The day was as good as gone, and she decided that she wasn't going to bother getting dressed. She would spend the evening in her robe, watch some TV, and order a pizza. With Joel absent, she rolled a joint from the little stash of pot that she kept hidden in her personal drawer and smoked it in the tub. Joel didn't approve of drugs, and although he had never tried to forbid her from smoking joints, he had made it clear that he didn't want to know about it if she did. For that reason, she tended to smoke only when he wasn't around, or when she was with friends.

After the bath and the joint, she felt better than she had in a long time. She looked at the earrings again, and decided to try them on. She piled her hair up on her head, wrapped herself in a clean white sheet, then stood in front of the mirror just to get a sense of how she might have looked in another time. She'd felt kind of silly doing it, but she had to admit that she appeared elegant, the earrings gleaming in the lamplight, fragments of yellow light falling like dust motes upon her face.

There was no way that Joel could afford a gift like those earrings, she knew, not unless he really was lying even more than she suspected about how much he was earning as a truck driver. The only conclusion to be drawn was that he was involved in something illegal, and the earrings were part of it: an exchange, perhaps, or a purchase with some of the proceeds. It took away some from the beauty of them. Karen had never stolen anything in her life, not even a piece of candy or some cheap cosmetics, the standard targets for the petty thieves among her high school friends when she was growing up. At the diner, she never took more than was permitted her under her food allowance. It was more than generous anyway, and she saw no reason to be greedy, even though there were one or two other waitresses who used the allowance as an excuse to take food home and gorge themselves, their boyfriends, and probably anyone else who happened to be dropping by their place too.

But the earrings were so beautiful. She had never been given anything so lovely, so old, so valuable. Now that they were on, she did not want to take them off. If he could convince her that he had come by them honestly, then she would keep them, but equally she would know if he was lying. If he did decide to lie to her about them, then their relationship would be under a real threat. She had already decided to forgive him for striking her again because she loved him, but it was time for him to be honest with her, and maybe with himself too.

She sat on the bed and turned on the TV. What the hell, she thought, and rolled a second joint. She watched a movie, some dumb comedy she'd seen before but that seemed far funnier now that she was a little high. Another movie followed, an action one this time, but she was starting to drowse. Her eyes closed. She heard herself snoring, and it woke her up. She lay down and rested her head on the pillow. The voices came again, but this time she had the peculiar sensation that this dream, and her nightmares about Clarence Buttle, had become conflated, because in the dream she sensed a presence nearby.

No, not in the dream.

In the house.

Her eyes opened.

"Joel?" she called, thinking that he might have come back earlier than expected. "Is that you?"

There was no reply, but she sensed that her words had caused a reaction elsewhere in the house: stillness where there had formerly been movement, silence where there had been sound.

She sat up. Her nostrils twitched. There was an unfamiliar smell: musty, but also faintly perfumed, like an old church vestment still suffused with the scent of incense. She found her gown and slipped it on, covering her nakedness, and was about to walk to the bedroom door when she reconsidered. She returned to her own bedside table and opened the drawer. Inside was a LadySmith 60 in a .38 special.

Joel had insisted that she keep a gun in the house, and he had taught her how to shoot out in the woods. She didn't like the gun, and had largely agreed to have it just to placate him, but now she was glad that, with Joel absent, she was not entirely defenseless.

She waited at the top of the stairs, but heard nothing, not at first. Then, slowly, she became aware of it.

The whispering had started again, and this time she was not asleep.

CHAPTER

XXXIV

Karen stood at the basement door, and listened. She felt like a sleepwalker, for her mind was still fuzzy from the sleeping pill, and the pot, and the aftereffects of dozing through the day. Everything was slightly off-kilter. When she turned her head, it seemed to take a split second for her eyes to follow the movement, and the consequence was a dizzying blurring of her vision. Now, tentatively, she placed the palm of her hand against the basement door, then knelt until her ear was close to the keyhole. Strangely, it made no difference to the volume of the voices she was hearing, even though she was certain that the whispering originated from behind the door. The voices were at once inside her and beyond her, resulting in an alteration in perception that she visualized in almost mathematical terms: an equilateral triangle, with her at one apex, the source of the voices at another, and the transmitted sound of them at a third. She was overhearing a conversation either carried on with no awareness of her presence or, more correctly, with an awareness of its inconsequentiality. It reminded her of when she was a very young girl, and her father and his friends would gather on a sunny day and sit around the table in the garden, drinking beers, while she sat in the shade of a tree, watching them and picking up on certain words and phrases, but unable to follow or fully understand the substance of their discussions.

Despite her dislike of dark spaces, and her concern at how Joel might react if he found that she had trespassed in his basement—for she knew that was how he would view it if he discovered that she had entered it without his permission—she wanted to see what was down there. She was aware that he was storing something new under the house for she had watched him moving the boxes from his truck. She experienced a frisson of excitement at the thought of such an incursion, spiced by a degree of apprehension, even fear.

She began to search for the key to the basement. While Joel kept one on a chain with his other keys, she guessed that there had to be a spare nearby. Already she knew her way around all the shared areas in the house. One of the kitchen drawers contained a jumble of old junk, including stray keys, locks, and screws. She went through it all, but could find no key that looked like it would fit the basement lock. After that, she searched in the pockets of Joel's coats that hung in the hall, but discovered only dust, a couple of coins, and an old receipt for gas.

Finally, aware that she was about to cross a line, she went through Joel's personal closet. Her fingers probed in suit pockets and shoes, beneath piles of T-shirts and through stacks of socks and underwear. Everything was clean and neatly folded, a holdover from Joel's time in the military. Halfway through, she began to forget about the key and started enjoying the intimate nature of her search, and what it revealed about the man she loved. She discovered photographs from his time in the military, and letters from a former lover, only a few of which she read, finding herself distressed by the possibility that someone could have thought that she loved Joel as much as she, Karen, did, and irritated by the fact that he had kept these letters. She flipped through them until she found the one that she sought, a simple "Dear John" letter advising Joel that their continued enforced separation because of his military service was too difficult for her to bear, and she wished to end their relationship. The letter was dated March 2007. Karen wondered if the woman, whose name was Faye, had found someone else before she wrote that letter. Some sixth sense told her that she had.

In a steel case on the floor of the closet was a Ruger pistol and a number of bladed weapons, including a bayonet. The sight of the knives made her shiver, the dreadful intimacy of their penetrative capacity, the potential for a brutal connection between victim and killer, separate entities briefly joined by a shard of metal.

Beside the knives lay what looked like a key to the basement door.

She carried it downstairs and placed it in the lock. She twisted the key with her left hand, the little LadySmith held in her right. The key moved easily, and the door unlocked. She opened it, and was suddenly aware of the silence in the house.

The whispering had stopped.

Before her, the basement stairs stretched down into darkness, only the first three illuminated by the light from the hall. Her fingers found the pull cord that dangled from the ceiling. She yanked it, and the overhead light came on, so that now she could see as far as the bottom of the stairs. Down there was another pull cord that lit the rest of the basement.

She took the steps slowly and carefully. She didn't want to trip, not here. She wasn't sure which possibility was worse: that Joel might come in and find her on the floor, her leg broken, or that Joel might not come back, and she would be left there, waiting for the voices to resume their whispering, alone in their presence.

She brushed the thought from her mind. It wasn't going to help her nerves any. At the second to last step, she stretched up on her toes, holding on tightly to the rail, and tugged the second cord. Nothing happened. She tried again, pulling once, then twice. There was still only darkness before her, and darkness behind and to her left where the basement stretched to most of the width of the house.

Hell, she thought, then remembered that Joel, always practical, kept a flashlight on the shelf immediately beyond the last step in case of just such an eventuality. She had seen it when he had first shown the basement to her on the day she had moved in with him. She trailed her fingers along a joist, surprised by how cold the metal felt, then allowed her hand slowly to run horizontally along the shelf, worried about dislodging the flashlight and knocking it to the ground. Eventually, her grip closed upon it. She twisted the head, and a beam shone on the ceiling, catching cobwebs and sending a spider scuttling into a corner. The beam was weak, though. The batteries needed to be replaced, but she would not be down here for long, just for long enough.

She spotted the new additions almost immediately. Joel had stacked the wooden crates and cardboard boxes in the far corner. She padded over to them in her slippered feet, shivering at the cold of the basement. All the boxes were open and filled with packing material: straw in most cases, foam chips in the rest. She reached into the nearest and felt a small, cylindrical object, protected by bubble wrap. She withdrew it from the box and unwrapped it in the flashlight's beam. It shone on the two gemstones inlaid into the gold disks at either end, and the unfamiliar signs carved into what she was certain was ivory.

She searched in the box again, and found another of the items, and a third. Each was slightly different from the last, but all had gold and gemstones in common. There were more of the cylinders down there, two dozen or more, and at least as many old gold coins in individual plastic sheaths. She rewrapped the cylinders that she had removed, and restored them to their place, then moved on to the next box. This one was heavier. She cleared away some of the straw packing to reveal a beautifully decorated vase. Beside it, in a crate previously used to transport wine, was the gold head of a woman with lapis lazuli for eyes. She ran her fingers across its face, so lifelike, so perfect in appearance. Although she was not someone who generally troubled museums with visits, here, in this musty basement, she began to understand the appeal of such artifacts, the beauty of something that had survived for so long, a link to civilizations now long vanished.

It made her think again of her earrings. Where Joel had gotten them from, she had no idea, but she knew now that this was the big score about which he had spoken, and in these items lay his hopes for both of their futures. She felt angry with him, yet also strangely relieved. If it had been drugs that she had found, or counterfeit money, or expensive watches and gems stolen from a jewelry store, she would have been disappointed in him. But these objects of beauty were so unusual, so unexpected, that she was forced to reconsider her opinion of him. He didn't even have pictures hanging on his walls until she came to live with him, yet this was what he stored in his basement? She wanted to laugh. It bubbled up from deep inside her, and she covered her mouth to stop it, and in doing so she was reminded of the sight of Joel seated cross-legged by the basement door, speaking intently to someone on the other side of it, and in that moment she recalled why she had come down here. The smile disappeared from her face. She was about to move on to the other crates when a shape on the shelf to her left caught her eye. It was clearly a box, loosely covered in bubble wrap, and it stood incongruously amid paint cans and jars of nails and screws. Yet even disguised as it was, and in such undistinguished surroundings, she was drawn to it. As she touched it, she felt it vibrate against her fingers. It reminded her of a cat purring.

She laid the flashlight on the shelf, and began to undo the wrapping. She had to lift the box to do so, and something inside seemed to shift slightly. Any concern she had that Joel might discover she had been down there was gone: she felt a burning desire to view the box, to open it, understanding the moment she touched it that this was what she was seeking, that this was linked to the voices in her nightmare, to the sensations of confinement and imprisonment, to

Joel's nocturnal conversations. When the bubble wrap stuck she tore at it with her fingers, hearing it pop as she shredded it, until at last the box was fully revealed to her. She stroked it, caressed it, marveling at the detail of its carvings. She lifted it, and was surprised by its weight. She couldn't begin to imagine how much the gold that went into its construction might be worth alone, regardless of the age of the box itself. With the tip of a finger she examined the intricate series of locks, shaped like spiders, that held the lid fixed to the base. There were no keyholes that she could see, merely clasps that would not move. She grew increasingly frustrated, picking with her fingernails at the metal, all sense of reason and patience gone. Then one of her fingernails broke, and the pain of it brought her back. She dropped the box as though it had suddenly grown hot in her hands. She was overcome by a profound sense of evil, a feeling that she was close to an intelligence that wished her only harm, that resented her touch. She wanted to run, but she was no longer alone in the basement, for there was movement in the corner to her left, directly across from the stairs.

"Joel?" she said. Her voice trembled. He would be so angry with her. She could already see the confrontation playing out: his fury at her trespass, hers at his hoarding of stolen artifacts in the basement of their home. They were both in the wrong, but her transgression was minor compared to his, except she knew that he would not see it that way. She did not want him to hit her again. Sense began to return to her: this was a serious criminal enterprise in which Joel was engaged, and that was bad enough. But the box . . . The box was another matter entirely. The box was foul. She had to get away from it. They both did. If Joel would not come with her, she would leave alone.

If he lets me leave, she thought. If it stops at just hitting when he finds out what I've been up to. Her mind went back to the weapons in his closet, and the bayonet in particular. Joel had shown it to her once before when she found him slumped in the corner of the room, his eyes red from weeping for his lost comrade, Brett Harlan. It was an M9 bayonet, just like the one Harlan had used on his wife before cutting his own throat.

Because the box made him do it.

She shuddered at the imaginative leap that she had just made, even as she strained to peer into the darkness before remembering the flashlight. She grasped it and pointed its beam at the corner. Shadows moved: the outline of garden tools and stacked bottles, the frames of the shelves, and one other, a figure that danced away from the light, melting into the blackness beneath the stairs; a deformed shape, distorted by the action of the beam but also, she knew, unnatural in its essence, contorted in its physicality. She could almost smell it: musty and aged, with an acrid edge, like old cloth burning.

This was not Joel: this was not even human.

She tried to follow its progress with the flashlight. Her hands were shaking, so she gripped the Maglite with both hands, holding it close to her body. She shone it under the stairs, and the shape danced away again, a shadow without a form to cast it, like smoke rising from an unseen flame. Now there was movement to her right as well. She swung the beam, and briefly a figure was framed against the wall, its body hunched, its arms and legs too long for its torso, the crown of its skull misshapen by outgrowths of bone. It was both real and unreal, the shadow seeming to stretch from the box itself, as though the essence of whatever was contained within it were seeping out like a bad smell.

And the whispering had started again: the voices were speaking about her. They were disturbed, angry. She should not have touched the box. They did not want her desecrating it with her fingers, with her woman's hands. Filthy. Unclean.

Blood.

She was having her period. It had started that morning.

Blood.

Tainted.

Blood.

They knew. They smelled it on her. She retreated, desperate to get to the stairs, aware now of three figures circling her like wolves, trying to stay out of the reach of her light even as they closed upon her. She waved the flashlight like a flaming torch, using it to probe at the darkness, to keep them at bay, her back to the shelves, then the wall, until at last she was facing the basement and her foot was on the first step. Slowly she ascended, not wanting to turn her back. Halfway up, the bulb above her head flickered and went dark, and then her flashlight too gave up the ghost.

They're doing it. They like the darkness.

Now she turned, stumbling up the final steps, and as she reached the door and slammed it closed she caught a final glimpse of them ascending toward her: shapes without substance, bad dreams conjured from old bones. She turned the key and pulled it from the lock, tripping as she did so and falling painfully on her coccyx. She watched the handle of the door, expecting it to turn like it did in those old horror movies, but it did not. There was only the sound of her breathing, and the beating of her heart, and the rustle of her robe against her skin as she pushed herself along the floor and came to rest against an armchair.

The doorbell rang. The shock of it made her squeal. She saw the figure of a man outlined against it by the night-light. She looked at the clock on the wall. It was after 3 A.M. Where had the hours gone? Rubbing the base of her spine where she had landed so awkwardly, she walked to the door and pulled the drape to one side so that she could see who was there. A man in his sixties stood in profile on the step. He wore a black hat, which he raised politely, revealing a bald cone misted by wisps of gray hair. She opened the door, relieved at the presence of another human being, even a stranger, but she still kept the security chain on.

"Hello," said the man. "We're looking for Karen Emory." He still had not turned toward her, so she could see only one side of his face.

"She's not here," said Karen, the words emerging before she even realized that she had spoken them. "I don't know when she'll be back. It's late, so she probably won't be home until morning."

She didn't know why she was lying, and was conscious of the weakness of the falsehoods she was uttering. The man looked unthreatening, but her survival instincts had been shocked into action by what she had seen in the basement, and he was making her skin crawl. She had been wrong to open the door to him, and now it was crucial that she lock it against him as soon as possible. She wanted to scream: she was trapped between this man, and the entities in the basement. She willed Joel to return, even as she understood that this was his fault, that the man was here because of him and what was stored in the basement, because why else would such an individual be on their doorstep at three in the morning. Joel would know what to do. She'd take her chances with his anger if he'd only return to help her.

"We can wait," said the man.

"I'm sorry. That won't be possible. Anyway, I have company." Lies were piling up on lies, and she sounded unconvincing even to her own ears. Then she thought about what the man on the doorstep had just said. *We're* looking for Karen Emory. *We* can wait.

"No," said the man. "We don't think you have company at all. We think you're alone."

Now she looked around to see if there was anyone else outside, but there was only this odd, creepy man with his hat in his hand. Only then did she realize that she had left her gun in the basement.

"Go away," she said. "Go away, or I'll call the police."

Now his head turned, and she saw how ruined he was, how damaged, and she felt that this was as much a spiritual as a physical decay. She tried to close the door, but his foot was already jammed in the gap.

"Nice earrings," said Herod. "Old, and too good for one such as you."

He reached through the gap, his hand a white blur, and ripped out one of the earrings, tearing the lobe. Blood sprayed on her robe and she tried to scream, but his hand was on her throat, his nails digging into her skin. His shoulder struck the door with massive force, and the chain came away from the frame. She fought against him, scratching at him with her fingers, until he slammed her head against the wall.

Once: "Don't . . ."

Twice: ". . . tell . . ."

The third time, she hardly felt it at all.

". . . lies!"

XXXV

Karen did not lose consciousness, not entirely, so she was aware of being dragged by her hair across the floor and thrown in a corner. Her ruined earlobe burned with pain, and she felt blood dripping from the wound. She heard the door locking, and saw the drapes being partially drawn on the windows, but she felt nauseated, and she was having trouble with her vision because, when the man walked to the window, she thought that she saw two reflections in the glass. One was the intruder, and the other—

The other was Clarence Buttle. There was something about his gait and posture that had ingrained itself upon her memory, even had the reflected figure not been wearing the shabby dark jacket that Clarence had been wearing that night in her bedroom, with the red-and-black-checked shirt beneath it tucked into baggy jeans that looked like they belonged more properly on a fatter person. Clarence's jeans had been held up with a brown leather belt, its battered silver buckle shaped like a cowboy hat. That was how she remembered him, because that was how he looked in the photographs that were taken of him as his true nature was revealed by the police investigation.

But Clarence Buttle was dead. He had died in prison, taken by stomach cancer that had eaten away at his insides. The reflected Clarence certainly looked like someone who'd been eaten away, except it was his face that had been consumed, because the Clarence that she glimpsed in the glass before the drapes closed had holes where his eyes should have been, and his lips were gone, revealing black gums and the stumps of rotted teeth. But in those final seconds, his lipless mouth had moved, and she heard the words, and smelled the foulness of his insides polluting the room.

"I've been a bad, bad boy," said the reflection, both Clarence and Not-Clarence, and Karen, struggling to hold back her bile, knew, deep down in the special hidden place where she kept all that was truly herself, that what she was seeing was the entity that had made Clarence Buttle what he was, the voice that had spoken to him of the pleasures of playing with little girls in old storm drains, the malign visitor that had put Karen Emory's name into Clarence's mind.

"She'll play with you, Clarence. She likes boys, and she likes dark places. And she won't scream. She won't scream no matter what you do to her, because she's a good, good girl, and a good, good girl needs a bad, bad boy to bring out the best in her . . ."

The intruder was looking at her in amusement, and she knew that he had seen something of what she had glimpsed, because he was rotting too, inside and out, and she wondered if the entity brought the cancer with it, if that degree of spiritual and mental decay somehow had to find a physical expression. After all, evil was a kind of poison, an infection of the soul, and other poisons, if absorbed slowly over time, brought changes to the body: nicotine yellowed the skin and blackened the lungs; alcohol damaged the liver and the kidneys, and scoured the face; radiation made your hair fall out; lead, asbestos, heroin, they all affected the body, bringing it closer to its final ruination. Was it not possible that evil in its purest form, the quintessence of it, might do the same? Because the sickness had been in Clarence, just as it was in the man who now held her in his power.

"What was his name?" he asked, and she felt compelled to reply.

"Clarence," she said. "His name was Clarence."

"Did he hurt you?"

She shook her head.

But he wanted to. Oh yes, Clarence had wanted to play, and Clarence played rough when it came to little girls.

Karen drew her knees up beneath her chin, and wrapped her arms around them. Although the reflection was no longer visible, she was afraid of what had created it. It was in here. She could feel it. She could feel it because there was a connection between her and Clarence Buttle. She was the one who escaped. Worse, she was the one who got him caught, and he would never forgive her for that, never forgive her for leaving him to rot painfully in a prison hospital with nobody to visit him, no one to care about him, when all he'd wanted to do was play.

The intruder approached her, and she shrank from him.

"My name is Herod," he said. "You don't have to be afraid of me. I'm not going to hurt you again, not as long as you answer my questions honestly."

But she was looking past him, her eyes flicking around the room, her nostrils twitching, alert for the approach of Not-Clarence, and his cancerous breath, and his filthy, probing fingers. The old man peered at her curiously.

"But you're not frightened of me, are you?" he said. "Because you've seen *him,* and that's quite the thing, quite the thing. Oh, you can call him Clarence, if you like, but he has lots of names. To me, he's the Captain."

He put a hand on her head and stroked her hair, and she trembled at his touch, because whatever had been in Clarence was also in him. "Though you don't have to be scared of the Captain either, not unless you've done something wrong, something very, very wrong."

He shifted his hand from her head to her shoulder and dug his nails in hard, causing her to wince and look him in the face, her eyes drawn to the arrow-shaped decay in his upper lip, and the virulence of its infection.

"But I suspect that even a little whore like you, all warm breath and hot britches, has no cause to worry, because the Captain has more pressing concerns. You're inconsequential, girly, and as long as you stay that way then the Captain will mind his distance. And if you don't, well . . ."

He cocked his head, as though listening to a voice that only he could hear, then grinned unpleasantly. "The Captain says to tell you that there's a storm drain with your name on it, and a friend there who's just aching for someone to join him." He winked. "The Captain says that old Clarence always did like warm, wet places, and the Captain saw him right on that score, because the Captain always keeps his word. Clarence now has a deep, dark, damp hole all to himself where he waits for the girl who got away. But that's the thing about the Captain's promises: you have to read the small print before you sign on the dotted line. Clarence didn't understand that, which is why he's been alone for so long, but I do. The Captain and I, we're real close. We speak with one voice, you might say."

He pulled hard, his grip still tight upon her so that she was forced to her feet.

"Now I have some bad news for you, but you're going to take it like a trooper: your boyfriend, Joel Tobias, isn't going to be the meat in your bun again anytime soon. He and I, we tried to have a talk, but he was a reluctant conversationalist, and I was forced to exert a little pressure on him."

He placed his left hand upon her cheek, and pinched it gently. His skin was cold to the touch, and she let out a little animal whine.

"I think you know what I'm talking about. To be honest, it was a blessing for him when the end came."

Her legs went weak. She would have fallen had Herod not held on to her. She tried to push him away, but he was stronger than her. She began to weep, but suddenly his hand was in her hair again, pulling her head back so far that she heard her neck crack.

"None of that," said Herod. "No time to grieve now. I'm a busy man, and time isn't on my side. We have things to do, and then you can mourn him all you like."

He led her to the basement door. He reached out his right hand and placed it against the wood.

"You know what's down there?"

Karen shook her head. She was still crying, but there was a numbness to her grief, like pain fighting to break through the diminishing effect of an anesthetic.

"You're lying again," said Herod, "but in a way you're also telling the truth, because I don't think that you *do* know what's down there, not really. But you and I, we're going to find out together. Where's the key?"

Slowly, she reached into the pocket of her robe and handed the key to him.

"I don't want to go back in the basement," she said. She thought that she sounded like a little girl, sobbing and wheedling.

"Well, missy, I can't very well leave you up here all alone, can I?" he replied. He spoke reasonably, even kindly, but this was the same man who had called her a whore earlier; who had left marks in her skin where his fingers had dug into her shoulder; who had torn her earlobe; who had killed Joel and left her alone again. "But you don't need to worry, not when you've got me to take care of you." He handed the key back to her. "Now go ahead and open it. I'll be right behind you."

To encourage her further, he showed her his gun, and she did as she was told, her hand trembling only slightly as she inserted the key in the lock. He stepped back as she opened the door, revealing the darkness beyond.

"Where's the light?" he asked.

"It doesn't work," she said. "It broke when I was down there." *They broke it,* she almost added. *They wanted me to trip and fall, so that I'd be forced to stay down there with them.*

Herod looked around, and saw the flashlight lying on the floor. He bent to retrieve it, and as he did so she kicked him hard on the side of the head, sending him to his knees. She ran for the front door, but she was still fumbling for the latch when he was on her. She cried out, and he covered her mouth with his hand and pulled her backward, then tossed her to the floor. She landed on her back, and before she could raise herself up he was kneeling on her chest. His hand reached into her mouth and grabbed her tongue so hard she thought that he was going to rip it out. She couldn't speak, but her eyes begged him not to do it.

"Last warning," he said. The wound on his lip had torn and was starting to bleed. "I don't cause pain without reason, and I have no desire to hurt you more than I have already, but if you make me do it, then I will. Cross me again and I'll feed your tongue to the rats, then leave you to choke on your own blood. Do you understand?"

Karen gave the faintest of nods, fearful of moving her head too much and tearing her tongue. He released his grip, and she tasted him in her mouth, sharp and chemical. She got to her feet, and he turned on the flashlight.

"Seems to be working fine now," he said and gestured for her to go ahead of him. "You first," he said. "Keep your hands away from your body. Don't touch anything but the stair rail. If you make any sudden moves while we're down there, it will go hard on you."

Reluctantly, she moved forward. The beam of the flashlight illuminated the stairs. Herod let her get three steps ahead of him, then followed. When she got halfway down she paused and looked to her left, where the darkness was deepest and the gold box rested on its shelf.

"Why have you stopped?" asked Herod.

"It's back there," she said.

"What is?"

"The gold box. That's what you're looking for, isn't it: the gold box?"

"You're going to show me exactly where it is."

"There are things down there," she said. "I saw them."

"I told you: you're in no danger. Keep going."

She continued descending until she reached floor level. Herod joined her, the flashlight searching the corners of the basement. Shadows jumped, but they were caused by the beam, and she might almost have been persuaded that she had imagined the earlier forms were it not for the fact that the whispering had returned. This time, it sounded different: puzzled, perhaps, but expectant.

She led him to where the treasures lay, but he showed no interest in the exposed seals, or the beautiful marble head. He had eyes only for the box. He allowed the light to play upon it for a time, tutting softly at some of the damage that it had incurred, the small dents and scuffs that marred the decoration on its sides, then pointed to a canvas bag that lay on top of some old suitcases stacked beside the shelf.

"Pick it up and put it in that bag," he told her. "And be careful."

She didn't want to touch it again, but equally she wanted all this to be over. He would leave when he had the box. If he was a man of his word, he would let her live. Despite her fear of him, she believed that he did not want to kill her. Had he wished to do so, she would be dead already.

"What is it?" she asked. "What's in there?"

"What did you see when you were down here?" Herod replied.

"I saw shapes. They were deformed. Like men except . . . not men."

"No, not men," said Herod. "Have you heard of Pandora's box?"

She nodded. "It was a box that contained evil, and it was opened and all that evil escaped into the world."

"Very good," said Herod, "except it was a pot, a *pithos,* not a box. The term 'Pandora's box' derives from a mistranslation into Latin."

He was glad that there was someone with him, now that he had that for which he had long been searching. He wanted to explain. He wanted someone else to understand its importance.

"This," he continued, "is a true Pandora's box, a prison of gold. Seven chambers, each with seven locks symbolizing the gates to the netherworld." He pointed to the arachnid clasps. "The locks are shaped like spiders because it was a spider that protected the prophet Mohammed from assassins by weaving a web in front of the mouth of the cave in which he was hiding with Abu Bakr. The men who constructed the box hoped that the spider might protect them in turn. As for what the box contains, well, let's call them ancient spirits, almost as old as the Captain himself. Almost."

"They're bad," said Karen. She shuddered. "I felt it from them."

She glanced around, but there was no sign of her gun, and she wondered if those malevolent shadows had found a way to hide it from her.

"Oh, that they are," said Herod. "They're very bad indeed."

"But what are you going to do with it?"

"I'm going to open it and set them free," said Herod, speaking as if to a child.

Karen stared at him. "Why would you do that?"

"Because that's what the Captain wants, and what the Captain wants, the Captain gets. Now pick up the box and put it in the bag."

She shook her head. Herod drew his gun and placed it against her lips.

"I have what I want," he said. "I can kill you, or we can both live. It's your choice."

Reluctantly, she lifted the box. Once again, she felt it vibrate in her hands. There was a tapping from inside it, as though a rodent were trapped in there, scratching vainly at the lid. It very nearly caused her to drop the box. Herod hissed in vexation, but said nothing. Carefully, she placed it in the canvas bag, then pulled the zipper closed. She tried to hand it to him, but he shook his head.

"I'll let you carry it," he said. "Go on. We're nearly done."

She led the way up the stairs, Herod close behind her this time, one hand resting lightly on her shoulder and the gun at her back. When she reached the living room, she stopped.

"Keep—" Herod began to say, before he saw what Karen had seen. There were three men in the room, all armed, their guns now pointing at his head.

"Let her go," I said.

XXXVI

If Herod was surprised to find us waiting for him, he hid it well. He pulled Karen Emory in closer to him, using her body as a shield, his gun pressed hard against the side of her neck, pointing upward into her brain. Only the right side of his head was visible to us, and even Louis wasn't going to take that shot. Blood was coursing from the terrible wound on Herod's upper lip, staining his lips and his chin.

"Are you okay, Karen?" I asked.

She tried to nod, but she was so afraid of the gun that the movement was little more than a tremor. Herod's eyes gleamed. He paid no attention to Angel and Louis. His gaze was fixed on me.

"I know you," said Herod. "I saw you at the bar."

"You should have introduced yourself. We could have saved a lot of time and energy."

"Oh, I don't think so. The Captain wouldn't have liked it."

"Who's the Captain?" But I recalled the second figure that I thought I had glimpsed in the car, a wraith with a clown's face.

"The Captain is very curious about you, and it takes a lot to pique the Captain's interest. After all, he's seen so much that there's little left to rouse him from his torpor."

"He's screwing with you," said Louis.

"Am I?" said Herod. He cocked his head, as though listening to a voice that only he could hear. "*Dominus meus bonus et benignitas est.* Ring any bells, Mr. Parker?"

I shifted my grip on the weapon in my hand. I had heard that phrase before. It functioned on a number of levels: as a coded greeting; as a dark joke, a declaration of faith in an entity that was far from benign; and as a naming of sorts. "My master is good and kind." Good and kind. Goodkind, or Mr. Goodkind. That was what his followers called him, or some of them, but now here was Herod implying that Goodkind and the thing that he called the Captain were one and the same.

"It doesn't matter," I said. "I've no interest in your ghost stories. What's in the bag?"

"Another ghost story," said Herod. "The prison box. I intend to leave with it, and you're going to let me."

"I don't think so." It was Angel who spoke. He was resting almost languidly against the frame of the door. "You may not have noticed, but there are three guns pointing at you."

"And I have one pointing at Ms. Emory's head," replied Herod.

"You kill her, and we kill you," said Angel. "And then you don't get to play with your box."

"You think that you have all the moves worked out, Mr. Parker, you and your friends," said Herod. "It pains me to disabuse you of that notion. Ms. Emory, reach very slowly into the outside left pocket of my coat, and take out what you find there. Do it gently, now, or you won't get to discover how this particular story ends."

Karen fumbled in his pocket, then threw something on the floor between us. It was a woman's pocketbook.

"Go ahead," said Herod. "Take a look inside."

It had landed close to Louis's left foot. He kicked it back to me, never taking his eyes from Herod. I opened it. It held cosmetics, some pills and a wallet. The wallet contained Carrie Saunders's driver's license.

"I buried her," said Herod. "Oh, not too deep. The box is steel— military in construction, I expect; I found it in her basement—but I didn't want it to buckle under the weight of the dirt. She has air too, courtesy of a hole and a plastic breathing tube. But it can't be pleasant, being trapped in the darkness, and who knows what might happen if her tube became blocked? A falling leaf would be enough, or a clod of dirt dislodged by a passing animal. By now, she must be close to panic, and if she does panic, well . . . Her hands are tied. If she doesn't keep her lips on that tube, she'll probably only have fifteen minutes to live, at most. They will be fifteen very long minutes, though."

"Why her?" I said.

"I think you know why, and if you don't then you're not as clever as I thought you were. I'd love to stay here and fill you in on all of the details, but suffice it to say that Mr. Tobias and his friends were very busy earlier killing Mexicans, and when they were done they went to Ms. Saunders's house to regroup. I learned a lot from Mr. Tobias before he expired: about a Jimmy Jewel and how he died, and someone called Foster Jandreau. It appears that Ms. Saunders could be quite the seductress when she put her mind to it. I guess you could call her the brains of the operation. She killed them all: Roddam, Jewel, Jandreau. Maybe you'll have the opportunity to question her yourself, if you let me go. The longer you prevaricate, the lower her chances of survival become. Everything is an exchange. Everything is a negotiation. I am an honorable man, and I keep my promises. I promise you the life of Ms. Emory, and the location of Carrie Saunders's makeshift coffin, in return for the box. We both know that you're not going to let Ms. Emory die. You're not the kind of man who could easily live with that knowledge."

I looked again at the license, and at Karen Emory's terrified face.

"How do we know that you'll keep your part of the bargain?" I said.

"Because I always keep my bargains."

I gave it a couple of seconds before nodding my assent.

"You're not serious?" said Angel. "You're going to take that deal?"

"What choice do we have?" I said. "Put your guns down. Let him leave."

Both Angel and Louis hesitated for a moment, then Louis slowly lowered his weapon, and Angel did the same.

"You have a cell phone?" asked Herod.

"Yes."

"Give me the number."

I did so, then said: "You want me to write it down for you?"

"No, thank you. I have an exceptional memory. In ten minutes, I will drop Ms. Emory at a pay phone, and I'll tell her where Carrie Saunders is buried. I'll even give Ms. Emory the money to make the call. Then you can ride to her rescue, and our business will be concluded."

"If you renege, I'll hunt you down. You, and your Captain."

"Oh, you have my word. I don't kill unnecessarily. I already have enough stains on my soul to last a lifetime."

"And the box?"

"I'm going to open it."

"You think you can control what's in there?"

"No, I don't, but the Captain can. Good-bye, Mr. Parker. Tell your friends to step away. I'd like all three of you in the far corner, please. If I see any of you emerge from the house, or if you try to follow me, our arrangement is off. I will kill Ms. Emory, and Carrie Saunders can take her chances in her own prison box. Do we understand each other?"

"Yes," I said.

"I don't believe that we're going to meet again," said Herod. "But you and the Captain, that's another matter. In time, I'm sure that you and he will have the chance to become more intimately acquainted."

Angel stepped away from the door, and he, Louis, and I moved into the corner of the room diagonally opposite the front door. Still keeping Karen as a shield, Herod backed out of the house, Karen closing the door behind them at his instruction. I had one last sight of her, and then they were gone. Moments later, there was the sound of a car starting up and driving away.

Louis made a move to the door, but I stopped him.

"No," I said.

"You trust him?"

"In this, yes," I said.

"I wasn't talking about Herod."

"Neither was I."

XXXVII

I don't know if Carrie Saunders panicked. I don't know if the tube slipped from her mouth and, trapped as she was, she was unable to reach it again. Sometimes, I find myself imagining her final moments, and always I see Herod tossing aside his spade and staring down at the compacted dirt, then gently tugging the breathing tube from the mouth of the woman buried below. He did it because she had breached some unwritten contract with him, but also because it pleased him to do so. For all his talk of honor, and negotiations, and promises, I believed that Herod was a cruel man. He kept his word about releasing Karen Emory, and he told her where Carrie Saunders was buried before he left her, but the autopsy concluded that Carrie Saunders had been dead for hours when she was found.

I do know this: Carrie Saunders killed Jimmy Jewel, and she killed Foster Jandreau. A gun, a Glock .22, was found in her house. The bullets matched those used to kill Jimmy and Jandreau, and her fingerprints were the only ones found on the weapon. As for Roddam, there was no way of knowing for certain if she was responsible for his death, but Herod had told the truth about her involvement in the other killings, so there was no reason to believe that he had been lying about Roddam.

After Saunders's body was found, there was some speculation that the man responsible for her death might have framed her for the other killings, but it was dismissed when Bobby Jandreau came forward and told of how he had spoken with his cousin Foster about his belief that the death of Damien Patchett, and those of the Harlans and Bernie Kramer, were linked to a smuggling operation being run by Joel Tobias, although he had no formal evidence to offer in support. Foster Jandreau was ambitious, but he wasn't advancing fast enough through the ranks for his liking. If he could find evidence of illegal dealings on the part of Joel Tobias, then he might have been able to resuscitate a moribund career. But Bobby Jandreau had made the mistake of discussing the matter with Carrie Saunders during one of their therapy sessions, and then she had killed Foster to stop him from delving further into the operation, and sullied his reputation with drug vials. Whether or not she did so with Joel Tobias's knowledge and consent I could not say, and those who might have been able to tell me were all dead. I remembered what others had said about Tobias: he was smart, but not that smart. He was not capable of running an operation potentially involving millions of dollars worth of stolen antiquities, but Carrie Saunders was. In Paris, Rochman revealed that his contact for the purchase of the ivories and the seals had been a woman who used the pseudonym "Medea," and that the money had been wired to a bank in Bangor, Maine. Rumors emerged that Saunders and Roddam might have been lovers during their time together at Abu Ghraib, but they were an unlikely couple. War created such odd unions, but it was probable that Roddam and Saunders were using each other, and Saunders had come out on top, because Roddam had died. Saunders and Tobias had gone to the same high school in Bangor, Saunders graduating the year after Tobias. They had known each other for a long time, but if she had been the guiding intelligence behind the operation, then she wouldn't have required the permission of Joel Tobias or anyone else to do whatever she had to in order to ensure its success.

I was there when they broke open the lock on the box, and I saw Carrie Saunders's face. Whatever she might have done, she did not deserve to die in that way.

Shortly after the discovery of the body, I gave my statement to the police, with two agents from ICE, the Bureau of Immigration and Customs Enforcement, in attendance. Behind them hovered a small man with a beard and dark skin, who introduced himself as Dr. Al-Daini, late of the Iraq Museum in Baghdad. The agents were part of the JIACG, the Joint Interagency Coordination Group, a grab bag of military, FBI, CIA, Treasury, ICE, and anyone else who happened to be passing and had an interest in Iraq, and how terrorists might be financing their operations. They had been drawn to the looting of the Iraq Museum by concerns that the stolen items were being sold on the black market to raise funds for the insurgency. The man who had interrogated me at the Blue Moon was lying, both to me and to himself: people were being hurt by what they were doing, but they were dying on the streets of Baghdad and Fallujah and anywhere else in Iraq that American soldiers were being targeted. I told the agents and Dr. Al-Daini everything, with only one detail concealed. I did not tell them of the Collector. Dr. Al-Daini seemed to sway slightly at the news of the loss of the box, but he said nothing.

When we were done, I got in my car and drove south.

XXXVIII

Herod sat in his study, surrounded by his books and his tools. There were no mirrors, no reflective surfaces. He had even placed his computer in another room so that there was no chance of a face being glimpsed. The Captain was a distraction, his desire to see the box opened so compelling that Herod had been forced to banish him from its presence by covering every reflective surface. He needed peace in which to work; to have done so in the presence of the Captain would have driven him insane. Figuring out the mechanisms of the locks would take time: days, perhaps. They had to be opened in a certain combination, for there were cells within cells. It was a puzzle box, an extraordinary construct: whatever relics had been concealed in the final chamber were bound with wire, and the wire was connected in turn to every lock. Simply to have broken the locks by force would have torn the presumably fragile relics apart, and if someone had gone to such efforts to secure them then it meant that it was important that the relics remain intact.

The box stood on a white cloth. It no longer vibrated, and all the voices within had ceased their whispering, as though wary of imposing on the concentration of the one who might free them. Herod was not afraid of them. The Captain had told him of what lay in the box, and the nature of the bonds that restricted them. They were beasts, but chained beasts. Once the box was opened, they would be revealed, yet still constrained. They would have to be made to understand that they were the Captain's creatures.

He was about to prise off the first spider, and reveal the mechanism of the lock, when the house alarm went off, shocking him with its suddenness. Herod did not even pause to assess the situation. He hit the locks on the safe room, sealing himself inside. He then picked up the phone, pressed the red button on the handset, and was immediately connected with the security company responsible for monitoring the alarm. He confirmed a possible intrusion and notified them that he had locked himself in the safe room. He walked to a closet and opened it to reveal a bank of monitor screens, each revealing one aspect of the house, both internal and external, and its grounds. He thought that he now caught the Captain's reflection on the screens, and felt his intense curiosity as he tried to glimpse the box, but Herod ignored him. There were more pressing issues for now. He could see no evidence of intrusion, and the gates to the property remained closed. It might well have been a false alarm, but Herod was disinclined to take chances with his personal safety or with his collection, especially when such a valuable and rare addition had just been made to it.

After four minutes, an unmarked black van appeared at the gates. A numerical security code, changed weekly as an added safeguard, was entered on the pad by the gatepost, which Herod duly confirmed. The gates opened, and the van entered the property, the gates immediately closing again behind it. Once the van reached the front of the house, its doors opened and four armed men appeared, two of them immediately moving to check the sides and rear of the building, one man training his weapon on the grounds, while the last approached the door and activated the main intercom.

"Dürer," said a voice. Like the numerical code, the word confirming the security team's identity was also changed weekly.

"Dürer," repeated Herod. He remotely activated the front door lock, opening it and allowing the security guards access to the main house. One of them, the one who had given the code word, immediately entered. The man who had been watching the grounds moved to the door, but remained outside until the main search team had joined him, after confirming that the rest of the house was secure, at which point he too entered the house, leaving them outside. Herod tried to follow their progress from screen to screen as they deactivated the main alarm and checked the log, then proceeded to move through the house. Ten minutes after the search had commenced, the intercom buzzed in Herod's office.

"You're clear, sir. Looks like it was something in zone two: dining room window. There's no sign of attempted entry, though. Might be a fault. We can send out a technician in the morning."

"Thank you," said Herod. "You can leave now."

He watched the four-man team leave. When they were gone, and the gates had closed behind them, he deactivated the locks on the study door and hid the screens, and the Captain, from sight. Although the room was well ventilated, and he often worked with the door closed, Herod disliked keeping it locked. The thought of imprisonment, or long-term confinement of any kind, terrified him. He thought that was why he had enjoyed inflicting it on the Saunders woman. It was a kind of transference, but also a punishment. He had offered both her and Tobias a deal: their lives for the location of the trove, but they had been greedy, and had commenced a negotiation for which he had neither the time nor the inclination. The second deal was offered to Tobias alone: he could die slowly, or quickly, but he was going to die. Tobias had trouble believing that at first, but Herod had managed to convince him in the end.

As he opened the door of his study, he was still mildly troubled by what might have caused the alarm activation, and was not concentrating fully on the room beyond, so that the Captain's voice sounded like a siren in his ears as soon as he began to emerge, an incoherent burst of anger and warning and fear. Before he could respond, there was movement in front of him. There were two men, both armed. One of them smelled so strongly of nicotine that his presence in the room seemed immediately to pollute the air. He pushed Herod to the ground and placed a blade against his neck.

Herod stared up at the face of the Collector. Behind him was the detective, Parker. Neither man spoke, but Herod's head was filled with noise.

It was the sound of the Captain, screaming.

XXXIX

I kept Herod under my gun as his eyes moved back and forth between the Collector and me, as though uncertain as to which of us posed the greater threat. Herod's own gun had been tossed to the floor by the Collector, and now lay out of reach. The Collector, meanwhile, was examining Herod's shelves, picking up items and examining them admiringly before restoring them to their place.

"You possess an impressive array of treasures," said the Collector. "Books, manuscripts, artifacts. I have been following your progress for some time, but even I had not imagined that you were so assiduous, and possessed such exquisite taste."

"I am a collector, like you," said Herod.

"No, not like me," came the reply. "My collection is very different."

"How did you find me?"

"Technology. Your car was fitted with a tracking device while you were in Ms. Emory's house. I believe it might have been cobbled together by the late Joel Tobias, which is ironic under the circumstances."

"You were outside his house all the time?"

"Yes."

"You could have taken me then."

"Mr. Parker was anxious to ensure the safety of Ms. Emory, and I wanted to see your collection."

"And how did you get in?"

"Sleight of hand. It's hard to keep track of so many men moving through one's house across different screens, especially once the alarm system has been deactivated."

"You intercepted the security detail."

"Yes. You may sit, but keep your hands on the desk. If they disappear from sight, Mr. Parker will shoot you."

Herod did as he was instructed, laying the palms of his hands flat on either side of the box.

"You're trying to open it," said the Collector.

"Yes."

"Why?"

"Because I'm curious to see what is inside."

"Such trouble you've gone to, all for the sake of idle curiosity."

"Not idle. Never idle."

"So this is purely a matter of personal interest?"

Herod considered the question. "I think you already know the answer to that."

The Collector pulled up an armchair and settled himself into it, his hands clasped in his lap, the fingers intertwined and the thumbs crossed, as though he were about to pray.

"Do you even know who it is that you serve?" he said.

"Do you?"

One corner of the Collector's mouth raised itself in a smile. "I settle accounts. I collect debts."

"But for whom?"

"I will not name Him here, in the presence of this . . . *thing*."

His fingers unfolded themselves as he indicated the box. He reached into a pocket and produced a gunmetal cigarette case and a matchbook. "Do you mind if I smoke?"

"Yes."

"That's a shame. It seems that I am set to impose still further on your hospitality."

The Collector put a cigarette between his lips, and struck the match. Soon, a foul-smelling gray smoke curled toward the ceiling. Herod's face tightened in distaste.

"I have them specially made," said the Collector. "I used to smoke generic brands, but I found their ubiquity crass. If I'm going to poison myself, I'd prefer to do so with a modicum of class."

"How admirable," said Herod. "Do you mind if I ask where you plan to put the ash?"

"Oh, these are slow burning," said the Collector. "By the time it becomes an issue, you'll already be dead."

The atmosphere in the room changed. Some of the oxygen seemed to be sucked from it, and I heard a high-pitched whine in my head.

"By your hand, or by your friend's?" said Herod softly.

"Neither."

Herod looked puzzled, but before he could pursue the matter further the Collector spoke again.

"What name does he go by, the one whom you serve?"

Herod shifted slightly in his chair.

"I know him as the Captain," he replied, "but he has many names."

"I'm sure. The Captain. The One Who Waits Behind the Glass. Mr. Goodkind. It hardly matters, does it? He is so old that he has no name of his own. They are all the constructs of others."

The Collector's right hand moved gently, taking in the room, smoke trailing from his fingers.

"No mirrors here. No reflective surfaces. One might think you were tiring of his presence. It must be wearying, I admit. All of that anger, all of that *need*. To work with it in your head would be next to impossible." He leaned forward and tapped the box. "And now he wants this opened, to add a little more chaos to an already troubled world. Well, no sense in disappointing him, is there?"

The Collector rose. He placed his cigarette carefully on the arm of the chair, then leaned over the desk and began moving his fingers along the locking mechanisms, the tips dexterously exploring the spider legs, the twisted bodies, the gaping mouths. He did not look at the box as he did so. Instead, his eyes never left Herod's.

"What are you doing?" said Herod. "These are complex mechanisms. They need to be examined. Their order needs to be established . . ."

But even as he spoke, a series of clicks and whirrs began to sound inside the box. Still the Collector's fingers moved, and as they did so the mechanical noises were drowned out by another. It was a whispering that seemed to fill the room, rising in terrible joy, voices clambering over one another like insects in a nest. One lid opened, then another and another. A shadow appeared against one of the bookcases, hunched and horned, and quickly it was joined by two others, a prelude to what was about to be revealed.

"Stop!" I said. "You can't do this!" I moved to my right, so that the Collector could see me, and I shifted the muzzle of the gun from Herod to him. "Don't open that box."

The Collector lifted his hands in the air, not in a gesture of surrender, but of display, like a magician at the end of a particularly fine conjuring act.

"Too late," he said.

And the final lid sprang open.

For a moment, all was still in the room. The shadows on the wall ceased to move, and what had for so long been without substance assumed concrete form. The Collector remained standing, his hands still raised, a conductor waiting for the baton to be placed between his fingers so that the symphony might begin. Herod stared into the box, and his face was illuminated by a cold white light, like sunlight reflected from snow. His expression changed, altering from fear to wonder at what was revealed to him, but concealed from the Collector, and from me.

And then Herod understood, and he was lost.

The Collector spun away, diving toward me in the same movement, forcing me to the ground, yet I was compelled to look. I saw a black back curved like a bow, its skin distorted and torn by the eruption of sharp spinal bones. I saw a head that was too large for the torso that supported it, the neck lost in folds of flesh, the top of its skull a fantasy of twisted yellow bones like the roots of an ancient tree stripped of bark. I saw yellow eyes glitter. I saw dark nails. I saw sharp teeth. One head became two, then three. Two descended on Herod, but one turned to me—

Then the Collector's fingers were pressing into the back of my head, forcing my face to the floor.

"Don't look," he said. "Close your eyes. Close your eyes, and pray."

There was no sound from Herod. That was what struck me most. He was silent as they worked on him, and though I was tempted to look again, I did not, not even when the Collector's grip upon me eased, and I felt him stand. I heard a series of mechanical clicks, and the Collector said, "It is done."

Only then did I open my eyes.

Herod sat slumped in his chair, his head tilted back, his eyes and mouth open. He was dead, but appeared uninjured except for a thin trickle of blood than ran from his left ear, and the fact that every capillary in his eyes had exploded, turning his corneas red. The box on his desk was closed once more, and I heard the whispering return, now filled with rage, like a hive of bees shaken by an outside force.

The Collector picked up his cigarette from the arm of his chair. A long finger of ash hung from the tip, like a building about to fall. He tapped it into Herod's open mouth, then returned the cigarette to his own lips and drew lengthily upon it.

"If you're going to taunt the dogs, always check the length of the chain," he said. He picked up the box and tucked it under his arm.

"You're taking it?" I said.

"Temporarily. It's not mine to keep."

He wandered over to one of the shelves and removed a tiny ivory statue of a female demon. It looked oriental, but I was no expert.

"A souvenir," he said, "to add to my collection. Now, I have one more task to accomplish. Let me introduce you to someone . . ."

WE STOOD IN FRONT of the ornate mirror outside Herod's study. At first, there was only my reflection and that of the Collector, but in time we were joined by a third. Initially, it seemed little more than a blur, dark gray absences where eyes and a mouth should have been, but then it formed itself into recognizable features.

It was the face of Susan, my dead wife, but with holes burned into her skin where her eyes once were. Then, like a rattle being shaken, the face blurred again, and it was Jennifer, my murdered daughter, but also eyeless, her mouth filled with biting insects. More faces now, enemies from the past, changing faster and faster: the Traveling Man, the one who had torn Susan and Jennifer apart; the killer of women, Caleb Kyle; Pudd, his face wreathed in old spider webs; and Bright-well: the demon Brightwell, the goiter on his neck swollen like a great womb of blood.

For he was in all of them, and they were all of him.

Finally, there was just the figure of a man, one in his early forties, of a little more than average height. There was gray seeping into his dark hair, and his eyes were troubled and sad. Beside him was his twin, and next to him was the Collector. Then the Collector stepped away, the two reflections became one, and I stared back only at myself.

"What did you feel?" asked the Collector, and there was an uncertainty to his voice that I had not heard before. "What did you feel when you looked upon it?"

"Rage. And fear. It was afraid." The answer came before I had even become aware of the thought. "Afraid of you."

"No," said the Collector, "not of me . . ."

I saw thoughtfulness in his face, but there was something else.

For the first time, I felt the Collector's own fear of me.

EPILOGUE

I wish I lived in my house with only a third part of all
these goods, and that the men were
alive who died in those days
In wide Troy land . . .

Homer, *Odyssey*, Book 24

The warehouse in Queens was known as the "Fortress," an art storage facility guarded by the U.S. government. The Fortress had already seen many antiquities from the Iraq Museum pass through its doors. It was there that the headless stone statue of the Sumerian king Entemena of Lagash had been taken after it was retrieved, and there that 669 items from the museum, seized by U.S. Customs at Newark Airport in 2003 were brought for authentication. Now, in the Fortress's gloomy confines, Dr. Al-Daini began the process of cataloging what had been recovered during the raids in Maine and Quebec, even as he mourned that which he had most fervently sought, and which had now been lost to him again.

When he found himself tiring, he left the Fortress and wandered to a nearby coffee shop, where he ordered soup and read an Arabic newspaper that he had bought that morning. Later, he would say that he smelled the man who sat down opposite him before he saw him, for Dr. Al-Daini did not smoke, and the stink of nicotine had tainted his soup.

Dr. Al-Daini looked up from his newspaper and his meal, and stared at the Collector.

"Excuse me, but do I know you?" he asked.

The Collector shook his head. "We have moved in similar circles, that's all. I have something for you."

He laid a box wrapped in string and brown paper upon the table, and Dr. Al-Daini felt his fingertips vibrate as he ran them over the outside of the parcel, then glanced around him before he used his knife to cut the string. He pushed aside the paper before opening the top of the long white box that was before him. Gently, he examined the locks. He frowned.

"The box has been opened."

"Yes," said the Collector. "The results were most interesting."

"But they are still trapped there?"

"Can't you feel them?"

Dr. Al-Daini nodded, and closed the top of the white box. For the first time in many years, he felt that he might sleep well.

"Who are you?" he asked.

"I? I am a collector." He slipped two pieces of paper across the table to Dr. Al-Daini. "But there is a price to be paid for relinquishing such a unique item to the proper authorities."

Dr. Al-Daini examined the papers. On each was the image of a small cylindrical seal.

"Consider them destroyed, or irretrievably lost."

Dr. Al-Daini was a man of the world. "Agreed," he said. "For your own collection?"

"No," said the Collector, as he stood to leave. "In recompense."

THE AIR WAS STILL. Rain had fallen earlier in the day, and the grass in the Maine Veterans' Memorial Cemetery gleamed in the sunlight. Bobby Jandreau was beside me, his girlfriend waiting on the path behind us. We were alone among the dead. He had asked that I meet him in this place, and I had been happy to do so.

"For a long time, I wanted to be here," said Bobby. "I wanted it all to end."

"And now?"

"I'm with her." He looked back at Mel, and she smiled at him, and I thought: she will be buried here next to you.

"They'll save a place for you both. No need to hurry."

He nodded. "This is our reward," he said. "To lie here, with honor. There is nothing more—not money, not medals. This is enough."

His gaze was fixed on the nearest stone. A husband and wife were buried there, side by side, and I knew that he was seeing his name alongside Mel's, just as I had.

"Their intentions were good," he said. "At the start."

"Most of the bad situations I've encountered began with the best of intentions," I replied. "But they were right, in a way: the injured, the scarred, they deserve better than what they're getting."

"I guess there was so much money that, in the end, they couldn't bear to give any of it away."

"I guess so."

He reached out to me, and I shook his hand. When we were done, there were two small cylinder seals in his palm, each decorated with gold and gemstones. A fragment of paper was bound to one with a rubber band.

"What are these?"

"Souvenirs," I said. "A man named Dr. Al-Daini has crossed them off his list of stolen items, in return for a certain gold box. On the paper is the name of someone who'll pay a high price for them, with no questions asked. I'm sure you can find a way to put the money to good use."

Bobby Jandreau closed his fist upon the seals. "There are men and women worse off than I am."

"I know that. That's why they've been given to you: because you'll do the right thing. You need any advice, talk to Ronald Straydeer, or just ask your girlfriend."

They left before I did. I stayed for a time, among the dead, and then, as the shadows lengthened, I crossed myself, and left the fallen to their own.

HERE THE DEAD LAY down their burdens, for a time. Here are names etched in stone, and bouquets on cut grass. Here husband lies next to wife, and wife next to husband. Here is the promise of peace, but only the promise.

For the dead alone can speak of what they have endured, and just as sleep may be punctuated by restless dreaming, so too the final repose is sometimes uneasy for those who have seen too much, who have suffered too much. The dead know what the dead know, and soldiers know what soldiers know, and they can share their torments only with their own kind.

At night, figures emerge from the shadows, and dark forms move in sheltered glades. One man sits beside another on a stone bench, listening quietly to his comrade as a night bird sings lullabies above their heads. Three men walk softly through the first fallen leaves, disturbing none, leaving no trace of their passing. Here, soldiers gather, and speak of war and of what was lost. Here, the dead bear witness, and witness is borne in return.

And the night breeze carries whispers of consolation.

ACKNOWLEDGMENTS

This book could not have been written without the generosity and patience of Tom Hyland, a veteran of the Vietnam War and a good man, who answered many questions over the course of its completion, and who improved the manuscript immeasurably with his knowledge.

I am grateful too to the contributors to Truckingboards, the truckers' forum, who took the time to explain the nature of their work between the United States and Canada.

I consulted a great many newspapers and journals in the course of writing *The Whisperers,* in particular the committed, sensitive reporting of *The New York Times* on the issues of PTSD and the treatment of returning veterans. Meanwhile, the following books proved invaluable in filling in the gaps in my knowledge: *My War: Killing Time in Iraq* by Colby Buzzell (Putnam, 2005), from which much of the detail of serving in a Stryker squad originated; *Trigger Men* by Hans Halberstadt (St. Martin's Griffin, 2008); *In Conflict: Iraq War Veterans Speak Out on Duty, Loss, and the Fight to Stay Alive* by Yvonne Latty (Polipoint Press, 2006); *War and the Soul* by Edward Tick, Ph.D. (Quest Books, 2005); *Blood Brothers* by Michael Weisskopf (Henry Holt and Company, 2006); *The Forever War* by Dexter Filkins (Vintage Books, 2008); *The Secret Life of War* by Peter

Beaumont (Harvill Secker, 2009), which filled in many gaps about life under fire in Baghdad, and the impact of conflict on the psyche; *Sumerian Mythology* by Samuel Noah Kramer (Forgotten Books, 2007); *Ancient Iraq* by George Roux (Penguin, 1964); *Thieves of Baghdad* by Matthew Bogdanos (Bloomsbury, 2005); *The Looting of the Iraq Museum, Baghdad,* edited by Milbry Polk and Angela M. H. Schuster (Abrams, 2005); *A Terrible Love of War* by James Hillman (Penguin, 2004); and *Catastrophe! The Looting and Destruction of Iraq's Past,* edited by Geoff Emberling and Kathryn Hanson (The Oriental Institute Museum of the University of Chicago, 2008).

Many books have been written about the experience of war, but few modern authors have written as beautifully, and incisively, as Richard Currey, who served as a combat medic during the Vietnam War. *Fatal Light,* his classic novel of Vietnam, was reissued last year in a special twentieth-anniversary edition by the Santa Fe Writers Project, and *Crossing Over: The Vietnam Stories,* from which this book quotes, has been in print for three decades. Further details are available from www.richardcurrey.com.

My thanks, as always, to my editor at Hodder & Stoughton, Sue Fletcher, and my editor at Atria Books, Emily Bestler, as well as to all those at Hodder, Atria, and elsewhere who help to get my odd books into the hands of readers; to my agent, Darley Anderson, and his staff; to Madeira James and Jayne Doherty; to Clair Lamb; to Megan Beatie; and to Kate and KC O'Hearn.

Finally, love and thanks to Jennie, Cameron, and Alistair.

Oh, and Sasha.